Oh, he had the perfect right to bed her now.

With a low groan of frustration, Rory grasped Joanna's slender wrists and brought them upward, where he held them imprisoned against his naked chest. She looked up in surprise, innocence glowing in her marvelous eyes.

She belonged to him by the king's command, and no one could say otherwise. Not even Joanna. The fact that she'd attempted to hide herself from him gave Rory all the more justification for taking her at once and without the benefit of clergy.

But first, Rory wanted to win her affection. Though he didn't believe in romantic love, a bride should display some tender esteem for her groom. He knew with demoralizing certainty that if he attempted to seduce her tonight, he'd become the villain in her preposterous make-believe tale.

He refused to play the role of the monster.

She waited, looking up at him in bemusement. "Milord?"

Her soft whisper seemed to compress Rory's heart into a tight leaden lump.

He knew they had to stop.

Kathleen Harrington

Highland Lairds Trilogy

The MacLean Groom

AVON BOOKS ◆ NEW YORK

This is a work of fiction. Names, characters, places, and incidents either are the product of the author's imagination or are used fictitiously. Any resemblance to actual events, locales, organizations, or persons, living or dead, is entirely coincidental and beyond the intent of either the author or the publisher.

AVON BOOKS, INC.
1350 Avenue of the Americas
New York, New York 10019

Copyright © 1999 by Kathleen Harrington
Inside cover author photo by Debbi DeMont Photography
Published by arrangement with the author
Library of Congress Catalog Card Number: 99-94452
ISBN: 0-380-80727-0
www.avonbooks.com/romance

First Avon Books Printing: November 1999

AVON TRADEMARK REG. U.S. PAT. OFF. AND IN OTHER COUNTRIES, MARCA REGIS-
TRADA, HECHO EN U.S.A.

Printed in the U.S.A.

WCD   10 9 8 7 6 5 4 3 2

With love to my "good-sister"
Leona Curtis.

Your sweet presence has brightened
all of our lives.

O, my luve is like a red, red rose,
That's newly sprung in June.
O, my luve is like the melodie,
That's sweetly played in tune.

As fair art thou, my bonie lass,
So deep in luve am I,
And I will luve thee still, my dear,
Till a' the seas gang dry.

Till a' the seas gang dry, my dear,
And the rocks melt wi' th sun!
And I will luve thee still, my dear,
While the sands o' life shall run.

And fare thee weel, my only luve,
And fare thee weel a while!
And I will come again, my luve,
Tho' it were ten thousand mile!

ROBERT BURNS

Prologue

∽∾ᏍᎧ∽∾

September 1496
Finlagan Castle, Isle of Islay
Inner Hebrides, Scotland

Rory MacLean stood on the quarterdeck of the *Sea Dragon* and watched the flames leaping from sawtoothed holes in the walls of Finlagan Castle. His gaze followed the billowing smoke that drifted lazily across the cerulean sky, then returned to the scorched, blackened stones with satisfaction.

It had taken a week of steady pounding from their longrange cannons before they'd breached Finlagan's barbican. Once inside the outer bailey, they'd stormed the island fortress, cutting down the rebels with great two-handed claymores like wheat before the scythe.

Rory turned from the sight of the smoldering wreckage to glance indifferently at the captives who stood nearby, watching their stronghold burn. Then he met the pale blue eyes of his chief mate. Unlike his cousin, Rory's own eyes were a deep, dark green. And while Fearchar came close to seven feet in height, Rory stood a mere four inches above the six-foot mark. Though not a giant like his kinsman, he still looked down on most men. And his strength in combat had been proven many times over.

"'Tis done, what we came to do," Rory said. "Let's return to Edinburgh and make our report to the king."

1

Fearchar MacLean grinned, the wide gap between his front teeth giving him a boyish air despite his sharp, battle-scarred features, fearsome black eye patch, and huge frame. "'Tis done, Captain," he echoed jubilantly. "And we wouldn't want these treacherous whoresons to be late for their own hangings, would we?"

The clank of heavy chains brought Rory's attention back to the two prisoners about to be taken below. Iain Mor, known to the English as Sir John Macdonald, would be turned over to the Prosecutor for the Scottish Crown and tried for treason. His kinsman, Somerled Macdonald, the notorious Red Wolf of Glencoe, would be executed for murder.

Rory met Iain Mor's gaze, untroubled by the hatred burning in his bleary, deep-set eyes. With a snarl of disgust, the laird of Finlagan Castle spat on the deck. "The King's Avenger! Pah! May your merciless soul be damned for what you did in this place."

Neither the sobriquet given him by the Scots people nor Iain Mor's contempt marred Rory's sense of accomplishment. He and his half-brothers, Lachlan MacRath and Keir MacNeil, had crushed the rebellion in the South Isles with the ease of a mailed fist smashing a slug.

"The fault for what happened on that island lies at your feet, not mine," Rory replied. "'Twas you who risked the lives of your family and clansmen to protect a fugitive from the king's justice. I've no pity for traitors."

Iain Mor's bearded chin lifted arrogantly. "We fought for the rights of the chieftain of the Glencoe Macdonalds."

"The Red Wolf has no rights," Rory told him. "He relinquished them the day he killed Gideon Cameron and ran from the law."

Despite the irons that bound him, Somerled glowered with the ferocity of a cornered bear. The Red Wolf of Glencoe had a great beak of a nose, shoulders as wide as a yardarm, and a massive chest. Beneath the full gray beard that hid his craggy features, his mouth curved in a taunting smirk. "You're naught but a landless beggar, MacLean, with no home except this paltry ship. You hope to ease the sting of your shame by destroying the castles of honorable men, but greedy bastards like you aren't fit to lick a Macdonald's boots.''

In less than a second, Fearchar's dirk pressed against Somerled's throat. ''You'll not talk to The MacLean that way, you miserable worm,'' he warned with a low growl, ''or I'll split your gullet easier than filleting a fish.''

Rory laid his hand on his cousin's arm. ''Leave the fellow be,'' he said calmly. ''Let's not cheat the king of a legal execution. They'll both be hanged in due time. Now send them below.''

As the prisoners were led away, Rory gazed across the water at the two warships awaiting his orders. ''Signal the others to weigh anchor,'' he told his chief mate, then added with a wry smile, ''It's time to show my younger brothers which of us is the finest sailor. We'll leave both ships floundering in our wake before nightfall.''

Fearchar shook his head, his flaxen hair whipping about in the salty air. ''Keir's got half a league on us already, and he's carrying the castle's women and children. With all that caterwauling going on, he'll be spreading every inch of canvas he's got. We won't have a chance to catch the *Raven*.''

''Damned if I'll let Keir make port first,'' Rory replied with a good-natured laugh. ''No one outsails the *Sea Dragon*, not even my cocksure baby brother.''

The command to get under way sent the nimble-footed seamen scrambling up the ratlines to loose the sails. Nearby, the *Sea Hawk* returned the *Dragon's* signal and prepared to come about. The *Black Raven* replied from a greater distance, her topgallants already unfurled in the strong breeze.

''Light out to windward!'' Rory ordered the helmsman. ''Full-and-by!''

The *Sea Dragon* leaped forward, her sails full and close to the wind.

In tight formation, the three galleons sailed out of the

Sound of Islay, heading for the open sea. The full-rigged ships sliced through the gray water in a fiercely competitive race that pitted brother against brother. Sails bulged and boomed as they caught the gusts blowing over the curling whitecaps. Rigging creaked and tall masts shuddered. Each crewman knew his captain would award him an extra fifty crowns, if his vessel reached port first.

Then, after their doomed cargo was discharged and their stores reprovisioned, the three men-of-war, commissioned by James IV to protect Scottish merchantmen from Dutch and English pirates, would set sail for the Continent and the untold booty that awaited them.

Chapter 1

May 1498
Kinlochleven Castle
Western Highlands

Surveying the formidable forty-foot stone wall, Fearchar grinned mirthlessly. "Welcome to your new home, laird."

Rory's scowl deepened. "And 'tis a damn strange feeling I've got about it."

If he'd hoped to find festive banners and a joyous celebration to welcome Kinlochleven's future laird to his castle, Rory would have been sorely disappointed. Not given to flights of fancy, he rode across the lowered drawbridge with a wary gaze on the ramparts overhead and his hand on his sword hilt.

The lack of resistance made him edgy.

An heiress's fortune wasn't a prize easily relinquished to a foe, and he hadn't expected the Macdonalds to submit to the king's decision without a fight. He'd brought along fifty of his kinsmen, armed and ready for battle, in the event he'd have to force his way into the fortress. If a long siege was required, he would send to his uncle's castle in Appin for reinforcements.

Damn it to hell, marrying into a nest of treasonous vipers hadn't been *his* idea. The preposterous scheme to bring the Glencoe Macdonalds peaceably under the authority of the

5

Scottish Crown had been hatched by James IV.

Once through the arched gateway and inside the eight-foot-thick sandstone walls, Fearchar seemed to feel the same disquiet. His gaze moved constantly about, skimming the outer bailey for any sign of a trap.

But the inhabitants of Kinlochleven barely looked up from their tasks at the large party of horsemen. The blacksmith continued to swing his hammer, his brawny apprentice beside him at the fire. A cooper sauntered leisurely across the grassy courtyard with an ale barrel perched on his shoulder. Two dairymaids ducked into a barn with frightened backward glances, as though sighting Satan and his legions on Judgment Day. From the bakehouse, the tantalizing aroma of fresh, warm bread lingered on the still air.

Not a blasted soul offered a word in greeting.

At Rory's signal, his men dismounted and followed him into the keep's dim vestibule, where a man in his early sixties, with thinning brown hair and stooped shoulders, appeared to be waiting for their arrival. He rose from a carved bench the moment he saw them. The fellow suffered from what appeared to be an old leg injury and moved with an obvious limp.

"I'm Kinlochleven's bailiff, David Ogilvy," he told Rory as he inclined his head in a brief salute. His gaze quickly assessed their strength, and his bristly brows met in a frown over his slightly protruding eyes. "Please follow me, laird."

With a brusque nod, Rory motioned for Ogilvy to proceed. The bailiff led them with a slow, shuffling gait up a flight of stone stairs to the castle's upper hall, where the Macdonalds stood waiting in small groups, their weapons sheathed. About twenty were men-at-arms, the rest, castle retainers along with a handful of menservants. A thin, ascetic priest stood at the edge of the gathering, his hand on the shoulder of a dirty-faced lad.

Brilliant colors adorned the vaulted timber ceiling; rich tapestries covered the walls. Ornately carved cupboards held silver tankards and jewel-encrusted plates. Even the floor boasted thick carpets from the Levant, as glorious as any made for an Ottoman's harem.

To a man used to the spartan furnishings of a ship, the magnificent display of household comforts in a Scottish castle should have been a pleasant surprise. But the setting's opulence only increased Rory's uneasiness. Anything this fine had to come at an exorbitant price. And as the new laird of Kinlochleven, he wasn't about to pay with his own blood—or that of his kinsmen.

With a flick of his hand, he signaled his men to be prepared for an attack from all sides.

At the far end of the hall, a middle-aged lady in a gold-trimmed black headdress sat waiting, her embroidery on her lap. She shifted nervously in her chair as they approached. Standing next to her, a maiden about the age of Rory's bride-to-be cradled a plump white cat in her arms.

"Laird MacLean," the woman said before they'd quite reached her, "welcome to Kinlochleven Castle. I am Lady Beatrix, Lady Joanna's cousin." Without offering her hand for his salute, she added briskly, "I'm sorry that my husband isn't here to greet you. The king's letter arrived only yesterday, and Laird Ewen remains at Mingarry Castle, unaware of the proposed alliance."

As Rory inclined his head in curt acknowledgment of the chilly greeting, he studied the younger female from the corner of his eye. The king had told him the heiress favored her notorious grandfather. Her large nose, square body, and frizzled hair made the resemblance to Somerled Macdonald unmistakable.

Having no lands of his own to bring into the marriage, he was scarcely in a position to quibble about the lassie's face and form. But somewhere in the back of his mind, Rory had always hoped his future bride—chosen for prudent reasons, of course—would be easy to gaze upon.

His wife-to-be's English blood was another disappointment. Her father, Alasdair Macdonald, had married Lady Anne Neville, whom he'd met in London while trying to enlist the aide of Edward IV against the former King of Scotland, James's father. And the lass herself had spent half her life in Cumberland. So now Rory was forced to mate with the offspring of a traitorous devil and a Sassenach witch.

But here he was, at Kinlochleven—the dutiful future bridegroom—ready to present his gifts to the bride-to-be.

Hell, he hadn't come expecting a bonny lassie, any more than he'd expected a festive welcome. Rory glanced up at the resplendent ceiling. For a castle such as this, most men would gladly marry a toothless hag. Determined to get the worst over, he turned to greet the heiress.

"Laird MacLean, this is my daughter, Lady Idoine," Beatrix said.

For the first time since he'd entered Kinlochleven, Rory smiled. "Milady," he said warmly.

Idoine froze beneath his gaze. In her obvious fright, she squeezed the cat, and the outraged pet scratched her hand and leaped down. "Ouch!" she squawked, kicking out at the scurrying ball of fur with the toe of her silken slipper. Her lumpy features darkened in a sullen glower as she watched the feline scamper across the hall and out the door to freedom.

With a sense of relief, Rory looked about the room filled with men and boys. "And the Lady Joanna?"

"My cousin isn't here," Beatrix answered brightly.

"Not here?" His gaze snapped back to the woman. "You said you received the king's letter yesterday. I expected the maid to be waiting to welcome her future husband."

Beatrix's eyes glittered suspiciously beneath his glare. Twin spots of scarlet stained her cheeks. "And s-so she should be, laird," she replied, her voice high-pitched and quivering, "b-but I'm afraid that's not so. When the contents of the letter were read to Joanna, she immediately disappeared."

"Disappeared?"

Beatrix looked to her daughter for verification, and Idoine nodded vigorously. "She's gone, laird."

Rory stepped closer to tower over the two cringing females. "Just where did Lady Joanna go? Mingarry Castle?"

"I have no knowledge of my cousin's whereabouts," Beatrix answered with a nervous flutter of her ringed fingers. Her embroidery hoop slid to the ground, and she reached down to retrieve it, then reluctantly met his gaze once again. "We searched everywhere for her, once we discovered her missing. But when the lass is upset she frequently vanishes without an explanation, only to be found later, wandering about the forest or glen in a daze." Beatrix touched the middle of her forehead with the tip of one shaky finger. "Joanna's a little slow. I'm sure His Majesty warned you about that."

"I was given no such warning," Rory growled.

Directly behind him, Fearchar moved restlessly. "Shall we search the castle?"

"Oh, please do!" Beatrix exclaimed. "I worry about the poor dear when she's missing like this. Sometimes we can't find her for days—till she's half-starved and caked with dirt. She's as helpless as a child, you know, without someone to care for her."

Rory drew his sword with an oath. His men immediately followed his lead, showing the steel of their broadswords and dirks. He turned to face Lady Joanna's kinsmen, and his words rang out in the still hall. "I am The MacLean. By order of His Majesty, King James of Scotland, this fortress now belongs to me, as does all the property and goods of my future wife."

The Macdonalds watched him with sullen faces, but made no attempt to draw their swords. Clan MacLean's reputation for savagery in battle was known throughout Scotland. The hall's fancy carpets would be soaked with Macdonald blood should they try to resist.

"Take their weapons," Rory ordered. "Then search all

the buildings within the castle walls. I want every blasted female in Kinlochleven brought to this chamber at once.''

The women and girls spilled into the upper hall from all directions, like a flock of sheep driven before a pack of hungry wolves. Clearly terrified of the large, ferocious MacLeans, many buried their faces in their aprons and wept. Others held the hands of the frightened children they'd brought with them, or drew the halflins close to their skirts with maternal protectiveness.

"Line them up," Rory said as he jammed his sword back into the scabbard.

Hands locked behind his back, he marched up and down the rows of females, searching for a lass of about seventeen with the beak nose and grizzled locks of the Red Wolf—and the empty eyes of a simpleton.

They came in every shape and size. Tall, thin household servants with pursed lips and pointy chins. A cook and her daughter, both round as haystacks. Middle-aged women who sewed and bleached linen. Dimple-cheeked dairymaids whose work-roughened hands proved their occupation. Hook-nosed crones who did the spinning and weaving. And fresh-faced lassies with long braids and freckles who tended the ducks and geese.

Rory stopped and asked each her name and position in the household. Most of them were bawling so hard, he couldn't understand a word they said. When he asked them to repeat their answers, they averted their eyes, as though addressing a fiend from hell.

"Jesu," he muttered to Fearchar, "I've never seen such a gaggle of puling, timid-hearted wenches. All this wailing is enough to unnerve a man."

" 'Tis true," his cousin replied, his teeth flashing in a cheery grin. "Ten of them together wouldn't equal one MacLean woman in her dotage."

'Twas easy to see that not one of them could be the mistress of this splendid castle. The king had told Rory that the future bride's maternal grandparents were the Marquess and Marchioness of Allonby, and along with her aunt, she was their co-heiress. As part of her inheritance, Lady Joanna had been awarded Allonby Castle in Cumberland. Dull-witted or not, Lady Joanna would have all the haughty pretentiousness ingrained in the Sassenach nobility.

"This is all of them?" he asked Fearchar, who nodded glumly.

Rory strode back to where Idoine stood clutching her mother's arm and studied her. Of average height, the coarse-featured young woman looked to be about nineteen, but she could be younger. Her stubby fingers showed no sign of toil, and the gown she wore was rich, its red velvet sleeves and ermine trim fit for the wardrobe of a queen.

Beneath his inspection, Idoine broke into a nervous, high-pitched giggle. She clapped both hands over her mouth, and her watery blue eyes glistened with fear.

His hopes sinking, Rory realized that Lady Idoine was the only female in the castle of the right age and rank. And she clearly resembled the Red Wolf of Glencoe.

Yet the obviousness of such a trick made him cautious.

There'd be no righting the error, should he wed the wrong lady at his own insistence. Once having taken the maiden to bed, he might be obliged to honor the marriage contract, regardless of her true identity. The girl's real terror would be understandable, considering his anger if he found out later that he'd been deceived.

Rory reached a quick decision. Since his future bride's kinsmen thought of him as a fiend from hell, he'd act like one. He caught hold of a child about two years of age and dragged him out of his mother's arms. The woman let out a startled yelp, then covered her mouth to smother her cry, lest she frighten the wean.

Drawing his dirk, Rory brandished it near the innocent head. "If Lady Joanna doesn't reveal herself at once, the laddie dies," he told the shocked assemblage. He repeated the threat in English, uncertain if the Maid of Glencoe could understand her native Gaelic after so many years in Cumberland with her Sassenach relatives. Surely, if she were listening from a place of concealment, she'd now give herself up.

Though Fearchar must have been as stunned by Rory's brutal announcement as the rest of their men, he calmly folded his arms and stared straight ahead of him. From the look of boredom on the giant's face, with its scars and sinister black patch, it appeared as if the two of them habitually hacked up wee bairns for the sheer pleasure of it.

The other MacLeans held their tongues as well. Rory had purposely chosen a laddie so young, he wouldn't understand what was being said, nor have dreadful memories to haunt him.

An agonized silence descended on the hall, broken only by the muffled sobs of the frightened mother. Motionless, the Macdonalds gaped at him. Every violent tale they'd ever heard about the King's Avenger must have rattled through their empty brains.

For a long, torturous moment, no one spoke. Then at the back of the hall, a bedraggled serving lad stepped forward from his place beside the priest. His cheeks covered with soot, his deep blue eyes wide with fright, he held out one dirty hand in a pathetic bid for mercy. He opened his mouth to speak, but appeared too terrified to form the words.

"Wait!" Beatrix shrieked. "Wait! I'll tell you the truth. Don't harm the baby."

Rory swung his gaze back to the frantic woman. Beatrix caught her daughter's arm and dragged the struggling girl to where he stood in the center of the hall. "This is the Lady Joanna," she declared breathlessly. "My daughter, Idoine, remained at Mingarry Castle with her father."

Rory handed the child back to its mother and nodded in dismissal.

Joanna slumped against Father Thomas's side, her heart beating a painful tattoo against her breastbone. Disguised as a serving lad in a frayed plaid, ragged shirt, and torn stockings, with a knit cap pulled down over her ears to cover her hair, she watched The MacLean with morbid fascination. She'd had no idea he'd be so stalwart and virile. But then her tutors had warned her that even Lucifer had been beautiful before his fall.

Well over six feet, MacLean soared above her kinsmen. All of the MacLeans were large and fearsome, but their chief exuded an almost diabolical power. And though fortune had blessed the Sea Dragon with golden hair and piercing green eyes, he was as cunning and ruthless as everyone had warned her.

Joanna had been certain he'd fall for their trick and hurry off to Mingarry Castle in search of the missing heiress. After reading the king's letter yesterday morning, commanding her to marry the chief of the MacLeans, her shock had quickly turned to indignation.

"You are wondering why I invited you to my chamber this morning," she'd said, meeting the curious gazes of her loved ones. Holding the missive between the tips of two fingers, as though it were a loathsome insect she'd just removed from the hem of her gown, she shook the vellum, and the sheets rattled portentously. "This is why."

Seated on a large chest at the end of Joanna's bed, Beatrix and Idoine had watched her with hands folded neatly in their laps. Father Thomas stood on one side of them, Joanna's former nurse and present companion, Maude Beaton, on the other.

"This missive is from the king," Joanna had explained. "The very villain who made me his ward after hanging my grandfather on false charges of murder and treason. James Stewart writes to inform me that he's chosen my bridegroom."

"Oh, dear God!" Beatrix cried, wringing her hands. "This can't be! You're to marry Andrew, my dear—though it will take time to arrange for permission from Rome."

"She can't marry my brother," Idoine stated with a careless shrug. "Not if the king says otherwise."

Beatrix shot her daughter a furious look. At eighteen, Idoine resented the fact that, in spite of her advanced age, her parents hadn't found her a husband before arranging her younger sibling's marriage.

Joanna's cousin, Ewen Macdonald, planned to wed the clan's new chieftain and heiress to his sixteen-year-old son Andrew. But the future bride and groom were too closely related according to canon law, and a papal dispensation had to be obtained before the nuptials could take place.

"I won't marry as the king decrees," Joanna had stated. She ripped the pages in half before their astonished eyes, then ripped them again for good measure. "I shall throw myself from the top of the battlements before I do."

"Whom has the king chosen for your husband, milady?" Father Thomas asked kindly. Like the others at the castle, he'd known Joanna as a small child—before she'd left for Cumberland with her mother at the age of seven. He didn't seem the least alarmed at either the treasonous gesture or the heroic threat of self-immolation.

Joanna dropped the torn sheets to the floor and ground the pieces under her heel. "According to this letter, I am to marry the vile, wretched, blackhearted, pig-faced lout who captured my innocent grandfather and delivered him to his executioners."

Beatrix gasped. She jumped up from the chest, her hands clasped to her breast, her face drained of color.

"God's truth, you've the right of it," Joanna said, somewhat mollified by their looks of horror. "I am betrothed to none other than the vicious, salacious, perverted chief of Clan MacLean."

"Dear Lord, save us all," Maude muttered under her breath. She quickly made the sign of the cross, then withdrew the holy medal of St. Maelrubha from under her bodice and kissed it fervently.

Idoine stared at Joanna in stupefaction. Suddenly a sparkle of joy flared in her narrowed eyes, and Joanna knew exactly what her cousin was thinking: *Thank God, it isn't me.*

Beatrix finally found her voice. "All our plans are ruined!" she wailed.

His thin face creased with concern for Joanna, Father Thomas shook his head. "How could the king betroth you to our ancient foe?"

Joanna snapped her fingers. "As easily as he made me his ward against my wishes."

"You'll have a husband with a tail," Idoine said with a gleeful smirk. She smoothed the velvet on her sleeve, her thick fingers caressing the soft blue material with lingering satisfaction.

"Hush!" Maude told her sharply. "My lady is upset enough. Don't make matters worse."

Joanna flung her arms wide in exasperation. "Oh, don't try to hide the truth from me. What Idoine said is certainly no secret: I know very well what's hidden beneath that contemptible fiend's plaid."

For every Macdonald child had heard the tale of how the MacLeans were once evil sea dragons, who'd changed to human form and come to the coasts of Scotland from the north in long ships with dragon heads at their prows, sacking and pillaging remorselessly. The shocking story was told by firelight that every MacLean chief was born with a dragon's scaly tail, which was clipped at birth so its stub could be concealed beneath his plaid. It was why, even now, the chief of their wicked clan bore the name of Sea Dragon.

Joanna had paced back and forth, trying desperately to think of a solution. As the heiress of two great families, she'd been taught that she must marry whomever was chosen for her. The chivalrous knights in the English ballads sung by the troubadours were only figments of her imagination.

This was real.

As real as that terrible day last spring when Somerled Macdonald stood on the gallows in Edinburgh. Joanna despised James Stewart. But even more than her grandfather's murderer, she loathed the hellhound who'd captured him and turned him over for execution.

"What will you do, milady?" Maude asked. She crossed

her arms and waited with staid resignation. As always, Joanna's companion was her usual down-to-earth self, the one rock of stability in her charge's otherwise unpredictable life.

"Somehow, I must gain time. I must delay my marriage to The MacLean until the dispensation comes from Rome."

Idoine straightened the silk cap perched on the back of her head, then coyly twined one wiry brown curl around her finger. "To openly defy the king's orders would be treason," she reminded her cousin.

"Then I'll have to do it secretly," Joanna declared.

"Why not try hiding in the secret staircase?" Beatrix urged. " 'Tis cleverly concealed."

The stairwell had been built by one of Joanna's ancestors for reasons no one could now explain. Its entrance was a false back in a large service cupboard in the laundry room, and the stairs led to a movable wall of oak paneling in one of the private chambers on the third floor. Joanna and her cousins had played in the staircase as small children, but it'd been many years since anyone had used it.

Joanna considered the idea for a moment, then shook her head. " 'Tis possible The MacLean might discover it, and then I'd be trapped." She stared down at the rug, pondering her limited choices. "But if he thinks I've already escaped to Mingarry," she continued, half to herself, "he'd likely ride off after me on a fool's errand." She turned to Father Thomas and clasped his arm. "Ask everyone in the castle to gather in the great hall at once."

The priest frowned. "What are you thinking, my child?"

"I have a plan, Father. But everyone in Kinlochleven, from the youngest bairn to the eldest grandfather, must help to carry it off. If but one soul betrays me, I'm lost. I'll either be hanged as a traitor for disobeying the king, or I'll be forced to marry The MacLean."

"I'd rather be hanged," Idoine had offered cheerfully.

Bringing her thoughts back to the present, Joanna stared at the very personification of wickedness now standing in the middle of her hall. The look of dismay on his face as he gazed at Idoine was enough to make a corpse snicker. MacLean clearly believed Joanna's cousin was his promised bride. And from the grimace contorting his sharp features, the idea must taste like gall on that forked dragon's tongue of his.

"This is the Lady Joanna," Beatrix repeated, holding Idoine tight to keep her from bolting. "She is your affianced bride."

" 'Tisn't true! 'Tisn't true!" Idoine bawled, nearly hysterical at the thought of being forced to marry the ferocious man. "I'm *not* Joanna." She tried to pull away, but her mother shoved her toward The MacLean.

Sarah Colson, the bairn's mama, took the opportunity offered by the commotion to disappear from the hall while MacLean's eyes were fastened on the sobbing female in front of him.

"Be still, you ungrateful wretch!" Beatrix snapped. "Would you have him murder the wee laddie, just to save yourself from an unwanted marriage?" She pinched Idoine's earlobe, and the girl howled in pain and humiliation.

Rubbing her injured ear, Idoine looked about the room as her eyes pooled with tears. "T-tell him," she implored her clansmen. "T-tell him I'm n-not the heiress he seeks. Tell him I'm n-not the M-Maid of Glencoe."

No one moved.

Not by a twitch of an eyelid did a single Macdonald give away the truth.

But the look of desperation in her cousin's eyes melted Joanna's resolve the way The MacLean never could have—even if he tortured her on the rack or chained her in his dungeon with only moldy bread and brackish water to eat for the rest of her woesome days.

Although Beatrix was willing to sacrifice her own daughter to save her niece for Andrew, Joanna couldn't allow Idoine to suffer the hideous fate that had been meant for her, and her alone.

Still, a shaft of pure terror struck Joanna's chest at the

thought of revealing her true identity. Like St. Agnes and St. Catrìona, she'd rather be a virgin martyr, willingly tied to a stake and riddled with a thousand arrows by her heinous foe rather than marrying him.

Joanna prayed she wouldn't bring shame on the ancient and honorable name of Macdonald. More than anything, she wanted her father's clansmen, once mighty Lords of the Isles, to be proud of her.

She was a Macdonald.

She was courageous.

She was invincible.

She was scared to death.

In an agonizing moment of self-revelation, Joanna realized she'd rather be given to Beelzebub himself than surrender to the perfidious, diabolical, dragon-tailed MacLean.

As she started to step forward, Father Thomas caught her hand. "Wait," he said under his breath. "Let's see what happens."

MacLean had the ears of a fox. He caught the hushed sound of the cleric's voice and turned his head to stare at them thoughtfully. He studied Joanna for what seemed like an eternity, then suddenly a light flared in his eyes. "Priest," he called, "fetch a holy relic from the chapel and bring it here."

Father Thomas left at once and quickly returned with the finger bone of St. Duthan enclosed in a small gold case. It was the chapel's most sacred relic, having been safeguarded by the Glencoe Macdonalds since the battle of Bannockburn.

"Open the box," MacLean commanded. When Father Thomas had done so, the tall warrior nodded to Idoine. "Now place your hand on the relic and swear by its saint that you are not Lady Joanna."

Choking back her sobs, Idoine gulped, then swallowed noisily. She looked at her mother with pleading eyes and her chin trembled.

A hush came over the chamber.

Even the angels painted on the ceiling seemed to hold their breath.

Beatrix narrowed her eyes and glowered at her daughter in wordless warning. A shudder shook Idoine and her gaze flicked to Joanna, then darted back to the powerful man in front of her.

What Joanna saw in her cousin's eyes in that brief second told her all she needed to know, and she offered a silent prayer of thanksgiving. Idoine had no intention of throwing herself on the sword for the sake of her brother's marriage to an heiress.

"Do it," MacLean ordered grimly. "Swear on this holy relic that you are not the Maid of Glencoe."

Her hand shaking, Idoine placed two fingertips on the bone. "I swear," she whispered, "I swear I am not the Maid of Glencoe. By the sacred finger of St. Duthan, I swear that I am not Lady Joanna Macdonald."

The merest hint of a smile flickered across the Sea Dragon's lips. "I don't believe you," he said softly. "Only a Macdonald would swear to a falsehood on the bone of a saint."

In the upper hall's candlelight, the earring in his ear glittered the same emerald green as his eyes, gleaming now in satisfaction. Joanna peeped at him from lowered lashes, unable to understand the strange feelings that swam through her insides, like trout darting about in a stream.

Godsakes, he had the most arresting mouth.

And his intelligent eyes, crinkled at the corners from the sun and wind, promised a quick and lively wit.

But then—she reminded herself sternly for the second time—even Lucifer had been beautiful before his fall.

She would have to continue to deceive The MacLean for as long as it took for Ewen to come and rescue both her and Idoine.

Rory sheathed his dirk and turned to survey the Macdonalds, fully aware of the trick they'd attempted to play on him. Lady Idoine had spoken the truth; the honest terror in her eyes was unmistakable. And he'd seen the frantic glance she'd cast the serving lad—who was no lad, at all, but a lassie. He'd wager his life on that. Christ, did they think he wouldn't notice the long curving lashes or the clear, creamy skin beneath the dirt stains on her cheeks? The lass was a peach, whoever she was.

As the supposed lad stared at the toes of his scuffed brogues, Rory noted the delicate features beneath the striped stocking cap that hid every strand of hair, the long, curving russet lashes—lowered now to hide the startling blue eyes—the arched brows, the graceful hands. Could this be the missing heiress?

The idea that this slim lass, barely over five feet, resembled the mighty Somerled Macdonald seemed preposterous. Then Rory remembered the gray-haired man's indigo eyes—eyes the deepest blue he'd ever seen.

Eyes exactly like this dirty-faced urchin's.

And the fierce chieftain had been named the Red Wolf in his youth because of his head of coppery hair.

The astonishing—nigh unbelievable—possibility that Lady Joanna might be attempting to hide right under his nose stunned Rory. If it were true, everyone in the whole damned castle had taken part in the deception. Once again, he looked around the great hall.

Could it be possible?

Had all these people connived to fool their new laird?

At that moment, the lass looked up to meet Rory's gaze. The brilliant blue eyes danced with mirth. He found it incredible that a Sassenach noblewoman—an heiress worth a damn fortune—would play the role of a servant. What would she do if he set her to mucking the stables?

Well, he'd go along with the ruse for now, pretending to believe Idoine was his future bride, while he sent messengers to Mingarry Castle to notify Ewen Macdonald of the marriage alliance and to make certain that Lady Joanna wasn't there. Meanwhile, 'twould prove an interesting diversion to learn the true identity of the little vixen dressed in a boy's shirt and plaid.

"Rather than return with my future bride to Stalcaire immediately as first planned," he told the Macdonalds coldly, "we'll await the arrival of your war commander." He favored Idoine with a brief glance. "He can accompany Lady Joanna and me to my uncle's castle, where we will be wed. From this moment on, I'll assume the responsibilities and privileges of your new laird."

Idoine started to protest, but Lady Beatrix clapped one hand over her daughter's mouth before she could utter a word. Grumbles of dissatisfaction swept through the hall. The Macdonalds' furious expressions told him they'd expected the chief of Clan MacLean to dash off to Mingarry Castle, thinking to find Lady Joanna with their clan commander, Laird Ewen.

"Place a guard at the gate and posterns," Rory told Fearchar. "No one is to leave without our consent, not even the lowliest serving boy. And send four men to Mingarry to invite Ewen Macdonald to his cousin's wedding."

With a nod, Fearchar left the chamber with several broad-shouldered MacLeans.

Next, Rory addressed the twenty weaponless Macdonald men-at-arms. "By order of His Majesty, King James, you are to travel to Stalcaire, where you will swear your fealty to him. Any man who does not appear there within the next two days will be charged with treason and dealt with accordingly. You have my permission to leave at once."

As the dispirited Macdonald soldiers filed out of the upper hall, Rory motioned to David Ogilvy, and the bailiff hurried as fast as his dragging gait would allow. "Have the chamberlain take my things to the castle's finest bedchamber." He glanced at Beatrix and Idoine, whose bottom lip was thrust out in a sulky pout. "I trust that won't inconvenience either of you ladies."

"Certainly not, laird," Beatrix answered sharply.

With a jerk of his head, Rory brought the brown-robed cleric a step nearer. "You may take the relic back to the chapel, Father."

"Father Thomas Graham," the priest replied, belatedly introducing himself.

"And have a candle lit before the Virgin's altar," Rory added as he turned to leave. "My gillie will bring you a crown for the offering as soon as my saddlebags are unpacked."

"For what intention, laird?" the priest asked in surprise.

"For the wedding couple," Rory told him with a frown. He'd thought the reason obvious. "That the bride and groom, soon to be joined in holy wedlock, will be blessed with a long and fruitful union."

Father Graham hunched his narrow shoulders as though caught in an embarrassing mistake. "Of course, milord. Of course."

Chapter 2

⌒⌒⌒⌒⌒

Later that evening Rory entered his new bedchamber, nearly certain that his future bride was masquerading as a serving lad called Joey Macdonald. He'd watched the lad—*lass, dammit*—seated by the fireside playing backgammon with Seumas Gilbride, Kinlochleven's steward, after supper. Each time the boy—*girl*—made a successful move on the board, he—*she*—would laugh out loud. The soft, husky laughter, filled with a naughty, irrepressible merriment, convinced him further of his suspicions.

He opened the low carved chest at the end of the fourposter. The scent of roses drifted up, enticing and evocative. Filled with costly and stylish robes, it brought to mind the image of a pampered Englishwoman whose world centered on her own shallow interests. This, then, was her chamber; these, her fine garments trimmed with fur. He lifted a lavender wool gown adorned with sable from the stack of folded clothing and held it out at arm's length.

Its owner was a tiny thing. The top of her head would barely reach the middle of his chest. He pictured Joey—the height would be correct for a twelve-year-old boy, but could also be that of a diminutive seventeen-year-old female.

Returning the gown to the pile, he went to the table that held an assortment of feminine trifles. Pulling open a drawer, he fumbled through the things, picked up a silver brush, and brought it closer to the candle flame. A strand of silken hair clung to the bristles, glowing like hammered copper in the moving light.

Christ! Blue eyes and red hair!

He'd been so damned sure Lady Joanna would look like Idoine, sour-faced and frizzled, that he'd never even considered the possibility the maid he would marry might be bonny.

Cold fury swept through him as he stared with unseeing eyes at the tapestry on the far wall. He'd like to turn the lying wench over his knee, lift up that tattered plaid she wore, and whale on her backside till her howls of outrage shook the rafters. If he attempted to thrash her as she so richly deserved, the Macdonalds would never stand by and allow him to lay one blow on her little bare butt. They'd stumble all over themselves confessing her true identity.

Hell, even the priest was in on the sham.

Rory sank down on the edge of the bed to remove his shoes and stockings, stopped, and smiled grimly. The Macdonalds weren't the only ones who could play this idiotic game of make-believe. They'd had a good laugh at his expense; now it was his turn.

He lay back on the mattress and stared up at the silk canopy. God, what a hellion, to try such a trick.

Meting out physical punishment would be letting her off much too easily. There'd be far more satisfaction in going along with the ruse till he'd evened the score.

He rose, crossed the room, and poured a glass of porter from the flagon on the side table. Twirling the ale, he stared into its dark brown depths. How much more gratifying to show Lady Joanna who really controlled Kinlochleven. He'd take the serving boy under his wing, and set all the Macdonalds wondering what they could do to protect their mistress from discovery and still not reveal her identity.

He smiled to himself in anticipation. His revenge would be slow and thorough, and all the sweeter for the waiting.

Rory sat up with a frown, uncertain how long he'd slept. He'd drifted off, fully clothed, on top of the coverlet and wakened with troubled thoughts.

Locked out of her bedchamber, what nighttime refuge had Joanna found that was completely safe? Not with any of the womenfolk; the sight of a lad going into the women's chambers in the evening and not coming out until dawn would be noticed and remarked upon.

Not the stables, either. Too risky.

Nor the great hall with his men-at-arms.

So where the hell was she sleeping?

He left the room, candle in hand, and descended to the ground floor. The snores of his soldiers, lying on the rushes, mingled with their grunts and groans as they tossed about in their sleep. The faint sound of male voices caught his attention, and he moved down the long gallery.

Two Macdonalds looked up in surprise when Rory entered the kitchen. Seumas and Jock Kean, the stable master, sat at one of the rough wooden tables, playing cards by the light of a tallow dip. They rose to their feet at the sight of him, their faces puckered in consternation.

"M-milord," Seumas said, his overwide smile splitting his whiskered cheeks, "is there something you're needing?"

Jock's eyes darted to the fireplace, and Rory followed his gaze. There before the hearthstones, cocooned in a swath of red and blue tartan, lay Joey, sound asleep.

"Nothing," Rory said. "I was merely restless. Rather than disturb any of the servants, I thought I'd check the pantry myself for something to eat." He looked at the tarots spread across the tabletop. "I enjoy a good game of cards. I'll join you, if I may." Without waiting for an invitation, he set his candle on the table and dropped to the bench across from Seumas.

"Certainly, laird, certainly," Jock said, and the two sat back down.

Rory pulled a crown out of his sporran and tossed it on the pile of coins in the center. "You men keep late hours."

"Ah, well," Jock answered, shuffling the tarots with his knotted fingers, "like you, we couldn't sleep, so we thought we'd bide the time with a bit o' harmless gamblin'."

They hadn't played for long when Kinlochleven's bailiff shambled into the kitchen. Rubbing his eyes, Davie came to a sudden halt at the unexpected sight of his new laird.

"You couldn't sleep, either, I take it," Rory said with a brief nod as he made his discard.

Abashed, the stoop-shouldered man adjusted the pleats of his belted plaid as though he'd dressed hastily in the dark. He peered at the fireplace from the corner of his eye; then, meeting his comrades' worried gazes, slipped onto the bench next to Rory.

Across the table, Seumas stretched and yawned. "Well, I'm for bed," he declared, picking up his winnings. "If you'll excuse me, milord?"

He nearly bumped into Father Thomas on the way out. The chaplain's dark brown eyes grew wide as he entered the room. "What in heaven's name—" He stopped short, his gaze flying to Joey, then nodded politely. "Evening, laird."

Rory smiled down at the king, queen, and knave in his hand. His few remaining doubts were completely wiped away by the changing of the guard. As Jock made his excuses along with Seumas and trundled off to bed, Davie and Father Thomas joined Rory at the table, ready to while away their shift.

What could look more innocent than two men sitting in the warmth of the kitchen over a friendly game of tarot, while a serving lad slept by the fire?

Laying his cards facedown, Rory stood, walked over to the wood box by the hearth, and picked up a log.

"Here, I'll do that for you, laird," Davie said, pushing himself up from the bench. He started to move toward the fireplace, favoring his lame leg.

"Sit down," Rory told him. "I can stir the fire."

He crouched over the sleeping figure and shifted the embers about with a poker, than added a log.

Illumined by the flickering light, Lady Joanna's translucent skin glowed with vitality. The delicate features had been scrubbed clean of the dirt smudges, and a sprinkling of cinnamon dusted her pert nose. Her soft, pink mouth had parted slightly in her sleep, and her long lashes rested on her silken cheeks. The knit stocking cap had been replaced by a lad's cotton nightcap, which had shifted in her nocturnal movements, revealing strands of lustrous red hair curving about her face.

Hell and damnation.

How could they think him so blind?

All the girl's innocence and sweet femininity lay right before him. He rose and turned to find her two clansmen, now both on their feet, watching him with sickly apprehension.

"The laddie sleeps like the dead, doesn't he?" Rory commented with a chuckle.

"He does, laird," Father Thomas replied, unable to manage the faintest of smiles.

Dusting his hands, Rory walked back to the table, sat down, and picked up his tarots. "Now, if you men are ready, let's get down to some serious card playing. And I warn you, I'm very hard to bluff."

The other men's eyes met, sharing a secret amusement. "Oh, we've no doubt you're a canny one, laird," Davie said, his protruding eyes lighting up like beacons. "But you'd have to get up fair early to outfox a Macdonald."

Rory returned his grin. "I'm glad to hear that. I wouldn't want to trounce you fellows too quickly—there's no pleasure in an easy victory."

"You told the men?" Rory asked Fearchar as he joined him in the library the next morning. Spread across the table lay the building plans of Kinlochleven, which he'd been studying. While the keep's interior boasted luxuries more common to an English manor house than a Scottish castle, the outer fortifications needed repair and reinforcement. He intended to renovate the fortress as quickly as new plans could be drawn up and masons hired.

"They all know," his cousin said, bracing his hands on his hips. The pale blue eye glistened with mirth, at odds with the somber black patch. "They could scarcely believe the truth at first, but I managed to convince them."

"And they understand my orders? No one is to touch her."

"I gave them your warnin', forbye," he replied. "If any man lays a finger on the lass, he'll beg to die before we're through with him."

Satisfied, Rory rotated his shoulders and massaged the back of his neck. He left the table and strode across the carpet. Bracing one hand on the edge of the narrow window, he looked out at the kitchen garden and paused for a moment to enjoy the bucolic scene.

Lady Joanna Macdonald, in her lad's clothing and carrying a large bundle of laundry, came into view. Making her way through the rows of peas and onions, she stopped for a moment to speak to the bairn Rory had threatened to kill the day he'd arrived. The child's mother, smiling with delight at the spate of cooing and gurgling from her youngster, continued to pick green peas and drop them into her cupped apron.

At Rory's sudden scowl, Fearchar spread his big, scarred hands across the building plans and braced his considerable weight on the table. "What's really eating your insides?" he asked. "The fact that the lassie's the granddaughter of Somerled Macdonald or the knowledge that she doesn't care to wed you any more than you wish to marry her?"

Turning from the window, Rory braced his shoulders against the wall. "Maybe 'tis both," he said, "maybe neither. Maybe 'tis just that I'd always planned to choose my own bride, not have one foisted on me by royal decree."

"You haven't tumbled arse over alepot for a bonny face and a braw smile when I wasn't lookin', have ye now? A fellow has to be sensible in spite of the urgings of his heart—or his loins."

Rory chuckled at his cousin's sly leer, but didn't bother to answer. They both knew he was far too pragmatic to believe in romantic love. Whatever the circumstances, his choice of a bride wouldn't be based on some fatuous myth perpetuated by bards and heartsick maidens.

"Dod, man," Fearchar said, "if 'tis bothering you that much, ride back to Stalcaire and ask the king to reconsider."

Rory folded his arms with a grimace of resignation. " 'Twould be a waste of time. I tried my damndest to talk James out of this asinine scheme the day he first proposed it. Lady Joanna is the granddaughter of the late Marquess of Allonby, and the Nevilles have always been close to the English throne—so doubtless the maid inherited their fierce loyalty to Henry Tudor. But none of this swayed the king. When I told him flat out that a MacLean could never wed a Macdonald, he refused to listen. To hear James Stewart tell it, he's the one making the sacrifice in allowing me to end my sailing days and take up the prosaic life of a landholder."

"There's a good many reasons for the king wanting these nuptials, as you damn well know," Fearchar said. "By uniting you and Lady Joanna in holy wedlock, her title and property will be safely in MacLean hands, rather than in the grasp of her misbegotten clan's pawky commander, Ewen Macdonald. And James isn't worried about the lass's loyalty, Sassenach or no—only her future husband's. Her English heritage makes the proposed alliance all the more desirable. Through your marriage, the Scottish Crown will gain a toehold in Cumberland."

"I'm fully aware of the political advantages to James IV and Scotland," Rory said sharply. "But have you forgotten the lady's grandfather murdered Gideon Cameron? I lost a brilliant mentor and ally due to nothing more than a cantankerous old man's spite and greed."

"If the lassie's willing to forget the fact 'twas you who captured the Red Wolf and delivered him up for the hangin'," Fearchar retorted, "you should be able to overlook the murder of your foster father. Lady Joanna had nothing to do with the plaguey affair."

"She's a Macdonald. That alone condemns her."

His face puckered in a scowl, Fearchar came around the table. " 'Tis high time you took a bride," he said bluntly. "You're not getting any younger. And a married man needs estates to leave his weans."

Rory clenched his jaw to stifle an oath. He didn't need to be reminded that he held no lands of his own. Since he'd been old enough to comprehend the full meaning of that unfortunate fact, he'd realized that as chief of Clan MacLean, he must one day wed an heiress, thereby providing a home for his dispossessed kinsmen, who'd otherwise end up as broken men, forced to sell their services as mercenaries in foreign lands.

In his years of faithful service on the sea, Rory had accumulated considerable wealth. And because of his loyalty to the king, he'd hoped to be awarded the estates that had once belonged to Somerled Macdonald. But that dream had been nothing more than an illusion. There was no gain without a price—and the greater the gain, the costlier the price.

"There are countless men who'd give their sword arm to be in your shoes," Fearchar reminded him. "And the lass needs a strong man who can protect her property from those who'd seek to take advantage of an ignorant female. As her husband, you'll be laird of thousands of acres, with tenants and livestock, granaries and mills, smithies and quarries. Not an opportunity to be tossed away lightly, my bucko."

"Oh, 'tis perfect," Rory agreed with a curl of his lip. "I get a bride who's descended from a long line of Scottish traitors on one side and our ancient enemy on the other. Hell, I don't know which is worse: the fact that she's half Macdonald or half Sassenach."

Fearchar clapped Rory soundly on the back. "God's bones, man! 'Tisn't the lass's fault she was born half-English. Or that her grandda was the Red Wolf of Glencoe."

Rory chuckled in spite of himself. "I have to admit, she is fair bonny. And she smells damn nice."

Fearchar's eyes twinkled with amusement. "How the hell would you know? You've never been that close to her."

"Her perfume lingered on the pillow," Rory admitted with a grin. "The Maid of Glencoe may spring from a long line of traitors, but she smells like my mother's rose garden."

Not just the pillow, but the entire bed—mattress, coverlet, and curtains—carried the intoxicating fragrance of a blossom-filled bower. He'd wakened in the night with the image of a sweet, supple body lying beside him and a cockstand that'd give credit to a sailor after ten months at sea. That morning he'd gruffly ordered a servant to put fresh linens on the bed and air out the chamber.

Rory picked up a letter he'd written earlier. He dusted it with sand, folded it, and sealed the missive with his ring; then he placed it beside a package wrapped in paper and tied with string, along with several other letters.

"Send Arthur to me," he told Fearchar. "I have an errand that will take my gillie to the *Sea Dragon*. On the way, he can deliver some letters to Stalcaire, along with a package containing one of Joanna's gowns. Lady Emma can use it to take the measurements for the little bride's wedding garments. Then Arthur can accompany her and my uncle back to Kinlochleven, along with Lachlan and Keir."

"Your family's coming here?"

At Fearchar's look of surprise, Rory leaned against the table and grinned. "We'll celebrate the wedding when they arrive. In the meantime, we're going to show Clan Macdonald that the MacLeans have a few tricks of their own. If the entire castle can conspire to keep Lady Joanna's identity a secret, we can convince them for a few days that we haven't discovered the fact that the stable boy is my sweet, bonny bride-to-be."

"You're going to pay them back in kind for their trickery," his cousin said with an approving nod.

" 'Tis part of it," Rory admitted. "But the most important reason will be to keep them off guard. As long as they're certain we believe Joey Macdonald is a lad, there'll be no attempt to sneak her away from Kinlochleven. I don't want to wake up one morning and find she's bolted. Until the wedding vows are said, I intend to keep my conniving bride-to-be right at my side.''

To Joanna's disgust, the Sea Dragon showed no sign of dragging his tail out of her castle. He slept in her bed, ate her food, and issued orders like he was the bloody king of England.

And as if that weren't bad enough, his men swarmed all over the fortress. Practicing swordplay in the bailey, marching up and down the battlements, stabling their ravenous animals in her barns, and nosing around the bakehouse with the boldness of greedy lads.

As Joanna made her way across the lower bailey, the Dragon's giant henchman called out to her. Fearchar's flaxen hair and full beard, along with the gold stud in his ear, the scars, black eye patch, and immense bulk, reminded her of a Viking. Maude had told her as a child of how the Norsemen had once been the scourge of the Scottish coast.

"The MacLean wants to talk to you at once, laddie," Fearchar said with a ferocious scowl. "Best hotfoot it into the keep, if you know what's good for you."

Joanna nodded and turned back. Geese and ducks honked and scolded, flapping their wings in outrage as she raced through their midst. It was a whole lot easier running in a kilt than a dress, and Joanna sprinted for the upper bailey and the door of the keep. She reached the donjon's open doorway, brushed past a startled Seumas, and skidded to a stop on the vestibule's stone floor in front of the Dragon himself.

MacLean stood with his feet planted solidly apart, his hands resting on his narrow hips. An engraved gold bodkin fastened the edge of his belted black and green plaid to the shoulder of his flowing saffron shirt. His shiny black brogues sported gold buckles that matched the rosette points on his checkered stockings. Beautifully carved Celtic designs adorned the hilt of his eighteen-inch dirk.

Godsakes, if he didn't look the portrait of a Highland laird, nobody did.

And the laird was scowling. Again.

Deciding he looked far too busy to be interrupted, Joanna quickly lowered her gaze and started to scoot around him.

"Don't leave," he said.

He'd spoken so softly, she looked up to see if he'd meant her.

He had.

With a wave of his hand, MacLean dismissed Seumas and turned his full attention on Joanna.

His stern, sea-weathered features had the mesmerizing appeal of a newly sharpened ax blade. A thrill of admiration, mixed with fear at the sight of a nearly invincible enemy, twanged through her. *Bonny* would never have described him—even if his name hadn't been MacLean. The fierce warrior standing before her brought to mind phrases like *awe-inspiring* and *frighteningly majestic.*

"Do you wish to speak with me, milord?" she asked, sending a prayer of gratitude heavenward that her voice was several octaves lower than that of most females. During Joanna's years at Allonby Castle in Cumberland, her Aunt Clarissa had told her more than once she had the voice of a whisky-soaked harridan.

His reply held the rumbling threat of far-off thunder. "I do."

"He's naught but a halflin," Seumas blurted out. "If he's doing something wrong, I'll see to it that he's properly instructed."

MacLean looked over at the steward in surprise. Instead of leaving as he was supposed to, Joanna's trusted retainer had hovered near the doorway, waiting to see what the fearsome man wanted with his mistress.

"If you please, laird," Seumas continued stubbornly, "I'll take the laddie with me and set him to work in the scullery."

MacLean stared at the portly, dark-haired man as though

unable to credit his ears that a lowly steward had dared to defy him. Beneath the Sea Dragon's icy regard, Seumas clamped his mouth shut and backed two slow steps to the door. Then with a quick, worried glance at Joanna, he hurried away.

To go for help, she fervently prayed.

Once Seumas had disappeared, MacLean turned back to Joanna. He jerked his head toward the small library just off the vestibule that he'd confiscated for his private office. "In there, lad."

Joanna swallowed painfully and tried to speak, but nothing came out. With no excuse to keep from being alone with him, she walked into the Dragon's lair on shaky legs, halted in the center of the fine Hindustan rug she'd brought with her from Cumberland, and waited for impending doom to follow her in.

With her teeth clenched to keep them from chattering, she stared at the warlord with all the bravado she could muster. She'd barely passed the five-foot mark in height, and at seventeen, there was no hope of ever getting any taller. She hooked her thumbs in her belt, tipped her head back, and met his frosty gaze.

God above! His eyes were cold enough to freeze Loch Leven in the summertime. But no matter what he threatened to do, she wouldn't reveal her true identity.

Like the king's daughter in the Celtic tale of the sea dragon, who'd been chained to a rock to be devoured for her people, Joanna would never forsake her duty.

He could burn her with hot pokers.

He could hang her from the rafters by her thumbs.

He could throw her into the moat, bound hand and foot!

No matter what hellish torment his lurid mind dreamed up, she'd never tell him she was the maiden he sought to despoil with his lecherous, debauched, lascivious MacLean hands.

Never.

Rory looked down at the dirty-faced lassie, trying so hard to act brave. The sprinkle of freckles across her nose and cheekbones could barely be discerned beneath the layer of soot. 'Twas all he could do to keep from smiling at her impudence.

"What's your name, lad?" he growled.

"Joey Macdonald."

"Who are your parents, Joey?"

Lady Joanna threw back her shoulders, and her dark blue eyes glistened with open defiance. "I don't have any parents. Nor grandparents, neither."

"You're an orphan, then?"

"That's what they usually call a child with no parents," she answered cheekily.

In spite of the brazen demeanor, Rory sensed her pain at the questions. "Who *were* your parents, laddie?" he asked in a milder tone.

"My da died on the Field of the Moss at Stirling fighting the old king. Mama died two years ago."

"So your father was a traitor."

The lass fisted her hands. "My da was a hero," she declared proudly. "He killed eight men with his claymore before being cut down by cannon fire from the hills above."

If the man hadn't died in the battle, he'd have been hanged with the rest of the rebels, but Rory didn't bother to point that out to his bride-to-be.

Joanna must have lost her father when she was only eight or so. The tattered shirt, several sizes too big for her, hung on her small frame. The frayed red and blue plaid she wore could have served a full-grown man. Even her worn-out shoes were overlarge.

Her tenacious pride touched something inside Rory. A memory of his own childhood flashed before him. He'd been fostered in the home of a Stewart ally at the age of eight. In his loneliness, he'd felt the need to prove himself to the other lads by acting as impertinent as Joanna. Gideon Cameron's patience must have been tested to the hilt.

"I've considered turning you over to Fearchar for training as a soldier." He paused to watch Joanna swallow back her dismay, then continued with a smile. "However instructive my kinsman's rigorous discipline might be, though, I'm not sure you've the makings of a warrior."

At that moment, Jock Kean appeared in the open doorway. "You sent for me, laird?"

Rory nodded and motioned for the man to enter, then turned back to Joanna. "Besides your household duties, lad, I'm going to have you work in the stables under the direct supervision of the stable master. In the afternoons you'll take orders from Jock, and your first duty today will be mucking out the stables."

Jock stepped forward and tugged off his coarse wool cap, revealing his smooth, hairless pate. His lively gaze darted to Joanna in reassurance and then back to Rory. "I'll take care of the laddie, then," he said, his round face splitting into a jaunty smile. "I'll see that he's kept busy and stays out of trouble."

Rory folded his arms and waited for the Sassenach heiress to confess her bloody secret.

Instead, Joanna edged closer to the cheerful, baldheaded gnome, then looked at Rory with huge blue eyes. "I'll do just as Jock says, laird," she promised. "I can handle the mucking—I know I can. And I'm real good with horses. You'll see."

He scowled at her. "What are you waiting for, then?" he snapped. "Get out to the stables and get busy."

She bowed low from the waist. "Very well, milord," she answered with a hint of mockery in her voice. "Thank you, milord."

All Rory could see was the top of the moth-eaten stocking cap, but he could have sworn the cheeky imp was grinning.

Before she had a chance to straighten up, Maude Beaton, who'd been identified as the missing heiress's former nursemaid, appeared in the doorway. She bobbed a curtsy the instant Rory glanced over. "Your pardon, milord," she said meekly. "The lad is needed in the scullery."

"Joey has work to do in the stables," he replied with a

frown. "And don't interrupt me again, woman, when I'm speaking with someone. No matter what the cause."

"I won't, laird," Maude promised. The tall, big-boned female looked at Joanna with solemn gray eyes, then turned and left, with Jock right behind her.

"You may go, lad," Rory said.

"Thank you, milord," she answered with a wide grin.

"Oh, and Joey," Rory said as she moved toward the door, her returning confidence obvious in her boyish swagger.

Joanna paused to look back.

"If you ever again answer my questions with such impudence, I'll discipline you myself. And if I do, you'll wish I'd let Fearchar strip the hide off your puny little bones, yank your ribs out of your chest, and beat your head into your shoulders with them."

The lass fled the chamber without a backward glance.

Rory grinned as he shook his head in grudging admiration. The confounded girl had spunk. The thought of bedding such a lively sprite sent an unexpected surge of lust flooding through his veins. Damn, if he wasn't starting to look forward to his wedding day.

Almost a dozen of her kinsmen were waiting for Joanna outside the library, listening for her cry for help, ready to rush to her assistance.

"Are you all right?" Davie Ogilvy asked in a hushed voice as he shuffled out of the vestibule alongside her.

"Did he hurt you?" Jacob whispered, his big blacksmith's hands fisted menacingly.

Safely wedged between her bailiff and the clan chaplain, Joanna strode down the south gallery that led to the chapel. "He didn't lay a hand on me," she said with a satisfied grin, "but I'd rather not have another private interview with the Sea Dragon for as long as I live."

Father Thomas placed his hand on Joanna's shoulder, and they came to a stop. "I'm afraid this farce is going to turn deadly," he said in a low voice, his dark eyes somber.

"When we agreed to your plan, Lady Joanna," Seumas added, stepping closer, "we thought the King's Avenger would be gone the same day he arrived, riding for Mingarry Castle in search of you."

"Don't give up so soon," she answered confidently. "All we have to do is fool The MacLean until Ewen arrives to rescue us."

Seumas rubbed his whiskered jowls, his mouth compressed in a tight line. "You can't keep up this deception much longer, milady," he warned. " 'Tis too dangerous."

"I can," she insisted. "I know I can. Why, MacLean wasn't a foot away from me and hadn't the least notion I was a girl. He's as easy to fool as the rest of those idiots."

Idoine squeezed closer to her mother. "If he does find out, he'll probably hang you."

"Let him," Joanna replied with a toss of her head. "Just as long as he doesn't marry me first."

Some of her kinsmen chuckled at the bold remark, but most regarded their mistress soberly. At the moment, the choice between a hanging and a wedding seemed an all-too-distinct possibility.

Pressing her hand to her ruddy cheek, Maude looked at Father Thomas with worried eyes. "Perhaps we should try to sneak my wee lamb out of the castle."

"That might be a very good idea," he agreed with a nod.

Although every member of her household staff was loyal to Joanna, she hadn't yet been fully accepted by the entire clan since her return to Kinlochleven two years ago with her grandfather. But she was their chieftain now, and she was determined to help them.

"My heart is in the Highlands and here I'll stay," she declared, clenching her hands with unflagging resolution. "Besides, if Joey Macdonald were to disappear now, The MacLean would guess who he really was, and then you'd all be in danger." She touched Beatrix's sleeve. "Have you received any word from Ewen?"

"Not yet," her cousin admitted. "But I'm sure we'll

hear soon. He may have gone to Stalcaire Castle to speak with the king. Hopefully, my husband is with His Majesty as we speak, begging him to reconsider this tragic misalliance and to give permission for you to wed Andrew instead.''

"Then we'll wait till Laird Ewen arrives," Joanna said. She met Idoine's worried gaze. "Don't be afraid, cousin. I won't let the Sea Dragon marry you. If it comes to that, I'll admit who I am."

At Idoine's halfhearted nod of agreement, Joanna tugged the knitted cap further down over her ears, making sure not a wisp of telltale red hair showed beneath its blue border. "Meanwhile, I'll continue to play the role of a serving lad."

Except for her recent encounter with the Sea Dragon, Joanna was actually enjoying herself. She'd much rather be free to roam the castle grounds than be relegated to the solarium, practicing her embroidery with Idoine.

"Be careful, my child," Father Thomas said to Joanna. "Stay away from all the MacLeans, unless it can't be avoided."

Joanna wasn't anxious to provoke the Sea Dragon's wrath a second time. She didn't want to get scorched by that fiery tongue of his—or frozen to death by that wintry glare. But like Jeanne d'Arc, her favorite heroine, she'd go to the stake before betraying her identity.

"I have to continue going about my duties, Father," she said. "If a serving lad doesn't look busy, someone will soon find him something to do. And if one of the MacLeans does come looking for Joey Macdonald, I'd better be mucking out the stables."

"Ah, lambkin," Maude said, "I'm afraid for ye." She drew Joanna into her arms and held her against her ample breast, then kissed her forehead.

At the gentle solace, Joanna blinked back tears. How often her former nurse had comforted her like this when she was a frightened child.

For a quiet moment, neither spoke.

Neither said what was uppermost in her mind: the true perversion of the MacLeans.

For it was whispered among the Macdonalds that their ancient enemies, inveterate sea raiders, were also said to fornicate with mermaids who called to them from the rocky shore.

If Joanna's stratagem didn't succeed, she would soon be married to Evil Incarnate.

Joanna's duties as serving boy included carrying wood into the castle's keep and piling it on the many hearths. The evening following her prickly conversation with The MacLean, Fearchar found her in the kitchen, perched on a table and munching an apple, and ordered her to take another armful of firewood to the laird's bedchamber. Resisting the urge to inform the bearded colossus that it was *her* bedchamber, not MacLean's, she scrambled up from the bench to do his bidding.

Joanna hadn't stepped foot inside her private quarters since the Dragon's arrival, and the idea of visiting her own room dressed as a servant tickled her sense of the ridiculous.

The door was ajar, so she entered without knocking. In front of the fireplace stood the large wooden tub used for bathing. Arthur Hay, MacLean's gillie, was pouring a bucket of hot water into the steaming receptacle.

Joanna halted just inside the threshold. Too late, she realized the reason for the extra logs.

The Sea Dragon was about to take a bath.

"Don't stand there gawking," Arthur called. "Put those logs in the wood box where they belong."

MacLean absently glanced over from where he sat on the edge of her high feather mattress, removing his shoes and stockings. Paying her no more heed than the deerhound that had come in with her, he rose and started to unbuckle his belt.

Beneath the hem of his plaid, his hairy calves were well-shaped and sinewy. The sight of his naked feet seemed so shockingly intimate, she nearly stumbled.

Joanna stared down at the logs cradled in her arms, fighting the paralyzing bashfulness that threatened to give her away. Her mind whirled dizzily as she moved to the fireplace with awkward steps.

The soft shush-shush of clothing being removed could be heard from behind, and Joanna's heart jumped to her throat. Godsakes! If she didn't get out of there fast, it'd be too late.

"Add some more wood to the fire, lad," MacLean told her.

"Very well, laird," she mumbled, her head bent over her chore.

On her knees before the grate, it suddenly occurred to Joanna that she'd just been blessed with a singular stroke of good luck. She now had the chance to discover if the stories she'd heard as a child were true! All she need do was linger just long enough to get a peek at MacLean's bare arse—not that she really *believed* he had a tail. Well, not totally and completely, anyway.

Her mouth went dry as she caught her lower lip between her teeth. What she planned to do was wicked. Shamefully so. When she whispered her sin to Father Thomas in confession, he'd give her a penance it'd take a year to complete. But the opportunity beckoned enticingly, too marvelous to pass up.

One by one, Joanna added the logs to the burning blaze, then slowly regained her feet. She stared down at the fire, red-orange and searing as the flames of hell.

"The water's ready, sire," Arthur told MacLean.

"*And so am I,*" Joanna whispered to the hearthstones. She straightened her spine like a pikeman and pivoted on her heel.

Her mouth dropped open at the sight of him.

St. Ninian protect her!

His skin bronzed from the sun, MacLean stood facing Joanna on the far side of the tub, a linen cloth draped loosely about his hipbones. His massive shoulders and arms bulged with muscles. Incredibly, he looked even larger disrobed and barefoot than he did fully dressed.

The heat of a flush rose up her neck and scalded her cheeks. Joanna couldn't drag her gaze away from MacLean, and could barely catch her breath.

On the warrior's right arm, a three-headed sea serpent had been dyed in greenish-blue ink. The elongated body wrapped itself completely around his bicep and tricep like a primordial, heathenish armband.

Crisp golden-brown hair covered his broad chest, where a holy medal hung between his nearly hidden nipples. The thick, triangular-shaped mat of hair tapered to a narrow line that led down his flat belly and under the scrap of white linen hiding his private parts. Beneath the lower edge of the toweling, his thighs resembled tree trunks.

He'd been badly scarred in battle. The jagged pucker of an old wound that must have nearly cost him his life ran from his breastbone down to the bottom of his right rib cage.

An unfamiliar ache spread through Joanna, a peculiar ache that made her restless and tense with expectation—though she hadn't any idea what she expected.

Golden-haired and golden-skinned, The MacLean was the most pagan creature she'd ever seen—and the most beautiful.

When his hand dropped to his waist to remove the linen cloth, she bolted for the door. The gentle splash of water as he lowered himself into the tub sounded like the clarion call of doomsday, and Joanna went flying out of the chamber and down the stairs as fast as her clumsy, too-big shoes could take her. To her consternation, the deep, rich sound of masculine laughter accompanied her hasty descent.

That night, she dreamed of the Sea Dragon. She lay sleeping in her own bed again, when he drew the curtains back with both hands and stood over her, arms upraised, long fingers grasping the edges of the heavy brocade.

"Wake up, lass," he called in silken seduction.

Dressed only in his belted plaid, he gazed at Joanna, his green eyes intense in the flickering candlelight with a raw, unexplainable hunger. The need she read there brought the tingling sensation of gooseflesh to her warm skin. She reached up and slipped her trembling hand beneath the tartan folds, her fingertips grazing the iron-hard sinews of his leg. He drew a quick, sharp breath at her touch, but didn't pull away.

The bare male flesh of his thigh awoke some latent wantonness inside her. Her breathing grew rapid and harsh. Her heartbeat speeded to a gallop as her body grew taut and vibrant with a primitive, instinctual energy.

Without knowing the reason, Joanna rose to her knees and lifted her night chemise over her head. Her long red hair fell about her shoulders and spilled over her breasts.

The Sea Dragon pushed her cascading locks aside to reveal their rosy tips. His gaze drifted over her vulnerable form with such lingering thoroughness, she could feel her skin's heated reaction, as though he scorched her with his smoky dragon's breath.

Currents of warm, honeyed air floated around them, tugging her closer to his lean, muscular form. She'd been caught in some invisible snare, like a sacrificial virgin enchained by a Druid wizard's magic. Beneath the compelling urgency of MacLean's bold gaze, she bent her head and lowered her lashes in a timeless pose of feminine timidity.

"Come with me, Joanna," he urged hoarsely.

"Where?" she whispered.

"Come swim with me in the loch, my wee nymph. I shall show you delights that only the mermaids know."

Her fingers twined around the gold chain of his holy medal. "I mustn't," she softly demurred. " 'Tisn't allowed for a virtuous maiden to go off with a wild sea dragon."

His smile was devastating. "Then we'll bathe together right here, love. Surely, you're not afraid of me in your own bedchamber?"

For the first time, she noticed the tub standing before the crackling fire.

His presence seemed to overpower her, to sweep away every vestige of maidenly decorum. "I'm not afraid," she declared with a harlot's abandon.

He turned and moved toward the steaming water. Releasing his belt, he removed his plaid and bent over the tub.

She stared in shock at his naked body. The broad expanse of his shoulder blades was superbly muscled. The lean, hard flesh of his torso showed every rib. She followed the curve of his spine down to his lower back, and her skin tightened with alarm and excitement.

God's truth, 'twas just as she'd dreaded.

A long, shiny green dragon's tail—the exact color of his eyes—swayed back and forth above his tight buttocks . . .

Joanna bolted awake with a shiver of horrified titillation. It had been nothing more than a dream, she assured her pounding heart. Merely the childish conjuring of her sleep-drugged imagination.

Appalled at her undeniable reaction to MacLean's dream image, she pressed a fist to her mouth and stared at the kitchen beams above her. Beneath her cotton garment, a damp warmth pooled at the juncture of her thighs. She arched her back as a long, shuddery ache rippled through her.

Some deep, inner part of Joanna wanted him to find her. To take her to their marriage bed and teach her the delights that only mermaids knew.

Joanna buried her face in her hands and groaned as the vision of a buck-naked MacLean floated before her closed lids.

By all the souls in Purgatory, she'd never be able to meet his astute, green-eyed gaze again!

Chapter 3

❦

The men sent to Mingarry Castle returned the next day to report that Ewen Macdonald wasn't there. Lady Joanna's cousin and clan commander had left before they arrived, apparently with the intention of riding to Stalcaire to request an audience with the king.

Rory received the news without comment. Ewen's appeal to James Stewart would be in vain. The political reasons behind the alliance uniting a MacLean and a Macdonald would prove to be uppermost in their sovereign's mind. Rory would soon wed the Maid of Glencoe, despite all pleas to the contrary.

The image of Joanna, standing wide-eyed and open-mouthed in his bedchamber, had been seared into his brain. Her innocent gaze had roamed over his near-naked frame, bringing a reaction so fierce and sudden, he'd been rendered all but speechless. 'Twas nigh unbelievable. Why had his body responded to that slip of a girl dressed in boy's garb? She'd gaped at him as if he were some rude barbarian. Dammit, the lass was as insignificant as a gnat and just as irritating.

Feeling restless and impatient, he decided to take Fraoch for a gallop. Remaining cooped up within the walls of a castle had lacerated Rory's nerves; he was used to the open sea. A moving deck beneath his feet, the sound of the wind whistling around the masts, and the soothing slap of the waves against the prow easily eclipsed the raucous hurly-burly of Kinlochleven's lower bailey.

Intending to harness and saddle his mount himself, Rory didn't bother to call out as he entered the cool, dim stables. The gentle nickers of the horses welcomed him as he strode past the stalls, his steps muffled by the loose straw on the dirt floor.

He stopped short at the sight of Joanna, crouched on a bundle of hay and peeking through the slats of one crib into another, her chores forgotten.

From his superior height, Rory could see easily over the top of the farther stall. Tam MacLean, his plaid shoved up out of his way, had one of the comely dairymaids nearly buried beneath him in a mound of straw. The lass's skirts had been lifted to her hips, and her plump white thighs cradled Tam's naked flanks as the soldier pumped rhythmically. The buxom girl buried her fingers in Tam's yellow hair and pressed his mouth to her exposed bosom, all the while emitting breathy whimpers of encouragement.

Grinning, Rory reached down and grabbed Joanna by the collar. Her surprised yelp alerted the two lovers, who quickly disengaged and repaired their disheveled clothing. With one meaningful look, he sent Tam and the scarlet-faced dairymaid hustling out of the stable.

Rory set his future bride on her feet. "Don't you know better than to spy on the grown-ups?" Rory asked with a feigned scowl.

"I wasn't spying," Joanna said defensively. "I heard Mary's sobs and thought that blackhearted devil was hurting her. I grabbed a pitchfork to stab him, but then she started moaning for him not to stop, so I waited to see what was going to happen next."

From the shock in the lassie's enormous eyes, Rory realized she was telling the truth. Apparently no one had ever bothered to explain the facts of procreation to the virtuous little maid.

He tried not to laugh at the comical look of stupefaction

on her face. "And when did you finally realize he wasn't hurting her?"

Joanna lowered her head and hunched her shoulders at the question. "I got a fair idea of what they were doing soon enough," she admitted to the toes of her scuffed boots, a blush of mortification spreading over her face. "Only they're supposed to wait till they're married."

Rory smiled at the indignation in the husky voice. "That's true," he replied, "but people don't always wait."

Joanna's russet brows drew together as she tugged her knit cap further down over her ears. "I don't understand why not," she stated bleakly. "I'd think you'd only do that if you *had* to."

Rory sank down on the stack of hay, thoroughly enjoying her outspoken nature and obvious inquisitiveness. But he didn't want his bride to come to their marriage bed frightened. "You'll find that when your own body starts to awaken, Joey, the idea won't seem so repulsive. And if you're lucky, the bonny lass your eye lights upon may feel the same way."

Joanna peeped up from under thick lashes for a moment, studying him with a thoughtful frown. "Is that what you intend to do to the Lady Joanna when you find her?" she asked suspiciously.

"After the wedding, I will," Rory said, sharp carnal need spearing through him at the thought. " 'Tis what a man does with his wife, laddie. There's no shame in it. Nor harm, either."

She took an involuntary step back, bewilderment on her dirty face. "What if the wife doesn't want to?"

He kept his voice soft and reassuring. "Then it's the husband's responsibility to make her want to."

Joanna stared at the golden-haired warrior seated on the bale of hay in front of her, frozen in sheer terror as the specter of torture rose up before her. The methods employed on common felons ranged from the boot to iron gauntlets. What would the notorious Sea Dragon inflict on a recalcitrant wife?

"By beating her?" she asked.

He smiled, and the crinkles around the corners of his eyes deepened. "There's no need to use a lash to get a lassie to do your bidding, Joey."

Joanna drew a quick, steadying breath. She knew the magnificent, broad-shouldered creature before her was wicked, but did he possess sorcery, too? Perhaps the magical power of the sea dragons had descended, along with their scaly green tails, from father to son in an unbroken line. 'Twould account for the strange effect he had on her. Her words rasped in her dry throat. "How, then?"

MacLean gestured toward the chestnut mare in the next stall, watching them with curious eyes. "The same way Jock taught you to handle the horses by coaxing them with carrots and apples to eat out of your palm. Once they get used to the smell and feel of you, they come round."

Her crushing disappointment at the bald, unromantic description of courtship tempered Joanna's relief.

Godsakes—carrots and apples?

Where were the ardent serenades sung beneath the lady's window, the poetry and flowers, the pledges of undying love?

The thought of MacLean doing to her what she'd witnessed between Tam and Mary wasn't at all the romantic rendezvous she'd envisioned for her wedding night. God's truth, such earthy sensuality left her breathless and trembling.

The sudden memory of the Sea Dragon's large, sinewy male body, naked except for the scrap of white linen, flooded her with embarrassment. Her heart did a funny little skip. Just imagining the touch of his lips on her bare breasts sent a tingling sensation curling through her inner parts. Even the sound of his deep baritone brought goose bumps to her skin. Though she'd ruled out torture as his preferred method of seduction, the use of magical powers couldn't be so easily dismissed. There were definite physical changes in her body whenever she was near him that couldn't be explained in any other way.

"Have you tamed many lassies with apples and carrots?" Joanna inquired, determined to squash the fluttery response in her belly.

MacLean gave a short, good-natured laugh, which she assumed was a modest affirmative.

She frowned at him skeptically. "Without once thrashing them?"

His emerald eyes sparkled with amusement. The thick golden hair framed his ax-sharp features, softened now by his devastating grin. "For a halflin, Joey, you've a man-sized curiosity," he said with a chuckle. "A wise man doesn't use a whip on his woman any more than he does on a fine horse."

Now he'd thoroughly confused her. As a young girl, Joanna had dreamed of a knight in shining armor coming to Allonby Castle and carrying her away on his magnificent white charger. Instead, she'd been betrothed to a man who equated courtship to horse training. "You'd treat your wife like your livestock, then?"

"That's not what I meant, lad," MacLean said patiently. "But a man's wife does belong to him, just as his land and his cattle. And he takes good care of what belongs to him, just as he protects it from rapacious neighbors' raiding parties."

At Joanna's mystified silence, he continued in an amused tone, quoting an old Highland proverb. " 'My own goods, my own wife, and we will go home are the three finest sayings in Gaelic.' "

The fact that he considered both her and Kinlochleven Castle his property couldn't have been stated more boldly or clearly.

"Seumas told us you're planning to make changes in the castle's fortifications," she said. "Don't you think you should discuss it with Lady Joanna first?"

Leaning forward, he braced his elbows on his knees and clasped his hands loosely in front of him. "Why would I?"

"Because she might not agree with your plans."

"What would a woman know about fortifications?" he asked in a bewildered tone.

"You could explain it to her."

He flashed her a lopsided smile as he shook his head. "And have her explain how she supervises the candlemaking to me? Or the bleaching of linen?"

Appalled at his intention to shut his wife out of the most important decisions affecting her own castle, Joanna tucked her thumbs in her belt and scowled at him. "You think because she's a maid she couldn't understand?"

He eyed her for a moment, then shrugged. "Lady Joanna's a bit slow," he said, tapping a fingertip to his temple, "even for a female."

She stared at him, indignation burning inside her. "What makes you say that?" she demanded.

"I was told so the first day I arrived. And Lady Joanna hasn't said three words to me in the time I've been here. The moment I come into view, she looks at me as though I've two heads and scurries away like a frightened wee mouse. So I assumed Lady Beatrix had spoken the truth, when she said the simpleminded heiress sometimes wanders about the glen, lost in a daze."

"Oh," Joanna replied. She bit her lip and looked down at the straw covering the floor. She'd forgotten that part of their plan.

"That is true, isn't it?" he questioned.

She looked up to find him watching her intently. "Why, of course," she replied. "But I still think you should discuss your plans with her. She might understand more than you think."

"Whether she'd understand or not isn't the point, lad," he stated. "I wouldn't debate the emplacement of the castle's artillery with my wife any more than I'd discuss a battle strategy with her. Protecting a fortress from its enemies is a man's responsibility."

Her low voice dropped another octave as she said tightly, "And a woman's responsibility is to see to her husband's comfort, produce a batch of bairns, and keep her nose out of his bloody business.''

MacLean plucked a piece of hay from the stack he sat on and rolled it between his thumb and forefinger. ''For a wee laddie, you're taking this discussion very seriously.''

Joanna caught herself just in time. She plopped down beside him and shrugged indifferently. ''I was only supposing. I'll never have to worry about castles or lands—or womenfolk, either, for that matter.''

He whacked her on the back, nearly dislodging her from the bundle of hay. ''Consider yourself lucky,'' he advised. ''You'll be able to choose your own bride, instead of having one chosen for you.''

She looked up at him in surprise. ''Don't you want to marry Lady Joanna?''

''Why would I?'' he asked with a lift of his brows. He rose to his feet before she could ask another question. ''You'd best be getting back to your chores now,'' he said briskly.

As Joanna poured oats into the feed troughs, she watched MacLean saddle Fraoch and lead him out of the stables. She prayed that Ewen would arrive soon. For she could never allow poor Idoine to be shackled for life to an ignorant jackass, who had all the romantic sensitivity of a door.

Rory's conversation in the stables with his irrepressible bride-to-be heightened his curiosity. He wanted to learn more about her. Hell, he wanted to learn *everything* about her, starting with what she'd look like without her boy's disguise—or anything on at all, for that matter. He found himself thinking of their wedding night and the delights that lay in store. Since he couldn't question Joanna directly, he decided to send for Maude Beaton.

''I'm told you were Lady Joanna's nursemaid when she was small,'' Rory said when the woman arrived. He stood in front of the fireplace in the library, one arm resting on the granite mantelpiece.

Maude sat down stiffly in the ladderback chair he'd indicated, a basket of colorful yarns she'd carried into the room resting in her lap. Attired in a fine wool gown, with a black headdress banded in velvet, she watched him with thoughtful gray eyes. Her costume and bearing bespoke a highly respected member of the household, and she showed no sign of fear in his presence, as did the other females.

"That I was, laird," she replied. "Though as for nursing her through illnesses and such, there wasn't much call for that. Joanna came into this world screaming her lungs out, her wee arms flapping and her short legs kicking, and she hasn't been still a moment since. 'Twas her mama who was the sickly one. From the day Lady Anne learned her husband had been killed in battle, her broken heart never healed."

"And that's when the Englishwoman returned to Cumberland with her daughter?"

Maude nodded and breathed a long, cheerless sigh. "I insisted on going with them. Couldn't stand the thought of being parted from my wee lamb, though it meant going to live among the Sassenachs. In the seven unhappy years we were there, I thanked God every day, for her sake, that I did."

"Why unhappy?"

Maude looked at the powerful laird standing before her and wondered just how truthfully she should answer him. When Joanna had concocted her ridiculous scheme to pose as a lad, Maude had been certain the King's Avenger would be as cruel and savage as legend portrayed. But after the first day, he'd shown great patience and understanding with his kinsmen-to-be. Not one Macdonald had been molested during his brief time as their new laird.

From the charts on the table, she surmised that MacLean planned to make improvements in his new home, not merely drain it of its resources for his own aggrandizement. And his leadership of men was unquestionable. Though stern and short of words, he conducted himself with decorum. To her knowledge, not a chambermaid—or a dairymaid, either—had spent a night in his bed, though more than a few willing lassies had succumbed to the blandishments of his hearty men-at-arms.

And Maude felt certain that Joanna's ruse would soon be discovered. The shrewd, sardonic green eyes watching her now convinced her of that. Lady Joanna and Laird MacLean would spend the rest of their lives bound to each other. It made no sense for the lass's future husband to think less of her than he already did, simply because she was a Macdonald.

"Och, the Nevilles never accepted her—Joanna being half-Scot and all," Maude said at last. "They criticized her accent and her uninhibited ways. Even the servants were needlessly cruel. I once overheard an uppity chambermaid call my sweet lassie a mongrel behind her back. I boxed the nasty chit's ears good for her, I did."

Intrigued, Rory sank down in the chair across from the ruddy-cheeked woman. "The Nevilles allowed this kind of treatment of their only granddaughter?"

"Joanna's grandparents were seldom at Allonby," Maude explained. "The marquess remained in London until his failing health caused him to retire to the country. He died a few weeks later, and his wife returned to court, only to follow him very shortly to the grave." She waved her hand in contemptuous dismissal. "Not much loss there. Neither one of 'em was worth a ha'pence, if you ask me."

Rory steepled his fingers, his elbows resting on the chair arms, and searched her perceptive gaze. The day the king of Scotland had commanded Rory to marry Joanna, he'd explained that George Neville, Marquess of Allonby, had been a trusted courtier in Henry Tudor's court, and the marchioness a lady-in-waiting to the English queen.

Rory motioned for Maude to go on.

"Lady Anne loved her daughter dearly," she assured him, "but her ladyship was an invalid for the remaining years of her life. So the poor dear lassie grew up alone and pretty much forgotten."

"No one saw to the future heiress's training in deportment or the running of a household?'' he asked in surprise.

"My faith, Joanna had tutors, right enough. Mean, pinch-faced men who'd rap her wee knuckles for the least mistake in her recitations.''

"And did she make mistakes often?'' he asked quietly, though his jaw tightened at the thought of anyone purposefully inflicting pain on the spirited lassie.

"Often enough to reduce her to tears at the sight of them,'' Maude replied, her eyes flashing with scorn. "Scholars. Hah! There was no pleasing any of those self-righteous hypocrites. 'Twas no wonder she'd sneak out to the stables, saddle her pony, and ride for hours through the countryside all by herself. The only solace she had was her daydreams and the stories I'd tell her in the evening just before she fell asleep. Mostly, she lived in a world of her own creation, filled with knights and their ladies fair and evil dragons needing to be vanquished.''

"I see.''

But he didn't see at all. *Knights. Dragons. Ladies fair.* None of it made much sense. And Rory was, above all, a sensible man.

Maude glanced over at the sheets of parchment spread across the library table. "Are you planning to make changes, laird?'' she asked with the inherent aplomb of a trusted retainer.

Drumming his fingers on the arms of his chair, Rory nodded absently. He'd imagined the Maid of Glencoe as a pampered Sassenach noblewoman, given everything her heart desired. The possibility that she'd been mistreated because of her Scottish blood hadn't occurred to him. His lack of awareness pricked his conscience—he wasn't generally that obtuse. He'd let the fact that she was a Macdonald overshadow everything else.

"Was her maltreatment the reason Lady Joanna decided to return to Scotland when her mother died?'' he questioned.

Maude smiled reminiscently. "Bless us, milady didn't

make that decision. 'Twas made for Joanna by her Uncle and Aunt Blithfield.''

That surprised him. Usually relatives were anxious to hang on to an orphaned lass born with a silver spoon in her mouth.

"They sent the heiress back to Scotland?"

"Not exactly." Her gaze on the colorful basket in her lap, Maude smoothed her fingers over the balls of brilliant yarn. Her smile spread into an irrepressible grin.

"Tell me what happened."

"Well, now," she said, "shortly after Lady Anne died, Lord Philip and Lady Clarissa came to take Joanna back to London with them. Clarissa was Lady Anne's younger sister. As far as the Blithfields were concerned, Allonby Castle was the farthest outpost of civilization, and they couldn't wait to shake its dust from their fancy shoes. But before they could pack Joanna up and hustle her off to their manor in Surrey, an army of Scotsmen appeared at the gate. Their leader demanded they turn the heiress over to him or he'd storm the fortress and slay every living soul. Rather than risk losing their own lives, those two cowardly Sassenachs agreed to hand her over, with not so much as a sword being drawn or a hackbut discharged."

Rory scowled, scarcely able to believe the tale. "Her own relatives relinquished Joanna without a fight?"

"Humph," Maude said, as she made a distasteful face. "You must remember, laird, the English aren't known for their honor. Nor their courage, either."

That much he knew to be true. "Was she held for ransom?"

Maude chuckled and shook her head. "The Scots' leader was none other than the lassie's grandpa, old Somerled Macdonald. The Blithfields had never seen him, and when he identified himself as the Red Wolf of Glencoe, the two imbeciles still didn't realize who he was. They simply had the portcullis raised and shoved the wee lassie outside."

"No one in the castle tried to stop them?"

"Oh, the officer of the guard tried to reason with the

Blithfields. Captain Pechell told the lass he and every last one of his men were willing to give their lives defending her. But when Joanna heard that the armed force outside the walls was too large to repel, she insisted on sacrificing herself to save the others.''

Rory leaned forward in astonishment. "Didn't she know who the Scots leader was?"

Maude shook her head. "Not till she stepped outside the gate. No one had bothered to tell her 'twas the Red Wolf. Then Somerled opened his arms and called her by name, and Joanna ran to him. He said he'd come to take her home to Scotland.''

"Why hadn't he told the Blithfields who he was in the first place, instead of threatening the castle?"

"Because Somerled knew they'd never give her up unless they feared for their own lives. 'Tis a fortune she's worth, as you very well know, milord. The last thing they wanted was to let the golden goose slip through their fingers. But their terror of the Scots was greater than their greed.''

Maude's emphasis on the maid's fortune made Rory realize exactly how the loyal nursemaid viewed him. In her eyes, he was just another avaricious person who coveted the girl for the wealth and lands she represented.

Dammit, he had tried to throw the proposed alliance back in the king's teeth, but he wasn't going to admit that to Maude now. She'd never believe him, anyway.

"If what you say is true," he stated skeptically, "Lady Joanna showed uncommon valor."

Maude lifted her brows at the inference she'd been lying. "Faith, 'tis true, right enough. The lass has more pluck than most men. But then, she *is* a Macdonald.''

His eyes thoughtful, the laird rose to his feet. "That's all for now. You may go."

She dipped a curtsy and left The MacLean to his quiet contemplation, with the hope that her words would soften his wrath when he discovered just who his impetuous bride-to-be really was.

Chapter 4

R ory paced the sloping embankment, counting his steps aloud as he went. Just as he'd expected, Joanna came hurrying over.

"What are you doing, laird?" she asked with a quizzical smile. Her violet-blue eyes were wide with concern, her long lashes, ruby-tinged in the sunlight, fluttered becomingly in her agitation.

He barely spared her a glance. "Measuring."

She had to skip to keep up with his long strides. "Measuring what?"

He stopped, his hands propped on his hips, and looked at her with a show of impatience. In spite of the soot on her cheeks and chin, the sight of her upturned face filled him with pleasure. God, she was bonny. Small-boned, bright-eyed, and enticing as the perfume that drifted from her pillows.

And she belonged to him.

All five feet of her.

He wanted to snatch off that tawdry knit cap and release the coppery hair hidden beneath. To take her in his arms and taste the soft lips and discover if they were really as sweet as they looked. But Rory wasn't about to enter marriage as the duped bridegroom. He'd no intention of playing court jester to Clan Macdonald.

First, he'd establish firm control over the wily Sassenach heiress and her equally deceitful kinsmen. Then he'd teach

57

Joanna just how easily a MacLean tamed a recalcitrant wench too clever for her own good—carrots and apples be damned.

"We're going to start the renovations on the barbican," he told her and promptly turned away.

She caught hold of his sleeve. "Aren't you planning to wait till you've wed Lady Joanna?"

He looked down at the tapered fingers clutching the saffron material of his shirt.

That's it, lass, touch me.

As no lowly stable boy would dare touch his laird.

And before I'm through, you'll have forgotten who you're even supposed to be.

She snatched her hand away as though she'd read his thoughts. "You . . . you really should wait," she added lamely. "At least till after the wedding."

"I see no need to wait, Joey," he replied in an absent tone. "I might as well get the masons and wrights started on the work while the weather's still fine."

The consternation in her eyes was laughable. Hooking her thumbs in her belt, Joanna squinted up at him. Her delicately arched brows drew together in displeasure. "And you're determined to go ahead with your plans for the new fortifications without discussing them with Lady Joanna?"

Rory strode briskly along the edge of the barbican once more. "What good would it do?" he tossed over his shoulder. "The Maid of Glencoe appears too ignorant to comprehend the need to have towers stand astride the curtain walls or the emplacement of artillery in the gatehouse."

He stopped, and Joanna, who'd been half-running to keep up, almost plowed into him. "She is simpleminded, isn't she?" he inquired gruffly.

"Oh, very!" Joanna exclaimed with an adorable smile, then sobered, trying her best to look properly downcast at the heiress's misfortune. " 'Tis sad to be born that way, but such things happen now and again, I've been told."

"I've been told you can read and write."

The abrupt change of subject caught her unprepared.

"Who said that?" she demanded. She raised her chin in cautious deliberation, uncertain if she should deny it.

"I'm not sure," he lied. He looked up at the tower above them as though calculating its height. "Perhaps Father Graham mentioned you'd received some scholastic training. Is that true?"

From the corner of his eye, Rory could practically see her devious little mind whirling, trying to decide if she should tell the truth or fabricate another tale of folderol.

Come on, my wee lass, step right into the trap.

She wavered for the space of a moment, and he commenced walking once again. Just as he'd hoped, the opportunity to portray the fractious stable lad as the complete opposite of the half-wit heiress proved too enticing. She nodded. " 'Tis true. Why do you ask, laird?"

"I think your talents may be wasted in the stable. You're a clever laddie. Come with me to the library. I've a letter I'd like you to write."

"Oh, Seumas usually writes all the letters," she said, following at Rory's heels as they crossed the lower bailey.

Curious eyes watched their progress, each Macdonald halting in his chores to make certain his mistress wasn't in trouble.

Flashing a brief smile and nodding reassuringly, Rory swept Joanna along in his wake. He didn't want a crowd of bystanders listening outside the library door.

"The steward has enough to do keeping the estate accounts, tallying sacks of seed, overseeing the planting of oats and barley, and preparing shipments of wool and hides," he said. "I'm not going to burden him further with my personal correspondence."

"Father Thomas can read and write, too," she offered with helpful enthusiasm. "He knows English and Greek, as well as Latin."

"The letters I send can be written in plain, everyday Gaelic," he replied. "And the priest is busy at the moment. I've asked him to remain in the chapel for the next few days. Did you know that someone keeps blowing out the candles lit for the wedding couple in front of the Virgin's altar?''

''That's terrible!'' she said in a scandalized voice. She tugged the ridiculous knit cap further down over her ears and made a moue of distaste. ''Who'd dare do a sacrilegious thing like that?''

''Some wicked varlet who isn't afraid of burning in hell for all eternity.''

She halted, staring at him with a stricken expression. ''Do you think the sin is mortal, then?''

''I can't imagine anything more serious than interfering with another man's prayers. Can you?''

She gulped, big-eyed and apprehensive. Her reply came out in a whisper. ''I never thought of it that way.''

''When I catch the culprit,'' Rory said, lowering his voice to a threatening growl, ''he'll wish he were in Hades instead of my dungeon.''

Joanna's heart started to work its way up into her throat. ''Why?'' she squeaked. ''What will you do to her—*him*?''

''Hot pincers. Thumbscrews. The rack.''

She wrung her hands. ''You'd torture a man because he blew out a holy candle?''

One hand caressing the hilt of his dagger, MacLean leaned over her and grinned malevolently. ''That's what happens to heretics.''

She staggered backward a step, nearly speechless. A cold chill whistled down her back. *''Heretics?''*

''Don't dally, lad.'' He caught her elbow and hustled her along beside him. ''We've lots to do.''

Joanna accompanied The MacLean into her grandfather's library. *Her* library now, though the tall man dragging her like a felon insisted it belonged to him.

He sank down in a caned armchair behind the table piled with charts and pointed to a sheaf of vellum, a quill pen, and a small bottle of ink. ''Let's see how well you can write,'' he said in a dubious tone. Obviously, he had no confidence in the schooling of a scruffy orphan.

Well, she'd show him.

Her tutors at Allonby Castle had insisted on a grandiose script befitting a monk given the task of copying the Holy Book for future generations.

Joanna took a large atlas from a nearby shelf to use as a writing desk, positioned herself cross-legged on a cushioned bench in the window embrasure, and waited with exaggerated politeness.

"Dear Lady Emma . . ." he began.

"Who's she?"

Godsakes, did he plan to dictate a letter to his ladylove? And him a promised bridegroom! Evidently sea dragons never learned of chivalry and honor and self-sacrifice. They were too busy taking carnal lessons from the water nymphs.

MacLean glowered at her. "What difference does it make who the lady is? Go on, write it down."

Biting her lip to keep back the scathing retort burning the tip of her tongue, Joanna wrote the salutation: *Dear Lady Emma.*

Satisfied with her belated compliance, he leaned back in his chair, clasped his hands behind his head, and stretched out his long legs. "Dear Lady Emma," he continued, "my plans have changed. I'd like you to bring the rest of the family here to Kinloch—"

"Slow down!" Joanna called, scribbling furiously. "You're going much too fast."

He stopped and waited for her to catch up.

Her quill poised above the parchment, she glanced over at him. "How large is Lady Emma's family?"

"Never question your laird and chief about his personal affairs, Joey," he admonished.

She stiffened at the imperious remark. "I haven't had a laird since the mighty Somerled Macdonald died."

"Well, you have one now."

Joanna glared at the obnoxious, thick-skulled, condescending libertine. The day a MacLean became *her* laird and chief was the day she grew wings and flew about the chapel, trilling alleluias and plucking on a harp.

Seemingly unaware of her indignation, the Sea Dragon

rose and strode lazily across the carpet to stand beside her. Folding his arms across his broad chest, he looked down from his great height at the vellum sheet. Sunlight from the window gilded his hair, forming a halo around his head. Lucifer in all his glory couldn't have been more alluring.

Humph. He could use all the sorcery within his power. She'd no intention of succumbing to the bronzed warlord's physical charms. Why, at that very moment, his scaly green tail was probably twitching with self-approval beneath that green and black plaid.

Green.

She hated green.

It was the color of toads and frogs and slimy moss.

Joanna shifted uncomfortably beneath his steady gaze. If the obvious display of beauty, size and strength was meant to intimidate, it succeeded. She could feel the back of her neck start to prickle, and her scalp grew tight beneath her striped cap.

"Are you ready to continue?" he inquired, his tone brusque.

She moistened her lips and swallowed. "I am now."

"The wedding will take place at Kinlochleven," he dictated, "not at Castle Stalcaire as we'd planned. Invite whomever you wish to accompany you here, including His Majesty and the entire court. King James sets great store in this alliance, and he should be present to witness the nuptials as he'd intended."

She made a strangled sound.

"Is something wrong?" he asked.

"Umhm. That's a lot of people."

He lifted one golden brow sardonically. "Not for a wedding."

"Tell that to Ethel," she muttered.

"Who?"

"The cook."

A smile flickered over his lips as he indicated for her to continue writing. "I'll be waiting for your arrival," he concluded. "Your son."

Joanna stared up at him in befuddlement.

"Go on," he said with an impatient flick of his finger. "Write it down."

Drops of ink splashed on the parchment from the shaky nib, and Joanna hastily blotted them with her fingertips. "Lady Emma is your mother?"

"What other woman would I invite to my wedding?"

"I-I had no notion," she replied. "I thought . . . perhaps . . . a sweetheart."

"Joey, Joey, Joey," he scolded with a slow, disbelieving shake of his head. "Would a bridegroom invite one of his light-o'-loves to his nuptials? Where did you get such a bizarre idea?"

"I haven't been out in the world much," she admitted grudgingly as she hunkered over the atlas. She could feel a blush creep up her cheeks. "I'm not sure what a man forced to wed against his wishes would do."

"What makes you think I'm marrying against my wishes?" he demanded, his tone incredulous.

"You said so."

"I never said any such thing."

Dismayed at his pathetic memory, she tipped her head back and gazed into his bedazzling green eyes. Eyes the color of mountain forests. Dark and deep and mysterious as a Druid's spell.

Inexplicably, the fresh scent of pine trees washed by the rain seemed to linger about him. She might hate green, but she loved the smell of juniper and spruce. Something shivered and bubbled inside her. Something as warm as mulled wine and as sweet as treacle.

"When we were talking in the stable," she insisted with a gulp, "you said I was lucky that I'd never have my bride chosen for me."

"Ah, well, I think you misunderstood me, lad. I'm very pleased to be marrying Lady Joanna."

"You are?"

He flicked the tassel of her stocking cap with one finger and smiled disarmingly. "I am."

Joanna squirmed on the bench, strangely affected by this show of playfulness in the fearsome warrior. "Even if she's a simpleton who wanders away and can't be found for days—weeks, really?"

Rory left the window seat and dropped back down in his chair. Propping an elbow on its arm, he rested his chin on his fist and studied Joanna. There was no mistaking the bewilderment on her expressive face. Her youth and inexperience shone like starlight in those mesmerizing blue eyes. A thousand candle flames couldn't equal their glow.

She was so damn easy to mislead, he should feel guilty.

What he felt was pure delight.

"Once I'm married to the lass," he said softly, "I'll put a leash on her."

"You'll do *what?*" Joanna leaped up from the bench, the letter and book falling to the floor at her feet. She held the quill in one hand and the vial of ink in the other, clutching them like lifelines in a stormy sea.

"Oh, I'll tether her on a long chain," he assured her. "She won't be confined to one room, only the castle grounds."

"How could you be so cruel?"

"I can't have my wife wandering off," he replied reasonably as he brushed a speck of lint from his sleeve. "How will she ever see to my comforts and produce a batch of weans if she's forever tromping through the woodlands in a daze?"

Joanna's small frame trembled with barely suppressed ire. "Well, she *won't* see to your comforts."

"She won't?" He reached down, retrieved the atlas and ink-splattered parchment, and waited for her to be seated again.

"The maid's far too dull-witted."

"I'll teach her how to serve me," he replied with a complacent grin.

Her eyes shooting sparks, her jaw clenched, she fairly spit out the words. "She'll never learn."

"She'll learn, lad, I promise you. With enough apples

and carrots, I'll teach the ninny to jump through hoops before I'm done.''

Devastated by his complete lack of sympathy for the tragic heiress, Joanna sank back down on the velvet seat. She'd have to warn Idoine to stay well out of sight till her father arrived. "You should see the lady's embroidery," she said halfheartedly. " 'Tis a mass of knots and tangles. And she lacks all the skills for running a household.''

He leaned over and set the large volume on her lap, then placed the sheet of vellum on top of it. "We'll all get along fine here at Kinlochleven, regardless of my wife's many drawbacks.''

Joanna gazed at the obtuse man, and her shoulders slumped in defeat. 'Twould do no good to argue with him. He was more stubborn than a donkey with a load of bricks on its back and a field of clover behind it. She looked down at the letter in front of her and sighed. "Are you sure you want to begin with 'Dear Lady Emma'?''

MacLean looked at her in surprise. "That's her name.''

"But it sounds too . . ." She paused, searching for the right word.

"Too formal?''

She nodded. "What do you usually call your mother?''

"Mother.''

Joanna leaned forward and smiled encouragingly. "Then why don't we change the salutation to 'Dear Mother'?''

He thought about it for a moment. "All right. Go ahead.''

She drew a line through the words and corrected them. "Actually," she said, "I think it sounds better, 'My dearest Mother.' ''

He quirked an eyebrow as she scratched out the correction and rewrote it, but didn't protest.

Joanna chewed her lower lip, still not satisfied. Then above the word *dearest* she added *darling*. "There," she said, pleased at last with her work, "that sounds much better.''

MacLean rose and walked over to stand beside her once

again. The salutation, crossed and recrossed and crossed out again, finally read: *"My dearest, darling, angel Mother."*

" 'Tis fortunate I'm signing the letter," he said dryly. "Otherwise she'd never guess who'd sent it."

"If I can make another suggestion," Joanna said, "I thought it would be better to end it this way." Without waiting for his assent, she scratched through the ending and wrote: *"Your loving, devoted, and dutiful son."*

He took the letter and perused it without comment, and Joanna realized, too late, that her handwriting appeared much too ornate for a mere orphan lad. The script was embellished with elaborate curlicues and grand flourishes.

"Naturally, I'll have to copy it over," she said, reaching out to take the sheet of parchment.

"No need," he told her, a tiny smile playing about his lips. "My mother will enjoy it just the way it's written."

His eyes gleamed with humor, and their sudden warmth took her breath away. How could she have thought his gaze frigid? Looking up at him now, she found it hard to believe he was only part human, a spawn of the sea monsters that roamed the ocean depths.

MacLean seemed different this morning, though she couldn't exactly say why. For one thing, he was standing much closer than he'd ever stood before. Godsakes, she could almost feel the heat of his large, well-muscled body. She scooted back on the bench before the scent of fresh pine could fog up her brain.

He took the ink and quill from her and set them on the desktop, then lifted the book from her lap and caught her hand.

Joanna flinched at his touch, expecting a sea dragon's skin to feel cold and scaly. She tried to squirm away, but he placed the atlas on the brocaded window seat and drew her up to stand in front of him.

His warm, firm clasp seemed to set off the clanging of bells that warned of a fire amid the haystacks. Her first reaction was to run to the well in the upper bailey and douse herself with a bucket of cold water.

MacLean turned her palms over and surveyed the signs of the toil she'd been doing since he'd arrived. Along with the blisters, fresh inkstains marred her fingers. "Jock's been working you too hard," he said with a frown.

"He's not," she denied. "I like working in the stables."

"I've changed my mind about that, laddie," he stated, ignoring the fact that she was trying desperately to escape his hold. "You'll make a better clerk than an ostler. From now on, I'll have you work here in the library with me."

Joanna couldn't believe what was happening. In spite of her best efforts to break free, the laird held her fingers in his strong grasp and looked down at her with the strangest expression—a mixture of amusement and affection.

What the devil was he up to?

If she didn't know better, she'd think he actually liked her—well, Joey. The last thing she'd anticipated was the ferocious Sea Dragon developing a brotherly attachment for an impudent, dirty-faced orphan boy.

A firm step interrupted her useless struggle, and Joanna looked over to see Fearchar standing in the open doorway. She expected to be released at once, but the chief of Clan MacLean continued to hold her hand as if it were the most normal thing in the world.

Godsakes, what would his second-in-command think? Lairds didn't show a personal interest in lowly serving lads.

But Fearchar gave no sign of surprise. He merely flashed his good-natured smile and waited.

"You can run along now, Joey," MacLean said, finally releasing her. "But plan to spend the afternoon working with me."

She turned on her heel the moment he freed her, darted around the tall, bearded titan, and raced out the door.

The next morning, Father Graham stood at the chapel door, his opened breviary in his hand. When he looked up to watch the hunting party mount, his face grew pale. Prayers abandoned, he hurried across the bustling lower bailey.

"Milord," he exclaimed as he approached Rory, already seated on Fraoch, "you can't mean to take Joey with you!"

Rory continued to tug on his leather gauntlets, unperturbed by the cleric's outrage. He glanced at the slim youth astride a capricious chestnut mare and then back to Father Graham. "Why not?"

Joanna's eyes flashed a warning to her chaplain, who paid her no heed. "Because he's—he's too young to mingle with a group of rough soldiers. And he's never been hunting in his life."

" 'Twill do the laddie good to be in the company of grown men," Rory said. "And with Arthur gone, I can use a bright lad to serve as my gillie."

"But not Joey!" Father Graham implored. His dark eyes betrayed his alarm. "There are other boys in the castle who could serve you better, laird."

Rory gathered the reins in his hand and shifted restlessly in the saddle. "Whom would you suggest?"

Father Graham looked wildly around the bailey, scanning the listening Macdonalds, till his gaze lit on two burly figures standing in front of the smithy. "Jacob's apprentice would be an excellent choice."

"And who, then, would work alongside the farrier?" Rory inquired in a bored tone. "Joey's not nearly as robust as the man's own son."

By now, several Macdonalds had left their work and come to stand near the small hunting party. The sandy-haired blacksmith reached up and grabbed the prancing chestnut's halter in his large, work-roughened hand, then looked over at Rory. "I'd be proud to lend you my son Lothar, milord, until your gillie returns. He's fifteen and stronger than most full-grown men."

Lothar hurried to stand beside his thickset father. Whisking off his brown wool cap, he bowed his head and waited hopefully.

Rory looked at the strapping fellow, then back to Joanna's slight figure, seated on the restive chestnut. "And I'm to leave the wee laddie to take Lothar's place at the forge?'' He rubbed his chin, pretending to consider the idea.

Joanna patted Bebind's graceful neck in a soothing gesture as she tried to hide her own nervousness. If she could slip away from the men-at-arms in the woods, she could put miles between them before they realized she'd disappeared. "Let me ride out with the hunters," she implored. "I'll come to no harm."

Father Thomas hurried to stand beside her, the long, white cord that tied his robe swinging briskly with each stride. Anxious to stretch her legs in a gallop, the pretty mare sidestepped and tossed her head at the sudden movement.

Joanna bent down to address the priest in a low, urgent tone, praying he'd read the message in her eyes. "I want to go, Father."

But her chaplain wasn't convinced. " 'Tis too dangerous, my child. You might take a spill and break a bone."

'Twas a lie, of course; Joanna was an expert horsewoman.

MacLean drew on his reins and turned his black stallion toward the raised portcullis. "You've coddled the halfling for too long, Father," he said. "But if you think the laddie might fall off his horse, I'll stay right beside him. Don't worry, I'll make a man out of Joey yet."

Without waiting for a reply, the laird led the hunting party through the gate and across the drawbridge. Then the horsemen urged their mounts to a canter in the direction of the heather-covered hills above the loch and the forest beyond. Four deerhounds gamboled beside the curvetting horses, barking ecstatically.

'Twas a glorious May morning, the sun seducing the spring flowers with its kiss. Wild daisies and clover bloomed on the hillsides. Overhead, the new leaves of the silver birch shivered in the gentle breeze.

Joanna could hardly contain her exhilaration. 'Twas wonderful to be out riding again. The opportunity to accompany the MacLeans had come in answer to her prayers to Jeanne d'Arc, and she assured the Maid of Orléans that she wasn't going to waste it. She'd be patient and wait for her chance to lag behind. When the men galloped off into the trees, chasing after the hounds, she'd simply ride away in another direction.

Ballachulish was only a day's journey, and she knew the way. From there, she could hire an escort to Mingarry Castle. She wasn't afraid; this was her land and her people. She'd be safe enough as long as she didn't happen upon strangers, which would be very unlikely. Once she was at Mingarry, Ewen would protect her. Clan Macdonald's courageous war leader would fight to the death before letting the chief of the MacLeans capture her again.

The barking of the deerhounds shattered Joanna's happy reflections. With cries of elation, the men kicked their horses' flanks and the chase was on. But the diabolical chief of Clan MacLean ruined everything.

Blast the man for a perverse, blackhearted scoundrel.

True to his promise to Father Graham, he stayed right at her side, till the two of them were moving at a slow walk and his men had disappeared, whooping and hollering, into the forest.

"There's no need for you to miss the chase, laird," she said, trying not to disclose her chagrin. "I won't fall off Bebind. She's spirited, but Father Thomas was being overcautious. Ride on and catch up with your men. I'll be quite all right."

He ignored her suggestion. "I was told that the chestnut is Lady Joanna's favorite mount, but you handle the little mare well. Almost as though you've ridden her before."

"Oh, I'm certain she won't mind my choosing Bebind," she asserted with all the aplomb she could muster. "Milady rarely rides out. She doesn't like the exertion."

Rory watched Joanna with concealed admiration. She had a fine seat and controlled the lively animal with expertise.

His future bride pleased him immensely. He'd expected

a haughty, petulant Englishwoman, not this intrepid Scottish lass. Quick-witted and resourceful, Joanna displayed a winsome charm and an endearing, albeit irreverent, sense of humor.

"Tell me, Joey, does Lady Joanna look forward to the wedding with anticipation?" he inquired offhandedly.

His sprightly companion gazed up at the cloudless azure sky and pretended to ponder the question. Then she turned her head to look at him, and a smile played about her kissable lips. Her blue eyes danced with hilarity. "I don't believe she's one bit happier about her marriage than on the day you first met."

He frowned in apparent disappointment. "I see."

"Well, Lady Joanna wouldn't be quite so reluctant," she offered bracingly, "if it weren't for the far better offers she's received."

"Better offers?"

"Umhm. For her hand." She lifted one gloved hand and waggled it tellingly.

"Ah hah," he said, staring at her dainty fingers. "From better men than my own humble self, I gather."

Her perfect smile revealed her delight at his frown of concern. "Oh, from warriors far more valiant, more chivalrous, and . . ." She paused and looked at him as though afraid she might hurt his feelings.

"Go on," he insisted. "Say it."

With a shrug of appology, she continued. "Far more handsome."

Rory wanted to reach over and drag Joanna off her mount and set her in front of him, so he could cuddle her small, lithe body close to his and cover those naughty, lying lips with his own.

But as captain of the *Sea Dragon*, he'd learned to bring recalcitrant sailors in line with iron-fisted authority. Swift and sure punishment for a man's wrongdoing prevented mutinous behavior in the future. Rory had no intention of allowing his bride-to-be to think she could mock him and not pay the price.

And in any event, he dared not risk her realizing he'd discovered her secret, lest she try something foolish in an attempt to escape before the wedding.

He set his jaw and fought back the surge of raw lust that coursed through him. "Anything else I should know?" he asked with appropriate misgiving.

She sat up straighter in the saddle, clearly enjoying his discomfiture. "Apart from the fact that she'd rather marry another man? Not really. But the most unfortunate fact for Lady Joanna is that one of her other suitors has lots and lots of gold."

"That's important to her, then, I take it?"

Joanna nodded tellingly. "Don't you wish you were extremely wealthy, milord?"

"I am," he said.

She cocked her head to one side and frowned. "You are?"

"I am."

"Well, you can't possibly be wealthier than all her other suitors, laird," she declared. "Are you certain you wish to marry a lady who's heart has been given to another."

"I do."

"Why, for God's sake?"

He smiled at her incredulous expression. "Because the king commands it."

Joanna urged her chestnut forward, irritated beyond belief by his smug, self-righteous reply. The black stallion immediately kept pace with Bebind.

She studied MacLean covertly. Sometimes it was hard to remember he was the lecherous, evil Sea Dragon, especially when she gazed into his thick-lashed green eyes.

The three eagle feathers on his bonnet, pinned with the clan badge, fluttered and dipped in the breeze. He'd pulled his golden hair back and tied it with a leather thong, and the sharp edge of his profile could have cut glass. Beneath the hem of his plaid, his massive thighs tautened as he guided his bad-tempered stallion effortlessly.

Though she knew he'd spent years on the sea, capturing

pirate galleons for King James, MacLean rode like a centaur, part man and part horse.

"We appear to have lost the rest of the hunting party," she pointed out with a nonchalant smile.

"There's no need to worry, Joey," he assured her. "After they've brought down the deer, we'll meet the others by the mill at the edge of the loch and have some midday refreshments."

She gazed at him in surprise. "How do you know your men will wait for us at Rannoch Mill, laird?"

"I told them to."

With a confident smile, he reached over and slapped Bebind's flank. Both horses broke into a gallop and tore across the hills.

Chapter 5

❧ ⌒∽◯◯∽⌒

Rannoch Mill sat on the confluence of the River Leven and Loch Leven beneath the shadow of Garbh Bheinn's rocky peak. From the grassy bank, one could see Kinlochleven's imposing walls above the rugged cliffs that plummeted down to the cold waters of the loch.

Joanna looked around with a sigh of pleasure as she nibbled on a pastry. This was surely one of the loveliest places in Scotland. The pristine reflection of puffy clouds in the lapis lazuli sky, snowcapped mountaintops, and verdant forests shimmered in the turquoise water.

The pastoral scene reminded her of the tapestry hanging in her bedchamber. Only the knight and his lady were missing from this colorful tableau, but her vivid imagination could easily conjure them out of the crisp spring air.

A handsome, stalwart, courageous knight attired in shining armor would ride up on his mighty steed, dismount in a graceful leap, and stride to where she sat alone amid the primroses . . . In his hand, he'd carry a bouquet of wildflowers that grew along the riverbank. He'd drop to one knee and pledge his undying devotion . . . Shyly, she'd take the violets and bluebells and softly demur, but his courtly manner would overcome her maidenly resistance . . . He'd come to rescue her from—

"Och, what a shot!"

"Blood and bones! The one-eyed devil never misses!"

The raucous sound of the soldiers' cheers disrupted

Joanna's daydream. The MacLean men-at-arms had fastened a painted deerskin to the trunk of an ancient oak and now vied with one another, showing off their skill with bow and arrow. Time and again, Fearchar had bested any man who stood up against him.

After Joanna had served The MacLean, he'd insisted that she sit beside him on the wool plaid spread on the grass, in case there was anything else he needed fetched from his horse. So far, his wants had been few and simple: a slice of mutton pie and a flask of ale from his saddlebags. Then, setting his green bonnet aside, he'd stretched out his long length, folded his hands on his flat belly, and closed his eyes for a midday nap.

Arthur Hay had an easy job serving such a self-sufficient master. Even when Joanna had spilled the porter on the blanket and dropped a piece of the golden-brown pastry on the ground, MacLean hadn't lost his temper.

God's truth, 'twas no wonder she'd felt nervous. He'd watched her with a lazy smile curving his generous mouth and spoke to her in a low, easy tone. As soon as MacLean drifted off, she'd turned her back to keep him out of her sight—and out of her wayward thoughts.

The resonance of his deep voice did peculiar things to her insides. She told herself that any maid would react to the presence of a licentious satyr with queer, unfamiliar feelings. Especially a satyr who practiced the art of black magic. Hadn't her tutors warned her that the Prince of Darkness spoke with honeyed words? Sweet, sugar-coated syllables thick with the enticement of unsurpassed pleasures and unimaginable delights.

"What say you, laird?" Tam called out. "Will you give us a demonstration of your skill?"

She turned to find MacLean had wakened and lay watching her beneath lowered lids. Completely relaxed, he leaned back on his elbows, his legs crossed at the ankles. "Not this morning," he answered. "Let Joey show us what he can do."

Joanna met his genial gaze and tried to hide the fact that

her stomach had just tied itself into knots. "I don't know how to shoot a bow and arrow," she admitted. "No one ever taught me."

"Then 'tis time you learned, lad," MacLean said.

"Truly?" She scrambled to her feet and looked at the men, who nodded their encouragement. "Would someone show me?"

MacLean rose lazily from the plaid. "I'll teach you myself."

"Will you, milord? Oh, I would love to learn!"

But when Joanna measured Tam's long yew bow against her own limited height, she wanted to wail in frustration. She'd never have the strength to draw it back.

"There's a bow rolled up in the blanket behind Fraoch's saddle," MacLean told her. "Go fetch it, lad, and you'll have your first lesson in archery."

Certain the warlord's weapon would be far too big, Joanna did as he ordered with a sinking heart. If she couldn't draw the string and bend the bow, she'd feel like a first-rate fool. To her surprise, though, inside the tartan wool she discovered a shorter bow of lemonwood made especially for a youth, along with a leather armguard and a small archer's glove.

Thrilled, she whirled around to find the men gazing at her with wide smiles. Their golden-haired chief had already taken his place before the target and waited for her with an amused air.

Rory watched Joanna hurry to him, bow, armguard, and glove in one hand and Tam's quiver of arrows in the other. He met her eager eyes and knew his assumption had been correct. Not only would she willingly play the role of his gillie rather than admit her true identity, she was enjoying it.

"Did you bring these for me, sire?" she asked artlessly.

"I did, lad. I thought we'd have time at midday for you to practice."

Laying the quiver on the grass, he showed her how to fasten her glove and string the bow. Then he drew her in front of him and demonstrated the correct way to grip the bow and nock the arrow. With his arms around her, he guided her hands, helping her draw the string and aim for the makeshift target.

"Loose the arrow smoothly," he said. "Just let the bowstring slip off your fingers."

Following MacLean's guidance, Joanna loosed one arrow after another. He bent his head and spoke patiently, teaching her how to concentrate on the target, not just with her eyes, but with her mind as well.

"Try to burn a hole in the target's center," he said softly, "and let no other thought intrude."

He explained how to predict the trajectory the arrow would take on its flight and how to hold her position until the arrow struck its mark.

Only when MacLean helped her aim did she hit the target with consistent accuracy. But Joanna didn't mind: the thrill of learning to use the weapon blotted out every other consideration. The men rewarded her efforts with heartening cheers. When she struck the center of the painted deerskin, they shouted vociferously, just as though she were one of them.

Her tutors in Cumberland would have toppled over, dead of shock, had they seen her. Those narrow-minded pedagogues had berated her interest in anything except deportment, languages, and religion. Though they'd tried their best to squelch her fascination with the Celtic legends and the tales of chivalry during King Arthur's time, Joanna had held fast to her dreams.

Now she was practicing archery like Robin Hood!

She wanted to flap her wings and cry *cock-a-doodle-doo* like a rooster bragging in the hen yard.

Rory could feel Joanna's slender body quivering with excitement. She bit her lower lip in concentration, so engrossed in the lesson she seemed unaware that he held her lightly against him.

His own body responded with rampant awareness of her femininity as the soft curve of her bottom, hidden beneath her faded plaid, came into contact with his thigh. The heat of carnal desire spread through his groin. He savored the feel of her, vibrant and sweet; and the knowledge that she was his forever sent his spirits soaring.

His.

His to keep.

His to enjoy and to pleasure through the bright summer days.

His to hold and caress during the long winter nights.

His for all the years that lay ahead.

An unfamiliar joy filled Rory as he looked down at his indomitable wife-to-be. He'd never known any lass like her.

Joanna's resilience and pluck were remarkable—there seemed to be nothing she wouldn't dare. Her lively nature promised a frank, open playfulness he'd never before met in a female.

The noble ladies of his acquaintance flirted and simpered with fervid intensity, their one goal, marriage to a suitable partner. Born a landless bastard, he'd been spared their guileful lures.

And while the earthy women he'd bedded had encouraged his attentions with lusty vigor, they'd never exhibited the kind of buoyant expectation shining on Joanna's innocent face.

His cheek brushed against the wool of her stocking cap, his mouth mere inches from her soft pink lips, and a tingle of sweet anticipation danced down Rory's spine. Lust clutched and pulled at his loins, bringing with it an ache so deep inside he had to stifle a groan.

With a silent oath, he counted the days before his family arrived and he could put an end to this ridiculous farce and take Joanna to his bed where she belonged.

When it was time to resume the hunt Joanna couldn't hide her disappointment, so MacLean promised to practice archery with her the very next day.

Holy hosanna! Who would have thought being the Sea Dragon's gillie could be so blessed wonderful?

"When will you teach me to use a sword, laird?" she asked, barely able to keep from skipping across the grass.

He laughed softly as he walked beside her toward the horses. "When you're strong enough to lift my claymore."

They came to a halt beside her chestnut mare, and Joanna caught MacLean's sleeve before he could move to Fraoch's side. "What about using a dirk?" she pleaded. "Will you teach me how to fight with a dirk?"

He shook his head in disapproval, but his eyes glittered with merriment. " 'Tis a bloodthirsty lad you are, Joey."

She squeezed his forearm insistently. "But will you teach me?"

"Perhaps."

Having to be satisfied with the noncommittal reply, Joanna placed her foot in the stirrup and started to mount. Bebind chose that moment to play one of her skittish games.

"Here, I'll toss you up," MacLean said unexpectedly. Without waiting for her response, he lifted her off the ground. Somehow, in his attempt to be helpful, his hand slipped beneath her plaid.

Shocked by the feel of his big palm curving over her bottom, Joanna bolted into the saddle. Too stunned to speak, she clasped Bebind's reins in her taut fingers and looked about the grassy embankment.

None of the men appeared to have noticed what happened. Or if they saw, paid no heed. They were all busy checking their girths and halters as they prepared to leave.

Even MacLean appeared completely unruffled by the accident. After all, Joey was only a lowly gillie-in-training, scarcely worth a second thought. And such trifling mistakes happened at times, with no need to apologize.

A flush scorched Joanna's cheeks. Godsakes, she could still feel his callused fingers sliding up the back of her bare thigh. If she hadn't tied the tails of her long shirt between her legs that morning, the ruse would have been over in an instant.

MacLean calmly met her gaze, unaware that her heart

was slamming against her rib cage like a battering ram against a castle gate. "When I think you're ready, Joey, I'll teach you how to use a dirk," he said, misinterpreting her stricken expression.

She lowered her lashes and stared down at her trembling hands, knowing she had to escape. If she stayed at Kinlochleven, 'twould be only a matter of time before he discovered her secret. And a small, insidious voice inside prayed that he'd do just that.

Her throat constricted with embarrassment, Joanna choked out a reply. "As you wish, laird."

The men were scarcely in their saddles when the deerhounds bolted for the woods, howling ecstatically. With a hue and cry, everyone galloped after them.

In the ensuing commotion, Joanna seized her chance. She kicked Bebind's flanks and the spirited mare leaped forward, delighted to be in the race at last.

Peeling away from the MacLeans in an oblique line, Joanna guided the chestnut into the nearby pines. She climbed upward, away from the loch, urging Bebind deeper and deeper into the forest. Riding at a bruising pace, she crouched in the saddle to avoid the low-hanging branches of spruce and fir.

A family of black grouse exploded from the bracken in front of her, beating their glossy wings angrily at the disturbance. The high-strung mare shied, and Joanna soothed her with an urgent whisper.

As the sound of the hunt grew fainter, she slowed her blowing horse to a walk. She was determined to put as much distance as possible between her and the chief of Clan MacLean before stopping to rest.

Her tasseled cap had been partially dislodged during the wild ride, and she anchored the striped wool further down on her head, then gave Bebind an encouraging pat. Following a half-forgotten trail along the river's precipitous edge, she continued her steep ascent into the mountains.

Only the noisy *chup chup* of crossbills and the rustle of leaves in the soft wind disturbed the silence. She'd finally eluded the clever MacLean. But for some reason, the exultation she ought to be feeling eluded her as well.

Rory cursed under his breath. He'd been so aroused by that one fleeting touch, he'd been slow to climb into the saddle. Then the sound of the men's shouts and the dogs' maddened barking had startled his fretful stallion. By the time he'd calmed the rearing, pawing Fraoch, Joanna had disappeared.

While most of his men chased after the deerhounds, Rory had shouted to Fearchar and Tam to follow him and flew after Joanna. The two were behind him now as he tracked the path of broken branches and crushed leaves.

She was riding at a fast pace, too fast for the dangerous terrain. At this elevation the river flowed through a rocky gorge, its banks falling in steep cliffs. Should she become rattled and make the wrong turn, Joanna and her mare would soar into space. And if she somehow evaded her pursuers, darkness would overtake her before she could reach any kind of habitation.

Though the brown bears that once roamed these mountains had disappeared long ago, the forest still harbored wild boars, wolves, and lynx. And the weather remained unpredictable in the spring. A storm could blow in with gale force, toppling tall trees in its path.

Rory burst into a small clearing and reined Fraoch to a halt. Still mounted, Joanna waited near the cliff's edge, giving her lathered horse a rest. She glanced about with frightened eyes when she heard him, then started to urge the chestnut onward.

In that instant a lone wolf, separated somehow from its pack, sprang from behind a jumble of rocks. Fangs bared and snarling, it leaped at Bebind's neck.

The frightened mare reared and plunged, striking out with her hooves and neighing frantically. Joanna tumbled to the ground and landed on her back with a bone-jarring thud. As Bebind raced through the trees, she struggled to her feet.

The wolf recovered in mid-air and immediately turned its lethal attention to the small figure backing slowly toward the edge of the cliff. The injured animal, a large male, had been sliced across the shoulder by the sharp tines of a stag and left behind by the pack when it couldn't keep up. Half-starved and desperate, the wolf lowered its head, bared its fangs, and crept forward in a menacing crouch.

"Don't move!" Rory shouted as he urged Fraoch forward.

Broadsword in hand, he jumped from the saddle and landed between Joanna and the wolf. The next moment, the huge beast charged.

Rory met it with the full force of his strength, plunging his blade to the hilt in its thick chest. The wolf dropped to the ground with an agonized yelp.

Rory pivoted to find Joanna teetering on the brink of the cliff, her eyes huge with terror, her face white beneath the splotches of soot. Dropping his bloody sword, he grabbed for her just as the loose rock gave way beneath her feet.

She threw her arms around Rory's neck and clung to him, gasping with fright in his ear. Her eyelids screwed shut in her frantic struggle for safety, she held on with every ounce of her strength.

It felt so damn wonderful, Rory smiled.

Beneath the oversized garments, her small, firm breasts pressed against his chest. The supple curves of waist and thigh enthralled him. All thoughts of retribution for her past misdeeds scattered like shot from an exploding hackbut. The need to end this absurd masquerade throbbed inside him.

He stepped back from the precipice and turned with her still in his arms. " 'Tis all right. You're safe now," he said soothingly.

The sound of MacLean's voice, calm and reassuring, penetrated Joanna's panic. She opened her eyes and tipped her head back to meet his gaze. "You . . . you saved my life," she whispered.

Stunned by the clash of emotions warring inside her, she

lifted her face to his. She yearned to brush her lips across his firm, generous mouth, parted slightly now in a warm smile. His face, so bold and cleanly cut, hovered only inches above her.

A spear of longing went through her, and suddenly Joanna admitted to herself what those strange feelings inside really meant. She wanted to trace the hard planes and angles of his features with her fingertips, to bracket his stern, unyielding jaw in her palms.

Godsakes, she wanted him to kiss her!

She actually wanted to kiss the Sea Dragon.

Impossible.

But true.

MacLean held her so tightly, she could feel the tautened muscles of his arms. Only the bunched material of her over-large shirt and the thick folds of tartan wool draped across her chest kept her small bosom and girlish figure a secret.

She gazed into his eyes and recognized the heartfelt concern for her. Shame at tricking him so completely burned inside her. She'd never expected this. Not only did he believe her a lad, but he sincerely wanted to help her—*Joey*—grow into a fine young man.

If she told MacLean that she'd deliberately hoodwinked him, he'd never forgive her. He'd be thoroughly disgusted by her behavior—but not so disgusted that he'd refuse to wed an heiress and acquire her wealth and estates. She'd be forced to marry a man who couldn't bear the sight of his wife. And the Glencoe Macdonalds, who were depending upon her to wed their war commander's son, would never give her the respect and allegiance she so longed to earn as their chieftain.

MacLean slowly lowered Joanna to her feet. His hands skimmed up her sides and bracketed her shoulders. "It's time we—"

The sound of horses crashing through the underbrush interrupted whatever he'd planned to say, and Fearchar and Tam rode into the clearing.

"You've found the laddie!" Fearchar called. His gap-toothed grin lit up his scarred, bearded mien, the black eye patch dark against his long blond hair with its two narrow sidebraids.

"And not a moment too soon," MacLean replied, as he released Joanna and turned to greet them.

Fearchar dismounted along with Tam and dropped to one knee to examine the wolf's carcass. Both men looked over at Joanna, the shocked realization that she'd been seconds from death written on their faces. The sincere concern in their gazes touched Joanna's heart. For whatever reason, the unqualified devotion they felt for their chief had been transferred, in some small part, to his impudent gillie.

MacLean retrieved his sword, wiped the blade on the dead wolf's thick pelt, and jammed it back in his scabbard.

Watching his methodical movements in dazed silence, Joanna told herself she must be mistaken. How could the MacLeans feel anything but hatred for a Macdonald? And how could she feel anything but contempt for their chief? Clan MacLean had been her clan's ancient enemy since time immemorial. And The MacLean was the hellish Avenger who'd hunted down her fugitive grandfather and dragged him back to Edinburgh in chains.

"You'll have to ride with me, Joey," MacLean said. "Bebind is probably halfway back to the castle by now." He mounted his great black stallion and reached an arm down for her.

Joanna allowed the warlord to pull her up behind him. Belatedly, she realized she'd offered no excuse for riding off alone. "Bebind was startled by a rabbit," she called to him over his shoulder. "She bolted into the trees, and all I could do was hang on."

"Is that right?" he replied.

Before she had a chance to catch her breath and embroider the fabrication, Fraoch took off at a gallop. Then 'twas all she could do to wrap her arms around MacLean's waist, grab hold of his wide leather belt, and hang on for dear life.

Chapter 6

~~~⌒⌒⌒~~~

That evening, Joanna sat cross-legged on the chest at the foot of her bed, polishing MacLean's dirk. She'd taken off the clumsy, scuffed brogues Jock had loaned her and wiggled her toes in her patched and faded stockings.

When the laird came into the bedchamber, she looked up in surprise. "I thought you were playing chess with Fearchar, milord," she said and started to return the blade to its sheath. "Is there something I can fetch you?"

"Nothing, lad," he replied. "Stay where you are and finish your work."

Rory walked over to a side table and set down his tankard of ale. Removing his sword belt and tossing the weapon on the bed, he dropped into a carved armchair nearby. His chin propped on his fist, he studied Joanna thoughtfully beneath lowered lids.

Today he'd come damn close to losing her. By God, he wouldn't allow his audacious bride to take such a foolish risk again.

Maybe putting her on a leash wouldn't be such a bad idea . . .

On their return to the castle, he'd intended to tell Joanna that he'd discovered her identity the moment he could get her alone. He knew she'd be shocked and possibly frightened, and he'd reassure the plucky lass that he wasn't going to punish her for her ridiculous charade. He was certain she'd done it out of loyalty to her clan.

No doubt it'd been some asinine Macdonald man-at-arms who'd convinced her to try the ruse in the first place, then left his mistress in the lurch when he'd ridden off to Stalcaire to pledge his loyalty to the king.

Rory wanted to give her a chance to prepare for their coming nuptials. He knew a bridal gown was an important thing to a lassie. In the letter he'd written, he'd asked his mother to bring an especially bonny one for Joanna. As well as some finely made undergarments and a night robe trimmed with fur.

The thought of removing a lacy chemise from his bride's slender white shoulders brought the deep ache of carnal desire.

God above, he wanted her.

The feel of her supple body brushing against his as he taught her to use the small bow had been sublime torture. If it weren't for the fact that their wedding would take place in only a few days, he'd be sorely tempted to take her that very night.

But on his return to Kinlochleven, Rory had been met by a self-appointed committee of the castle staff, headed by Father Graham. The men had insisted on speaking to him at once, and in private. So he'd dismissed Joanna, led the anxious group into the library, and listened to their pleas.

Seumas, Davie, Jock, and Jacob, along with the supposedly pious cleric, did their best to convince him that Joey shouldn't be trained as his gillie. They cited the lad's youth, his past record of irresponsibility, his puny size, and his penchant for playing nasty pranks.

Rory had given the castle's steward, chamberlain, blacksmith, and stable master every opportunity to tell him the real reason Joey shouldn't be his personal servant. He'd listened politely to their suggestions for Arthur's temporary replacement; then refuted every choice with a reason why the other lads wouldn't do.

The Macdonalds clearly intended to deceive him, and the more they contrived to spin their false web, the angrier he'd become. Their damnfool plotting had endangered their mistress's life that day.

Let them play the farce out to the end, he decided, if that was their wish. He'd teach them to respect and fear their new laird's authority, whether they chose to give him their heartfelt devotion or not.

After the evening meal, Rory had sent Joanna upstairs with chores to be done in his bedchamber. Her loyal servants had watched her go with gloomy faces, but not one tried to stop her or to confess the truth.

Every so often now, Joanna peeked at Rory from under her lashes, and he wondered what she was thinking. No doubt she prided herself on how clever she'd been in fooling the King's Avenger.

Disgruntled at the thought, he sipped the porter, watching her covertly over the rim of the pewter tankard. He propped his feet on the edge of the low chest she sat on, and she inched away as though he were some kind of monster.

Hell almighty, what was it about him she found so damn repugnant?

"Joey," he said, and she jumped at the sound of his voice.

"Aye, lord."

She was so flustered by his nearness she didn't even realize she'd answered in English. He chose to ignore it.

"You said Lady Joanna had many suitors. What kind of a man do you think she would like to marry?"

"Milord?" she asked, this time in Gaelic though she was clearly shocked at his question.

"Every young maid, even a simple one, must think about her wedding day and try to picture the bridegroom standing at her side."

Joanna bent over the dirk, polishing the sharp eighteen-inch blade as though her life depended on it. He frowned, suddenly worried she might slice off one of those dainty wee fingers.

"I'm sure I wouldn't know," she mumbled. But her frenzied movements slowed, and he quietly exhaled.

"Well, if *you* were the Maid of Glencoe, what kind of husband would you choose?"

Joanna's russet brows drew together as she rubbed the cloth furiously over the weapon once again. "The Maid of Glencoe *has* no choice. She'll marry whoever is chosen for her—either by the king or by her clan commander, Ewen Macdonald."

Rory leaned forward, ready to snatch the dirk from her hands, if necessary. "Use your imagination, lad," he urged in a soft, soothing manner. "Pretend the heiress does have a choice. Whom would she choose?"

To his relief, Joanna laid the dangerous weapon aside. Palms resting on her bent knees, she stared up at the ceiling and pursed her lips in concentration. "I can't imagine that, milord," she declared at last, "me being an orphan laddie and all."

Rory rose and moved to a tall court cupboard that stood against one wall. Opening its double doors, he withdrew a square gold casket from a shelf, then walked over and handed it to her.

"What is this?" she asked, her luminous eyes alight with curiosity.

"A wedding present," he said. "I brought it for my bride. Go on, lad. Open the box and tell me if you think she'll approve."

Joanna slowly lifted the lid, and her mouth opened in a silent *oh* of amazement.

Resting on the gold satin lining lay a necklace once intended for a Spanish infanta, recovered from the booty onboard a pirate ship. In the soft light thrown by the candles overhead, sapphires twinkled amid the piece's fine gold filigree, reflecting the brilliant hue of Joanna's violet-blue eyes. 'Twas truly a necklace fit for a queen.

"Well," he prodded when she offered no comment, "do you think Lady Joanna will like it?"

Joanna closed the case and set it beside the dirk. She shrugged her shoulders with casual indifference. "If your intent is to buy her affection with expensive jewelry, mi-

lord, you're destined to fail. The maid cares little for bau-
bles.''

He picked up the casket and gazed down at the royal
insignia embossed on the top. But he watched her carefully
from the corner of his eye. ''Does she now?'' he murmured.
''Why, do you suppose?''

'' 'Tis possible she thinks other things are more important.''

''Such as?''

''Such as gallantry.''

Rory laid his rejected bridal gift beside the tankard on
the table. ''Explain what you mean, lad.''

'' 'Tis obvious, sire, from the tapestry on the wall, which
Lady Joanna brought with her from Cumberland. I've been
told her mother's women made it especially for milady's
dowry.''

For the first time, Rory studied the colorful hanging with
a critical eye. The tapestry portrayed a knight dressed in
immaculate armor, not a dent or a ding anywhere on it. His
unmarred face, as comely as any lassie's, shone with the
idealism of the very young. If he or his armor had ever
seen a battle, it'd been from far in the rear. This magnificent
flower of chivalry looked up at a finely attired lady who
stood on a balcony and held a glowing candle to light his
way in the dark.

''Do you mean that Lady Joanna hopes to wed a Sassenach knight?'' he demanded.

''Whether the knight's English or Scots isn't the point,''
she replied testily. She jumped up from the chest and joined
him in front of the tapestry. With an exasperated sigh, she
waved her hand in an eloquent gesture. ''Look at the entire
scene and try to feel the emotions they're feeling. The valiant knight has brought his fair lady a bouquet and a ballad
he's written especially for her.''

Rory looked closer. The green, untried fledgling held a
bunch of posies in one elegant hand and a rolled parchment
tied with ribbon in the other. ''And what exactly are they

feeling?'' he growled, unaccountably disturbed by the look of enchantment on Joanna's dirty face.

"He's pledging his undying devotion," she said softly, her gaze fastened on the knight. "He's come to rescue the lady from a despicable, unwanted suitor forced upon her by a wicked stepfather."

Rory looked down at Joanna with dawning realization. *Knights and ladies fair.* Maude had told him that·as a child Joanna's only solace had been romantic tales and daydreams. His bride-to-be dreamed of a knight in shining armor who'd rescue her from her unwanted groom—namely, the despicable and repulsive Laird Rory MacLean.

He gazed once more at the tapestry. Hell, he wouldn't even need to draw his sword to best a mincing gallant like that. He could break the puppy in two with his bare hands.

"Can you compose a ballad to a lady's beauty, grace, and wit?" the lass beside him inquired with an expectant smile. "You could sing a tribute to Lady Joanna's virtues to the accompaniment of your lute."

"I don't play the lute," he stated, his words curt.

She compressed her mouth in mute disappointment, then suggested buoyantly, "What about the vielle or the guitar?"

"I don't play any musical instruments," he answered with a scowl.

Taken aback, she stared at him as though he'd just grown a third eye. "Well, surely you've written poetry in praise of a lady's melodious voice or lovely hair."

He felt a muscle jump in his cheek as he spoke through clenched teeth. "Wrong again."

Realizing a bit late that she'd been sailing straight into a gale, the intrepid lass trimmed her sails, came about, and deserted the ridiculous pair in the tapestry for the safety of the far side of the room.

Joanna walked back to the carved oak chest, picked up MacLean's dirk and returned the blade to its sheath. Conscious of his thunderous expression, she carefully placed his weapon on the nearby table. "Was there anything else you needed this evening, laird?'' she asked respectfully.

Before he could respond, Abby hurried through the open doorway, carrying two buckets of water. She set them down, pulled the empty wooden tub from its spot behind a screen, and placed it in front of the fireplace.

''What are you doing?'' MacLean asked the servant with an impatient frown.

Abby stared at him in astonishment as she dipped a quick curtsy. ''Before you left on the hunt, milord, you ordered a bath prepared for this evening.''

''Very well,'' he replied in a distracted manner, his irascible gaze locked on Joanna.

While Abby went for more buckets of water, Joanna busied herself with the soap and cloths used for bathing. A tingling excitement began to rise inside her as she worked.

This was it!

This time she wouldn't throw away her golden opportunity like some chicken-hearted ninny.

MacLean's sharp words rang out in the quiet room, slicing through her happy contemplation. ''Does Lady Joanna expect to be courted with flowers and music and poetry by her future husband?''

He stood in front of the tapestry, glaring at the knight again. The scowl on his face could have turned the finest wine in the castle into vinegar instantly.

''If she does,'' Joanna called over her shoulder, ''the maid's likely to be disappointed, isn't she, milord?''

She whistled softly to herself as she laid out a clean tunic for sleeping and a fresh pair of short hose for the next day. This time she'd discover if the Sea Dragon really had a tail or if the story was mere foolish blather.

His low voice rumbled like storm clouds over the loch. ''Why do you say that, Joey?''

Joanna could scarcely believe his question. MacLean hadn't gone near Idoine since the first day he'd arrived. Since his notion of paying court to a lady seemed to center around training horses, he must have been waiting for his bride-to-be to wander into the stables.

"Because you haven't so much as kissed her little pinkie," Joanna replied with a chuckle.

"I'll kiss a lot more than her little finger, when the time's right," he said gruffly.

Humming under her breath, Joanna dumped a pitcher of cold water into the steaming bath and swished it around with her hand. The thought of seeing MacLean's big, muscular body stark naked had her heart pumping and her insides shaking.

But she wasn't going to run out of the room this time.

Not even if she felt nauseated and woozy.

Not even if she keeled over in a dead faint at the sight of his scaly green tail.

Abby entered again with two more pails of water, one hot and one cold. "Lady Beatrix says Joey's needed in the solar, laird," she announced as she emptied them into the tub.

"I'm needed right here," Joanna said before MacLean could dismiss her. She sent Abby a quelling look, warning her silently not to contradict.

The serving girl cast a furtive glance at the mighty warrior before answering her mistress. "Lady Beatrix is going to be terribly upset if you don't come with me, Joey," she insisted. "She needs you right away for something very important."

"I'd like Joey to stay," MacLean stated. "Since Arthur's not here, the laddie can help with my bath."

Abby's brown eyes nearly popped from their sockets. "Lady Beatrix says I'm to assist you, milord—that is, if you really need someone to stay and help, your being a grown man and fully capable of undressing yourself, milord." Looking down at the toes of her sturdy shoes, she crossed herself and bobbed another curtsy.

"There's no need for you to help him, too," Joanna told the girl, her words crisp and emphatic. "I'm the laird's gillie. I'll serve him. Now go back and tell Lady Beatrix that everything's fine."

Abby leaned closer and whispered behind her cupped

palm. "I'm not supposed to come back without you."

"You may leave, Abby," MacLean said, the quiet authority in his voice ending any further discussion. "And close the door behind you, girl. I don't want to suffer from a draft while I'm bathing. Tell Lady Beatrix that I'm not to be disturbed by anyone for the rest of the evening."

The befuddled servant did as he commanded. God's truth, she had no other choice.

Joanna looked over at the tall, broad-shouldered warlord expectantly. Her limbs grew taut and tense; her belly clenched in anticipation. An inner fire heated the blood in her veins, till 'twas a wonder steam didn't flare from her nostrils. Destiny had brought them together, and no one could wrench the moment from her now.

For now she'd finally learn the truth.

Did he or did he not have a tail?

MacLean sat down on the edge of her soft feather mattress. "You can start by removing my brogues, lad."

Startled by the unexpected command, Joanna clasped her hands tightly in front of her. "Is . . . is that what Arthur does?"

The laird smiled encouragingly as he untied the leather thong at the nape of his neck and the golden waves fell loose about his collar. The sparkle in his green eyes sent tingles of exhilaration shimmying through her.

"Always."

Godsakes, she knew *that* to be an exaggeration. The man had removed his own shoes the time she'd carried in the firewood. But if he insisted on being coddled this evening, she'd humor him.

She went over to where he sat, and when he held out one foot and then the other, she pulled off his shiny black brogues with their fancy gold buckles. Then she stepped back, took a deep gulp of air, and waited.

Joanna told herself her heady anticipation came from a purely academic interest only. Once she determined the truth of the story, she'd never need to see him naked again. Or want to, for that matter.

But MacLean sat as though expecting her to do something else.

"The water will get cold, milord," she reminded him as she glanced at the steaming tub.

"Then what are you waiting for, lad?" he replied in a patient tone. "Take off my stockings."

A smile played about his mouth, just as it had when she'd served him the mutton pie and ale earlier that day. God's truth, he'd been a patient man then, especially when she'd spilled the ale all over the blanket. And he'd taught her how to shoot the bow and arrow with painstaking care. She wasn't sure why he'd taken such an interest in a slip of a boy, but she'd never forget his kindness.

"Do you have any younger brothers, laird?" Joanna asked as she knelt down in front of him.

The question seemed to catch MacLean off guard. He lifted his straight golden brows in bewilderment. "I have two brothers, as a matter of fact, both younger than me. Why do you ask?"

"No reason," she replied, peeling off the checkered short hose.

The sight of his bare feet and well-formed calves wasn't quite as shocking as it had been the first time, but her heart did a strange little hop-and-skip dance at the thought of what lay ahead. The memory of his scarred, hairy chest and massive shoulders sent prickles of excitement up and down her skin. Goose bumps popped out along her forearms.

"There must be some reason behind the question," he insisted with a lazy, devastating grin. "Why did you ask if I had younger brothers?"

"Well," she responded shyly, peeping up at him from beneath her lashes, "I thought maybe I reminded you of one of them."

Chapter 7

Thunderstruck, Rory gazed down at Joanna.

She thought of him as an older brother.

Shock and frustration warred within him.

Christ, he'd never known any female to affect him the way she did. His blood pounded in his ears, his sexual craving growing huge at the sight of her on her knees in front of him, looking up with sweet submission. He was hard and swollen and insistent with a need that couldn't be denied. He wanted to pull her onto his lap and pleasure her in a hundred different ways with his lips and teeth and tongue. To explore the feminine curves and hollows of the supple form hidden beneath those ludicrous clothes with his skilled and knowing fingers.

And she'd asked if she reminded him of a younger brother.

What in the whole breadth and depth of Scotland could have given her such a preposterous idea?

"Do I, milord?" Joanna persisted with a winsome smile.

"My brothers are nothing like you, Joey," he answered brusquely. "Lachlan and Keir are fighting men like me."

She blinked in amazement. "Are they as big as you, too?"

"Nearly." He clenched his jaw, fighting a sense of acute and bitter disappointment.

Damn! That's what came from being so understanding and patient. From allowing her to keep up her audacious pretense instead of exposing her immediately and punishing her for her willfulness—an unparalleled and headstrong willfulness that kept her here in his bedchamber, alone with him and perfectly willing to see him up close and bare-arsed in order to continue her outrageous deception.

Hellfire and damnation!

He'd never experienced anything so erotic as the thought of her dainty fingers removing every stitch of clothing from his big, aroused body. By the time she'd undressed him, she'd no longer see him in quite the same brotherly light.

"The bath is waiting, laird," Joanna reminded him as she bounced to her stocking feet.

Rory rose to stand in front of her, and the top of her shabby knit cap barely reached the middle of his chest. "Unfasten my plaid, Joey," he ordered quietly.

Her eyes grew enormous in her small, heart-shaped face. She glanced at the closed door, wondering, no doubt, if she should make a hasty retreat as she had on the evening she'd brought the firewood.

If she tried to run, he'd stop her.

Joanna wasn't going to leave this time.

Not if their lives depended on it.

But the diminutive lass surprised him. Violet-blue eyes darting sparks of rebellion, she clamped her lips shut as though squelching a defiant reply. With graceful hands, she reached up and unfastened the pin that held the green and black tartan folds draped across his shoulder. She stood so close he could feel her lithe body brush against his clothing as she placed the bodkin on the small table by the bed. Every fiber in Rory's being ached to move closer still.

Joanna's face glowed with curious expectation as he pushed the corner of his plaid over his shoulder and let it fall down his back. Only the wide leather belt about his waist held the rest of his plaid in place around his hips and thighs.

"Now my shirt, lad."

Her smooth brow furrowed in a dubious frown. "I don't remember seeing Arthur do that," she complained.

Rory lifted one eyebrow sardonically, and his low words were edged with sarcasm. "How many times did you watch my gillie attend me when I was bathing?"

"Only once," Joanna admitted. She lowered her head, and her long russet lashes fluttered against her smooth cheeks as she ran the pink tip of her tongue over her lips in agitation.

Her delicate femininity rocked him. His lungs constricted, and his breath grew short. She'd made a frail, unmanly boy-child, but as a seventeen-year-old lassie, her slim figure and graceful movements were enchanting.

"Remove the shirt before the water gets cold, Joey," he said, his voice amazingly calm despite the way his eager body was reacting to her nearness.

Her dainty fingers trembled as she fumbled with the laces that tied the ruffled collar of his billowing shirt. Then she pulled the long saffron tails out from under the black belt, her lashes still lowered to conceal her thoughts.

Rory drew the linen garment up over his head and dropped it on the comforter behind him. He could hear Joanna's quick in-drawn breath at the sight of his bare chest so close in front of her. Clad only in the belted plaid that reached nearly to his knees, he looked down on the top of her frayed blue and white cap and willed himself not to move.

He'd been certain that Joanna would never go through with the task of disrobing him, but she remained where she stood, not budging an inch. When she slowly lifted her gaze to meet his, her eyes sparkled with a mixture of wariness and determination. Beneath the layer of dirt, the color had drained from her cheeks. He could count every freckle on that delightful soot-covered face.

Rory traced a fingertip down the narrow bridge of her nose. "You're the one who needs a bath, Joey," he murmured. "Why don't you use the tub when I'm through bathing? The water will still be warm and soapy. You can scrub some of that grime off while I'm getting dressed."

A vision of lathering her slender white body and rinsing

the satiny skin with his bare hands sent a lance of desire spearing through him. Vivid thoughts of their wedding night and what he planned to do to his naughty bride nearly stole his breath away.

At his offhand suggestion, sheer terror glittered in her eyes. "I don't like baths, milord," she announced in a tone of unqualified rebellion. " 'Tis much too dangerous. You can catch a chill and die."

"Not on a warm spring evening like this," he said with a low chuckle.

"Any evening's too dangerous," Joanna replied. "My da took a bath one fine summer night, went to bed, and never woke up."

"I thought your father died on the battlefield."

She didn't even blink. "That was my real father. My stepfather died of a chill after bathing, just like I said."

"Come on, lad," Rory goaded, "where's your gumption? You were the one who asked if you could learn to fight with a dirk."

"Fighting's one thing," she declared. "Bathing's another."

He drew a line down the middle of her smudged cheek, then rubbed the dirt between his thumb and forefinger. "A little soap and water never hurt anyone."

"Holy hosanna," she grumbled. "By the time you get in the bath, the water will have already turned cold. I'm not washing in a tub of ice."

Rory braced his hands on his hips to keep from seizing Joanna and lifting her up to eye level. He wanted to cover her mouth with his, to whip off that absurd cap and bury his fingers in her coppery hair. He wanted to bury himself in her soft warmth.

At the thought of tasting her sweetness, of caressing her bare skin, of pinning her slender form beneath him and gazing into her expressive eyes while she felt him swollen and turgid inside her, the blood raged in his veins.

"Then unbuckle my belt," he said softly, "and slip it off."

This time Joanna would surely try to break for the door. If she made a move to leave, he'd stop her. He'd sweep her up in his arms and lay her on the bed behind him, where he'd worship her delicate femininity with his hard male body. He'd teach her the pleasures of the marriage bed and listen with satisfaction to her breathless cries of surrender.

There'd be no wrong in seducing her that evening; they were betrothed. Many couples shared a bed before their wedding day with no shame involved.

Joanna reached toward the large gold buckle. He tensed as her fingers fumbled with the clasp, fighting the primitive urges that gripped him.

Over the top of Joanna's head, Rory's gaze lit on the fanciful tapestry. He hadn't noticed before, but the resplendent knight seemed to be smirking. That arrogant pup appeared certain the lady would tumble off the balcony and land at his feet, overwhelmed by his courtly manner, his handful of blossoms, and his mawkish love song.

With a low groan of frustration, Rory grasped Joanna's slender wrists and brought her hands upward, where he held them imprisoned against his naked chest. She looked up in surprise, innocence glowing in her marvelous eyes. He realized with demoralizing certainty that if he attempted to seduce her tonight, he'd become the villain in her preposterous make-believe tale.

He needed to win her affection. Though he didn't believe in romantic love, a bride should display some tender esteem for her groom. Hell, his mother had been so entranced with his father, she'd run away with him regardless of the consequences.

Rory suspected that all young lassies harbored maudlin fantasies—the kind of fatuous, sentimental myths that bards sang about. He didn't want to shatter Joanna's childhood dreams and leave her disillusioned and regretful.

On the contrary, Rory wanted Joanna to think of *him* as her protector. He wanted to see that look of enchantment on her radiant face when she gazed at him—the same damn dreamy-eyed look he'd seen when she gazed at that untried whelp hanging on the wall.

How ironic that a man who'd always scoffed at the idea of romantic love desperately wanted a lass to romanticize about him. To see him as some mythic warrior who'd come to rescue her from a fire-breathing dragon. Devil take it, what was happening to his pragmatism? His forthright common sense?

But he refused to play the role of the monster.

She waited, looking up at him in bemusement. "Milord?"

Her soft whisper seemed to compress Rory's heart into a tight, leaden lump.

If he felt Joanna's inexperienced and openly curious gaze move over his buck-naked body, he'd never be able to keep himself under control. The thought of her seeing him like that, reading in her eloquent eyes the startled realization of how massively aroused he'd become, struck him with incredible force.

His mouth suddenly bone-dry, Rory concentrated on breathing in a slow, rhythmic pace. He clenched his jaw and ignored the heated blood steaming in his veins. As he struggled to conquer the primal beast inside, raw, unequivocal lust wrapped itself around his entrails and squeezed painfully. It was fortunate his plaid had been fashioned from over seven yards of wool. At the moment, his manhood stood erect, huge and heavy with need for the engaging, high-spirited lassie before him.

"Leave," he said hoarsely. "I'll finish disrobing by myself."

Joanna's heart stumbled as MacLean released her hands and pushed her gently away.

She'd told herself that only dispassionate curiosity had kept her there for so long.

She knew better now—now that he'd ordered her to go.

So close she could breathe in the masculine scent of him, Joanna gazed, enthralled, at MacLean's broad shoulders and deep chest. The three-headed dragon's long, slinky body wrapped itself around the bulging muscles of his upper arm in a permanent, barbaric display. The jagged scar of his old wound lay white beneath the crisp golden-brown hairs. The golden holy medal hanging between his flat nipples honored St. Columba, one of Scotland's most revered religious heroes.

She longed to see the bronzed warlord's magnificent figure completely unclothed. And it wasn't simply because she hoped to discover if he had a dragon's tail. Joanna yearned to rake her fingertips through the thick mat of hair on his chest. To press her lips against his sun-gilded flesh and inhale the tangy scent of the forest.

The sight of Tam and Mary in the stable flashed before her. She wondered what it would be like to be held in MacLean's powerful arms, to have his mouth exploring the sensitive tips of her breasts, to have his huge body pressing against hers as she sank down, down into the soft feather mattress of her canopied bed—just as Tam had pressed Mary down into the loose straw.

Would she whimper and plead for the rugged, virile man to continue as the dairymaid had done?

A thrill of excitation twanged through Joanna.

Godsakes, she couldn't leave.

Not now.

Joanna slowly raised her eyes to meet his, but MacLean stood perfectly still, looking over the top of her head at the wall behind. Her lips trembled as she offered an ingratiating smile. "I don't mind helping with your garments, milord. Not if that's what Arthur usually does. I won't be fully trained as a gillie unless I do."

"Go!" he commanded, and a shudder went through his large frame.

"Are you ill?" she asked in genuine concern.

MacLean braced one palm on the post of the canopy bed, his head lowered, his gaze fixed on the rug at his bare feet. "Joey," he said, his deep baritone terse and threatening, "if you don't get the hell out of here, I'm going to dump you in that tub of quickly chilling bathwater. Do you understand?''

She didn't wait for him to repeat the threat. She hurried to the door and swung it open, startling Beatrix, who had one ear pressed to the heavy oak panel. Maude and Abby stood behind her in the corridor.

Joanna quickly shut the door and held her finger to her lips to signal for silence.

"How *could* you?" Lady Beatrix hissed. Her features contorted in outrage, she planted her hands on her hips and leaned closer to Joanna. "How could you stay in there alone with that fiend? You're daft taking such foolish chances. What if he'd found you out? What then?''

"Are you all right, child?'' Maude questioned in a whisper.

Joanna tried to hide her vexation at being ordered from the room. "I'm fine," she said with a defensive tilt of her chin.

Abby wrung the corner of her apron in her plump hands, her pretty brown eyes filled with tears. "What did he do to ye, milady?''

"Nothing, dammit," Joanna replied. "And I wasn't taking any chances. MacLean thinks of me as his little brother.''

The serving lass clapped her hand over her mouth, horrified at her mistress's bad language and incredulous at her reply. *"His little brother?''*

"Thank heavens,'' Beatrix muttered crossly.

Maude said nothing, merely giving Joanna a penetrating look from narrowed eyes. Beneath the silent scrutiny, Joanna could feel the heat of a blush creep up her cheeks. The realization of just how close she'd come to seeing the mighty chief of Clan MacLean in all his bare-arsed splendor struck her with a near-paralyzing impact.

Godsakes! What in the names of all Scotland's saints had she been thinking? She could have given herself away and ruined everything.

Joanna had to keep her identity a secret until Ewen came

to rescue her. She wouldn't fail her clansmen and prove herself unworthy to be their chieftain.

"Let's go," she said with a weak smile, "before the Sea Dragon changes his mind and wants me to scrub his scaly back."

Rory unbuckled his belt and let his plaid drop to the floor. Then he picked up his tankard of ale and padded to the tub. Stepping into the warm water, he sank down with an agonized groan. Jesu, he felt like a rutting stallion, locked out of a pen holding twenty mares. His balls hadn't ached this way since he was a fifteen-year-old cub dallying with a milkmaid who liked to play tease and tickle in the hay.

He lifted the pewter cup in a salute to the damn puling knight in the tapestry. "You won that joust, you mealy-mouthed sonofabitch," he taunted with a mocking grin. "The fine, fair lassie standing on that balcony may be captivated by your bonny face, but Lady Joanna won't be for long."

Rory had never been any good at pretty speeches. He'd never engaged in devious intrigues or devised clever strategies to capture a reluctant lady's attention. He'd certainly never misled any woman to make a sexual conquest. There'd never been the need.

The chief of Clan MacLean had always prided himself on his honest, straightforward behavior, and the females he'd bedded had been just as forthright in their sexual desires.

In a few more days his family would arrive at Kinloch-leven, and Lachlan could teach him everything there was to know about courting a fine lady. The man was a goddamn genius at wooing. He could play the rebec, harpsichord, and lute; compose ballads and poetry; dance with consummate grace; and twist any lass around his finger with disgusting ease.

Of course, Lachlan was much comelier than his older brother. Slimmer, more graceful, with a face almost as braw as the knight's on the wall there. When it came to the lassies, Lachlan made Rory feel like a great, lumbering brute.

The thought that Joanna might see a resemblance between Lachlan and her fantasy hero brought a scowl. Rory sipped his ale and stared in rueful cogitation at the tapestry. Outwardly, his brother was the image of the illusory knight, but Lachlan was intrepid in battle and had the scars to prove it beneath his clothing. Inwardly, Rory's brother hadn't escaped life's emotional scars either, though his charming ways with the lassies kept them well-hidden.

Since the Maid of Glencoe was already betrothed to Rory, his brother would never purposely set out to court her; there was nothing to worry about there. But he didn't want Joanna to pay more attention to Lachlan's refined, gentlemanly talents than she did to her eager bridegroom.

This evening she'd almost discovered for herself how eager he was. He smiled at the memory of her ingenuous eyes when she'd asked him that cockamamie question.

She'd find out on her wedding night if he thought of her as a younger brother.

Rory tipped his head back and gave a sharp bark of laughter.

"Ah, Joanna," he said, lifting his tankard to the gentlewoman on the balcony, "you're about to discover how romantic and chivalrous the chief of Clan MacLean can be when he puts his mind to it."

Two mornings later, the expected guests arrived with the skirling of bagpipes and beating of drums. Joanna watched the cavalcade ride beneath the raised portcullis from her perch on the keep's castellated parapet.

King James rode a magnificent caparisoned steed beside a beautiful woman she assumed was Lady Emma MacNeil, MacLean's widowed mother. On the sovereign's right rode the arrogant and ambitious Archibald Campbell, second earl of Argyll, whom Joanna had seen from a distance in Edinburgh. Directly behind them came a middle-aged gentleman with two younger enormous warriors, who could only be MacLean's uncle and brothers.

They were followed by what appeared to be the entire Scottish court. James's household included over a hundred personal retainers, many of them of gentle birth. In addition to the richly clothed lords and ladies, there were grooms, clerks, a barber, a tailor, and a falconer—for the king was inordinately fond of falconry. Musicians, singers, dancers, acrobats, mummers, and minstrels swarmed into Joanna's lower bailey. Even a dozen Observantine friars from the nearby monastery and a small group of Poor Clares, apparently on a pilgrimage, had attached themselves to the royal retinue for safety while traveling.

The twenty Macdonald men-at-arms, who'd been coerced into swearing their fealty to the king, were also now returning to Kinlochleven. Joanna's heart lurched painfully when she spotted her clan's war commander, Ewen Macdonald, and his brother, Godfrey, with Ewen's sixteen-year-old son Andrew riding between them.

Andrew's handsome face looked up to the battlement where she sat, but he didn't recognize her in disguise. His dark brown eyes swept the upper bailey, then moved back to his father for guidance, as they always did.

Joanna pressed her hand against her waist and told herself it was the very size of the entourage that caused the sharp pain in her belly. What had MacLean been thinking to invite so many people?

The past Sunday, Father Thomas had read the banns at Mass exactly as MacLean ordered. Poor Idoine had squirmed in the pew, her face white and drawn with fear. Joanna had assured her cousin again that she'd never allow the Sea Dragon to force her into marriage with him. Upon her father's arrival, Ewen would identify Idoine as his daughter, and The MacLean would have to accept the fact that he'd been outfoxed from the start.

After greeting the king, MacLean lifted his mother down from her horse. She threw her arms around him in an openly affectionate greeting and said something in his ear that made him laugh. Then he shook the older gentleman's hand with a welcoming smile. His brothers whacked him on the back with blows that would have sent any other man flying. She suspected by their animated conversation that they were congratulating him on his upcoming nuptials.

MacLean grinned as though he hadn't a care in the world. He'd soon have to explain to all these people that the bridegroom was ready and willing, but the elusive bride-to-be—whom he'd mistakenly believed to be Idoine— was nowhere in sight. The thought made her cringe. In a strange, bittersweet way, she actually felt sorry for him.

When the King of Scotland entered the donjon with a fanfare of trumpets, Joanna knew she could dally no longer. She'd need to go down and see that Ethel and Peg had everything running smoothly in the kitchen and buttery. She prayed her mercurial cook hadn't become so flustered by the influx of the king's cup-bearers, turnspits, kitchen var- lets, and head chef that she'd started nipping from a bottle of spirits again. And that Davie had assigned the guest bed- chambers on the fourth floor in the correct order of status. If James Stewart ended up in a smaller room than one of his vassals, heads would roll. And her chamberlain's would be the first.

Joanna scowled with annoyance at all the trouble that stiff-necked MacLean was causing, and climbed down from the edge of the parapet.

Arms folded across his massive chest, Fearchar stood directly behind her, engrossed in the pageantry below. She hadn't heard him join her on the battlement, but she wasn't surprised by his quiet presence. The giant often appeared nearby, as though he'd nothing better to do than keep his cousin's apprentice gillie company.

"What was MacLean thinking to have invited the entire court to his wedding?" she asked crossly as she tripped down the stairs beside him.

The huge warrior's wide smile split his bearded face. "Forbye, laddie, he'd be thinking how proud he is of his lovely bride."

"Humph," she sniffed. "Lady Joanna will be lucky if that mass of malingering humanity doesn't eat her out of house and home before they finally leave."

"Och, there's naught to worry about there, lad. The lassie's bridegroom is a wealthy man. He could feed the chattering apes for a month and never see a dent in his coffers."

She stopped on the stone step and stared at him, horrified. "A month! You don't think they'd stay that long, do you?"

Fearchar puckered his lips and scratched the bristly flaxen whiskers beneath his chin. "Well now," he said, "I doubt they'll stay more than a few days. But I've fought alongside The MacLean for the last ten years, and I've never known him to count the cost when it came to getting something he wanted."

"Godsakes, what has that got to do with it?" she snapped in exasperation.

He grinned complacently, his one eye twinkling merrily. "Not one of the fortresses he vowed to conquer lasted a month beneath the assault of his cannons."

Joanna groaned and resumed her descent to the ground floor. "Fortresses and cannons," she muttered under her breath. "That's all warriors think about."

Chapter 8

Rory joined his family in the solar early that afternoon after speaking at length with the king. He found his mother in front of a large wooden frame, which had been turned toward the light of one of the tall, narrow windows that graced the tower room.

When he entered, Lady Emma smiled in welcome, then returned her gaze once again to the tapestry. "Rather a fantastic depiction, don't you think?"

Rory had never been in the castle's solar, the common retreat of gentlewomen. He'd certainly never had the inclination to join Lady Beatrix and Lady Idoine as they plied their needles. Expecting to find another insipid portrayal of a knight offering tokens of love to his lady fair, he went over to stand beside his mother.

The nearly completed scene showed a ship of ancient origin with a gruesome dragon's head on its prow. In the vessel a row of men-at-arms stood along the rail, looking out across the curling whitecaps. A bevy of bare-breasted water nymphs sat on the rocky shore, combing their long silken locks.

Rory glanced indifferently at the tapestry, then looked closer. In the foaming waves, a naked man with a green scaly tail the size of a sea monster's frolicked with a voluptuous mermaid, his intentions clear from the lascivious look on his evil face.

"Something from mythology, I suppose," Rory said

with a puzzled frown. "Lady Joanna's companion, Maude Beaton, seems to have a special interest in yarns and dyes. This must be her creation, though I admit it surprises me."

Curious, Keir and Lachlan left their game of chess and came to join them in front of the unfinished wall hanging.

Lachlan grinned at the blatantly erotic images. "It doesn't look like any story told by the Greeks that I ever read. But 'tis rather unique. I'd like to have van Artevelde's artistic opinion."

Rory glanced at his handsome brother before returning his intrigued gaze to the engrossing seascape. "I was sorry to learn the little Fleming didn't come with you. I'd hoped to have him paint a portrait of Joanna in her wedding gown."

"The poor man had to remain at Stalcaire," Lady Emma explained. "He's nursing a putrid throat."

Six months ago, Lachlan had brought the renowned Flemish painter, Jan van Artevelde, to Castle Stalcaire to render the earl of Appin's portrait. On board the *Sea Hawk*, the two men, so different in physical stature and temperament, had shared their mutual gift for languages.

"Is he still trying to master the Gaelic?" Rory asked.

"He's made phenomenal progress," Lachlan commented absently, his attention still fastened on the wall hanging with its resplendent blues and greens.

Grinning, Keir moved closer to study the titillating scene for a moment. "Maybe 'tis something from the Macdonald clan history," he suggested with a bawdy leer. "If Rory's bride starts trilling a siren's song on his wedding night, he could be in for a wild ride. He'll be lucky if she lets him come up for air."

Lady Emma clucked her tongue at her youngest son's ribald humor, then looked inquiringly at Rory. "When do we meet your intended bride?" she asked for the third time that day.

This time Rory didn't put her off with the excuse that Joanna was busy at the moment and he'd introduce them to his betrothed later. "You've already met her."

Duncan Stewart, earl of Appin, who'd been gazing disinterestedly out the window at the loch below, turned in astonishment. "We have?"

Rory's family looked at one another in mystification as his uncle, a dapper man with graying brown hair and perceptive hazel eyes, came to join them before the large wooden frame.

During the sumptuous repast set out for the guests in the great hall earlier that day, Rory had waited impatiently to see if one of them would discover the truth. His impertinent bride-to-be had been right in front of his family the entire time.

Joanna had helped the servants serve the food. Zipping from one trestle table to the next like a bumblebee working a garden of blossoms, she hadn't lit in one place long enough for any visitor to even speak with her. Not a single person had given the disheveled, ragtag laddie a second glance.

Rory nodded as he met the perplexed gazes of his loved ones. "My betrothed is parading around the castle in disguise," he explained dryly.

Keir and Lachlan exchanged looks of wry amusement. "Which lass is she?" Keir asked.

"I'd rather you puzzled it out for yourself," Rory replied.

Duncan left the tapestry to sink down in a chair beside the table holding the chessboard and its carved ivory pieces. "We've been told the heiress favors the Red Wolf of Glencoe," he said with a quizzical lift of his brows.

Rory was genuinely fond of his uncle. When Duncan's tightfisted father had died, leaving him a title and wealth at the age of thirty-four, Duncan had provided for his young bastard nephew with openhanded generosity. When it came time for Rory to be fostered at the age of eight, the earl had sent him to the Camerons, who were caring Stewart allies. Later, he'd paid for Rory's university schooling in Paris and provided the funds for his initial venture into shipbuilding.

"And you were expecting Somerled Macdonald's bulbous nose and frizzled hair," Rory replied softly, unable to suppress a grin.

Lady Emma's brilliant eyes clouded. She lifted her hand to her throat, an expression of maternal sympathy on her lovely face. "Surely not . . . not Lady Idoine?"

"I suspected Idoine myself, at first," Rory conceded. "She was the most logical guess. But the sullen lass with the coarse features and bristly hair is definitely not the Maid of Glencoe."

"But who—"

A soft tap on the door interrupted Lachlan's question.

Rory lifted his hand in warning. "Don't say a word about this in front of anyone. Not a soul."

At his call, Fearchar swung open the door, and Joanna, a scowl creasing her smudged forehead, stepped past him into the chamber. Rory's cousin closed the door quietly behind them. He crossed his arms and leaned one hefty shoulder against the doorjamb, making certain they wouldn't be disturbed.

"You wanted to see me, laird?" Joanna asked, her harried expression telling Rory she had more important things to do than play the role of his gillie-in-training. Today of all days, she didn't have time to be at his beck and call.

The mangy striped stocking cap, pulled low over her ears, covered every wisp of her hair. Her frayed, overlarge plaid hung down past her knees, held in place by a decrepit belt, and her tattered, raveling stockings, fastened by worn garters, fell in loose folds around her calves.

That morning she'd taken care to smear her face heavily with soot from the hearth. The impression of her slender fingertips could still be seen on one cheek, where she'd hurriedly dabbed it on.

"Come in, Joey," Rory said, motioning her forward. He waited till she stood beside him, wanting his family to get a good, long look at the bedraggled serving lad before he continued. "My mother has several chores she'd like you to do for her."

'Twas the first Lady Emma had heard of it, and she glanced at her eldest son in surprise, but didn't say a word to the contrary.

Though there were already enough tasks to keep her busy till sunset, Joanna smiled at the pleasant lady standing beside MacLean and bowed politely. "Whatever milady wishes."

MacLean placed his hand on Joanna's shoulder and gave her a friendly squeeze. "Lady Emma was so impressed with the letter you wrote for me, Joey, that she'd like you to write one for her."

"I'll be happy to, milord," Joanna replied as she gazed at the Sea Dragon's mother in wonderment.

In her mid-forties, Lady Emma had light brown hair and soft, rounded features. Like her brother, the earl of Appin, she was somewhat taller than average and slender in form. MacLean must have inherited his great height and Herculean physique from his father's people.

Joanna wondered what else he'd inherited from the former chief of Clan MacLean. A green dragon's tail, perhaps? And knowledge in the black arts?

She shifted nervously from one foot to the other as she met the combined gazes of the four newcomers, who watched her in absolute silence. Beneath the layer of grime on her cheeks, she could feel the creeping warmth of a blush.

Didn't they know it was impolite to stare—no matter how small and filthy and insignificant the other person appeared?

Standing shoulder to shoulder, the trio of Highland lairds would have filled anyone with foreboding. Even if she weren't a chieftain of the rebellious Macdonald clan, whose power had been broken by these three ferocious warlords, Joanna would have been shaking in her overlarge shoes.

God's truth, they were awesome.

Known to the Scottish people as the Sea Hawk, Lachlan MacRath stood nearly as tall as his older brother. Leaner of build, he had a whipcord strength and a handsome mien with finely chiseled features. His reddish-brown hair curled about the embroidered collar of his white linen shirt. A friendly, inquisitive smile curved the corners of his mouth, giving him a more gracious, urbane appearance than MacLean. He was the comeliest man she'd ever seen— even bonnier than Andrew, and that was saying a lot. But the undeniable power and unquestioned authority were there, and the intelligent gaze fastened upon Joanna was exactly the same.

In fact, all of MacLean's family, with the exception of his uncle, had eyes the precise color of the Sea Dragon's. A deep, piercing green that seemed to look into the inner-most places of your soul.

Swallowing convulsively, Joanna shifted her gaze to Keir MacNeil and shivered. The Black Raven had the soaring height and immense build of The MacLean. But there was something even more sinister in the cast of his blunt-cut features, enhanced by a battle scar that slashed through one eyebrow and crossed the broken bridge of his nose. Though approximately eight years younger, he had an aura of ruth-lessness that matched MacLean's for sheer intimidation.

The fondness for earrings appeared to be another family trait. A faceted ruby sparkled on MacRath's right earlobe, while MacNeil sported a large gold hoop that dangled and swayed malevolently. Joanna knew without being told that a black raven, the sacred bird of Woden, decorated one burly arm.

"Wait for Lady Emma in her bedchamber, lad," MacLean instructed Joanna with a dismissive pat on the back. "My mother will join you shortly."

Casting them a last, furtive look from beneath lowered lids, she sent a quick prayer to Jeanne d'Arc for her deliv-erance from such formidable enemies.

Rory watched his intended wife beat a hasty retreat with Fearchar at her heels, then turned to his family with a smile of satisfaction.

"The charming wee vixen . . ." Lachlan murmured the moment the door closed behind her. "You lucky seadog."

The light in Lachlan's laughing eyes told Rory he'd noted the delicate features, the smooth skin beneath the layer of soot, the long, silken lashes. Trust Lachlan to spot a bonny lassie.

Keir's gaze remained mystified. "You jest," he said with a disbelieving frown, and Rory shook his head in reply.

Hope lighting her soft features, his mother reached out and touched Rory's sleeve. "You don't mean that quaint child is . . ."

"She's no child," Rory told his loved ones with a wide grin. "Though she's as naughty and impudent as any laddie playing pranks on Hallowmas Eve, she's seventeen years old and a Sassenach noblewoman to boot. That scamp, my dear family, is my bonny wee bride-to-be, the irrepressible Lady Joanna, Maid of Glencoe and chieftain of the Glencoe Macdonalds."

"But . . . but why is the heiress dressed in boy's clothes? And ragged ones at that?" Lady Emma touched a fingertip to her temple. "Is she simpleminded?"

Rory chuckled. "That's exactly what the Macdonalds would like me to believe. But Joanna's as bright as a new-minted crown. Someone or something convinced her to take part in this ruse, and the rest of the castle has aided and abetted her in the deception. Lady Beatrix and Lady Idoine; Father Graham, the clan chaplain; her companion and former nurse; her household staff—everyone."

"Have you told the king?" Duncan asked, his astute eyes dark with misgiving.

"I have," Rory told his uncle. "Fortunately, since I was the butt of the joke, His Majesty chose to find the entire escapade amusing."

"Thank heavens for that!" Lady Emma said, her voice bright with relief.

"I'd stake my reputation that Ewen Macdonald is the real culprit," Duncan shrewdly observed as he picked up a discarded bishop lying next to the chessboard. "I've learned that he's filed for a dispensation in Rome so he can marry Lady Joanna to his son Andrew."

Rory had met the youth for the first time that morning, and it'd taken only minutes to see the callow immaturity in his dark brown eyes. "You must be mistaken," he growled. "The boy's an idiot."

"There's no mistake about it," his uncle replied. He placed the bishop beside a rook on the checkered board. "One of the friars traveling with us translated the papers into Latin after Ewen filed the petition with the Archbishop of Appin. The Macdonalds hope to keep Kinlochleven under their control by wedding the two cousins. But nothing can be done until they receive permission from the Vatican."

"Any dispensation from Rome will come too late," Rory said grimly. "The wedding takes place the day after tomorrow. Lady Joanna will marry me just as the king has commanded. And the Macdonalds will attend the ceremony and offer their cheerful congratulations, or face charges of treason. There's not a damn thing they can do about it now."

"Be wary of a plot," Lachlan cautioned. The diplomat among them, he had his finger on the pulse of Scottish politics. "James Stewart wants this alliance in order to bring the Macdonalds of Glencoe securely under his rule by wresting their allegiance from Donald Dubh Macdonald and transferring it to a new chieftain loyal to the Crown."

Keir braced one foot on a low stool and rested his large hand on the hilt of his broadsword. "And every member of that infernal clan secretly supports the heir to the deposed Lord of the Isles," he added with a grimace of disgust, "regardless of how many oaths of fealty they've sworn to King James."

"Exactly," Duncan agreed. He moved a knight forward to protect the white king, then looked up, his gaze pensive. "Which is why His Majesty wants Kinlochleven Castle and the surrounding countryside securely under Rory's command."

"But Donald Macdonald's no more than a lad," Lady Emma protested with a wave of her elegant hand. "And held under lock and key by the earl of Argyll. He'll never lead a rebellion in the Hebrides."

"Don't be too sure," Lachlan replied. "The laddie will one day be a man, and there'll always be disgruntled chiefs of the Isles willing to flock to Donald Dubh's banner—if it holds out the promise of enough reward for them."

"And never, ever trust Argyll," Duncan warned them. "His one and only goal is the spread of Campbell rule throughout the Western Highlands."

"But he'd never release Donald Dubh," Keir argued. "The Campbells detest the Macdonalds almost as much as we do."

Rory clapped his youngest brother's shoulder. "Nothing is certain in this life, Keir, least of all the loyalties of Archibald Campbell. Argyll will do whatever it takes—using statecraft, legal cunning, and force when necessary—to achieve his aims."

Lady Emma moved to the table, poured wine into a goblet, and gave it to her brother. "What do the Macdonalds of Glencoe think of their half-Sassenach chieftain?"

Taking the silver cup she offered, Duncan rose to stand beside his sister. "Except for her immediate staff here at Kinlochleven, Lady Joanna's clansmen are suspicious of her. Before Somerled died on the gallows, he named his granddaughter as his heir by law of tanistry, and there's been no open talk of disputing her right to the chieftainship."

Keir scowled as he shoved the low stool aside with his foot. "But by marrying the maid to his son, Ewen can consolidate all the power of the Glencoe Macdonalds in his own two hands."

Rory took the goblet his mother offered, then leaned against the table's edge. "That's one of the reasons I've kept my discovery of Joanna's identity a secret from everyone but my own men," he told them. "I'm taking no chances that the Macdonalds will try to spirit her away before the wedding. As long as they believe I think Joey Macdonald is an orphan serving lad, they'll bide their time.

They plan, no doubt, to wait until just before the marriage ceremony to prove that Lady Idoine isn't the real heiress after all. And by that time, 'twill be too late for them to do anything but watch in respectful silence as Joanna and I take our vows.''

Lady Emma poured three more goblets of wine, handed one to Lachlan, one to Keir, and then raised her own. "Let's set the subject of plots and politics aside for now. The wedding morn will soon be here, and I propose a salute,'' she said with a happy sigh, "to the new bride and groom.''

"To the bride and groom,'' they chorused.

Rory straightened from the table and joined them in the toast. "To my bride.''

"What else can we do to help?'' Lachlan inquired, after draining his cup. "Outside of not killing any of your future relatives before the ceremony.''

"And not giving away the secret of your wee bride's identity,'' Keir added with a sly wink.

Rory met his brothers' amused gazes. There was no point in trying to conceal what he was about to say from his mother and uncle. They'd know soon enough, dammit. Hell, the whole blasted Scottish court would know at the wedding feast. He squared his jaw and scowled ferociously, daring them to laugh at his urgent request.

"You can teach me how to dance.''

Chapter 9

Rory's family stared at him, scarcely able to believe their ears.

"You heard me," he grated through clenched teeth. "I want to learn to dance."

Lachlan gave a long, low whistle of amazement. "After twenty-eight years of ignoring such flummery, you finally decide you want to dance with the ladies?"

"Not with the ladies, you ass," Rory said. "With my bride. Most bridegrooms dance with their bride on their wedding day. Is that a hanging offense?"

"You big lummox," Keir said with a chuckle. "You couldn't dance your way out of a prison cell if your life depended upon it."

Tucking his chin, Rory flexed his shoulders and glared at his younger brother. "I don't have great talent for tiptoeing across a dance floor, I admit. But if every imbecile in the court can learn the steps of a simple pavane, why can't I?"

"Why can't he, indeed!" his uncle admonished. "I've never seen any man match Rory's swordplay. He's light enough on his feet when it comes to skewering an opponent with dirk and broadsword."

Keir grinned wryly, a devilish gleam in his eyes. "Ah, but put my big brother around the fair demoiselles and his tongue and feet both stop working. Rory's never chosen a partner for the evening in his life. He's always waited till one picked him.''

"What the hell are you talking about?'' Rory gritted.

"Not your dancing, you thickheaded loon." Keir waved his goblet at Rory, amusement softening his rugged features. "You've been here for over a week, man. I'd have thought by now you'd have seduced the maid."

"Seduction's a trifle difficult," Rory said stiffly, "when the lassie's pretending to be a boy."

Lachlan and Keir looked at each other and burst into laughter.

"That's enough," Duncan rebuked mildly, though a smile skipped over his lips. "Let's not forget there's a lady present."

"A wise decision," Lady Emma concurred. Her eyes twinkled with merriment as she gazed at her eldest son. "And I think it's wonderful, my dear, that you want to dance at your wedding."

"I agree," said Lachlan. "Keir and I will be happy to teach you the steps of the pavane. Is there anything else we can do to help?"

"There is," Rory said, his words clipped and abrupt. He'd known this wasn't going to be easy, but he'd be damned if he'd scuttle his plans just to avoid his brothers' gibes. "I want you to compose a ballad in honor of Lady Joanna. It's to be sung at the wedding feast. Can you do it?"

"Of course," Lachlan replied with a shrug. "Do you intend to serenade your new wife or should I?"

Rory glowered at Lachlan. "You know I can't sing a damn note. And I sure as hell don't want you standing in the middle of the hall, looking like some fabled Adonis and warbling an ardent refrain to my impressionable bride. Joanna's not to know you had anything to do with it."

"Have Fergus MacQuisten sing the ditty," Keir proposed. "We'll swear the old bard to secrecy. He can announce at the wedding feast that Rory composed the ballad especially for Joanna and taught it to him. No one will know any different.''

Rory smiled at the brilliant suggestion. Twisted and gnarled with age, the seventy-year-old Fergus had a voice sweeter than birdsong in springtime. Joanna would be listening to the troubadour's lilting tenor, but she'd be looking at Rory.

"There's something else, isn't there?" Lachlan asked with canny intuition.

Setting his wine goblet on the table, Rory set his jaw and hooked his thumbs in his belt. "If either of you so much as snicker," he cautioned his brothers, "I'll knock the pair of you boneheads down and stomp on you."

Keir and Lachlan's eyes danced with hilarity, and their mouths twitched in barely suppressed grins. Till that moment, they'd never known their oldest brother to give a bloody damn about capturing any female's attention. Here was their chance to roast him on the spit.

"They won't laugh," Lady Emma quickly interjected. She frowned in admonition to her two younger sons, then turned to Rory with an encouraging smile. "What is it you wish them to do?"

"I want Lachlan to write a sonnet to my bride," he said with a defensive lift of his chin. "Something praising her beauty and charm. The kind of folderol that lassies like to hear."

"But wouldn't it be better to express your feelings in your own words, dear?" Lady Emma asked.

Lachlan put his arm around their mother's shoulders and gave her an affectionate squeeze. "Not unless you want to hear him compare his bonny bride's charms to the finer qualities of a siege engine."

Slapping her second son's hand playfully, she made a disapproving moue, but she didn't contradict his assertion.

"Will you have Fergus recite the poem at the banquet?" Duncan asked him.

"I'll memorize the lines myself," he said in a strangled voice, "and I'll recite them when the time is right."

Just as he'd expected, his brothers' mirth erupted into loud guffaws.

Lady Emma clasped her hands joyfully, her eyes shining. "Why, Rory, I think the lass has stolen your heart!"

He jerked his thumb toward his chest. "My heart's right here where it's always been," he stated. "But Joanna's young and filled with starry-eyed dreams, like many a lassie before her."

His mother stiffened, and he immediately regretted his careless words. He'd rather bite off his tongue than hurt her. But the truth remained: at the tender age of fifteen, she'd run away with his father in spite of her parents' objections, and her bastard son had paid dearly for her impulsive behavior.

"I have no regrets, Rory," she said, her gaze somber. "I only wish for once you'd allow your emotions to rule that hard head of yours. That you'd surrender your heart to that darling lass."

Rory scowled at her. "Don't be foolish, Mother. I'm marrying the maid because the king commanded it, and because I want estates to leave my future heirs. This alliance gives me a chance to build something permanent for my MacLean kinsmen and myself."

Coming to stand directly in front of him, she reached up and touched his cheek. "When I eloped with your father," she said, "I willingly gave up my family and my inheritance for the man I loved."

Rory met her entreating eyes. With a reluctant smile, he caught her hand and kissed the slender fingertips. Still beautiful at forty-four, she hadn't a single strand of gray in her lustrous brown hair, in spite of the fact that she'd outlived three stalwart husbands.

"Only a rosy-cheeked lassie with her head in the clouds would mistake the throb of physical attraction for a fancy called love," he told her gently.

" 'Tis true, I loved your father beyond reason," she admitted, her voice filled with sweet reminiscence. "Someday, Rory, you'll love a woman so deeply you'll forget everything but the need to be with her. And then you'll find it in your heart to forgive me." The absence of a matrimonial settlement had meant that her firstborn son was left illegitimate and homeless when his father died on the battlefield at the age of eighteen.

"There's nothing to forgive," he denied. "No one could have a more wonderful mother."

She smiled pensively. "And what should I have Joanna do when I return to my chamber?"

Clasping her shoulders, Rory bent his head and brushed his lips across her forehead. "Anything you wish, Mother. Just keep her occupied and out of trouble while Lachlan and Keir teach me the rudiments of the pavane. I don't want her alone with Ewen Macdonald or that damnfool idiot son of his."

Joanna sat on the velvet pillows stacked in the deep window embrasure of Lady Emma's bedchamber. She'd brought along paper, pen, and ink, and waited impatiently for MacLean's mother to appear, her mind concerned with the preparations for supper.

"Here I am at last, child," Lady Emma said, as she entered with a rustle of rose satin. She sank down on a small cushioned settle and beamed at Joanna. "Isn't it exciting? There's nothing like a wedding! All the delicious sweetmeats and the frivolity and the guests dressed in their most colorful velvets and satins."

Joanna could hear the clank and clash of swords coming from the ground below, as men strove to exhibit their prowess before the admiring ladies. There'd be games of archery later that afternoon with long bow and crossbow. A papingo shoot was planned, with the best archers trying to knock the brilliant bird from the top of a high pole.

"Seems to be a lot of work for a few minutes of churching," Joanna said with acerbity. "Do you have a letter you wish to dictate, milady?"

The vivacious widow nodded, her gaze flitting to the small writing desk balanced across Joanna's knees. "I do.

And I see you came prepared. But there's no great hurry. We can get to my correspondence in good time.''

"I've many tasks to complete before the evening meal," Joanna informed her gravely. "In fact, I'm needed in the kitchen right now."

Lady Emma fluttered her hand in a dismissive gesture. "Mercy, don't fret about that, child. My son said you were to attend me for the rest of the afternoon and run any errands I needed. Some other lad can take over the chores in the scullery."

Joanna bit her lip to keep from uttering a protest. No one but the chatelaine of the castle could make the myriad decisions necessary that day.

With the fragrance of lavender drifting about her, Lady Emma rose from the bench and moved to the chamber's great bed. Its linen hangings had been tied back and the quilted comforter piled high with feminine clothing. She lifted a magnificent emerald gown and held it up for Joanna to admire.

"My faith, isn't it lovely?" she asked. "As mother of the groom, I'm expected to dress in my finest raiment. I don't want to disappoint my son. He's never been married before. What do you think?"

Joanna peered at the exquisite damask silk. "I think 'tis the finest gown I've ever seen," she answered abruptly. "MacLean won't be disappointed. Do you wish to dictate that letter to me now, milady?"

"I believe I'll wear my gold-trimmed headdress," Lady Emma mused. She laid the gown on the bed and smoothed her fingers along the fur trim. "Though perhaps the one with the pearls would be more appropriate."

Joanna rolled her eyes in exasperation. The entire family was demented. What difference did it make which finery the lady chose to wear on Sunday morning? There wasn't going to be a wedding without a bride.

"I think the gold one would be best," Joanna said, tapping the nib of her pen restlessly on the leather-covered desk.

Lady Emma returned to the settle. "Why don't we start?" she suggested with a smile.

With head bowed over the paper and her pen poised above the vellum, Joanna waited. "I'm ready when you are, milady."

"My dear Lady Joanna," the widow began in a dreamy tone.

Joanna's head flew up in surprise.

Oblivious to her lackey's astonishment, Lady Emma continued blithely. "By the time you read this, you'll be my daughter—"

"She can't read."

At last Joanna had the flighty woman's complete attention. The holly-green gaze flew to meet hers. "She can't?"

"She's had no schooling. She's simple."

MacLean's mother pressed her hand to her breast, sympathy written across her lovely features. "Ah, poor soul." Overcome with disappointment, she lowered her head and traced her fingertips over the embroidered edge of her girdle.

Joanna waited for Emma MacNeil to declare that her son shouldn't marry the poor witless soul. Once again, she'd misjudged MacLean's family.

The widow looked up and smiled reassuringly. "But I'm certain my son will be very gentle with the unfortunate lass."

"I doubt that," Joanna stated baldly. "MacLean said he planned to put a leash on her."

Lady Emma stood up, then sat back down, her eyes widened in shock. "Surely not!"

"He said he'd feed her carrots and apples, till she was eating out of his hand and jumping through hoops."

Lady Emma covered her eyes with a handkerchief, her words smothered and far away. "My son said that?"

For a moment, Joanna suspected the widow of laughing at her own son's unqualified callousness, then pushed the unlikely thought aside and continued in righteous indignation. "He did. He said he'd teach Lady Joanna how to see to his comforts, and that she'd eventually produce a fine batch of weans. God's truth, he talked as if she were a piece of furniture he'd purchased at the fair.''

Wadding the lace-edged square of linen in her hands, Lady Emma gazed out the window behind Joanna. Her lovely eyes sparkled with tears, but her voice was calm and sober when she spoke. "What . . . what else did he say?''

Somewhat mollified, Joanna leaned back against the pillows. The widow appeared sincerely moved by the unfortunate heiress's plight at the hands of her ruthless, diabolical son. That was more compassion than MacLean had ever shown for the tragic Maid of Glencoe. "He defended his harsh attitude by reciting an odious proverb.''

"Hmm,'' Lady Emma said thoughtfully as she dabbed at the corners of her eyes. "Let me guess. 'My own goods, my own wife . . .' ''

Joanna nodded. "That's the one.''

"I see what you mean, child. But my son also believes in the old Gaelic proverb, 'Say but little and say it well.' Rory's not given to flowery speeches, but you mustn't assume he hasn't deep feelings. Quite the contrary.''

Joanna could barely keep from snorting. "What do you mean, milady?''

"Rory's always been short of words,'' the widow replied as she tucked her handkerchief into the small purse that hung from her girdle. "But that doesn't mean he has no affection for others. Beneath that brusque exterior is a man yearning to be loved. You mustn't believe the terrible lies spread by his enemies, child. Time and again, he's demonstrated his willingness to risk his own life to defend others, but there are many people envious of his courage and unswerving loyalty to the king.''

Joanna gazed at the woman in speculation. "Is MacLean like his father?''

Lady Emma didn't seem perturbed to have a mere lackey ask such a personal question. "Oh, indeed,'' she replied, "and I loved Niall passionately.''

Joanna brushed the quill's plume under her chin, her

mind racing. Since the lady seemed so willing to share her intimate feelings, Joanna might as well ask the one question she was longing to have answered.

"When you . . . ah . . . when you spent your first night with Niall MacLean, were there any . . . er . . . surprises?"

The corners of Lady Emma's eyes crinkled just like her son's when she smiled so widely. "What do you mean by surprises, child?"

"Oh, anything at all. Anything you weren't particularly . . . expecting?"

"I was very young and very naïve, so I suppose I was a trifle surprised that night. What maiden isn't when she loses her virginity?"

Joanna probed gently. "But nothing repulsed you?"

Lady Emma tipped her head to one side, regarding her with a quizzical look. "Nothing at all.'

"That's a relief," Joanna murmured under her breath as she stared down at the sheet of vellum.

"What did you say, child?"

Joanna looked up to meet the lady's kindhearted gaze. "I said I'm relieved that you think the heiress will have no unhappy surprises on her wedding night. MacLean told me that when a man beds his wife, he treats her just like he treats his horse."

Lady Emma rested her forehead in her palm and shook her head in resignation. "He probably didn't mean that the way it sounded," she said. "But why was he discussing such a private matter with a wee laddie like you?"

"MacLean caught me peeking at Tam and Mary in the stables," Joanna admitted. "He picked me up by my collar and shook me till my teeth rattled, then lectured me on my behavior. One thing led to another and I asked him if he'd bedded any lassies. Next thing I knew, he was talking about slipping a bridle on Lady Joanna."

Lady Emma slapped her hands against her cheeks and bolted from the settle. She hurried across the room to a washstand, poured out a pitcher of water and proceeded to bathe her face. Her shoulders shook as she bent over the basin, splashing water like a wild woman.

Joanna set the lap desk aside and walked across the room. "I didn't mean to upset you, milady," she apologized, stricken at the effect her thoughtlessness had caused. After all, the insensitive, hard-hearted brute *was* her son.

Lady Emma buried her face in a linen towel. "You didn't upset me, child," she gasped, her words muffled. "I'm just so happy my son is being wed in two days, that I started to cry. Did you ever burst into tears from sheer happiness?"

Joanna shook her head in incomprehension. "I guess I've never been that happy."

Joanna had assumed that with Arthur Hay's return to Kinlochleven, her duties as MacLean's gillie would be completed, and she'd be free to oversee the castle's staff. But Lady Emma kept Joanna with her until it was time for the evening meal. Fortunately Maude undertook the supervision of the kitchen servants, and the vast array of food was prepared without Ethel threatening to slip a knife between the royal chef's ribs or sneaking into the buttery to guzzle a flagon of ale.

While the guests feasted on venison and suckling pig, musicians played in the gallery at the far end of the great hall. A group of mummers performed a farce that made everyone roar with laughter, and nimble acrobats demonstrated their astonishing abilities to leap and tumble across the rush-covered stone floor.

Every time Joanna came near MacLean, he was discussing plans for the improvement of Kinlochleven's fortifications.

"The size of the castle provides ample facilities for storing provisions that would last a year," he told the king, who was seated beside him. "Once the modifications are completed, we could hold out against an attacking force ten times our number."

When she poured his wine, MacLean paused to look up

and give her a brotherly smile. James Stewart smiled too, his brown eyes warm and friendly.

Considering that she appeared as bedraggled as ever, His Majesty's kindness to a mere kitchen varlet seemed astounding. She had to admit James IV of Scotland was much nicer than she'd ever imagined.

Ewen Macdonald caught Joanna's eye as she scurried around the great hall carrying an enormous tray of dirty trenchers. At forty-one, the Glencoe Macdonalds' war leader commanded the respect of his clansmen. Though not as tall and powerful as MacLean or his brothers, he'd proven his courage and strength in battle. Streaks of silver glinted in his walnut-brown hair and well-trimmed beard. He had the same dark eyes as his son, but his gaze glittered with a cunning intelligence.

"Meet me in the stables," he said in an undertone when she casually made her way to where he sat. "I want to speak with you alone."

"I'll sneak out as soon as possible," she whispered. She glanced cautiously at the dark-haired lad beside him.

Ewen shook his head, warning her silently not to speak to his son. Andrew's taut features betrayed his smoldering anger. He'd always taken it for granted that they'd be married one day, and Kinlochleven and all its lands and revenues would be his. 'Twas no wonder his father feared that, in his hurt pride, he'd reveal her secret and the game would be lost.

Godfrey Macdonald glanced up as Joanna took his empty trencher, a sneer curling his lips. He made no attempt to hide his disgust at her filthy male apparel.

"Hello, Godfrey," she said quietly.

Younger than Ewen by three years, he showed none of his brother's innate leadership or his nephew's bonny looks. Deep pock marks that even a scraggly beard couldn't conceal riddled his bloated face. A distended blue vein pulsed on his protuberant nose, and his breath reeked of alcohol.

"Go away," he responded in a hiss, "before someone

becomes suspicious.'' Tipping his head back, he drained his tankard in one long, greedy gulp.

In the crush of people, it should have been easy to slip out of the donjon unnoticed. But whenever Joanna tried to leave, either Fearchar or one of MacLean's brothers lingered nearby. Several times she almost walked into one of them. Standing eyeball to mammoth chest, she felt like she'd fallen asleep and awakened in a land of giants.

When supper was over, the menservants dismantled the trestle tables and pushed the benches to the side of the chamber. Rushes were swept from the stone floor for the dancing, and many of the lairds and ladies swayed and dipped in a stately branle around the chamber.

To Joanna's disappointment, MacLean didn't leave his chair on the dais beside the king. She wanted to see the fearsome warlord executing a courtly révérance to Lady Beatrix or Lady Idoine. From the sulky pout on her cousin's face, Idoine felt the same way.

But MacLean didn't even glance at the dancers. God's truth, the confounded man hadn't the tiniest spark of romance in his black soul.

Late in the evening, Joanna still could find no opportunity to meet the Macdonalds' clan commander. She'd hoped to creep out to the stables once everyone sought his bed, but MacLean and his two brothers joined Davie and Seumas in their nightly game of cards at the kitchen's large table.

The Sea Dragon had made a habit of spending half the night gambling with the men who stood guard over Joanna while she slept. Apparently the vice ran in his family, for Lachlan and Keir showed no more sign of retiring at a decent hour than he did. Exhausted, she fell asleep in front of the hearth to the drone of their quiet masculine voices as they made their bets over the tarots.

''Here's a crown that says you're bluffing, Davie,'' MacLean softly challenged. ''And I warn you, I can see through a Macdonald's blatherskite like the wings of a moth circling a flame.''

The last thing Joanna heard was the warrior's deep chuckle and the chink of a coin being thrown atop the pile of shillings on the table.

She smiled sleepily. The rich timbre of his baritone was just about the nicest sound a lass could hear as she drifted into slumber.

It wasn't until the next morning that Joanna finally had a chance to slip away unnoticed. She handed a note to Jock as she brushed by him in the stables, whispering that it was for Ewen, then hastened to the chapel.

Inside, everything glistened from Abby and Sarah's energetic cleaning. The warm oak of the pews glowed from being polished. The gold candlesticks on the altar gleamed. Sparkling white and freshly pressed, the altar cloths lay draped across the Communion railing in readiness for the next morning's ceremony. In the vestibule, huge bouquets of roses, lilies, and apple blossoms stood in buckets of water, waiting to be placed in the tall vases on the main and side altars.

Their perfume drifted about her, reminding Joanna of the floral-scented soap she'd been forced to abandon with MacLean's arrival. A hurried bath in the buttery using Ethel's hard, yellow cakes couldn't compare with lingering in a warm tub before the fire.

Joanna looked carefully around to be sure no one lurked in the shadows, then hurried up the aisle to the row of blue votive lights burning in front of the Virgin's altar. With another quick glance to be certain she was alone, she bent forward and blew out the flames. Crossing herself, she made a hasty genuflection and sent a prayer heavenward that she'd be forgiven for such a grievous sin.

A soft tread sounded behind her, and Joanna's heart leaped like a frightened roe bounding for freedom. If MacLean had caught her, she'd be led to the stake and set afire like a torch.

Chapter 10

"**B**lowing out candles isn't going to save you, Joanna."

She whirled and gasped in relief when she recognized Ewen's solid frame outlined in the rosy light streaming through the stained glass window behind him.

"Thank God, 'tis you," she croaked hoarsely.

"I got your note," he said as he strode up the side aisle. "We'd best speak quickly." He caught her elbow and drew her into a small alcove, out of view.

"Have you come to take me to Mingarry?" she asked, hoping he wouldn't detect the disheartenment in her voice. She should be thrilled to escape the Sea Dragon's clutches, yet the very thought of leaving Kinlochleven seemed to carve a hole in her chest where her heart should be.

'Twas her beloved castle she'd pine for, Joanna reassured herself, and most definitely *not* the ferocious Highland chief who intended to wed her on the morrow.

Ewen's dark brows met in a scowl as he released her arm. "Not right away. Your disappearance now would only cause alarm. They'd be searching the countryside, certain who you were, before we were halfway to Ballachulish."

A tremor shivered through her, and Joanna clasped her hands to keep them from shaking. "But what should I do?" she asked breathlessly. "MacLean plans to wed Lady Joanna in the morning."

"Just keep up with your excellent stratagem," Ewen

said. He offered her a brief, sour smile as his gaze traveled down the tattered shirt and worn plaid to the short hose sagging about her ankles. "When we announce that Idoine is truly my daughter, just as she claimed from the start, he'll be the laughingstock of the Scottish court. MacLean can't marry a bride he can't find. There'll be nothing left for the King's Avenger but to go back to Stalcaire empty-handed."

She breathed a sigh of relief. "And I'll be free to become Lady Joanna again."

Ewen stroked his short, pointed beard with calm assurance. "All we need do then is wait for the dispensation to arrive from Rome. Once it comes, you can marry Andrew. And that will be the end of James Stewart's plans to bring the Glencoe Macdonalds under his iron fist."

Joanna's heart plummeted at his words. "How soon do you think permission will come?"

"It could be a matter of months."

Ewen watched her through narrowed eyes, and Joanna turned away from his hard, discerning gaze.

He grasped her arm and pulled her around to face him. "It's what your kinsmen expect of you," he insisted curtly. "The entire Macdonald clan is depending on you to meet your obligation as their chieftain and marry the man chosen for you. You're not some tavern wench or poor crofter's daughter, Joanna. Whom you marry is of the utmost importance to your kinsmen. We can't allow Kinlochleven to fall into the hands of our foes."

"I understand," she said, lowering her lids to conceal her unhappiness. She'd never been fully accepted by her English relatives in Cumberland. Aunt and Uncle Blithfield had often scolded Lady Anne for her daughter's wild Highland ways, and her Neville grandparents had tried to curb her tempestuous Scottish nature. Joanna wanted desperately to be needed and loved by her clansmen, but her heart rebelled at the sacrifice she was being asked to make for their sakes.

Ewen's terse words bristled with an unmistakable warning. "Don't do anything to give yourself away, Joanna."

She rubbed her hands over her upper arms to ward off the shivers that plagued her, then raised her eyes to meet his cold stare.

"Now that the king is here, I'm frightened," she confessed. "Should my identity be discovered, I could be hanged for a traitor."

He caught her wrist and squeezed the bones in his unrelenting grasp. His sharp reply came like a headsman's ax, slicing through the peaceful stillness of the chapel. "Nothing will happen to you, lass, if you keep up the deception. But no Macdonald will ever forgive you if you betray yourself—purposely or otherwise."

Making no attempt to break free of his painful hold, Joanna bowed her head. Her shoulders slumped in defeat. "I know."

"Never forget," Ewen said, somewhat mollified by her easy capitulation, "MacLean captured Somerled and turned him over to his executioners. He hounded that old man unmercifully, till he ran the Red Wolf to the ground like a common felon. No Macdonald should ever feel anything but contempt for the King's Avenger." He paused, then added harshly, "Unless you believe your grandfather was guilty of the charges against him."

"Grandpapa was innocent!" Joanna exclaimed. "He'd never have killed anyone without just cause. I'm certain of it."

Convinced of her sincerity, Ewen patted her hand. "Place your loyalty to your clan above all else, Joanna, as your father and grandfather would have wished you to do. Once you're married to Andrew, I'll give the two of you free rein here at Kinlochleven."

Joanna knew what her cousin's promise implied. More concerned with his falcons and horses, Andrew would take little interest in the mundane duties of the laird of the castle. His frivolous attachment to heavy gold chains, velvet jackets, and fur-lined gauntlets would far exceed the attention he'd give to the deer parks, fishponds, rabbit warrens, and dovecotes on their estates. Though she'd have to take care that her self-indulgent husband didn't drain their coffers dry, she'd be free to make the day-to-day decisions over their far-flung holdings. As her clan's war leader, all Ewen would ask in return was that Joanna's men-at-arms remained loyal to the Macdonalds, if another rebellion should break out in the Hebrides and spread to the mainland.

"I'd better go now," Ewen said. "If any MacLean should see us talking like this, he might start to wonder." Without another word, he turned on his heel and strode down the aisle.

Joanna moved to a niche at the side of the chapel, where a stained glass window depicted a slender maid dressed in silvery armor holding a banner adorned with the lilies of France. With trembling fingers, she lit a candle in front of the Maid of Orléans, just as she'd done every morning since she'd first been told, after the death of her grandfather, that she was to marry Ewen's son. She looked up at Jeanne d'Arc's brave, shining face and fought the despair that tugged at her aching heart.

Day after day, Joanna had prayed for a gallant champion to come and rescue her from her betrothal to Andrew. Instead of a valiant knight-errant, though, the Sea Dragon had appeared at the castle gate. An ogre who'd been responsible for her grandfather's death.

Not really an ogre, she admitted. She'd seen what a strong and wise chief The MacLean could be in his dealings with her kinsmen. Forthright, just, slow to wrath, the bold Highland warrior had a natural ability to lead. Many of Joanna's loyal retainers had grown to admire him, and the practical, outspoken Maude was slowly but surely being won over to his side. As Joanna's husband and the laird of Kinlochleven, MacLean would protect their estates and increase their wealth.

His patience with the halflins in the castle—including the obstreperous Joey Macdonald—proved he'd never have killed the wee laddie as he'd threatened that first day. And the afternoon he'd patiently given a stripling lad a lesson in archery remained a delightful memory she couldn't erase. That very same day, he'd saved her life.

One thing seemed certain: though Joanna believed in her grandfather's innocence, she knew instinctively that MacLean must have been convinced beyond a shadow of a doubt that Somerled was guilty of murdering Gideon Cameron in cold blood. Otherwise, he would never have hunted him down so remorselessly.

There wasn't a shadow of a doubt, however, that someone in heaven had made a serious mistake when answering her prayers. For in sending this valiant Highland chief to rescue her from marriage to Andrew Macdonald, the saints had sent the one man she could never marry in his stead.

For if she married the chief of Clan MacLean, she'd earn the enmity of every member of her clan.

Joanna's heart fluttered like a bird caught in a net at the thought of becoming MacLean's wife. What would it be like to lie down beside the mighty warlord? To draw the bed curtains about them and be held in his muscular arms in the velvety stillness of the night? To feel his strength surround her as his determined lips sought hers in a possessive, all-conquering kiss?

A tiny shudder went through her, and she pressed her fingertips against her closed lids, trying to block out the enthralling image of that virile man lying beside her, their naked bodies touching intimately.

Holy heavens, she wouldn't allow herself to think of it.

For marriage to the chief of Clan MacLean was a path she could never go down.

The sound of footsteps broke the chapel's silence, and Joanna straightened, refusing to allow the tears to fall. Blinking furiously, she glanced over her shoulder to find Fearchar standing in the main aisle.

"Here you are, laddie," he said. "The last I caught sight of you, you were heading for the stables."

Brawny arms akimbo, he watched her with thoughtful regard. The black eye patch and ragged scar on his cheekbone, the gold stud in his ear, and the narrow braids that decorated his long blond hair no longer seemed so alarming, for she could read the concern in his one good eye.

Like the humble serving lad she portrayed, Joanna sniffed and wiped her nose on her dirty sleeve. "Were you looking for me, sir?"

"Is aught amiss, lad?"

She lifted a shoulder noncommittally. "I was cleaning and got a speck of dust in my eye, 'tis all."

Fearchar joined Joanna and looked at the brilliant stained glass in open admiration. "Forbye," he said, " 'twas brave and braw the Maid of Orléans was. She reminds me of another wee lassie I know."

"Does she?" Joanna asked in awe. She gazed up at the slim girl in chain mail, a helm at her feet and the light of undaunted courage glowing in her pale face. "I wish I knew someone like her."

The robust, gentle-hearted man beside her glanced down at the burning candle, and his teeth flashed white in his bearded face. "Lady Emma would like you to wait upon her again today, Joey."

"Please tell her I need to speak with The MacLean first," she said. "Do you happen to know where he is?"

" 'Tis up on the battlements he is, lad," Fearchar replied. "I'll accompany you there."

Rory stood with Lachlan on the barbican, looking out over the valley below. He'd laid the plans for the castle's improvements across the wide stone parapet and was pointing out the changes he intended to make.

"As you can see," he told his brother, "Kinlochleven is impenetrable on the west, where the cliffs drop straight down to the loch. But the south-facing curtain wall, the barbican, and the main gate are all highly vulnerable. I plan to reinforce the existing stone curtain with buttresses, put gun loops along the walls, replace the aging portcullis with a much stronger one, and build a new gate. All the posterns will be reinforced and another well dug in the lower bailey.

When the alterations are complete, we'll be able to withstand anything thrown by catapult or cannon.''

Lachlan nodded his agreement and clapped his brother on the shoulder. ''You may not be much of a dancer, Rory, but you're a blasted wizard when it comes to fortifications.''

Rory met his teasing gaze with a crooked grin. ''I've stormed enough castles to know every weakness imaginable. And now, thanks to you and Keir, I'll be able to dance at my wedding banquet without stomping on my bride's wee toes—or her fancy gown.''

The three brothers had spent most of the previous afternoon locked in the solar, while Fearchar guarded the door and Lady Emma kept Joanna occupied.

Lachlan had played a lute, calling out instructions like a persnickety French dancing master, and Keir took the part of the lassie. It'd been damn awkward for Rory, pointing his toe and mincing about like a popinjay, while Keir, who stood well over six foot in his stocking feet, curtsied and simpered and pretended to drag a train five yards long behind him. Rory's brothers had guffawed hilariously every time he'd stepped on the imaginary swath of white satin.

Lachlan chuckled at the ridiculous picture they'd made. ''Just remember, Rory, you don't merely glide around the floor with a lady, holding her hand. You *dance* with her. Gaze into her eyes and will her to come closer than propriety allows. Let the damsel read your hunger for her in every move you make.''

Rory scowled. He might hunger for Joanna, but he wasn't about to expose his feelings to the entire court.

''Don't look so uncomfortable at the thought of showing your tender regard for the lassie,'' Lachlan said cheerily. '' 'Tis only natural, given she's such a peach.''

''You misread my intentions,'' Rory informed his brother, who merely grinned and shook his auburn head, unimpressed and unconvinced. ''Certainly, I feel admiration and respect for Joanna—and desire. Hell, who wouldn't? But I'm far too sensible to make a fool of myself over a slip of a lass like some idiots do.''

Lachlan laughed. ''Don't try to tell me you haven't fallen for the delectable wee maid, Rory. I know you better than that. Why else the dance lessons and the ballad and the sonnet? Which, by the way, are almost finished.''

Rory bristled at his sibling's smug assumption. ''Joanna believes in the myths of chivalry portrayed in the troubadours' ballads, that's why. And if she wants to be swept off her feet by a knight in shining armor, I'm more than willing to play the part—and reap the obvious rewards. But that doesn't mean I'm in love with her. Wives are chosen for pragmatic reasons.'' He flung up his hand in mounting irritation. ''So you can wipe that smirk off your face, dammit.''

Lachlan shrugged concedingly, but his eyes never lost their sparkle of amusement.

''Joey wishes to speak with you, laird,'' Fearchar called from behind them. The brothers turned to see him climbing the outside stairs with Joanna, who looked as ragged and unwashed as ever.

Lachlan stepped forward to greet his future good-sister with a warm smile. ''Good morning, Joey,'' he said, his voice filled with fraternal affection. ''I hope we didn't keep you awake with our card playing last night.''

''I slept through it all,'' Joanna replied. She bestowed an answering smile on the debonair chief of Clan MacRath, but when she turned her bonny blue eyes on Rory, her expression grew solemn. ''I'd like to speak with you in private, laird. 'Tis about something important.''

''Very well,'' Rory said, glancing at his brother and cousin. ''If you gentlemen will excuse us?''

Joanna watched the two men leave, then joined Rory at the battlement's parapet. ''I like your family,'' she confided with guileless sincerity. ''They're very nice.''

''I'm glad you like them,'' he replied as he rolled up the building plans. ''My brothers think you're a lad of parts, and Lady Emma couldn't say enough kind things about you. It seems you kept her highly entertained with your frank observations yesterday.''

Joanna's long lashes fluttered at his words, and she turned stiffly to face the scene before them. She clasped the edge of the stone wall and stared straight in front of her. ''Did she tell you what we talked about?''

''She didn't,'' Rory answered truthfully.

His mother had refused to indulge his curiosity, telling him only, between bouts of bubbling laughter, that his lucky star must have risen in the night sky that year, because no man could ever be more fortunate on his wedding day than Rory would be on his.

At the crimson rising on Joanna's cheeks, he had a hunch their conversation was all about him—and none too flattering at that.

Anxious to redirect the conversation, Joanna pointed to the ruins of an ancient island fortress in the loch. ''Eilean Ceilteach is said to be the place where Fraoch slew the fiendish monster that guarded the magic fruit. My nursemaid told me the story when I was just a wee bairn.''

Rory smiled as he recalled the tale his mother had told him of the Celtic hero, who'd brought back the healing berries to his ailing lover, the exquisite Mai.

''But you must know the story already,'' Joanna added happily, ''since you named your stallion after the valiant warrior.''

''I didn't,'' he replied. ''My mother had already named the mean-tempered brute when she presented him to me.''

Joanna wrinkled her impudent nose in disappointment, but made no comment. 'Twas clear she'd hoped Rory had been as enthralled with the legend as she.

Together, they looked out across a glen surrounded on three sides by mountains. Splendid woodlands of oak and birch wound like ribbons along the foothills. The great Mamore Forest stretched across the higher ranges to the north. Through the eastern gorge, with its bold granite crags overhanging steep slopes, the river cascaded down to the floor of the valley and the cold saltwater loch, teeming with fish and studded with islets. The Observantine monastery could be seen on one island, with its chapel dedicated to St. Findoca.

" 'Tis very beautiful," she said quietly.

He glanced down at her. Thick curving lashes hid the magnificent indigo eyes. The fine bones of her gamin face defied the application of soot from the hearth. In spite of the tattered clothes, her slim figure stood straight and proud, betraying her noble birth. He asked himself for the hundredth time how anyone could think she'd be able to fool him for the space of a day, let alone one full week.

Looking out at the vista once more, he spoke with suppressed intensity. "I've sailed the seas and visited countless foreign cities, and I've never seen a sight fairer than the one before my eyes this morning."

"I would like to travel to faraway places," Joanna said, a wistful note in her low contralto. "Especially France. I'd like to visit Paris and Orléans." She canted her head and looked up at him. "Have you been there, laird?"

"I have."

He patted her slender shoulder in his best brotherly fashion, though his fingers ached to follow the enticing curve of her nape beneath the ribbed edge of her stocking cap. He wanted to lift her stubborn chin with his fingertips and gaze into those thick-lashed, wondering eyes as he bent to kiss her.

He wanted Joanna to want him.

Tomorrow the detested cap would come off. And the decrepit shirt and frayed plaid. Until then he'd have to content himself with just having her near, and the sure knowledge that they would be married the next morning.

He'd laid his plans carefully, wanting her to be swept away. He wanted their wedding day to be as romantic as every starry-eyed lassie's dream. As for their wedding night . . . His body hardened at the thought. Well, that promised to be a dream come true for the randy, hot-blooded bridegroom.

"With your spunk, Joey," he continued conversationally, "you'd make a fine sailor."

"Do you really think so?" she asked with a puckish grin.

"I do. Someday I'll take you aboard the *Sea Dragon*. We can sail to the outer isles in the springtime, then spend the summer calling on ports from Le Havre to Cadiz."

"Where is your ship now, milord?"

"She lies at anchor in Loch Linnhe, near Stalcaire."

The longing for adventure glowed in Joanna's eyes. "It must be wonderful to own a fleet of ships and be able to go anywhere you wish."

His gaze fixed on her radiant face, he spoke in a low tone. "Many men would covet what I now possess. I intend to guard it wisely."

Her arched russet brows drew together as she searched his eyes with a puzzled expression. " 'Twould have to be a very strong foe to wrest your possessions from you."

"No man will ever take what is mine," he told her bluntly. "Not while I'm alive." He tapped the rolled parchment lightly on the top of her cap and smiled indulgently. "Now, what was it you needed to talk about, lad?"

Her head bent, she scuffed the toe of her oversized shoe across the rough stones of the battlement. " 'Tis about the wedding," she replied in a smothered voice.

"What about the wedding?"

Too uneasy to meet his perceptive gaze, Joanna fidgeted with her belt buckle. "I was wondering what you planned to do tomorrow, if 'tis proven that Lady Idoine really isn't Joanna Macdonald after all."

Folding his muscular arms across his broad chest, he spoke with absolute conviction. "I'm not mistaken about Lady Joanna's identity. And I'm going to marry her in the morning."

Joanna planted her hands on her hips and glared at the pigheaded, stiff-necked man. "Godsakes, MacLean! How can any creature on God's green earth be so obtuse? We've told you that Lady Joanna is missing. She's wandering about somewhere in a daze!"

He met her obvious dismay with a dazzling smile that deepened the creases around the corners of his eyes and displayed his even white teeth. "Now that the king is at Kinlochleven, I expect the truth from everyone at the wedding."

Joanna flung her hands wide in exasperation. "What if you're mistaken? Won't you feel foolish standing at the altar without a bride?"

"I'm counting on the Maid of Glencoe to be at the wedding," he stated. He strode along the barbican, the wide pleats of his belted plaid swinging about his bare thighs. The breeze ruffled the three eagle feathers in his green bonnet and stirred the lace at his throat.

Joanna stayed right beside him, hoping to make the intractable man see reason.

"By now," he continued, "the news of our marriage celebration has spread through the countryside. If Idoine isn't the Maid of Glencoe, my future bride will have heard the reports. She'll know about the preparations taking place at this moment—the banquet, the flowers in the chapel, the large number of guests, including the King of Scotland, who'll be present at the ceremony."

Joanna had to take two steps for every one of his, but she refused to be left behind. "Won't it be rather . . . humiliating . . . to stand in front of the altar before all those guests, if she doesn't appear?"

" 'Tis my hope that very fact will motivate her to attend her own wedding."

"And what if she doesn't?" Joanna demanded, catching his sleeve and tugging persistently. "The maid is simpleminded, if you recall."

He halted and with a smile of absolute confidence tapped the rolled parchment on her shoulder as though bestowing knighthood. "I appreciate your concern, Joey, but I've made alternate plans."

"You have?" She gaped at him in shock. Disappointment threatened to choke her, and her contralto dropped to a hoarse croak. "You'll marry someone else?"

Rory chuckled at the look of consternation on Joanna's dirty face. He wanted to lift her up and twirl her around in a circle, informing her bluntly that she was the most outrageous little minx in Scotland. Then he'd lower her soft, supple form inch by sweet inch, till he could nuzzle the valley between the firm young breasts hidden beneath that overlarge shirt, and tell her she belonged to him. To him and no other.

"I hadn't thought of choosing another bride," he said, pretending to give the idea some consideration. "But I'd best honor the king's wishes and marry Lady Joanna."

"But how can you marry her, if she's not at the wedding?"

"She'll be there."

Scowling, Joanna turned to go, and Rory clasped her shoulder to hold her in place beside him. "Everyone's to be attired in his best garments for the ceremony."

She glanced down at her shabby clothing. "This is my best," she declared stubbornly. " 'Tis the only plaid and shirt I own."

For once, she was undoubtedly telling the truth.

"Then make certain you take a bath this evening," he warned her. "Don't appear at my wedding with a dirty face and grimy hands, laddie, or I'll take it as a personal insult. Just because you have an aversion to bathing doesn't mean you don't have to clean up for the celebration like everyone else in the castle. Tomorrow's going to be a very special day."

The blue eyes flashed with ire. "I'm not sure I'm even coming to your stupid wedding," she retorted.

"Everyone in Kinlochleven has been ordered to attend," he said in a low, threatening voice. He bent closer for emphasis. "You be there, Joey, or I'll skin the hide off your wee frame and nail it to the chapel door."

Joanna shrugged his hand away and started toward the stairs. "All right, I'll be there," she grumbled. "All scrubbed and shiny. But you're going to feel like a first-class jackass standing at the altar all by yourself."

"You let me worry about that," Rory called to her back
with a grin.

After the guests had retired for the night, Joanna dragged
a laundry tub into the buttery with Maude's help. She
washed her long hair with her companion's assistance and
wrapped it in a large linen towel that had been warmed
before the kitchen fire. Then Maude left the small service
room, locking the door from the outside and dropping the
key into her pocket to make sure her young charge
wouldn't be disturbed.

Lolling back in the steaming water, Joanna enjoyed the
luxury of an unhurried bath at last. She propped her heels
against the smooth wooden staves and wiggled her toes in
ecstasy. She'd had to forgo the perfumed soap she loved;
she couldn't risk anyone noticing at the wedding tomorrow
that Joey Macdonald smelled like a bouquet of roses. But
that small sacrifice didn't spoil the pleasure of the moment.

Joanna released a long, drawn-out sigh as she gazed
about at the bottles of wine and flagons of ale stored on
the shelves along the wall.

The Sea Dragon had bathed earlier in the evening. She'd
seen Abby hustling up and down the stairs to his bedchamber with buckets of hot water.

The image of MacLean stepping into his bath naked as
the day he was born brought a warm, tingly feeling inside.
Scooting down in the water, she rested her turbaned head
against the back of the tub and closed her eyes, imagining
what it would be like to touch him. She longed to smooth
her hands over his bare male flesh, bury her fingertips in
the thick mat of golden-brown hair on his chest, and learn
the strength of his corded muscles. Would his solid, imposing frame feel as hard and unforgiving as it looked?

Like Cuchulainn in the old Celtic ballads, the mighty
warlord seemed the epitome of courage and strength.
Whether he had a sea dragon's tail no longer seemed to
matter, though the possibility that he'd cavorted with mermaids brought a sudden frown.

Joanna clicked her tongue and shook her head in censure. She could imagine the scandalous sight of him entwined with a voluptuous water nymph, his muscular limbs enclosing the willing, nubile form. The creature's soft, lush breasts pressed against his hairy chest as he ran his questing hand over her smoothly rounded rump and pulled her even closer.

But mermaids didn't have rumps, smoothly rounded or otherwise; they had tails like a fish.

Godsakes, MacLean wasn't holding a water nymph in his arms.

He held Joanna—Joanna Macdonald without a stitch of clothing on.

Like a seductive sea maiden, she wrapped her arms around his naked body. His fingers tangled in her long red hair as he kissed her—a hot, scorching, passionate kiss that branded her as his mate. Forever.

An unfamiliar ache spread through Joanna, so intense, so compelling, she could feel her nipples tighten and her breasts grow full and taut. A pulsing sensation spread at the juncture of her thighs as the warm water lapped against her secret places. What would it be like if he were to touch her there?

Her eyes flew open, and she sat up straighter in the tub. A flush scalded her cheeks.

Good Lord! Her tutors at Allonby had warned her of the dangers of an idle mind.

Pursing her mouth resolutely, Joanna picked up the yellow soap on the stool nearby and briskly lathered a small cloth, scolding herself for her wanton thoughts.

Her kinsmen still regarded her with skepticism because of her English blood. If they suspected her enthrallment with the Sea Dragon, they'd renounce her as their chieftain. Black magic or not, she hadn't proven immune to MacLean's physical charms. Seeing him beside Andrew, Joanna had been forced to admit that she'd much rather wed the golden-haired chief than the callow sixteen-year-old lad, whose world centered solely around himself and his amusements. But more than anything, she yearned to be loved and accepted by her clansmen—even if it meant marrying Andrew.

MacLean was the hellhound who'd captured her grandfather.

She mustn't ever forget that.

After Joanna's mother had died, Somerled Macdonald had come to Cumberland to rescue his granddaughter from her restricted and circumscribed life with her aunt and uncle. He'd arrived before Allonby Castle's gate with his men-at-arms, threatening to raze the fortress if they didn't turn the Maid of Glencoe over to him at once.

Wakened from a sound sleep, Joanna had been frightened at first, not knowing which fierce Highland chieftain demanded her person. Aunt Clarissa begged her to save them all from certain death, while Uncle Philip assured Joanna she'd merely be held for ransom and not tortured and killed.

Joanna knew better. If the hostile Scots on the other side of the walls were MacLean clansmen, her ancient foes would inflict a great deal of pain and humiliation on her before they killed her.

The walk across the outer bailey had seemed to drain Joanna of whatever courage she possessed. With each step she invoked a different saint to save her, in a litany motivated by sheer cravenness.

The castle gate had opened slowly, creaking on its thick iron hinges, and Joanna walked beneath the raised portcullis, her heart pounding, but ready to face her enemies as a true Macdonald.

Standing several paces in front of the other Highlanders, the huge, gray-bearded chieftain stood waiting for her. The moment she appeared within the glow of their torches, he held out his gloved hand.

"Child," he called softly in the Gaelic, " 'tis really you."

At the sound of his familiar, beloved voice, she stopped short and peered at him through the darkness. "Grandpapa?" she squeaked.

" 'Tis me, lass," he said with a broad smile. "I knew those blasted Sassenachs would never let you come with me unless I threatened to destroy the whole blessed castle first." With a raucous burst of laughter, he opened his arms, and Joanna flew to him.

Somerled Macdonald, labeled the Red Wolf because of his implacable resistance against the Stewart kings, enclosed her in his welcoming embrace. Lifting her completely off the ground, he kissed her temple and cheek as he hugged her tight.

" 'Tis time to be going home, darling of my heart," he'd said, using his pet name for her. "Time to go home to the Highlands."

Through the buttery door, the sound of male laughter in the kitchen brought Joanna back from her bittersweet memories.

Even on the eve of his wedding, MacLean was participating in the nightly game of tarots. She heard his deep chuckle as he won a pile of coins.

Well, let the notorious Sea Dragon laugh. Tomorrow he'd face the ultimate humiliation of standing alone at the altar like a pathetic and rejected buffoon.

Godsakes, she'd tried to warn him.

If the arrogant laird believed that Lady Joanna would appear at the church steps to save him from his self-inflicted mortification, he was sadly mistaken. No Macdonald could ever feel anything but contempt for a MacLean.

Joanna would squelch every trace of tender feeling for the King's Avenger from her heart. Her duty lay with her clan. She could never marry the man responsible for Somerled's death on the gallows.

Chapter 11

The morning of the wedding bloomed as sweet and delicate as the apple blossoms in the May sunshine. An azure sky dotted with puffs of white clouds promised a day the inhabitants of Kinlochleven Castle would long remember—some with immense pleasure, others with deep resentment, depending on whether they were MacLeans or Macdonalds.

Lairds and ladies in costly velvets and taffetas paraded down the center aisle of the chapel and took their places in the pews, as though this were just another ordinary marriage ceremony.

Joanna slipped into her seat alongside Maude, apprehension slithering around in the pit of her belly like the evil serpent in the Garden of Eden. Ewen and Godfrey planned to wait until the last possible moment before announcing to the entire congregation that The MacLean's intended bride was missing. His mistaken assumption that Lady Idoine was the Maid of Glencoe hadn't been their doing. Ewen's daughter had sworn to her true identity on a sacred relic, but the King's Avenger had refused to believe her. There were several impartial witnesses present in the chapel who could verify their statement.

For the tenth time that morning, Joanna reminded herself that MacLean's coming humiliation wouldn't be her fault. God knew, she'd tried to warn him from this demented farce.

She clenched her hands in her lap and watched from the corner of her eye as Keir MacNeil, splendid in his green and blue plaid, escorted his lovely mother to the front pew. His straight black hair, tied with a thong, hung to the middle of his back. The MacNeils were descended from a long line of Celtic sea rovers, and his rugged features, swarthy complexion, scarred brow, and broken nose gave him the roguish air of a pirate. Attired in red and black tartan, Duncan Stewart, second earl of Appin, followed his sister and nephew.

Lady Emma had chosen the pearl-studded headdress to go with her green satin gown, after all. Ladies Beatrix and Idoine proudly displayed their finest ensembles as well. Loaded down with gold chains, brooches, and bracelets, with tasseled purses hanging from their girdles and elegant gloves on their hands, they took their places in the front pew of the chapel.

That morning, Idoine had completed her toilette with special care, tinting her round face with skin whitener and pink rouge. 'Twas a shame the sulky frown that creased her forehead ruined the sought-after effect of meek and mild virginal maid. Joanna knew that if MacLean actually tried to marry her cousin, Idoine would throw a fit, kicking and screaming and pointing out Joey Macdonald as the real bride.

Tugging her stocking cap snugly over her ears, Joanna glanced down at her threadbare apparel and edged closer to Maude's large, reassuring frame. Her companion had been delayed with last-minute tasks and hadn't been able to meet Joanna in the pantry at sunup as planned.

There hadn't been enough time for Maude to weave Joanna's unruly mane into a tight braid as she'd done every other morning since the Sea Dragon's arrival. Together, they'd hastily scooped up Joanna's long hair, piled it on top of her head, and anchored it loosely in place with two combs.

Joanna prayed the wayward locks would remain hidden throughout the lengthy High Mass. Afterward, she and

Maude could slip into one of the small service rooms off the kitchen and braid her hair securely. She couldn't chance having her hair tumble down past her shoulders in front of the entire Scottish court during the banquet to follow.

That would put every Macdonald at sword's point and herself in the shadow of the hangman.

After MacLean's explicit instructions the previous afternoon, she hadn't dared to apply soot to her face and hands. She felt almost naked without the dirt to hide behind. Several Macdonalds had glanced at her that morning and grimaced, certain the deception was over. But the MacLean men-at-arms only smiled and waved a friendly hello to the worried-looking serving lad.

Good Lord! Clan MacLean was easier to dupe than a wagonload of country bumpkins at a fair.

The congregation rose when James Stewart, King of Scotland, entered, decked out in traditional Highland garb in honor of his trusted friend. His close advisers accompanied him, attired in tawny satin doublets and coats of blue velvet. Everyone waited in respectful silence as the dignified procession wended its way up the aisle and His Majesty, facing the gathering, settled himself in a large wooden chair on the altar's dais beneath a blue and gold canopy.

Joanna's breath caught when MacLean entered from the side of the chancel, accompanied by Father Thomas and his brother Lachlan.

Tall and resplendent, the bridegroom wore a fine linen shirt with lace at the collar and cuffs, and a green velvet jacket. A jeweled bodkin fastened the corner of his green and black belted plaid to his shoulder. A sealskin sporran, jewel-encrusted dress sword, silver mounted dirk, checkered short hose with rosette points, and black brogues with shiny gold buckles completed his costume.

There was no mistaking the power and wealth of this forceful Highland chief on his wedding day.

There was no mistaking the confusion written across Father Thomas's gaunt face either. The priest looked around the chapel at the assemblage, his dark, deep-set eyes betraying his bafflement.

"My dear friends," he began after a minute's painful hesitation, "earlier this morning, His Majesty, King James, as Lady Joanna's guardian, signed the marriage contract, as did the chief of Clan MacLean. Laird Lachlan MacRath and Lady Emma MacNeil witnessed the signing. The banns having been duly read, there is no legal impediment to the marriage of Joanna Macdonald and Rory MacLean."

The congregation shifted in their seats, looking at one another in wonderment. From where Joanna sat, she could see Ewen turn to his brother and son with a smirk and murmur something under his breath. Godfrey's shoulders shook with silent laughter, but Andrew's chin jerked upward in an unconscious display of nervous tension.

"Laird MacLean had hoped," Father Thomas continued in a stilted manner, "that Lady Joanna would choose to attend the wedding this morning, but to his disappointment, she has not come forward. So at the request of The MacLean, and by permission of His Gracious Majesty, the vows for the absent bride will be said by a proxy."

A startled silence descended on the assembly for one long, incredulous moment, then the rustle of satins and silks and the whisperings of astounded men and women filled the chapel. Everyone looked around in astonishment, trying to discover which lass had been chosen to take the part of the missing bride.

In the front pew beside her mother, Idoine preened in her garish orange velvet, certain that as the Maid of Glencoe's cousin, she'd be the obvious choice. Joanna sent a plea heavenward that this time the presumptuous damsel was correct.

Clasping his prayer book so tightly his knuckles turned white, Father Thomas cleared his throat, and the crowd gradually quieted. "His Majesty has left the selection of the substitute bride to the groom, who informed me this morning that he'll chose another Macdonald to say the vows for Lady Joanna during the ceremony." Hollow-eyed, the spare, grim-faced cleric turned to MacLean expectantly.

Joanna slouched down beside Maude, attempting to hide behind Davie, who was seated in front of her, so she couldn't be seen from the altar. She peered cautiously around the nave, and the back of her neck prickled with fear. MacLean men-at-arms stood at every portal, their brawny shoulders filling the door frames. Even in the hallowed sanctuary of the church, they bristled with weapons.

Stealthily, she straightened her spine and peeked over Davie's stooped shoulder.

A confident smile curved the corners of MacLean's mouth as he stepped down from the altar's dais. He moved through the open gates of the chancel railing and stood at the front of the center aisle.

The brideless groom gave no sign of the abject mortification he should have been feeling. Truth was, he appeared to be in complete control of the entire situation.

"For the person who will stand at the altar beside me and recite my bride's vows," he said in a clear, ringing tone, "I have chosen my wee friend, Joey Macdonald."

Joanna gasped in dismay and slunk lower in her seat. She could feel her scalp tighten beneath the frayed cap, as the serpent in her belly sank its fangs into her vitals.

Rory moved to where Joanna sat cringing beside her former nursemaid. The deep violet-blue eyes grew wider with each step that brought him closer, till he stood beside her at the end of the pew.

Bowing her head, she closed her eyes, folded her hands, and started to pray in earnest. Had she bothered to look over at Maude, she'd have seen the glow of happiness shining on her companion's face.

"Since you were so concerned for me yesterday," Rory said to the crouching demoiselle, "I was certain you'd be willing to assist me this morning." He extended his hand to her. "Help me out of this dilemma, lad. Come say the vows for Lady Joanna."

"Surely not me, laird," she mumbled, her head still bent. The long lashes fluttered like silken fans above her rosy cheeks. "You don't want a poor orphan lad to take the place of your heiress bride."

"Ah, but I do," he quietly insisted.

She slumped farther down on the bench, refusing to meet his gaze. "I can't, milord. 'Twouldn't be right."

This time his words carried an uncompromising conviction. "I insist."

Joanna's russet lashes flew up and she stared at him, speechless with horror. Her gaze locked with his, she slowly reached out her fine-boned hand, and their fingers touched. He drew her up, and she accompanied him past the congregation to the altar as though in a daze.

The Scottish courtiers gaped in disbelief, confusion apparent on their stunned faces. In his seat in the front pew, the haughty earl of Argyll frowned at the startling turn of events. Then he folded his arms and waited with calm indifference for the ceremony to proceed with a mere wisp of a lad taking the vows for the absent bride.

Ewen and Godfrey glared at Rory, the creases deepening on their foreheads. Beside his father, Andrew followed Joanna's slight form with worried, questioning eyes. But the trio did nothing to give the secret of her identity away— exactly as Rory had predicted.

As he and Joanna made their way to the front of the chapel, the Macdonald men-at-arms stirred restlessly on the hard benches. Short of open rebellion against the king, there was nothing they or anyone else could do. To draw arms in a church would be just cause for excommunication.

Rory was well aware that his own men, stationed before every exit, were grinning broadly at the wee bride attired in boy's clothing. From the moment they'd learned of her disguise, they'd been mesmerized by the indomitable lassie. The ferocious MacLeans considered her attempt to deceive them a hilarious jest. Their chief's new lady was a plucky Scots lass with more spunk than any Sassenach maid had ever shown.

Side by side, Rory, in full Highland splendor, and

Joanna, in a serving lad's shabby garments, stood before the priest at the altar, and the chapel grew eerily silent.

Joanna's muddled mind could scarcely comprehend what Father Thomas was saying as he opened his prayer book and made the sign of the cross over them.

Great Lord above!

What an incredible stroke of bad fortune to have MacLean choose Joey Macdonald to be his bride's proxy!

She could almost feel Ewen's infuriated glare boring into her back. If her clan's commander thought she'd bravely refuse to speak the vows and risk hanging as a traitor, he was woefully mistaken. Jeanne d'Arc couldn't help her now. Not all the angels and saints in heaven could deliver her from this debacle.

Joanna's body trembled from shock and a burgeoning awareness of what was about to transpire.

Godsakes, this wasn't the wedding she'd always dreamed of!

Blindly, Joanna looked up at the rose window above the altar and blinked back tears of disappointment and chagrin. Dressed like a lowly servant in boy's garb, with a hideous stocking cap covering her long hair, she felt her cheeks flame with embarrassment.

Exasperation at MacLean's obtuseness, resentment at Ewen's selfish scheming, but most of all, anger at herself burned inside Joanna. The ruse had been her own idea; she now had only herself to blame. Certainly not MacLean, who believed her the lad she pretended to be.

Why did he have to be so blasted trusting?

Gathering her scattered wits about her, she realized that MacLean had taken her shaky hand in his firm, warm grasp and drawn her close beside him. The sheer size of her bridegroom took her breath away. His broad shoulders blocked out the sight of her disgruntled kinsmen. All she could see was the magnificent Highland laird she was about to marry.

Timidly, Joanna looked up to find his gaze upon her, and

though she wanted to look away, she could not. He held her enthralled with his dragon-green eyes.

At the sight of the tears clinging stubbornly to her lashes, he drew her even nearer. A tender smile flickered across his mouth, and he rubbed his callused thumb across her knuckles in a reassuring gesture.

Though she'd carried her deceitful guise through to the end, Joanna was going to marry the chief of Clan MacLean, after all. She would soon be his wife. A sudden, inexplicable tingle of excitement coursed through her at the thought, making it hard to breathe. A fragile yet undeniable thread of longing tightened around her heart.

The truth, so long denied, sprang forth like the tender shoots of the snowdrop through the late-winter snow.

She wanted to be his wife.

Father Thomas had been speaking for some time, though she hadn't heard a syllable he'd uttered. But now the priest raised his voice, slicing through Joanna's dreamlike trance as he addressed the entire assembly. "If anyone knows of any just cause or impediment as to why this wedding should not go forward, speak now, or forever hold thy peace."

Throughout the chapel, every man, woman, and child strained to hear, each anxious to know if an accusing voice would be raised in protest.

The muffled sound of a disturbance came from behind Joanna. Numb with dread, she turned her head to peek at the front pew. Andrew was attempting to rise, fury contorting his finely chiseled features. With Godfrey's help, Ewen held the struggling lad down, his hand clamped over his son's mouth.

For a moment, everything seemed frozen in time.

In the deafening silence that followed, Joanna swayed dizzily on her feet, and MacLean's hand slipped beneath her elbow to hold her up.

But no Macdonald dared to stand in front of the king and utter false reasons why Joanna and MacLean could not be legally joined in marriage.

Without another sound, the breathless urgency passed.

Triumph gleaming in his eyes, MacLean took both her hands and enclosed them in his much larger ones.

Through a haze of wildly conflicting emotions, Joanna heard the fearsome warrior repeat Father Thomas's words calmly and distinctly.

"I, Rory Niall MacLean, take thee, Joanna Màiri Macdonald, to my wedded wife . . ."

The ardency in his rich baritone made her tremble. He spoke as though to his bride, and Joanna listened in mesmerized wonder.

". . . to have and to hold . . . for fairer, for fouler . . . for better, for worse . . ."

His golden head bent, he towered above her, a figure of awesome strength and undeniable charisma. Yet as she looked up at MacLean, the hard-edged angles of his face softened with an emotion she couldn't comprehend.

". . . for richer, for poorer . . . in sickness and in health . . . from this time forward . . . till death us depart . . . and if holy church it will ordain . . . hereto I pledge thee my troth."

Though MacLean couldn't know he'd spoken those words to the bride herself, for some strange, incomprehensible reason, it seemed as if he'd intended her—in spite of the boy's disguise—to be the recipient of that vow.

Unconsciously, she leaned toward MacLean, forgetting for the moment that she stood before the altar on her wedding day dressed in a lad's ragged shirt and plaid. The tangy scent of the forest drifted around him. His thick blond hair framed his proud features. The emeralds on the pin that fastened his plaid caught the May sunlight streaming through the stained glass windows and seemed to wink at her enticingly.

"Joey . . ." Father Thomas prodded. "Joey . . ."

Dragging her gaze from MacLean, she looked at the anxious clan chaplain and belatedly realized that he'd been trying to lead her in the bride's vows and she'd failed to respond.

MacLean tightened his grip on her hands, and Joanna gave him a tiny, tremulous smile. He needn't worry that she'd try to run away; her knees were knocking too hard beneath her plaid. God's truth, 'twas a miracle she hadn't collapsed to the floor.

Somehow, she managed to repeat the words after Father Thomas, though her heart thudded like a Celtic drum and the blood pounded in her ears.

"I, Joanna Màiri Macdonald, take thee, Rory Niall MacLean, to my wedded husband . . . to have and to hold . . . for fairer, for fouler . . . for better, for worse . . . for richer, for poorer . . . in sickness and in health . . . to be meek and obedient in bed and at board . . ."

As she spoke the words in a faint, quavering voice, a heart-stopping smile lit MacLean's face. His possessive gaze seemed to devour her, and it took all of her quickly fading willpower to continue.

". . . from this time forward . . till death us depart . . . and if holy church it will ordain . . . hereto I pledge thee my troth."

At a gesture from Father Thomas, Lachlan stepped forward and offered a ring. The priest blessed it and gave it to MacLean.

Joanna's bridegroom calmly held her shaking hand in his strong, sure one. Unable to meet his searing gaze, she lowered her lids. He held the ring between his thumb and forefinger, and it looked surprisingly small in his big hand.

Slipping the circlet of gold on her finger, MacLean spoke in a voice filled with unqualified assurance. "With this ring, Joanna, I thee wed, and this gold and silver, I thee give, and with my body, I thee worship—"

Her cheeks aflame, Joanna's gaze flew to meet his eyes. Sparks of delight seemed to dance in their emerald depths.

Rory lifted his bride's dainty hand to his lips as he continued with a smile of immense satisfaction, ". . . and with all my worldly cattle, I thee honor."

He drew her slender figure into his arms, and with a flick of his wrist snatched the striped stocking cap off her head and sent it sailing across the chancel. Freed of its bondage, her hair tumbled to her waist in a mass of glorious curls, the tortoiseshell combs that had secured it falling to her feet.

Rory had spent nights trying to imagine what shade of red Joanna concealed beneath that detested cap. Never in his most fantastic dreams had he envisioned the vivid, coppery sheen that glistened and beckoned before him. Strands of cinnamon and vermilion picked up the scarlet and crimson of the stained glass above them, creating a translucent halo of shimmering light around her head.

Of their own accord, his fingers delved into those silken locks, and his gut tightened in a need of jolting, primal intensity.

Bracing her hands against his shoulders, Joanna stiffened and leaned away from him, unable to follow the lightning turn of events. Her wary eyes revealed her complete confusion.

"I know who you are, Joanna," he murmured as he lifted her up for the bridal kiss. Grazing her smooth cheek with his open mouth, he sought and found her lips, parted slightly in amazement.

The carnal desire Rory had held in check with such determination during the past seemingly endless days burst forth like an unbridled stallion through an opened gate. He slipped his fingers into the lustrous curls at the nape of her neck. Cupping the back of her head in his palm, he covered her mouth with his.

Stunned into compliance, Joanna allowed MacLean to kiss her, feeling with shock the warmth of his tongue stroking hers.

Godsakes, this was no benedictional kiss; this kiss conveyed all the passion a man can feel for a woman.

MacLean knew who she was.

He knew Joey was really Joanna Macdonald!

With a whispering sigh of submission, she wrapped her arms around MacLean's neck, giving back his kiss and the passion, as she thrilled to the feel of his hard body supporting hers with such effortless ease.

In front of them, Father Thomas coughed. Joanna made a soft, plaintive sound at this gentle reminder that they were the focus of a dumfounded congregation's attention and slid her fingertips across MacLean's cheek to gain his concurrence.

Reluctantly, Rory broke the kiss and set his wife on her feet. With his hand about her slim waist, he turned to face the stupefied assemblage, grinning at them like a besotted fool.

"There was no need for a proxy," he explained to the confused Scottish court. "The Maid of Glencoe has just said her own vows for all to hear. Your Majesty, family and friends, may I present my wife, Lady Rory MacLean."

Joanna's bewildered gaze flickered over the watching faces.

Most of the courtiers had risen to their feet, clapping at the splendid development, though the seated Argyll remained impassive. The MacLean men-at-arms burst into laughter and shouted huzzahs. Rory's family beamed in satisfaction.

Joanna's loyal servants, including Ethel and her daughter, Peg, and Mary, the winsome, rosy-cheeked dairymaid, smiled sheepishly, as they realized the clever ruse had never really worked at all. Seumas, Davie, and Jock glanced at one another in growing apprehension, wondering if they'd be punished. Jacob and his burly son, Lothar; Abby; and Sarah, with little Teddy on her lap, all watched in pleased acceptance.

But the Macdonald soldiers scowled in thunderous disapproval. Ewen, Godfrey, and Andrew glowered in hatred, their rage transparent, though they remained still and silent in their pew.

There was nothing anyone could do.

MacLean had outfoxed them all.

In the confusion, Lady Emma left her place between Duncan and Keir and approached the bride and groom.

"Before the nuptial Mass begins, my dear," she said to Joanna, "we have a surprise for you. Come with me."

Joanna turned to MacLean in bafflement, and he nodded his assent. "Go with my mother," he said tenderly.

Lady Emma led Joanna into the vestry, where Maude stood waiting. A wide smile lit her ruddy face, and her gray eyes sparkled joyously.

Beside a tall cupboard, an exquisite gown of white satin lay draped over an armchair. Joanna walked slowly across the room and touched the fine material in amazement.

"But how . . . ?" She looked at her childhood nurse and shook her head in wonderment. "You knew about this?" she asked with a quavery smile.

"Only since this morning, my wee chick," she replied. She waved her hands to shoo Joanna along. "Now hurry! Everyone's waiting. Let's get you dressed for your wedding Mass."

Joanna, still dazed, allowed Lady Emma and Maude to peel off her shirt and plaid. A chemise of exquisite fragility quickly replaced the plain, shortened smock underneath.

Blue satin garters held up the long, delicate stockings she slipped over her legs. And the heels of her white satin shoes were encrusted with diamonds.

Over all this feminine finery came the long, embroidered petticoat, followed by the silk kirtle trimmed lavishly with lace.

Then the two older women lifted up the heavy gown, made of yards and yards of satin, and helped her slip it on. The narrow sleeves were fitted and came over the backs of her hands in a point.

Joanna looked down at herself in surprise. The décolleté bodice, cut square and low to reveal the kirtle's shirred under-bodice, also revealed the tops of her breasts. "Perhaps 'tis a wee bit—"

"Tch, tch," Maude warned, clicking her tongue in admonishment. "Don't say another word. Your groom asked his mother to bring a beautiful dress for you to wear on your wedding day. 'Twas Lady Emma's women who fashioned your gown.''

Tying the satin girdle snugly around Joanna's waist, MacLean's mother laughed, reading the unspoken question in her eyes. "I chose white for a virginal maid," she explained. "But also because I knew it would look exceptionally fine with red hair."

"How did you know the color of my hair?" Joanna asked in astonishment.

Lady Emma lifted a lock and let slide it between her fingers. The green eyes grew thoughtful as they gazed into hers. "Rory wrote that you favored your grandfather's coloring."

Before Joanna could utter a word, the widow gently patted her cheek. "I pray you find it within yourself to forgive my son, child. For only through forgiveness will you both find your heart's ease."

Tears stung Joanna's eyes, and she looked down, unable to respond.

Over the magnificent gown, they slipped a sleeveless robe of white velvet, its immense train trimmed with ermine.

Next, Lady Emma and Maude arranged Joanna's hair, letting it fall loosely past her shoulders and down to her waist. They carefully pinned a crown of white roses on her head.

Maude stepped back to eye their handiwork, and nodded approvingly. "Stunning," she said with a satisfied nod.

Joanna turned to face the tall mirror on the cupboard door and gasped in delight. The effect of her red hair against the white roses and white satin proved stunning indeed. The image reflected in the glass fulfilled all her girlish dreams.

Stepping behind her, Lady Emma fastened a rope of pearls around Joanna's neck. "Rory told me that you weren't particularly pleased with his sapphire necklace," she said with a wink to Joanna in the mirror. "I informed him that these are a much better choice for a young bride. This is my wedding gift to you, child.''

Joanna touched the pearls in awe. "Milady," she said, "how can you be so kind to me, when I've played such a despicable trick on your son?''

Lady Emma turned her around and cupped Joanna's face in her hands. "My darling daughter, had I the entire world to chose from, I could not have found a better wife for Rory. Not if I'd invoked a hundred magic spells, or searched for a thousand years." With a tender smile, she leaned forward and kissed her on the cheek.

Together, the two women took Joanna out a side entrance of the vestry and around to the front of the church, where Lady Emma handed her a bouquet of white roses.

Maude swung the door wide for her. "Go away in, chickie," she urged. "We'll hurry ahead and tell Father Thomas you're ready."

When Joanna entered the vestibule, James IV, King of Scotland stood waiting for her, along with a small entourage of courtiers. Tall and handsome, the king had a broad forehead, large eyes, and high cheekbones, complemented by a shock of straight reddish hair and a finely trimmed beard. He frequently adopted the Highlander's colorful attire while visiting them, and today he was splendid in red and black tartan.

She halted, suddenly terrified he was there to accuse her of treason. As her king and guardian, he'd ordered her to marry The MacLean, and she'd purposely attempted to defy his royal command.

Joanna's throat tightened as she took a tiny step back. Her mouth went dry, and her eyes blurred with sudden tears.

The entire purpose of His Majesty's sojourn through the Western Highlands was to secure the sworn fealty of the most powerful lairds in the area. What would he think of a maid who'd dared to defy him?

"Since you were our ward before you became Lady

MacLean," James Stewart said with a pleasant smile, "we have the honor of escorting you up the aisle."

Joanna released a shaky breath as she dipped in a low curtsy. "Thank you, Your Majesty. 'Tis my great honor, indeed, to be escorted by my sovereign."

He was the only Scots king who'd acquired the Gaelic. Though he wasn't letter-perfect, he could converse with those of his subjects who knew nothing of Scots-English. But James IV had a gift for more than just languages and the proper arrangement of the belted plaid. His liaisons were legendary. At the age of twenty-nine, he'd fathered several royal bastards by a long string of mistresses.

The king's brown eyes twinkled in his lean, pale face as he gazed at Joanna reassuringly. He took her hand and placed it on his crooked elbow. "No one appreciates the attraction of a bonny lass more than your sovereign," he said, patting her fingers. "Since we must one day choose our bride for political reasons, we can only hope that we shall be fortunate enough to find a lass as fair as Laird MacLean's."

"Your Majesty is too kind," Joanna replied with a shy smile. She could see why the king was so immensely popular with most of his subjects—the exception being, of course, the Macdonalds and their allies in the Hebrides.

At a nod from the king, two of his courtiers opened the main doors.

Joanna entered the nave alongside James Stewart, and the congregation rose to its feet. From the choir above them came the magnificently trained voices of the Observantine friars and Poor Clares, accompanied by the sweet lilting strains of a bagpipe. So this was why the friars and nuns had been included in the royal entourage.

Ahead, MacLean waited for her in front of the altar. His observant gaze took in her loosely flowing locks, the white satin gown, and the velvet robe with its long, elegant train. A slow, devastating smile spread across his face as he held out his hand to her.

Rory watched Joanna walk majestically up the aisle on

the arm of the King of Scotland, past the grinning Mac-Leans and the scowling Macdonalds, past Kinlochleven's faithful retainers and servants, past the entire Scottish court.

The sight of her heart-shaped, gamin face sent his spirit aloft. The wariness and confusion in her marvelous indigo eyes made his throat ache with a need to be tender. To cherish and protect her.

His mother had been right—his lucky star had risen. All the icy cynicism that encased his heart seemed to melt at the sight of his bonny wee bride.

When Joanna and the king reached the altar, Rory took his wife's hand and led her to the pair of prie-dieux. Together they genuflected and knelt on the crimson velvet cushions, and Father Thomas opened his missal.

From the choir came the hauntingly beautiful strains of *Kyrie eleison,* and Joanna and Rory MacLean's wedding Mass began.

Chapter 12

⌒⌒◯◯⌒⌒

Seated beside Rory at the wedding breakfast, Joanna looked about in wonder at Kinlochleven's great hall. Pink roses and white apple blossoms tied with green ribbons festooned the chamber, along with branches of rowan to ward off evil spirits and ensure the bridal couple's good fortune in the years to come.

Golden candlesticks with beeswax tapers lit every table. Elegant china plates from the Orient, embossed silver goblets, cups, saucers, knives, and rare spoons fashioned by Flemish silversmiths adorned the sparkling white cloths. The hall's herbed rushes had been swept up, and thick carpets from the Levant rolled out across the stone floor.

Great press cupboards sat against the high walls, their doors left open to display exquisitely embroidered linens, bolts of fine wool, taffeta, damask, and cloth of gold. Fine pelts of rabbit, miniver, otter, marten, fox, ermine, and sable spilled over from the low carved chests placed along the rear of the chamber beneath the gallery. Colorful Italian tapestries depicting scenes of ancient Rome hung in the hall's arched recesses. The munificence of the dowry gifts given by the groom and his family to his bride surpassed anyone's remembrance of weddings past.

Overwhelmed by the nearness of her husband, Joanna was barely aware of the others seated at the principal board on the canopied dais. On MacLean's left, King James conversed pleasantly with earls Archibald Campbell of Argyll and Duncan Stewart of Appin. Beyond them, Lady Emma, Lachlan, and Keir carried on an animated conversation.

Ewen sat on Joanna's immediate right, mute and stony-faced, while Lady Beatrix engaged Godfrey in a stilted conversation. A wrathful frown creasing his handsome visage, Andrew sat beside his sister in festering silence.

Although Andrew hadn't spoken two words to Joanna that morning, he'd followed her every movement with his irate gaze. Attired in red and blue tartan, he made a dazzling display of Highland bravura. The ladies of the Scottish court openly admired his perfect features and gorgeous dark locks, but today he paid them no heed.

Father Thomas had wisely chosen to join the visiting religious at their table on one side of the hall. He rose to say grace, and for a few brief moments, a peaceful quiet reigned. Then the servants wound their way through capering children, carrying enormous trays of roast beef, lamb, salmon, trout, sturgeon and porpoise, and platters piled high with crab, crayfish, oyster and eels. Lackeys in the royal gold and blue livery attended the guests with ewers of water, silver basins, and towels.

Joanna turned to her husband. Though she'd been tricked into saying her wedding vows, she felt good manners demanded that she express her gratitude for the wondrous gifts and, most especially, the thoughtfulness of having his mother bring the exquisite bridal gown. "MacLean, I—"

"Rory," he insisted as he slipped his arm about her waist. He leaned toward her and cupped her cheek in his large hand. His shimmering, sea-dragon's gaze drifted over her face with a lingering thoroughness. His thumb traced the line of her jaw, then rested lightly on her chin. "Call me Rory," he murmured, just before kissing her. His tongue followed the compressed seam of her lips, pushing boldly between, till it played an enticing game with her own.

Joanna's eyes flew open as his tongue teased hers. She stiffened at the brazen behavior, though it shouldn't have surprised her. He'd kissed her the same way in church.

Twice. Unconcerned with the sanctity of their surroundings, he'd gathered her in his arms at the close of Mass and kissed her with more blatant eroticism than any lass had ever imagined when dreaming of her wedding day. And that just after taking Communion.

Joanna had never heard of such scandalous tongue-kisses, and wondered wildly if he'd learned the shameless trick from a mermaid.

She tried to pull away, just as she'd done before.

Just as before, he wouldn't allow it.

His fingers tangled in the thick hair at the nape of her neck, holding her in place. "Meek and obedient in bed and at board," he reminded her with a deep, throaty chuckle as he playfully nibbled at her bottom lip. "You can't have forgotten the words you spoke such a short time ago, wife."

"'Tis just that I'm not certain we're supposed to be doing this," she whispered.

He whispered in return. "Doing what?"

Joanna lowered her head, too embarrassed to look at him, nearly too embarrassed to respond. Her words were scarcely audible. "What we're doing."

"You mean kissing."

Her lids flew up to meet his gaze. "Well, of course, we're expected to kiss," she answered with exasperation. "'Tis our wedding day. But not . . ."

The light in his green eyes fairly danced in amusement, as he bracketed her face in both hands. "Ah, that," he said in a serious tone, though the twitch at the corner of his mouth told her he wanted to laugh. "Don't worry, lass. 'Tis the way every groom kisses his bride."

"It is?"

"It is."

"No one told me to expect it," she complained with a dubious frown, then looked at him accusingly. "You took me by complete surprise."

"I'll have lots of surprises for you today, Joanna," he

promised, as he idly wound a strand of her long hair round his forefinger.

She gazed at him in wonder. A tingle of excitement zig-zagged up and down her spine. A whole field of butterflies took flight inside her belly.

Could it be that he was warning her about his dragon's tail?

"You . . . you will?"

"I will." He covered her lips with his and delved into her mouth once again.

Surrendering to his unequivocal demand, Joanna slid her arms around his neck. Seeking further knowledge of this strange way of kissing, she timidly ran the tip of her tongue along the edge of his teeth, then cautiously entered the warm, alluring cavern of his mouth.

The effect upon him was instantaneous. With a strangled sound deep in his throat, he clasped her even nearer, till her soft breasts were smashed against his hard chest. For a startled moment she thought he was going to lift her out of her chair and onto his lap.

Shouts of encouragement at this unbridled license filled the hall. The MacLean soldiers rose to their feet and saluted the bridal couple's passionate kiss with lifted tankards. Laughter and the excited chatter of the guests rose in a babble of voices.

At last, MacLean broke the kiss to nibble softly along her jaw.

Joanna breathed in the fresh scent of pine that mingled with the sweet perfume of her roses and gave a sigh of wonder. When they kissed, she seemed to forget everything but the feel of his lips on hers. "Mm. Thank you—"

" 'Tis my pleasure, milady," he said with a wry grin.

"—for the gifts," she finished primly. She drew away and sat straight in her chair, folding her hands in her lap. "And for asking your mother to bring such a beautiful gown for me to wear at my wedding."

He lifted a lock of her hair and threaded it loosely through his long fingers. "Since the sapphires I chose weren't to your liking, I hoped my mother would succeed where I failed.''

"When did you write her?'' Joanna asked in confusion. She lowered her lids and traced a pattern on the fine lace tablecloth with her fingertip. "How long have you known?''

"Would you believe from the start?''

She looked up to meet his gaze, and the laughter in his eyes made her shake her head doubtfully. "Should I believe that?''

He ran his thumb lightly over the bow of her upper lip. "Someday I may tell you, Joanna,'' he said in a low, silky tone. The hand at her waist moved to the small of her back, gently stroking the line of her spine. "But not today. Today I'll let you wonder.''

The heat of mortification crept up her neck. "Did you know the evening you ordered me to assist at your bath?''

"Most definitely,'' he assured her.

Joanna recalled how he'd allowed her to remove everything but his belt and plaid, then inexplicably ordered her from the room.

Holy heavens.

He knew she'd been perfectly willing to see him naked!

MacLean tipped her chin upward and planted a kiss on the tip of her nose. "Enjoy the celebration,'' he told her softly, "while I enjoy the pleasure of watching my wee bride blush.''

"I'm not blushing,'' she denied. "'Tis overwarm in here, that's all. And other people are watching, too.''

"Let them,'' he said. "They'd be disappointed if the bridegroom didn't kiss his bride.'' He followed his words with another scorching kiss, accompanied by the raucous cheers of his men.

MacLean drew away at last when a servant approached to pour more claret in their half-empty goblets. Joanna straightened the crown of roses that wreathed her head and, in an attempt to rein in her galloping heart, tried to concentrate on the conversation taking place on the other side of her husband.

"MacLean and his brothers are brilliant seamen," James IV was saying to Argyll. "We weren't anxious for him to end his sailing days and become a prosaic landholder like the rest of us. His fleet of ships made it possible for our trade with the Continent to thrive. And we understood why he'd hesitate to give up his adventurous life, considering the wealth and fame he'd acquired. But our mind was quite set on this match."

"The old hatreds are as outdated as the old ways," Archibald Campbell replied glibly. " 'Twould appear the invincible Sea Dragon no longer considers the idea of a MacLean marrying a Macdonald quite so distasteful." He glanced over at the couple and, realizing that the bride sat listening, offered an apologetic smile.

The second earl of Argyll and chief of the Campbells held one of Scotland's largest and most powerful clans in his unrelenting grip. Somewhere in his early fifties, he had the physique of a much younger man. And the wily, reddish-brown eyes of a fox. Those eyes assessed Joanna now with a detached, analytical thoroughness. If he disapproved of her masquerading as a lad, he gave no indication.

Joanna nodded coolly to the earl, then peeked at her husband from beneath her lashes. His jaw had tightened at Argyll's thoughtless words, but he made no comment.

She remembered their conversation in the stables. MacLean had indicated that day that he didn't want to marry the Maid of Glencoe. Later, he'd denied it. But perhaps by then he'd discovered her identity and didn't want to admit the bald, distasteful truth to the unwanted heiress.

The knowledge that he'd never wished to marry her brought the ache of disillusionment. The thought that all of this lavish display might simply be for form's sake came as a crushing blow to her pride.

She'd had no doubts, while living in Cumberland, that her personal worth had been based solely on the extent of her wealth. That the same remained true in the Highlands left a bitter taste on her tongue.

'Twas only her pride, though, not her heart that felt bruised.

After all, she hadn't wanted to wed him, either. Why else would she have spent the last week dressed as a boy?

Her own feelings bewildered Joanna. She'd willingly kissed the Sea Dragon, even though he'd been responsible for her beloved grandfather's death. God above knew, she shouldn't feel anything but hatred for this brash, over-confident male, whose formidable will swept everyone and everything before it. And she'd gravely disappointed her clansmen. From their end of the table, Ewen and his family's accusing glances reminded her that she'd failed in her most important responsibility as their new chieftain: to marry the man they'd chosen for her.

When MacLean's family had crowded around the bridal couple after Mass, offering their congratulations along with the rest of the Scottish court, only her personal retainers and servants had joined them. Ewen, Godfrey, and Andrew remained apart with the Macdonald men-at-arms, watching in frigid silence. It didn't seem to matter that the decision had been taken out of her hands.

If the Glencoe Macdonalds repudiated Joanna as their chieftain, there'd be a bloody battle as the two sides fought to gain control of Kinlochleven. She and the people of her castle would be caught like helpless pawns in the middle.

Course followed sumptuous course, each more elegant than the last; boars' heads, venison, peacocks, swans, suckling pigs, cranes, plovers, and larks. There were great bowls of rice, almonds, figs, dates, raisins, oranges, and pomegranates. Spiced wine and beer appeared in flagons on every table, and the drink flowed freely.

The trestles had been arranged to leave a large open space in the center of the great hall. While the guests feasted, dancers in Highland garb performed to the accompaniment of three bagpipers, Tam MacLean included, playing old Scottish airs. Then the king's striking, gray-eyed jongleur strummed a guitar and regaled them with tales of legendary Scots heroes.

During the morning's festivities, MacLean used every opportunity to fondle his new wife. He touched her arm, her waist, her shoulders, her back, and seemed to have a fascination with her long red hair. Twice his large hand drifted across her buttocks. How it found its way under her velvet robe Joanna wasn't quite certain.

The air left her lungs in a rush when she remembered the day he'd slipped his hand beneath her plaid, the long fingers gliding up the back of her bare thigh. 'Twas no accident, she realized now, though he'd pretended not to notice it had even happened.

A rising tide of physical awareness flooded her senses as his callused fingertips lightly caressed the bare skin between the base of her neck and her shoulder. His proprietary gaze repeatedly drifted to her breasts, where the low decolletage revealed the firm mounds rising and falling with each breath.

God's truth, MacLean *was* her husband, however bold he might be. There was nothing she could do in public about the ogling and fondling, short of boxing his ears—which his tutors should have done when he was naught but a lad. What she intended to do in private was another matter. For though he left no doubt that he intended to take his pleasure with her that night, he'd find that the Maid of Glencoe had more than one trick up her sleeve.

She leaned toward him with a docile smile and spoke behind a cupped hand. "Apparently no one taught you, milord husband, that 'tis considered poor manners to stare down the neckline of your table partner's gown."

He had the indecency to laugh out loud. "You're not merely my table partner," he replied, his gaze continuing its indolent scrutiny. " 'Tis my bed partner you are, Lady MacLean. Every man looks forward to the sugared dainties that follow the meal. I'm merely enjoying a glimpse of the sweet confections to come."

Using the pretext of examining the rope of pearls his mother had given her, MacLean brushed the back of his fingers across her exposed bosom. With a start of surprise, Joanna felt her breasts swell and her nipples tighten in response.

A faint, knowing smile played across his lips. "Who would have thought such bounty lay hidden beneath that overlarge shirt?" he murmured, his words a low, throaty rasp in her ear. "And now 'tis all mine for the plundering."

Belatedly, Joanna realized his intent.

Her husband was seducing her.

Right here in Kinlochleven's great hall.

It didn't seem to matter that the room was crowded with people. From the smoldering fire in his eyes, she wondered for a moment if he intended to throw her over his shoulder like a bundle of kindling and carry her up the stairs to their bedchamber.

Every part of Joanna seemed to come alive at the thought. She squirmed in her chair, warmth oozing through her like honey in the sunshine, and read the sure knowledge in his gaze.

She was his for the taking.

After the meal, the guisers performed a bawdy farce filled with innuendoes and sly allusions. The receptive audience roared with glee when the elderly husband greeted his toothsome young wife with a lascivious leer, then fell flat on his face as he lunged for her.

Next one of the king's Italian minstrels favored them with a pastorale in which the heroine was a charming shepherdess. The guests, replete with food and drink, listened in quiet appreciation.

Finally an elderly bard holding a Celtic harp took the floor. He bowed low to the king and again to Joanna, then settled himself on a high, three-legged stool.

"I have the privilege on this very special occasion," he announced, "to sing a ballad composed by the chief of Clan MacLean in honor of his lady wife."

Suddenly tense, Rory watched Joanna from the corner of his eye. He clenched his hand on the tablecloth, while his other hand remained fixed and still about Joanna's small waist.

Lachlan had refused to allow his older brother to hear the composition, saying there wouldn't be time to make any changes. Whether Rory was satisfied or not, the music and words would have to suffice as written.

Joanna leaned forward, her attention focused on the gnarled figure, wondering, no doubt, why her husband had chosen such an ancient, white-bearded man to sing the love song to her. When Fergus MacQuisten's magnificent full-throated tenor filled the hall, an awed hush descended over the company.

The words and music Lachlan had composed expressed an unrequited, nearly hopeless yearning of a lord for an exquisite yet unattainable lady. Like Venus shining in the night sky, she was the unreachable goal, the unattainable quest. The subtle yet unmistakably romantic praises for her beauty and intellect surpassed anything they'd ever heard.

Lofty and noble as the words were, an earthly hunger had been woven throughout. Plaintive and sweet, the song spoke to each listener's secret longing, the grand passion hidden within each lonely heart.

As Fergus sang, Joanna turned within the compass of Rory's arm and gazed up at him. He met her dreamy eyes, certain in the knowledge that she was seeing him in a whole new light.

Not as a rough, crude soldier, but a gallant champion.

A knight in shining armor.

Rory wasn't quite sure how, but in some way, his brother had managed to capture the aching need he felt for this tiny slip of a lass and yet could never hope to put into words. How he would ever repay Lachlan, he couldn't imagine. At this moment, nothing seemed enough.

As the last strains of the ballad faded away, Joanna leaned toward him. " 'Twas beautiful, Rory," she said on a sigh. She placed her fingers lightly on his cheek. "I've never heard anything so moving."

For the first time that day, she initiated a kiss. A kiss of such tenderness, such tentative, wondering exploration, Rory's heart nearly exploded. His entire body reacted to her shy, hesitant touch with a ravenous lust that pulsed through his veins and tightened every muscle.

Dammit, he couldn't give in to his rampaging carnal desires now. 'Twas barely past midday, far too early to make a seemly exit, though he longed to sweep his wife into his arms and carry her upstairs, ignoring the shocked looks of the guests. He yearned to lay Joanna on their bed and slowly, lingeringly remove the satin gown and the fragile chemise beneath.

But even greater than the need to slake his lust, Rory wanted this day, this moment, to remain in Joanna's memory forever as a magical dream come true.

Someday he'd tell her the truth—that the tenderly erotic love song had been written by his brother. And they'd laugh about it together, because by then they'd have a half-dozen weans, bonny daughters and sturdy sons, crawling over their bedcovers in the mornings, demanding attention.

But the nights . . . ah, the nights . . . they'd have all to themselves.

The stately strains of the pavane being played by the musicians in the gallery slowly impinged upon Rory's consciousness. He reluctantly released Joanna and rose to his feet.

"I think 'tis time for our wedding dance, Lady Mac-Lean," he said with a nervous smile. He need only perform this one last feat, then he could sit back and enjoy the rest of the day.

Rory led Joanna down from the dais and to the center of the hall, where he managed a passable bow. Aware of the curious eyes fastened upon them, he intended to concentrate on the instructions Lachlan had called out as he'd practiced with Keir. If his movements appeared somewhat labored and stilted, so be it. Most of all, he was determined not to step on her long velvet train.

Joanna rose from her deep curtsy and took the hand Rory held out to her. Her face shone with pleasure in the dance, the indigo eyes with their thick russet lashes sparkling like starshine. The glorious mane of coppery hair drifted past her shoulders and fell to her waist in lustrous silken curls. Petite and fine-boned, she moved across the floor with an unconscious elegance.

He'd known she'd be attractive once she set aside the boy's clothes and dressed befitting a lass, but even in his most vivid imaginings, he'd never dreamed how adorably feminine she'd be.

Joanna pointed her foot in a graceful, gliding movement, and Rory's blood ran cold at the size of the white satin slipper. One misstep and he'd break every bone in that dainty wee foot.

He'd lost count long ago of how many foes he'd slain on the field. In one battle alone, he'd brought down four-teen men with his sword and dirk. Yet this slight lassie had him shaking in his shiny dress brogues. A fine sheen of sweat broke out on his brow. He only hoped she wouldn't guess the effect she had on him.

"Our wedding feast was wonderful," Joanna confided. "I've never seen some of the exotic dishes the king's chef prepared."

Every time his wife sank low in one of the many curtsies required in the pavane, Rory bent forward in a courtly rév-érance. He discovered to his incredible delight that he was afforded a sight of her bosom that would have turned an eighty-year-old archbishop into a rutting stag. The smooth, dewy globes of her breasts rose firm and high above the low neckline, so creamy white and delectable they made a man salivate with just one peek.

Rory smiled. Dancing with Joanna was proving far more pleasurable than he could have possibly envisioned. If she'd only dip just a bit lower, he'd be blessed with a glimpse of those sweet, rosy peaks.

"Thankfully," he replied, "my mother took over the task of guarding you."

"Guarding me!" she exclaimed. "From what? Going into the kitchen?"

She dipped again, and Rory ran his tongue across his lips like a man parched with thirst. He gave a quick nod, his gaze fastened on the mouthwatering display. "Why else?"

Joanna tilted her head, fixing him with a quizzical look before she came to a graceful halt and dropped into a final curtsy.

The high rafters rang with applause. Rory realized in surprise that the music had stopped and the dance had come to an end. He released a pent-up breath of satisfaction. His wee bride still had all ten toes, and not a footprint could be seen on the pristine white velvet of her train.

Keir and Lachlan waited at the edge of the dance floor, wide smiles creasing their faces. They met the couple as Rory led Joanna toward the dais.

Lachlan grabbed his older brother around the neck, pulled him close, and spoke in a low, amused tone. "When I said to show your hunger for your bride, I didn't mean you were to strip the poor lass naked with your eyes on the dance floor, ye bloody fool."

Rory frowned. He hadn't realized his emotions were so blasted transparent.

"Why the hell not?" Keir asked with a chuckle. "She's his now. He can do as he damn well pleases with her."

Joanna had heard their exchange, and from the spark of indignation in her eye, was about to offer a scathing retort. Before she could say a word, Keir snatched his good-sister's hand and tugged her out of Rory's grasp.

"The next dance in the suite is a galliard," Keir said as he deftly slipped the sleeveless robe off Joanna's shoulders and handed it to her bridegroom. "I suggest you go have another glass of wine, Laird MacLean, while I gallop around the floor with your lady wife."

Rory scowled down at his youngest brother's big feet. "Just be sure you don't step on her," he warned.

*   *   *

In the afternoon, the guests were treated to a joust. To Joanna's obvious delight, the MacLeans had unearthed armor and weapons—captured from Sassenach soldiers nearly a hundred years before—in the castle's armory. They'd polished the steel helmets, breastplates, greaves, and gauntlets till the pieces gleamed like silver in the spring sunshine.

A pavilion had been erected in the grassy meadow outside the castle walls, where bright pennons snapped in the breeze. When Joanna and Rory took their places beside the king, Fearchar rode to the center of the field on his huge steed. Armed with shield and lance, he approached the three and tipped his weapon in salute.

"With my laird's permission," he said in his booming voice, "and if milady will allow, I will act as her champion."

Rory signaled his approval, and Joanna tied a green satin ribbon to the end of Fearchar's lance.

"For luck," she told her knight-errant. Blue eyes shining, she clasped Rory's arm in excitement and leaned closer to him. "How could you have planned all this without my knowing?"

"The MacLeans are rather good at keeping secrets," he said with a crooked grin. "Especially from Macdonalds."

She wrinkled her freckled nose and flashed him a puckish smile. " 'Tis very clever you'll be thinking yourself, milord husband. But the next time you try to surprise me, I won't act so surprised. That will serve you."

The men had blunted the weapons for safety. Even so, every time Fearchar unseated his opponent, a roar would go up from the enthusiastic crowd. As the toppled warrior hit the ground with a thud, Joanna would wince and cover her eyes.

Thick-necked and barrel-chested, Murdoch MacLean proved the blond titan's biggest threat, just as expected. At the first pass, Fearchar shattered a lance on his kinsman's shield without Murdoch even losing the stirrups. The second try proved more successful. The thud of iron-tipped lance against steel jacket resounded, and Murdoch flew from his horse to fall unconscious on the ground.

The prone man quickly regained his wits, though, and with a bow to his sovereign and the bridal couple, strode from the field.

"Thank God," Joanna said with a grateful sigh. She slipped her hand into Rory's and laced her fingers with his.

The simple move to seek his reassurance and strength stormed the keep of Rory's well-guarded heart. His chest compressed, as though the thick-walled bastions protecting his vulnerable emotions crumpled inward beneath her gentle onslaught. Her slightest touch carried more power, more potential for his own destruction, than a claymore wielded by a foe.

"My men are all battle veterans," he told her, his voice tight and strained with the need to maintain some small measure of distance. *She* was supposed to be swept away, not Rory. "This joust is no more than child's play to them."

Her eyes grew somber. "Still, I would feel terrible if one of them were seriously hurt, especially on my behalf."

"Why, Lady MacLean," he said, bringing her fingers to his lips, "I think you're starting to like us."

She lifted one shoulder noncommittally. "Some of you, perhaps."

"Which of us?" he prodded.

"Tam and Arthur, and Fearchar, of course," she said, idly measuring the length of her fingers against his own. "He even helped Maude gather lichens and brambles to make dyes for her yarn, so she can complete the tapestry she's making."

Rory recalled the hedonistic scene depicting a dragon-tailed sea raider sporting with a water nymph. "The one in the solar?"

"That one."

He arched an eyebrow quizzically. "We wondered if it portrayed some little-known Greek myth."

Joanna pursed her lips, as though to keep from laughing. Avoiding his eyes, she studied their clasped hands. "Not Greek," she said after a moment, "nor Roman, either. The tapestry was inspired by an old Celtic legend."

He smiled at her with open skepticism. "Not any I've ever heard of."

"Oh, 'tis a legend known only to the Macdonalds," she explained. When she met Rory's gaze, her eyes sparkled with naughtiness, warning him there was more to the tapestry than she was willing to reveal.

Rory touched his finger to the tip of her nose. "Someday you'll have to tell me this old Celtic legend."

"I'll tell you tonight, if you wish," she offered brightly, then frowned as she realized she'd blundered into uncharted seas.

"That's very sweet of you," he said, drawing her close for his kiss. "But I think tonight we may be a wee bit too busy for storytelling."

When the pageant was over, it was nearly time for supper. His curly brown hair ruffling in the late afternoon breeze, Tam piped *Creag-an-Sgairbh,* Stewart of Appin's lively march, as the animated, prattling guests returned over the drawbridge and into the castle.

Fearchar and Maude strolled side by side. Though little was spoken between them, she carried the helm and gauntlets he'd worn during the tournament. Earlier, they'd danced a branle together, swaying to left and right with a catlike grace belied by their large, sturdy frames.

The sight of the couple ambling along brought a smile to Rory's lips. Nothing would please him more than to have his huge cousin choose a wife from among the Macdonald kinsmen here at Kinlochleven. That Maude was Joanna's beloved companion made it all the better. The bond between the four of them would bind them closer through the years.

As the courtiers and clansmen entered the donjon's vestibule, Rory took advantage of the momentary confusion to draw his bride aside. "Come with me, Joanna," he urged. "I've something to show you."

His wife shook her head, her eyes suddenly wary. "I think we'd best return to the great hall with our guests."

Before she could protest further, Rory guided Joanna into the still library, where he leaned back against the door and quietly turned the key.

Chapter 13

Widening his stance, Rory pulled Joanna into his arms, lifting her up for a passionate kiss. He rocked her slowly back and forth against his aching body, savoring the feel of her soft femininity pressed snugly against him. His heart kicked against his breastbone with each breath-stealing jolt of pleasure.

Even through her layers of petticoat and satin gown she must have felt the hardened bulge beneath his sporran and plaid, for she broke the kiss and leaned back in his arms, her long-lashed eyes huge and wondering.

"What you feel, Joanna," he said thickly, "is hunger for my bride, but 'tis hardly any surprise."

He lifted her higher to nuzzle the tantalizing curve of her neck and the sensitive spot behind her ear. When she scrunched up her shoulder in a reflexive reaction, he took her earlobe between his teeth and, with a growl, tugged gently.

"God, you smell wonderful," he murmured as he kissed her temple. "Like honey and roses and everything sweet all rolled into one delicious pastry."

She tried to pull away, but he wouldn't allow it. "You sound like a starving man," she complained with a husky laugh.

"I am." With another low growl he let her petite form slide slowly down the length of him; then he reluctantly released her and moved to the library table, where he picked up a package. "This is for you, Joanna."

"Another present?" She lifted a hand to the milky pearls that hung round her neck, a diffident smile trembling on her lips. "But you and your family have given me so much already."

"Those gifts were for the household," he said. "This is for your personal enjoyment."

She lifted her russet brows in puzzlement.

"Come on, don't be shy," Rory urged. He propped his hip on the edge of the table and gestured for her to move closer. "Open it."

Taking the box from his hands, Joanna set it on the tabletop beside him, removed the twine, and lifted the lid.

"Why, 'tis beautiful!" she cried, her violet-blue eyes alight with pleasure.

Carefully she lifted out the small birdcage wrought of gold, with the figure of a yellow canary on a hanging perch. Leaves of jade and petals of amethyst adorned the top, where a shiny gold chain could be used to suspend the ornament from a window beam.

Rory brushed his fingers along the bottom of the cage and released the catch. A tinkling sound, surprisingly like the notes of a miniature clavichord, filled the room. With a gentle push, he set the perch in motion, and the porcelain canary swung back and forth to the musical vibrations.

"Oh," she gasped in delight. " 'Tis singing! The wee birdie's singing!" She looked up at Rory, her eyes wide in amazement. "Where did such a marvelous thing come from?"

" 'Twas likely made in India," he said, pleased with her obvious captivation. "Or Persia, perhaps. A French merchant must have brought the trinket back from a bazaar in the Levant. I saw it in a shop window in Paris three years ago."

The words were no sooner out of his mouth than he realized his mistake. Damn. When it came to romancing dreamy-eyed lassies, his straightforward, pragmatic nature always tripped him up.

A thoughtful frown creased Joanna's brow. "Paris?" She studied the dainty piece, clearly fashioned for a woman's diversion.

At the time, Rory had purchased the bauble for a current mistress. When he'd returned to Scotland, he'd found that, though the lady's interest hadn't waned, her staid, rich husband had taken grave offense at his young wife's more flighty affectations—taking a lover being one of them.

The trifle had remained in a straw-filled barrel deep in the *Sea Dragon*'s hold, all but forgotten, until he'd remembered it the day he'd sent the letter to his mother. Arthur had been given the responsibility of retrieving it from the ship and bringing it to Kinlochleven.

"Rory," Joanna began, her gaze fastened on the cage's finely crafted wires. She paused, then continued in a small, hesitant voice. "Have you ever lain with a woman?"

He waited for a breathless moment before answering. He didn't want to start their married life with a lie, but he wasn't sure how she'd react to the truth.

"I have," he said at last.

Her head drooped, making it clear she hadn't taken the truth well at well. Apparently valiant knights in shining armor never romanced any demoiselle but their one true love. During their talk in the stables, Joanna must have assumed, when he said he'd tamed a few lassies, that he'd been speaking of courting, not coupling.

Her reply was nearly inaudible. "I see." Touching a fingertip to a delicate jade leaf at the top of the cage, she tilted her head to one side as though listening in fascination to the tinkling notes. "Was she very bonny?"

He blinked at her assumption that his affirmative answer indicated only one female, but he was in no hurry to correct her error. Brutal honesty between him and his bride of a few short hours could clearly be stretched too thin.

He slid his hands over her shoulders and caressed the fragile bones at the base of her throat. She was so incredibly lovely, standing there in the white satin gown, with her reddish-gold hair drifting about her. All day long, he hadn't been able to keep from touching her, or from burying his fingers in that glorious, silken mane.

"Joanna," he said quietly, "do you remember when we stood on the barbican and looked out over the glen?"

Her curving lashes remained lowered, but she gave a quick nod.

"I said that I'd never seen anything so fair. 'Twasn't the castle or the lands that I spoke of that morning, lass. 'Twas you."

Her head snapped up, her eyes bright with disbelief. "Me? But I was covered with grime and dressed like a boy!"

He smiled as he took the trinket from her hands and set it on the library table. Then he sank into the caned armchair nearby and pulled her down on his lap. At her obvious skepticism, he tweaked her freckled nose playfully.

"I could see you were bonny," he said, "even in your ridiculous disguise and with your hair hidden beneath that hideous cap."

"Truly?"

At her sincere befuddlement, he realized Joanna had no notion of how adorable she really was.

"Truly."

Before he could confirm his answer with a kiss, the brass cylinder in the cage's hidden workings ceased its revolutions, and the notes slowly faded away.

"Oh, dear!" she said, squirming to sit up straighter, her mind on the now-silent ornament and not on the havoc she was wreaking below.

Rory's tenuous control started to slip as the firm curve of her rump moved against his thickened sex. With a smothered groan, he readjusted his sporran and eased her onto his thigh, relieving the pressure.

Unaware of his distress, Joanna reached for the plaything, her eyes narrowed in disappointment. "Is it broken?"

He shook his head. Turning the birdcage over, he showed her how to wind the key, then start it once again.

She watched in awe as he returned it to the tabletop, the music tinkling gaily around them. "You mean I can make it play over and over, as many times as I wish?"

"As often as you wish," he assured her with a chuckle.

"Thank you, Rory." She slid her arms about his neck and pressed her smooth cheek against his stubbled one. She brushed her lips across his mouth, her bashful hesitation sweetly enticing. "Thank you for everything."

He accepted her kiss of gratitude with greedy satisfaction and deftly slipped his hand inside the low neckline of her bodice. At the touch of his fingers on her silken skin, she jerked in a sudden, convulsive reaction, then shivered in breathless confusion.

"Oh . . . oh, my!" she whispered and sucked in a quick draft of air.

Rory smiled, certain no man—or bumbling sixteen-year-old lad, either, for that matter—had ever touched her so intimately.

'Twas more than his body that ached at the sight of his innocent bride in her lovely white wedding gown. His heart ached with tenderness at the sure knowledge that she belonged to him. Completely and forever. She was his wife, and one day would be the mother of his children. From that time onward, his life would be entwined with hers. The thought brought an unfamiliar and soul-satisfying gratification, a happiness so deep, so reverent, it was nearly pain.

"Did you enjoy your wedding banquet?" he asked, easing her gently over his arm till her head was tipped back.

" 'Twas perfect." She gazed up at him guardedly. But in spite of her obvious distrust, he could read the pleasure of his touch in the luminous depths of her eyes.

"I'm glad you feel that way," he said tenderly. Beneath his caressing fingers, her breasts grew firm and full. Her warm softness brought a throb of yearning so deep and intense he nearly groaned.

She drew a shaky breath, her breast lifting in his cupped palm, responding to the light caress of his thumb across the taut peak. "Mmm," she murmured. "We've been gone too long. Our absence will be noted."

"Let them notice." Rory bent his head and claimed her lips once again. He eased his hand from her bodice and moved it down the satin dress, relishing the feel of her feminine curves and the flat plane of her belly. His tongue played a game of enticement with hers as he slowly moved his hand beneath the embroidered hem of her petticoat and up one slender calf. His callused fingers snagged the delicate silk hose, and he vowed silently to buy her a dozen pair to replace it.

"We have supper yet to go, before the bedding," he said huskily as his fingertips circled the rosette on her garter. "But there's nothing to say we can't enjoy a bit of pleasure before we return to our guests."

When his hand slid beneath the lacy ruffle of her shift where it ended at her knee, Joanna wriggled and tried to sit up.

"Perhaps we should return to the hall now," she suggested, her throaty contralto breathless with alarm. "Everyone will be waiting for us to lead them into supper."

"Let them wait." He traced the curve of her ear with his tongue as he smoothed his fingers across her satiny thigh. "I'm going to touch you, Joanna," he murmured, aware of her growing tension. "Very carefully and very gently. Don't be afraid. Open yourself to me, little bride."

"We shouldn't be doing this before the bedding," she said in a worried tone, though she followed his soft-spoken directions.

He cupped her mound in his hand, thrilling to the feel of her fine-boned fragility. The heat of sexual need churned in his blood. Desire tautened every muscle in his feverish body.

" 'Tis a natural and normal thing for a betrothed couple to experience a taste of the pleasure to come," he assured her, his voice thick with tightly leashed passion. "Since our courtship was rather unconventional, I think it'd be wise for us to get better acquainted before the bedding."

"God's truth, I don't think we could get any better acquainted than this," she said brightly, struggling to scoot upward against the curve of his arm.

He smiled as he held her gently in place. "Ah, but we can, lass. And we will."

Joanna felt a pulsing sensation spread through her as his fingers delved into the tight curls at the juncture of her thighs. She wasn't certain that what MacLean was doing was as acceptable as he made it sound. Still, she couldn't find enough breath left in her lungs to protest.

He stroked her with exquisite tenderness, barely touching her, yet bringing such intense pleasure that Joanna sighed. Her body moved of its own accord, and she opened her legs wider.

"That's the way, darling," he said, his voice coaxing and deep. "Let me pleasure you."

He slowly eased a finger inside her, and as though she had no will of her own, Joanna's muscles automatically responded by clenching him. She closed her eyes, too embarrassed to meet his knowing gaze. Her hips undulated with his strokes, and her breathing grew ragged and heavy.

"Rory," she gasped, shaking her head, "I don't think . . ."

Joanna pushed against his shoulders, suddenly frightened by the unknown. She tried to shove aside the feelings that were swamping her, taking her to someplace she'd never been. Someplace she'd never dreamed of. "I don't think we should . . . right now . . ."

"Shh," he whispered, "don't talk, Joanna, just feel. Just feel me touching you. Feel me caressing your velvety warmth. You want me to touch you like this, lass. You know you do."

Nothing in Joanna's books or her studies had prepared her for what was happening now. Not her vivid imagination nor her daydreams nor the morality fables told by the scholars at Allonby.

Her heart pounded so wildly she thought it might burst. She clutched the soft velvet of Rory's jacket, trying desperately to hold on to her reeling, gyrating world. Flames of excitement licked through her, and she moaned low in her throat as her slumbering eroticism awoke beneath her husband's skilled tutelage.

"Open your eyes, Joanna," he commanded, his deep baritone hoarse and insistent. "Tell me you want me."

Joanna's lashes flew up, and she met his piercing gaze. He held her enthralled, and she couldn't look away. She reached up, her fingertips skimming the emerald gleaming on his earlobe, and threaded her fingers through his amber-hued hair, aware of only his touch and the green eyes that devoured her.

"Rory," she confessed, releasing a tortured breath, "I . . . I do want you."

The light of male conquest flared in his eyes, and a victorious smile curved his lips. "Not nearly as much as I want you, darling lass," he said, his voice rough with passion. "But you will. I promise, you will."

Her husband seemed to know with unfailing expertise exactly where to touch, where to fondle, where to stroke. The pleasure steadily built inside Joanna, and with it an unimaginable tension. She grasped his muscular arms and rose toward him, seeking and finding his lips.

Soaring on a wave of ecstasy she'd never known before, she called his name in wonder, and Rory covered her mouth with his to muffle her plaintive cry of fulfillment.

A feeling of lethargy drifted over Joanna as she rested in the protective circle of his arm. She took in a long, steadying draft of air and idly fingered the lace at his throat, waiting for her heart to gradually cease its frantic race.

Rory placed light, reassuring kisses on her forehead, her cheeks, her nose and chin. "Sweet little wife," he crooned as he readjusted her petticoat and gown and smoothed down the wrinkled satin folds.

Joanna met his heavy-lidded gaze, unaware of anything or anyone beyond the two of them. She traced his eyebrows and prominent cheekbones with her fingertips, studying each feature as though seeing it for the first time, then brushed her fingers over his lips.

"Ah, lass," he whispered against the pads of her exploring fingers, "do you know how your husband hungers for you?" He took one finger into his mouth and bit her lightly with his sharp, even teeth.

"Ouch!" Joanna exclaimed, resisting the urge to laugh at his playfulness as she jerked her hand away.

What had she been thinking to brook such familiarities on his part? She'd foolishly allowed herself to forget for the moment that he was her clan's sworn enemy. There'd be no bedding, no carnal pleasures to come. Once they were alone in her bedchamber that evening, she would inform MacLean that there'd be no intimacies between them. He'd tricked her into saying the marriage vows, and she intended to seek an annulment on those grounds.

Her bridegroom nipped the bridge of her nose. "I plan to keep you in bed for the next fortnight, Lady MacLean, and devour you like the tasty wee morsel you are."

"If you devour me like a tasty wee morsel, Laird MacLean," she told him with a skeptical frown, "there'll be nothing left for the second fortnight."

He grinned lecherously. "Then I'll have to take very tiny, wee bites, won't I?"

"My brother has everything planned," Godfrey told the solidly built man standing by the bartizan's narrow window. "Andrew will leave with her tonight."

Looking out across Kinlochleven's upper bailey at the battlements, Archibald Campbell, second earl of Argyll, took another sip of chamomile tea. He occasionally suffered from gout and had left the festivities in the great hall to retire early. Usually fastidious to a fault, this evening he received his clandestine visitor attired in a blue velvet chamber robe and comfortable slippers.

The earl had been allotted the castle's second-best suite of guest rooms—the best having naturally been awarded to the king. The spacious chamber boasted a thick carpet on the planked floor and several fine pieces of carved oak. A large court cupboard held an array of glassware and silver, along with decanters of expensive wine and brandy.

"You'll never get the lass out of this castle," Argyll said dispassionately. "MacLean, along with his two brothers and that behemoth kinsman of his, could slay every one of your men-at-arms without breaking a sweat. And from the gleam of lust in his eye today, I'd say The MacLean would gladly do all the killing himself, should any man try to steal his new bride."

Godfrey held a glass beaker between his palms, warming the cognac it held. "We've no intention of fighting our way out," he replied. "There'll be no alarm raised. Just make certain your men are waiting near Rannoch Mill when the two young lovers and their escort ride by."

"How many will there be?"

"Andrew and four men-at-arms, plus the girl. I've convinced my older brother that only a small party stands a chance of getting past the guards unchallenged. And don't worry about MacLean. By the time they reach the mill, he'll have already met his maker at the hands of his Macdonald bride."

"Never," Argyll scoffed. He turned away from the window and peered at Godfrey with open skepticism. "That tiny lass couldn't kill any man, let alone her able-bodied bridegroom."

Godfrey shrugged. "If she doesn't, 'twill not matter overmuch, for I can make it look as though she did. The king will be enraged, of course, when he discovers his favorite Highlander slain. But he won't hang Joanna. 'Twill look like a tragic accident. A panicked bride, frightened of being bedded by her ancient enemy, tries to protect her virtue and elope with her handsome cousin. Her attempt goes sadly awry, and the overeager bridegroom falls victim to virginal terror."

Campbell sank into a chair and placed the cup and saucer on a small table beside him. He steepled his fingers in quiet contemplation.

"It'd be best not to kill MacLean," he said at last. "If you can prevent the consummation of the marriage, 'twould be enough. There's no point in risking the king's retribution for the murder of his beloved friend. Not unless it's absolutely necessary."

"Now you sound like my faint-hearted brother," Godfrey replied with a chortle. He breathed in the fumes of the fine French cognac and took a sip. As the brandy burned its way down his throat, his determination to rid the world of the King's Avenger increased. He'd never feel safe until the bastard was planted in his grave.

The earl lifted his brows in polite inquiry, and Godfrey continued. "My brother wants it to look as if Joanna and Andrew were the only two people involved. Ewen has instructed the lad to leave MacLean trussed up like a suckling pig in the middle of his marriage bed for his brothers to find in the morning. That way if anything goes wrong, Ewen can plead that he had no knowledge of his son's intentions. He'll claim the two youngsters were carried away by their passion for one another, thereby playing on the king's sympathy. Everyone knows James Stewart is a romantic at heart."

"The king might be touched by the story," Argyll commented dryly, "but the spurned bridegroom will be a little less sympathetic. Just how do you intend to spirit the two impetuous lovers out of the castle?"

"There's a secret stairway."

Archibald Campbell smiled. It was a peculiarly humorless smile.

Ewen Macdonald wasn't the only man who coveted the Macdonald heiress for his son. Argyll's youngest boy, Iain, had barely turned fifteen, but he was man enough for his father's purpose: to marry the Maid of Glencoe and bring the mighty fortress of Kinlochleven and the vast estates of the Glencoe Macdonalds firmly under Campbell control.

"If I get the chance," Godfrey said malevolently, "I'll slit MacLean's throat. It's the only way we'll ever be free of him. I don't care to be looking over my shoulder for the rest of my life.''

The earl slouched back in the carved oak chair and propped his swollen foot on a tufted stool. ''You can't honestly think James will believe the maid killed her bridegroom. God's Mass, the two of them have been billing and cooing like a pair of turtledoves all day.''

Godfrey downed the rest of the cognac in one quick gulp and went to the cupboard to pour another. ''Kissing and fondling is a far cry from swiving,'' he tossed over his shoulder, ''especially for a frightened, inexperienced lass. Besides, she'll be gone when they discover his corpse. By the time the king learns that Joanna's at Inveraray and married to Iain, he'll be willing to overlook the death of MacLean. It'll be that . . .'' He paused to lift his glass in a salute. ''. . . or accuse one of the most powerful chiefs in Scotland of outright treachery.''

If Argyll appreciated the flattery, he gave no sign. ''Nevertheless, I want MacLean left alive. What time should my men expect the fleeing lovers?''

''Before midnight, if all goes well. Warn your men that they'll be dressed as Observantine friars. And remember, Andrew is not to be harmed. Is that understood? Otherwise I'll—''

''Otherwise you'll do what?'' Argyll asked softly.

Godfrey gripped the beaker's stem and stared down at the cognac. Silently cursing the misfortune that had put him in Argyll's clutches, he drained his glass without further comment.

Chapter 14

❦

Following supper, Rory's brothers stole the gold buckle off his left shoe in the old Highland tradition.

"'Tis to prevent witches from depriving your lusty bridegroom of the power of loosening the ribbons that fasten the virgin zone," Keir reminded Joanna with his hearty laugh. When she blushed charmingly, he added sotto voce, "Of course, I don't think there's much to worry about there."

Then everyone sipped the bridal posset, made of hot wine, milk, eggs, sugar, and spices.

Lachlan lifted his silver cup in a salute to the newly wedded couple. "The wine will give your bridegroom strength," he told Joanna after the toast, his eyes gleaming with mirth, "and the sugar will make him kind and tenderhearted."

"Now 'tis time for the bride to retire," Lady Emma said with a warm smile.

From his place in front of the enormous hearth, Rory watched Joanna make her way across the great hall with her escort of women. Lachlan and Keir stood on each side of him, making good-natured jests about their older brother's patent eagerness to follow in his wife's wake. He'd taken their ribald humor in stride that evening, though Joanna's ears would have been scorched had she heard even half of what had been said among the men.

He gave up trying to concentrate on the conversation

around him. As he stared at his bride's retreating back, he repeated over and over in his mind the lines of the sentimental poem Lachlan had written.

Rory wanted to get it perfect.

He wasn't going to botch this evening with his usual direct, plain-speaking ways. He intended to keep the lust that surged through his loins well under control, until he'd dazzled his bride with the magical words of romance penned by his clever brother.

> *My bride, my love, my shining star,*
> *Your beauty gleams like moonbeams afar . . .*
> Or was it . . . *glistens like moonlight from above*?

Rory pulled the piece of paper from his sporran and turned the writing to the firelight. He scanned it quickly, and before anyone noticed, shoved it back into his sporran.

> *My bride, my love, my shining star,*
> *Your shimmering beauty surpasses the moon . . .*
> *above . . . on far.*

Jesu, would he ever get the damn thing memorized?

While the guests enjoyed the dancing that followed the light supper, and the king dallied in the solarium with his mistress of the hour, Joanna's women led her toward the stairs.

Fearchar followed the ladies to the foot of the main stairwell. "Forbye, milady," he said to Joanna, "I'll see that the rest of your evening goes undisturbed."

She turned and smiled thankfully.

Arms folded across his broad chest, Fearchar was prepared to stand guard during the night, lest the more obstreperous celebrants decided to pay a midnight call on the bridal couple, banging kettles and tooting horns in a noisy charivari.

"Please make certain my husband is the only one allowed to come up," she said.

The large man winked at his new mistress. "That I will, to be certain. Sleep well, Lady MacLean." His gaze moved to Maude, on the step above. "And sweet dreams to you, demoiselle."

"Stuff and nonsense," Maude replied with a disapproving snort. "I'm too realistic to have dreams and too old to be addressed as a maiden."

He grinned mischievously, and his eye, the soft blue of a robin's egg, glimmered with gentle humor. "You've the tongue of an adder, Maude Beaton, but you're sonsy and braw for all that."

"My faith," she grumbled to Joanna, "the man's jaw clacks like a broken waterwheel." But a smile skirted her lips before she turned and continued upstairs.

Carrying a flambeau to light the way, Maude preceded her mistress. Lady Beatrix and Abby followed behind, while Idoine, being a virginal maid, remained in the great hall with Lady Emma and the others.

Her tension mounting, Joanna's breathing grew labored as they climbed the stone stairs. The intimate moments she'd shared with her groom that afternoon would have only added to the natural exhilaration felt by any other bride, for she'd now had a foretaste of the pleasures a man could give a woman. But she was no ordinary bride, and her wedding night would bring no sweet moments of bliss.

As Joanna and her companions turned from the dark stairwell to approach her bedchamber on the third floor, Ewen and Andrew stepped out of the shadows.

Maude stopped in her tracks, and Joanna almost bumped into her. Abby gave a squeal of surprise before clapping her dimpled hand over her mouth.

"What are you doing here?" Maude demanded. She lifted the candlestick higher and scowled at the intruders.

Lady Beatrix immediately stepped closer to Joanna and clutched her by the elbow, as though afraid she might try to run away. "Your cousins merely wish a moment of your time, dear," Beatrix said, her words barely above a whisper.

"Could this not wait until morning?" Joanna inquired, her thoughts on the night ahead. MacLean might protest, cajole, and wheedle, but all his blandishments would be for naught. Her mind was set, her decision unequivocal. She folded her hands in front of her and regarded the two men abstractedly.

The glow of the candlelight illuminated the strands of silver in Ewen's dark brown hair and beard. The day's strain had taken its toll. His lean face stark and unsmiling, he looked far older than his forty-one years. "As your war commander," he said tersely, "I have the right to speak with you about matters pertaining to the clan, Joanna."

If some problem demanded her immediate consideration, she had no choice but to attend to it. Married or not, she was still their chieftain. Though the delay in her confrontation with MacLean would stretch her nerves to the breaking point, she must put duty first and foremost.

"Very well," she agreed. She turned to Maude and Abby. "Go in and prepare my chamber while I speak with Ewen."

Maude wrinkled her nose disdainfully, as though smelling something rotten. "This is extremely inconsiderate on your cousin's part, milady." She turned her critical gray eyes on the two interlopers, and her uncompromising features revealed her displeasure. "Lady MacLean's bridegroom will be coming upstairs to join her soon," she told them bluntly. "Your intrusion on their evening had best be brief."

His hand on his sword hilt, Andrew stood, sullen-faced and silent, beside his father. He glared at the tall woman with overt belligerence, his jaw tight with anger.

"This won't take but a minute," Ewen replied smoothly.

Joanna motioned for the women to leave. "Pray, go on, ladies. I'll be there presently," she urged with a reassuring smile.

She waited until the trio of females entered her room and Beatrix had shut the door behind them. Then she turned to her two cousins. "You could have chosen a better time," she chided. "Why didn't either of you speak to me about this matter before now?"

"Because every time Andrew or I tried to get near you today," Ewen answered with a snarl, "a MacLean came between us. They made it bloody impossible for any Mac-donald to have a moment's privacy with you. We had to sneak up here and lurk in the shadows like common thieves."

"Well then, what is it you wish to say?" she questioned, looking from father to son.

Andrew stepped closer. "Can you guess what it feels like to have your betrothed stolen away?" he asked petulantly. "I've been forced to watch MacLean paw you all day, when you never so much as allowed me a chaste kiss."

"You and I were never betrothed, and well you know it," Joanna replied in exasperation. "Our betrothal couldn't take place until the dispensation came from Rome."

Andrew braced his hands on his hips. A sneer marred his perfect features. "And you couldn't wait long enough for the papal permission to arrive."

On the rare times they'd been together alone since her grandfather's death, the sixteen-year-old had tried to press his clumsy attentions on her and been roundly slapped in the face for his efforts. He'd been the one who couldn't wait.

Joanna turned to Ewen, hoping for some common sense from the older man. "What was I supposed to do? I made every effort to hide my identity. I entered the chapel this morning believing that The MacLean thought me a lad. Once he led me up to the altar, there was nothing I could do but say the vows or be tried as a traitor for refusing to obey the king."

Ewen grasped her arm and pulled her deeper into the recessed arch along the stone wall. He lowered his voice, though they were entirely alone, his words a challenge. "But there is something you can do now, Joanna."

"I am fully aware of that," she replied tautly. What did

he think she intended to do—leap joyfully into bed with the Sea Dragon?

His dark eyes glittered in the faint glow of moonlight streaming through the slotted window. A smile curved his thin lips. "Then you'll leave with us tonight?"

"Are you insane?" She met their determined eyes and took a step back. "How could I possibly leave when every MacLean soldier in this castle would give his life to stop me? And kill any man who attempted to take me with him."

At Ewen's thunderous scowl, she continued smoothly. "My marriage is no more than lines written on a piece of paper. Until the vows are consummated, there is no marriage. When MacLean comes to my bedchamber, I'll forbid him to touch me."

Ewen laughed scornfully. "Do you really think you can stave off your bridegroom's attentions indefinitely?" He took a step closer and waved his hand toward the closed door. "Do you really believe, Joanna, that you can spend the entire night in that bedchamber with the chief of Clan MacLean and prevent him from consummating your marriage?"

She lifted her chin and glared at her cousin. "That's my intent."

"You won't have to hold him off all night," Andrew said eagerly. "My father has a better plan." He tossed back a thick lock of hair and sniggered like a defiant schoolboy. "I've hidden a weapon under your bed."

"A weapon!" she cried softly.

"You'll need our help, lass," Ewen said. "We'll see that you get away before he overpowers you."

Joanna shook her head. "He won't force me against my will."

"For God's sake, lass!" Ewen said, his voice dripping with sarcasm. "You're deluding yourself. MacLean hates anyone with the name of Macdonald. Don't you know what everyone is saying?"

At her look of bewilderment, he leaned toward her and

sadly shook his head. "MacLean never wanted to marry you in the first place. He outright refused the king's orders to take a Macdonald to wife. The slimy bastard only agreed to the alliance under threat of dire punishment."

Joanna straightened her spine and stared at the wall behind him. "I know he didn't choose to wed me," she replied through stiff lips. "I didn't wish to marry him, either."

Ewen caught Joanna's chin in his hand and forced her to look at him. "If you don't have any pride as a Macdonald," he grated, "or as the daughter of a valorous Highlander killed on the battlefield fighting the old Stewart tyrant, surely you must hold some tiny jot of pride for your Sassenach mother."

Joanna gazed into his infuriated eyes, and icy apprehension sliced through her belly. She shoved his hand away, fighting the tears that threatened, and spoke in a thin, reedy voice. "What has any of this to do with my mother?"

Ewen stepped back, his gaze raking her coldly. "Don't you know anything, girl?" he asked in disgust. "MacLean said he'd rather burn in hell before he married the spawn of the devil and a witch."

The accusation of witchcraft stunned her. A woman could be disinterred from her resting place in sacred ground if such a calumny could be proven against her. Joanna put out her hand as though to ward off the image of her mother's grave being desecrated, of Lady Anne's coffin being set afire or tossed into a pond to see if it would float. Her throat tightened till she could barely speak. "I . . . I don't believe you. He'd never accuse Mama of black magic. He never even knew her."

"You don't have to believe me, Joanna," her cousin said softly. "Ask your treacherous, bastard bridegroom." He jerked his bearded chin toward the stairwell. "Ask anyone down there celebrating the gullible Macdonald bride's easy capitulation to her clan's mortal enemy. MacLean's profane refusal could be heard through a closed door at Stalcaire. Everyone in the Scottish court knows of it. Hell, half of

them probably heard him. They were all laughing up their
sleeves as you minced around the dance floor with the very
man who labeled your heroic father a devil and your poor,
dead mother a witch.''

From the absolute confidence in his voice, Joanna knew
that Ewen spoke the truth. Rory had accused her sweet,
loving mother of witchcraft. Disillusionment invaded her
soul, crushing every hope of happiness. She could feel her
heart shatter into a thousand pieces, the pain almost beyond
bearing. All her childhood dreams came crashing down
around her. A man capable of slandering the good name of
someone as gentle and kind as Lady Anne was capable of
anything. Her belief that she could reason with MacLean
had been hopelessly naïve.

There were no knights, no ladies fair.

Only evil-minded dragons who delivered old, helpless
men to the gallows and slandered virtuous noblewomen.

Inhuman, despicable dragons who deceived and seduced
foolish, foolish girls.

Joanna rubbed her arms, suddenly shivering in the drafty,
unlit passageway. ''All right,'' she said through trembling
lips, ''I *will* ask him. I'll have the truth from him tonight.''

Ewen's teeth flashed white in his dark brown beard. ''I
only hope he has the balls to admit it.''

His eyes black in the night shadows, Andrew grabbed
her hand. ''There's a loaded weapon beneath your bed,
Joanna,'' he whispered excitedly. ''Wait until your women
leave and MacLean comes up. While he's disrobing, take
it out—''

''I won't kill him,'' she said with a stubborn lift of her
chin. ''No matter what he's said or done, I won't kill him.''

''You don't have to kill him,'' Ewen replied in a pla-
cating tone. ''Just keep the bastard at bay until Andrew
comes for you. It won't be long, I promise. While you hold
the weapon on MacLean, Andrew will tie him up and leave
him where he'll be found, all snug and safe, in the morning.''

Andrew couldn't contain his glee. ''We'll slip out of

Kinlochleven tonight," he said with an adolescent snicker, "then file for an annulment once we're at Mingarry Castle."

"I'll have the truth from that despicable coward's own lips," Joanna said firmly, "but I won't run away like a frightened little rabbit. This castle is mine. These lands are mine. I won't desert my kinsmen here at Kinlochleven who depend on me."

"Very well, Joanna," Ewen agreed. He stroked his beard as he sent a quick glance to his son. "We'll abide by your wishes for now."

Chapter 15

Rory opened the door of their chamber to find Joanna sitting up in the high four-poster, waiting for him. The blue damask bed curtains had been drawn back, framing her against the plump white pillows and the carved oak headboard.

He paused for a moment in the doorway, gazing at her with a feeling very close to awe. She looked so damn fragile in the middle of the massive bedstead. His throat grew constricted and his heart pounded as wildly as any anxious bridegroom's ever had.

Candles on the side table, on the press cupboard, and on the mantel filled the room with a lambent glow. Their flickering light played across the bed, bathing its still occupant in a rich golden hue. A cozy fire burned on the grate, creating a warm and beckoning welcome.

His gaze fixed on his enchanting wife, Rory stepped inside and shut the door quietly behind him

Joanna wore a voluminous ivory nightshift, its narrow yellow ribbons already loosened at the throat for her husband's pleasure. The age-old tradition of untying the love-knots on a bride's clothing was still practiced in the Highlands, and her women had seen that not a pin remained in her locks or a ribbon on her shift left untied.

Her hair, brushed to a glorious sheen, fell loose about her slim shoulders and spilled over the embroidered ruffles across her breasts and onto the bedclothes in lustrous curls.

Joanna's dark blue eyes appeared enormous in her small, heart-shaped face as she watched him enter in silence.

The need for her pulsed through his veins. A familiar tightening in his groin reminded Rory that he'd waited impatiently for this moment since the night he'd found her sleeping in front of the kitchen hearth, the firelight revealing the delicacy of her freshly scrubbed features.

Now the waiting was over.

"You look lovely," he said, then berated himself for the paltry understatement.

The armored knight in the tapestry on the far wall surveyed Rory with a conceited smirk, as though to say he surely could do better than that.

Joanna's bottom lip trembled, and Rory recognized her acute tension. She attempted a smile and, failing, gave a quick nod in acknowledgment of his inadequate praise.

Part of him felt a surge of relief. She looked far more nervous than he. Even if he stumbled a bit in his attempt to be gallant, she'd probably never notice. Still, he'd have to put her at ease, both physically and emotionally, or their wedding night would degenerate into a very awkward procedure for both of them.

Rory released a long, controlled breath, schooling himself for a painstakingly slow seduction. He'd try to make light conversation—though, God knew, frivolous discourse had never been his long suit, and tonight of all nights, the latest blather of the court was the last thing on his mind.

Nevertheless, he'd give Joanna all the time she needed to get used to the idea that she was alone in her private chamber with a man who was about to disrobe and climb into bed with her.

"I'll pour us some wine," he said with a heartening smile.

When Joanna opened her mouth to speak, nothing came out. Once again she nodded.

Rory moved to the tall cupboard, where a decanter and two engraved wineglasses had been set out for the bridal pair. He recognized the interlaced Celtic design on the crystal goblets, gifts from Keir. His mother must have brought them up earlier that afternoon. He'd have to remember to thank her in the morning.

His back to the bed, Rory poured the dark ruby claret, mentally rehearsing the poem Lachlan had written.

My bride, my love, my shining star,
Your beauty glimmers like moonbeams from afar.

He'd recite the words after they'd both had a little wine—when she wasn't quite so tense, but before the heaviness in his loins made him forget the lines completely.

My bride, my love, my shining star . . .

The brief recitation shouldn't be too hard—if he didn't trip over his own tongue in the process.

Rory grinned to himself. Who'd have believed he'd be spouting romantical gibberish to please a lady? Certainly no one who'd ever known him on the battlefield—or in the boudoir either, for that matter.

Holding a glass in each hand, he turned . . .

. . . to stare at the wrong end of a loaded crossbow aimed straight at his gut.

His bashful wee bride held the cocked and lethal weapon in her two shaking hands.

Christ! He'd heard of virginal trepidation, but this was carrying maidenly modesty a bit too far.

"Put it down, Joanna," he ordered softly, his fingers tightening around the goblets' fragile stems.

"Not . . . until . . . you answer . . . my questions," she replied, pure venom in her stilted words. Standing rigid and straight beside the bed, her shoulders thrown back, her chin lifted stubbornly, she glared at him.

Too late, he realized that Joanna hadn't been overcome by a bride's nervous qualms. For some unfathomable reason, she was so angry she could hardly speak.

She stood no more than five paces away. Too close to miss, even if she could barely see him through her tears.

And too far away to reach before she could release the triggering device.

He spoke in a voice that had commanded men three times her size in the heat of battle. "Put the goddamn thing down, Joanna, before it goes off."

Her diminutive figure quivered with rage. "First . . . MacLean . . . you'll answer . . . my questions," she retorted. "Did you . . . call my father . . . a devil?"

Rory's jaw clenched as he swallowed back a vile oath.

Who the hell had told her?

When he finished whaling on her little butt, he'd strangle the bloody bastard and then flay him alive.

The crossbow had to be cocked by means of a stirrup at the end of the crosspiece. Placing the weapon in a vertical position, the archer engaged the stirrup with his foot and shoved down with his heel to cock the bow, which was caught and held by a trigger mechanism.

There was no way in hell his indignant little wife could have accomplished the feat.

"Who loaded the bow, Joanna?" he asked quietly, gazing straight into her furious eyes.

She stared blindly at Rory, as though unable to understand his question. He could see she was close to hysteria. Though some man—and Rory had a pretty good notion who that man was—had to have cocked the weapon for her, all she need do now was squeeze the lever under the stock.

With a range up to four hundred yards, the crossbow's square-headed missile would strike him with such force he'd be impaled on the wooden cupboard behind him.

Tears streamed down Joanna's cheeks. Her husky contralto caught on a sob with each word she uttered. "Did you . . . accuse my mother . . . of being a witch . . . you . . . perverted satyr?"

Damnit to hell, he'd personally break the loudmouthed bastard on the rack, after first disemboweling the cur and severing every body part he owned.

"Who loaded the bow for you, Joanna?" Rory asked

pleasantly. He took a cautious step toward her. "I know you couldn't have done it yourself, lass. Now tell me who gave you that weapon, and I promise not to get angry."

She took a frantic step back, her agitation increasing tenfold. Apparently his calm demeanor wasn't what she'd expected. Christ, did she think he'd fall down on his knees and grovel at her feet, begging for mercy?

"Did . . . did you say it?" she continued insistently. "Answer me, you . . . you half-human freak of nature. And I want the truth, damn you! Did you call . . . my father . . . a devil . . . and my mother . . . a witch?"

The only thing more unpredictable than a frightened man was a hysterical woman. And her crazed words left no doubt Joanna was hysterical.

With a crooked smile, Rory lifted his shoulders in a noncommittal shrug. Then he hurled the goblet in his right hand against the stone wall, where it exploded in a shower of crimson drops and crystal shards.

At the sudden crash, Joanna jerked reflexively and spun around, releasing the trigger. The quarrel struck the chamber's heavy wooden door with a chilling thunk. Rory closed the distance between them in four quick strides.

As he yanked the spent crossbow from her lax hands and smashed it against the low chest at the foot of the bed, the door flew open and Andrew rushed in. The adolescent's dark brown eyes revealed his confusion. He'd expected to find the cowed bridegroom pleading for his life.

"I should have known," Rory growled. Flinging the disabled weapon aside, he caught the startled lad by the throat and shoved him against the wall. "You worthless, puling runt," he said, banging the boy's head viciously against the whitewashed plaster with every word. "I ought to kill you, you miserable worm."

Dazed, Andrew wobbled on limp legs and his arms went slack. His terrified eyes could barely focus on his infuriated attacker.

In his rage, Rory held the harebrained youth up and pounded his thick skull a few more times for good measure.

The knowledge that Joanna preferred the conceited whelp to her husband made Rory want to bash his flawless, bonny features into a bloody pulp.

But the idiot was only sixteen and infatuated with a maid so alluring that even Rory, a hard-bitten warrior, had been temporarily blinded to her true nature.

With an oath, he spun the lad around and shoved him toward the open door. "Get the hell out of here," he snarled as he administered a swift kick to the boy's backside.

Andrew landed on all fours, scrambled clumsily to his feet, and staggered down the dark passageway.

Joanna took Rory's guttural command to heart. Eyes averted, she tried to scurry past him and out of the room.

"Not you." He grabbed hold of the high frilled collar of her nightshift, dragged her back inside, and slammed the door. "You're not going anywhere."

Even in his wrath, he glanced down to make certain she wasn't wading through slivers of broken glass and splintered wood in her bare feet. He felt a stab of relief that her toes weren't cut and bleeding, and his unwarranted concern for her incensed him all the more.

"Let me go," she said, panting for breath and squirming like an eel. "Don't you . . . dare touch me . . . you . . . monstrous aberration. Not after what you said . . . about my mother and father."

He caught a handful of hair at the nape of her neck and brought her head back so he could look into those deceitful blue eyes. Their indigo depths were wild with anger and sparkling with tears. The long lashes clumped together in wet auburn spikes tipped with shimmering drops.

"I ought to turn you over my knee and give you a sound thrashing," he gritted.

"I should have shot you!" she cried.

With a pithy expletive, Rory lifted Joanna up in his arms and in two long strides moved to the bed, where he dumped her onto the quilted comforter.

Before she had a chance to scramble back up, he pinned

her hands on either side of her head and leaned over her.

"You want to know if I called your father a devil and your mother a witch?" he thundered. "Of course I did! What Scotsman in his right mind would willingly choose to marry a traitorous Macdonald?"

"You married me fast enough when you learned the size of my fortune," Joanna responded, a sneer curling her soft pink lips. "Pray, pardon me, Laird MacLean, if I'm not feeling flattered."

In her anger, her vibrant coloring was breathtaking, the scattered reddish-gold locks vivid against the pale nightshift and sheets. Her fine complexion shone translucent in the candlelight, the blue veins on her temple visible beneath the delicate skin. Her brilliant eyes were almost black in her rage.

The enticing perfume of roses drifted up from the rumpled bedclothes, and lust—unadulterated male lust—roared up inside him with the urgency of stone shot loosed from a catapult.

She must have read the gut-wrenching need in his gaze, for fear replaced the anger in her eyes. "Let me up," she said, her voice tight and quavering.

The air left his lungs in a whoosh. Rory took a deep breath through flared nostrils, struggling to maintain some semblance of sanity in this irrational turn of events. What had happened to the romantic wedding night he'd so carefully planned?

God Almighty, if any female could drive a man stark, raving mad, this tiny bit of willful baggage could do it.

"Meek and mild in bed and at board," he grated. "Don't Macdonalds ever keep their promises?"

"Not with vile miscreants who libel their parents," she taunted. "No one would expect them to."

"Goddammit, you little vixen, who else but a half-Sassenach, half-Macdonald harpy would try to murder her own husband on their wedding night?"

The shock in her eyes told him he'd struck a telling blow.

"I hate you!" she cried, teardrops glistening on her white cheeks. "I'll always hate you!"

Sick at heart, Rory looked down at her and silently cursed the ignorant, interfering fool who'd destroyed all the warmth and tenderness between them.

A feeling of emptiness squeezed his chest like a breastplate of cold, hard steel. Though he had every right before God and man, he couldn't take Joanna now. Not with the blood roaring angry in his veins and rage tightening every muscle. Not with Joanna rigid with fear and hatred.

If he tried to claim his marital privileges, she'd fight him. And with her stubborn courage, Joanna wouldn't quit fighting him until he'd completely subdued her. The thought that he might accidentally injure her in the process or break her magnificent spirit filled him with horror.

Christ, what the hell was wrong with him?

He was worried about hurting her after she'd just tried to nail him to the wall with a crossbow quarrel at four paces. A jumble of contradictory and warring emotions roared within him.

Rage.

Lust.

Tenderness.

And above all, a sharp, caustic disillusionment.

Rory released her hands and straightened, more furious at himself than Joanna or her sniveling, interfering milksop of a cousin. With a snarl of self-contempt, he strode to the side table, snatched up a flask from among his personal effects, and moved to the door, where he paused to glance back at the bed.

Joanna had rolled over on her stomach, buried her head in her arms, and was now sobbing as though her heart would break.

His sweet, innocent bride was probably devastated because she hadn't succeeded in killing him.

Without another word, he stepped into the passageway and slammed the door, leaving his treacherous Macdonald wife to nurse her disappointment with her salty tears.

*   *   *

The cool evening air and the warm aqua vitae acted like a soothing tonic on Rory's raging temper. Holding the silver flask in one hand, he rested the other on the parapet and looked up at the sky. A full moon hung just above the mountaintops, bathing the peaceful landscape in its silvery glow.

He hadn't wanted to return to the hall, where people were still celebrating his nuptials. A bridegroom rejoining the wedding festivities after spending such a short time with his bride would raise eyebrows and start tongues clacking.

So he'd taken the inner stairs to the keep's battlement two at a time and kept his own sorry counsel with the fiery Scotch brew and the dispassionate moon. In the solace of the whisky and the star-studded night, the irony of the situation occurred to him. While he'd been practicing the lines of his brother's addlebrained poetry, his wife had been conspiring to kill him.

God above. What a glorious ass he'd made of himself.

Lumbering around the great hall's floor with his bride, when everyone knew he couldn't dance any better than a trained bear.

Giving Joanna time to change into a lovely gown before proceeding with the wedding Mass, even though she'd tried to deceive him by pretending to be a stable boy for the past week.

Luring her into the library for a brief interlude of gentle seduction, where, like a wayward schoolboy, he'd felt compelled to admit that he'd slept with another woman. He was twenty-eight and had taken no vows of chastity. Did she think he'd lived like a priest before he met her?

Hell and damnation, he was through trying to act like someone he wasn't. Joanna would have to set aside her fanciful dreams of knights in shining armor and accept the harsh reality of life with the chief of Clan MacLean. At seventeen, 'twas well past time she grew up. Many girls were wed by fourteen, and mothers by fifteen.

Lady MacLean would have to learn she was married to

a man who placed practical considerations foremost—first, last, and always. He didn't believe in romantic love, and he sure as hell didn't intend to act as if he did. She'd have to settle for a husband who could administer their estates, secure their castle from marauders, and protect her and their children from harm.

Christ, what more could an intelligent wife expect?

Rory tipped the flask and took another slow, appreciative sip. Leaning against the parapet, he looked down at Kinlochleven's upper and lower baileys, at the thick curtain walls, the barbican and gatehouse, where repairs had already been started. He gazed across the battlements to the night-shrouded forest beyond and the still waters of the loch, reflecting a wide swath of moonlight.

He held everything he'd ever hoped for in the palm of his hand. A mighty fortress, far-flung lands, and incredible wealth. And a young, healthy wife to give him bairns.

But the taste of ashes remained, despite the scalding effects of the raw spirits he'd imbibed.

His bride saw him as some kind of inhuman monster.

Rory bitterly rued the day he'd let his temper get out of control and shouted the epithets about her parents. He could understand Joanna's indignation. Had any man ever been foolish enough to accuse Lady Emma of being a witch, he'd be rotting in his grave.

Back at Stalcaire Castle, Rory had made a grievous error. But it was surely a mistake that could be mended, given time. Although most marriages usually began under more auspicious circumstances, many couples started their life together as near strangers. Perhaps if he told Joanna he was sorry that he'd labeled her mother and father so harshly, she'd be willing to begin again, as polite acquaintances who'd only just met.

Taking a last swallow of whisky, Rory slipped the half-empty flask into his sporran. He'd given his unhappy bride enough time to cry herself to sleep. When she awoke to his presence in their large, soft bed, he'd apologize for what he'd said about her parents. Then he'd salvage what was left of his wedding night. And perhaps, if he were very fortunate, he'd sire an heir.

When Rory entered his bedchamber for the second time that evening, the candles were smoking stubs. The fire on the grate had died down to a few glowing embers. Only the shaft of moonlight coming in through the tall window illuminated the silent room.

The broken glass and spilled wine remained on the floor, along with the remnants of the crossbow. Its quarrel was still embedded in the door.

Joanna lay facedown atop the comforter just as he'd left her. Whether she'd fallen asleep or was only pretending, he'd soon discover. Avoiding the scattered debris, Rory crossed the rug to stand beside his bed. His bride didn't stir.

He moved closer to her motionless form and touched her shoulder. "Joanna," he said softly, "I'm sorry for what I said about your mother and father."

She remained still, and he smiled knowingly—now she was going to dish up a taste of the silent treatment.

Women were so damn predictable.

"Joanna," he repeated with quiet gravity. He wasn't going to let her goad him into nearly losing control again.

When she continued to ignore him, Rory eased her onto her back and stared down at her tearstained face. She was fast asleep. With a long, resigned exhalation of air, he pushed the covers aside and slipped her slender form beneath them.

He watched Joanna turn on her side and snuggle into the warmth of the bedclothes. Bending, he kissed her gently on the cheek.

Then he slipped off his clothing, crossed to the far side of the bed, and sank down on the mattress. Propped on several pillows, Rory stacked his hands beneath his head and stared at the silken canopy above him.

He could wake up Lady MacLean, of course, though he knew from previous experience that she slept like the dead.

He could then insist on his rights as her husband and laird.

But he wanted the spirited lass to come to him eagerly. He wanted to see the need that pulsed within him mirrored in her eyes.

Damn—'twould be a long, uncomfortable night. But tomorrow he'd launch a seduction that would prove irresistible. And his bonny bride would discover, with his guidance, the delights that awaited her in their marriage bed.

Chapter 16

❧❧❧

The next morning Joanna came slowly awake, not by the kitchen hearth, but in her big canopied bed. She had a vague memory of a large masculine body sleeping beside her during the night. The uncomfortable suspicion that she'd cuddled up to the warmth radiating from her bed companion's muscular frame made her eyes pop open.

Holy hosanna, he'd been naked.

She was sure of it.

Her cheeks burning at the thought, Joanna brought the covers up to her chin and cautiously surveyed the chamber. There was no sign of her enraged bridegroom. Only the broken glass on the floor and the crossbow quarrel embedded in the door proved that the previous evening hadn't been some horrible nightmare.

God above, he'd been angry.

She'd never really intended to shoot MacLean—just make him admit that he'd accused her mother of witchcraft. Well, bloody hell, he'd admitted it, all right. And without a single jot of remorse. Joanna sniffed self-righteously. 'Twas no more than could be expected from the fiend who'd captured an innocent man and carted him off to the gallows.

The muffled sound of hammers brought Joanna to her feet. She crossed to the window, opened the casement, and stared down in dismay at the scene in the lower bailey. A team of workmen was pounding on the old, rusted portcullis that protected the main gateway. From the tools and new iron grate lying on the ground nearby, 'twas clear they'd started the improvements that MacLean had talked about.

Skirting the shards of glass, Joanna threw on her clothes and raced down the stairs. She ignored the glances of her startled guests as she crossed the great hall, not pausing for a word of explanation.

Usually a new bride remained in seclusion the day after her wedding, too modest to face the knowing looks of others. This was one bride, however, who had nothing to feel immodest about.

Joanna left the keep and stalked toward her *supposed-to-be* husband, who was never going to be her *real* husband, no matter what he thought. His broad back to her, The MacLean stood watching the work in progress, as yet, unaware of her approach.

"Stop!" she called to the men, who glanced over their shoulders in surprise at their mistress. "Stop what you're doing this instant. All of you."

Her clansmen halted and turned their curious gazes first on her and then on MacLean, as though awaiting his orders.

"Go on," he told them quietly. "Take it down." He waited until they were once again at work, then turned to meet her furious gaze with an untroubled smile. "I see you're finally awake, Lady MacLean. I should have known, from the way you used to sleep through our card playing, that the only thing that could disturb your rest would be the clanging of hammers on iron bars. You look lovely this morning, by the way."

Joanna's cheeks burned. Every man within hearing had to assume that the very reason she'd slept so late that morning stood beside her with a look of blissful contentment on his smug face.

"This work has to stop," she declared with a scowl.

MacLean stepped closer and fingered a lock of her hair, which spilled loose over her shoulders. She hadn't taken time to do more than run a brush through her tangled curls.

"Just because I'm a new bridegroom," he said softly, "I can't loaf the day away. We'll have plenty of time this afternoon, lass, to enjoy a leisurely talk."

The light flashing in his lecherous green eyes matched the sparkle of his emerald earring. He didn't fool her for a moment: he planned to do a whole lot more than just talk. Good Lord, did the man think of nothing but debauchery?

While MacLean openly leered at his bride, the laborers, who were all Macdonald clansmen hired from the nearby villages, lifted the rust-covered iron grate down and laid it on the ground beside the new one.

Joanna propped her hands on her hips and glared at them. "Replace that old portcullis immediately."

Not a man moved. They stood still and silent, their apprehensive gazes glued on the chief of Clan MacLean. At his curt nod, they started knocking the corroded hinges off the dilapidated wooden gate that guarded the drawbridge.

In a state of near panic, Joanna looked around the bustling castle grounds. Everywhere, workmen scurried about. A master mason stood with his apprentices, going over a set of plans. A crew of laborers had started to dig a new well, while other men were busily removing all the postern gates. Quarried stone had been brought in by the wagonload and stacked near the south curtain wall.

Joanna clapped a hand to her forehead. Good God, she'd never be able to pay for all these improvements. Most of her tenants paid their rents with produce from their farms and fields. Cattle, hogs, and poultry populated her byres and yards. Baskets of grain and vegetables filled her overflowing storehouses. But at the moment, there were mighty few sillers in her coffers.

Joanna clutched MacLean's forearm. "What do you think you're doing to my castle?" she demanded. "I never gave permission for these repairs."

His determination was evident in the cast of his square jaw; yet his unruffled tone held a hint of amusement. "I'm doing what should have been done years ago. The outer walls need to be reinforced, and the old gates must be replaced.'' He pried her stiff fingers from his sleeve and lifted them to his lips for a brief salute. ''And Kinlochleven Castle is mine, Lady MacLean,'' he added. ''I determine what will and will not be done within its walls.'' Releasing her hand, he turned and strode away.

Joanna followed on his heels. ''Just wait one minute,'' she said, indignation tightening her throat. When he continued to ignore her, she raised her voice. ''I want to talk to you, MacLean. Now!''

Oblivious to her demands, he strolled into the armory, and Joanna stalked in behind him.

Inside the stone building, Fearchar was directing several MacLeans in the tallying of weapons and armor. Rory's cousin turned and greeted the newly wedded couple with a wide smile. ''Good morning, Lady MacLean,'' he said.

Joanna nodded absently, her attention diverted by the chaos inside. Stacks of outdated breastplates and greaves covered the workbenches, along with mounds of helmets, their silver blackened by time. Lances, pikes, and Lochaber axes lay piled on the floor.

''These can be turned over to the smithy,'' Fearchar told Rory, pointing to several ancient claymores. ''Jacob and Lothar can use the steel to forge new broadswords.''

MacLean nodded his agreement, seemingly unaware of the outraged female beside him.

With a belligerent toss of her head, Joanna crossed her arms and glared at them. ''I want these weapons put back where they belong,'' she announced. ''And I want all the old gates placed back on their hinges and the old portcullis rehung at once.''

Several MacLeans paused for a second to toss her a curious glance before resuming their tasks.

Fearchar gazed down at her from his great height, his pale blue eye alight with amusement. Then he motioned to the other MacLeans, who were watching their clan chief from the corners of their eyes in fascination. Without another word, everyone filed out of the armory. The last to leave, Fearchar quietly closed the solid door behind him.

Before she could say another word, MacLean caught Joanna round her waist and set her on a workbench. Shoving aside a stack of worn gauntlets, he placed a large hand on either side of her hips and leaned closer. "Now suppose you tell me exactly what's bothering you this morning, wife."

"Bothering me!" She swept her hand in an all-inclusive gesture. "You've removed every gate in the castle. Kinlochleven has been left open to any attacking force riding by."

MacLean chuckled softly. He slid his hands up her blue velvet bodice, his thumbs lingering just below her breasts. "Attacking forces don't usually ride by, Joanna. They remain to lay siege. And since all my enemies are *inside* the castle walls at the present moment, what difference does it make if the portals stand wide?"

Before she could answer, he brushed her tousled curls aside, bent his head, and nuzzled her earlobe. His breath felt warm and moist, and when he dipped his tongue into the hollow of her ear, the gesture seemed astonishingly intimate. A tingle of excitement caromed through her, and she stiffened her spine. She wouldn't allow him to take liberties with her person the way he'd done the previous day. This time she was ready for any guileful assault he might attempt.

Joanna placed her hands on the man's broad shoulders with the intention of pushing him away. In spite of her determination, he drew nearer with ridiculous ease.

"Most of my rents are tendered in livestock and produce," she said angrily. "I don't have the crowns to pay for these costly repairs."

"I do," MacLean murmured, leaning ever closer.

Joanna's heart did a strange little kick. His breath fanned across her face, and the tangy scent of pine engulfed her. He brushed his lips across hers, then delved into her mouth with his tongue, stroking and caressing in blatant enticement. He tasted of wintergreen and snow-covered mountaintops.

Joanna tried vainly to control the ripple of excitement unfurling inside her. Breaking the kiss, she resolutely turned her face away.

"I shall never be able to repay you for such a great expense," she warned him breathlessly. She squirmed and tried to edge away, only to bump against the heavy armor piled beside her.

"You won't have to," MacLean replied.

But Joanna knew he was wrong. She'd have to repay every blessed siller he spent on her castle, once their wedding vows were declared null and void. She tried to envision which household items she could sell to raise such an enormous sum. Her favorite Italian tapestries, brought all the way from Cumberland, would have to go. And the silver plate. And the gold candelabra. The dowry gifts, of course, would have to be returned to the rejected bridegroom and his family, so there'd be no help there, confound it.

While her mind whirled frantically, toting up what each piece might bring, the Sea Dragon buried his long fingers in the curls at the nape of her neck, holding Joanna captive in the most primitive manner imaginable. As he cupped the back of her head in his palm, his mouth trailed down the slope of her neck to her shoulder. The low, square décolletage of her gown provided ample opportunity for his questing lips, and when he nibbled on her bare skin, her mental calculations collapsed in a flurry of prickly sensations.

She gasped when his hands cupped her breasts. Joanna could feel the heat of his body through her layers of clothing. Lord, he'd felt so warm lying beside her while she slept that she'd dreamed of lying in front of a roaring fire, wrapped in his arms.

Rory inhaled the feminine scent of his bride, and a low, male growl of sexual intent rumbled deep in his throat. She'd burrowed against him in the night, and it had required all his willpower not to take her while she slept.

His decision to wait had nothing to do with chivalry, dammit. He was determined that Joanna would want him as much as he wanted her. And he was stubborn enough to hold out for her unconditional surrender.

"You smell nice," he murmured as he eased the sleeves of her gown off her shoulders. A scattering of cinnamon dusted her ivory skin. He pressed a kiss just below the fragile shoulder bone, then explored the hollow of her clavicle with his tongue.

Joanna tipped her head back, and her coppery hair cascaded over his hands. " 'Tis rosewater," she said nervously. "I'm glad you like it. Some find its perfume too light and elusive. They prefer lavender or jasmine or even musk."

"I like it," he assured her. "I like everything about you, lass, from the top of your red head to your bonny wee toes."

Rory edged Joanna's velvet bodice down to reveal the smooth globes of her breasts. The need for her brought an ache so deep inside he nearly groaned. He bent his head and laved the rosy peaks, savoring the feel of the taut buds against his tongue and the exquisite silk of her breasts in his sword-hardened palms. His heart lurched toward his throat as her long, drawn-out sigh of pleasure foretold her inevitable surrender.

The pagan urge to claim his wife there on the rough wooden bench, amid the rusty breastplates and mailed gauntlets, throbbed within him. As he suckled her, the lust that pooled in his groin nearly drove all thoughts of waiting from his mind. When it came to sex, he'd never been a patient man.

'Twas different now. Hell, he was more aroused kissing Joanna than coupling with any other woman. But he refused to rush her into something she'd later regret.

Rory raised the hem of her blue gown, pushing it upward inch by precious inch, till he could edge her knees apart and stand between her creamy thighs. Beneath his plaid, his engorged male member pulsed with heat and a primitive urgency that wouldn't be denied.

"God above, Joanna," he whispered thickly.

His lungs compressed as he drank in the sight of the pale, silken skin above the gartered stockings. She was the very essence of femininity, sweet and fragile and so small he could cup her little butt in his hands. He eased Joanna back till she lay before him on the bench's gouged planks.

"Remember when I touched you yesterday," he murmured. "Remember how good it felt, darling lass. I will be just as careful, just as gentle now, I promise you."

Rory bent again, this time to press his lips to her abdomen, kissing her through the thin chemise. He smoothed his fingers up her legs, then cupped the mound of springy curls at the juncture of her thighs.

With a ragged exhalation of air, Joanna threaded her fingers through Rory's golden waves, unable to find the words to command him to stop. The memory of the intimacy they'd shared in the library pushed aside all thoughts of duty to her clan. As his callused fingertips sought her secret place, she tensed in heart-stopping anticipation. He parted her smooth folds, and she grew swollen and slick beneath his touch.

"Oh, dear God," Joanna whispered as he caressed her.

She grasped the collar of his shirt with one hand and clutched the folds of tartan wool draped across his shoulder with the other, wanting the pleasure to go on and on. The sensual need within her spiraled deeper and ever more insistent. Tension and a nearly unbearable expectation swamped her, and she began to undulate beneath his caresses, wordlessly urging him onward.

She waited breathlessly for Rory to penetrate her with his finger, as he'd done before. Instead he withdrew his hand and straightened above her.

"Oh, dear God," she said once more, but this time it came as a tortured moan.

Joanna sat up and threw her arms around Rory's neck, clutching him tight. Her sensitive nipples pressed against the smooth cotton of his shirt and the thick, rough folds of his plaid. She wanted to arch her back and rub against him like a kitten in a blatant ploy to be petted. The ache of sexual frustration nearly made her sob, and she had to bite her lip to keep from whimpering in disappointment.

Rory bracketed Joanna's passion-drugged face in his hands. She looked up at him, the desire smoldering in her violet-blue eyes, the confusion and need written across her features. There was only one thing he wanted more than to continue to stroke his wife's trembling body until he brought her to fulfillment.

"Tell me you want me, Joanna," he said hoarsely. He kissed her delicate cheekbone and the corner of her mouth, his nostrils flaring as he breathed in her intoxicating perfume. "Tell me you want me to take you as a man takes a woman."

Her long lashes fluttered and fell to shadow her cheeks. She shook her head slowly and deliberately, as an involuntary shudder passed through her slender body.

"Please let me leave now," she said, her voice barely audible.

Every fiber in his body rebelled at the thought of letting her go, but Rory stepped back and allowed Joanna to smooth her skirts down about her ankles. He watched in silence as she slipped from the workbench and hurried out the door. Then he braced his hands on the bench's rough boards and took a deep, steadying draft of air. His head lowered, he closed his eyes and fought the compulsion to go after her. He wouldn't take his wife against her will. He would wait until she admitted she wanted him.

But he'd be dammed if he'd court her with ballads and poems written by another man. Joanna would have to accept her husband exactly as he was, a plainspoken Highland chief.

"You'd best discover what's happening in your private quarters," Fearchar said quietly as he joined Rory on the barbican's battlement later that morning. "On her way upstairs a few moments ago, Maude let slip a fascinating bit of information which will be the clack of the entire Scottish court by midday, if you don't do something to thwart it."

Rory turned from watching the master bricklayer measure the placements for the new gun loops and scowled at his cousin. From the hilarity lighting up the burly Highlander's features, Rory knew he'd soon be the butt of everyone's sly jests, if he didn't forestall his wife's latest stratagem—whatever the hell that was.

"What's Joanna up to now?" he asked as he and Fearchar moved out of earshot.

" 'Tis only that your docile wee bride has decided to rearrange some bedroom furniture," his cousin answered cheerfully. "And put several dozen household items on the auction block to be sold to the highest bidder. The sale will start in the great hall after the midday meal and continue till sundown. With some of the wealthiest Scots in the kingdom present for the bidding, plus assorted members of the clergy, the lassie's expectin' to raise quite a sum."

"Christ Almighty," Rory muttered under his breath. Not waiting for further explanation, he hurried down the outside stairs of the barbican and across the bailey to the keep.

He arrived at the open doorway of his bedchamber to find Seumas and Davie, under their mistress's supervision, removing the tapestry of the knight and his lady fair from the wall. Maude stood beside Joanna, clucking her tongue and shaking her head in disapproval.

"May I inquire what you're doing?" Rory asked his wife pleasantly.

Joanna whirled at the sound of his voice. Guilt tinged her cheeks with a rosy glow. "Holy hosanna, you startled me," she complained. "Don't you have anything better to do than spy on us? I thought you were measuring the battlements."

He lifted his brows at her blustering. She was clearly up to something. "I'm waiting for an explanation, Joanna. Why are you removing that tapestry from our bedchamber?"

"I'm going to sell it," she declared with a stubborn tilt of her chin. "I brought this wall hanging with me from Cumberland, and I'm going to sell it."

"Why?"

"Why?" she parroted, staring at him wide-eyed, as though he were daft. "Because I need the coins 'twill bring, that's why. Why else would anyone sell anything?"

"And use the money to pay for the repairs, I suppose," he said, making no attempt to hide his exasperation.

She lifted her shoulders in eloquent dismissal. "Of course."

Rory leaned one shoulder against the doorframe and folded his arms across his chest. "Put the tapestry back where it was," he told the two men, his imperious tone leaving no doubt that he expected their instant obedience. Seumas immediately clambered back up the ladder, while Davie unrolled the colorful hanging on the chamber floor.

Joanna strode toward her husband, her eyes sparking fire. "Why do you care if I sell it?" she asked. "You don't even like that tapestry."

"That's not true," Rory replied smoothly. "I happen to be very fond of it."

She turned her head to stare at the knight dressed in his shiny silver armor, then met Rory's gaze once again. "I don't believe you. Why should you be fond of it?"

"The young fellow reminds me of myself," Rory replied with a sideways grin.

Joanna snorted derisively. "He does not. You're not anything like him."

"Milady!" Maude exclaimed in reproach.

"Well, he isn't," Joanna gritted.

"You mean I'm far more handsome?" Rory inquired blandly. "Or far more chivalrous?"

"Neither," Joanna said. "You're neither."

"Joanna," Maude chided softly. "You're forgetting your manners."

Behind their mistress, Davie and Seumas were trying unsuccessfully to stifle their chortles as they replaced the wall hanging in its original position.

"Will that be all, milady?" Seumas inquired as he climbed down from the ladder.

Joanna gestured to the low oak chest, which held her furs and gowns. "You can move that as I directed earlier," she said, her rebellious gaze locked with Rory's.

"You're not selling the chest, either," Rory told her emphatically.

"I wasn't planning to," she replied with a brilliant smile. " 'Tis merely being moved to another chamber."

For the first time, Rory noticed the oak stand that belonged beside the bed was missing, as well as the feminine articles that had stood on the tall press cupboard against the far wall. He strode into the room, coming to a halt directly in front of his wife.

Joanna looked up at her large husband and swallowed nervously. She wondered frantically if the Sea Dragon had ever made some poor wretch walk the plank. She could imagine how it would feel, standing on the wrong end of a long, narrow board, with the frigid ocean waves crashing beneath and the implacable ship's captain, sword in hand, standing behind.

Thankfully, MacLean's words were calm and dispassionate when he spoke. "Your things, my dear wife, are remaining right here where they belong."

Joanna opened her mouth to speak, then thought better of it. His words were calm enough, but a muscle twitched in his cheek.

"Will that be all, then, milord?" Seumas asked warily, as he and Davie sidled toward the recently vacated doorway.

MacLean's gaze flicked to meet theirs, then returned to Joanna. "That will be all. Close the door behind you."

Maude didn't need a special invitation to leave. She dipped a curtsy and beat a retreat behind the two menservants, who'd fled without another word.

"Traitors!" Joanna called after them. Ignoring the irate Highland chief standing in front of her, she turned and walked over to the carved chest at the foot of the bed. "Well, if they won't move it, I will," she said. She bent and grabbed one of its handles.

Just as Joanna gave a determined tug, MacLean placed his foot on top of the chest. At the sudden, unexpected weight, she fell backward, landing with a plop on a thick fur rug.

"Ouch!" she squawked, rubbing her sore behind. She glared up at her husband. "You did that on purpose!"

Rory knelt on one knee beside his obstinate wife. Hell and damnation, he had no reason to be surprised at her devious schemes. He'd gone into this preposterous marriage with his eyes wide open. No one but a stubborn little donkey would attempt to masquerade as a member of the opposite sex and expect to get away with it. And no bride of one day would believe she could move out of her husband's bedchamber without encountering opposition—except his own vexatious little wife.

He caught Joanna's chin in his hand and tilted her face upward to meet his gaze. She glowered at him, her slight figure stiff with outrage.

"If I decide to administer punishment," he said softly, "you'll feel more than a wee smack on your butt."

Her eyes grew wide at the threat, but she wisely refrained from saying anything that would inflame him further.

"I've tried to be patient," he continued, "but God knows, my patience is starting to wear thin. There'll be no sale of our household goods this afternoon or any day hereafter. And by the time I return to our chamber this evening, Lady MacLean, I want every stick of furniture and every tapestry in its rightful place. I want to see your vials of perfume exactly where they belong on the cupboard. I want to find your silk ribbons and silver hairbrush on the table beside the bed." He leaned over her, his words sharp and precise, so there'd be no mistaking his meaning. "And I want to find you in it."

A large lump rose in her throat as Joanna watched the chief of Clan MacLean rise to his feet. For several long, heart-pounding moments he loomed over her like the angel of death. She wanted to contradict him, but the icy glitter in his eyes forestalled her. 'Twas best, sometimes, to listen to one's commonsense. Sometimes 'twas better still to keep one's intentions a secret, rather than make an outright declaration of war and throw it in the enemy's teeth. Especially when that enemy stood six-foot-four in his stocking feet and had the strength of a young bull.

Joanna swallowed back the retort burning the tip of her tongue and wisely waited until her irate husband had left the room before saying another word.

"If he isn't the most obnoxious, overbearing, high-handed human being I've ever laid eyes on," she muttered, "I'll stand in the middle of the lower bailey in the pouring rain and honk like a goose."

She lifted the chest's wooden lid, pulled out her clothing, and piled it on the bed. Then she took hold of one handle and dragged the heavy piece of furniture to the door. It'd take her a while, but she'd have her things moved to the empty bedchamber down the passageway before midday.

Rory returned to the battlements, where he found Tam MacLean marking the positions on the stones for the new gun emplacements.

"Wait until everyone's seated at the midday meal," he told the young man. "Then take Murdoch with you and move all my wife's belongings back to our private chambers. Maude Beaton will show you where they've been placed. And see that this isn't the clack of the servants' quarters. They've better things to do than gossip about their mistress."

Not daring to question his chief further, Tam gave a quick nod. "Very well, laird."

Chapter 17

Dropping to her knees in the loft's clean hay, Joanna lifted the tiny kitten and nuzzled its black and white fur. "Hello, pretty one," she cooed softly, delighting in the feel of its curious, whiskered nose against her cheek. "What shall we name you?"

Three days before the guests had arrived at Kinlochleven, the stable cat had given birth to a family of five. This was the first visit Joanna had managed to squeeze from her hectic schedule. Settling deeper into the hay, she crossed her legs beneath her gown and lifted the kittens, one by one, onto her lap. Tabby rubbed against Joanna's knee, proudly showing off her children.

"Oh, I know," she told the mother cat as she scratched her under the chin, "you've done a wonderful job. I'm so happy to see that mama and babies are all doing fine."

"I trust you've finished moving your things back into our bedchamber by now," MacLean said. At the sudden, unexpected sound of his deep voice, Tabby disappeared, abandoning her offspring to her mistress's safekeeping.

Joanna looked up to find her husband standing at the edge of the loft. She'd been so engrossed in the five tiny kittens that she hadn't heard him come up the ladder. She met his peremptory gaze with all the bravado she could muster in the face of his indisputable advantage in size and strength. The Highland chief might be taller than most men, and he might be even stronger, but she wasn't going to let any MacLean intimidate a Macdonald.

"You may as well learn the truth now as later," she told him. "I finished moving my personal possessions out of your chamber after you left this morning. I'm going to be sleeping in another room tonight and every night forthwith, until you leave my castle."

MacLean smiled with that unflagging self-assurance she'd grown to know so well. "Joanna, lass," he said, his voice tinged with amusement, "your predictability never ceases to amaze me. A good commander doesn't signal his moves to his enemy before the battle."

She'd been about to inform the imperious chief of Clan MacLean that she was going to sue for an annulment on the grounds that their two-day marriage hadn't been consummated—and never would be. At his words, she snapped her mouth shut so fast, she bit the tip of her tongue.

"Ouch," she cried, wincing in pain as she pressed her fingertips to her lips. She glared up at him as though it were his fault.

MacLean crouched down beside her. "Did you bite your tongue, sweetheart?" he asked sympathetically. "Let me see." He cupped her chin in his long fingers and gently tilted her face upward.

Tears welling in her eyes, Joanna tried unsuccessfully to push his hand away. "Since you're neither a barber-surgeon nor an apothecary, I don't see how 'twould help."

He bent his head and brushed his lips lightly across hers, and the tenderness of his touch made her skin prickle with goose bumps. "Show me, little wife," he coaxed in his low, velvety baritone. "I'll kiss it and make it better."

"Humph," she said with a derisive sniff. "If you want to make things better, you can stop interfering with my plans to entertain our guests. Everyone was looking forward to the auction until you ruined everything by canceling it."

MacLean dropped down in the hay beside her with a chuckle. " 'Tisn't considered good manners to invite guests into your home and then try to lighten their purses by offering your plates and linens to the highest bidder.''

She gazed at him pensively. "I hadn't thought about linens," she confessed. "Thanks to you, we must now stage an elaborate masque, so people won't be too disappointed. I've also asked Fergus MacQuisten to sing after this evening's supper. Do you think you could write another romantic ballad, this time in honor of Beatrix? 'Twould please her greatly and make up for the canceled sale.''

MacLean stretched out his long legs and propped himself on one elbow. Even in his relaxed position, an aura of power radiated from the body lying so close beside her. Stories of his valor on the battlefield were legendary, and peering at him from the corner of her eye, Joanna had no doubt of their veracity.

A lazy smile played about his lips as he stroked one of the tumbling kittens, which had crawled out of Joanna's lap and was playing with bits of hay. The black kitty wrapped its tiny paws around MacLean's forefinger and nipped the callused tip, and Joanna was forcefully reminded of her own vulnerability. MacLean had snatched the loaded crossbow from her with no more effort than it'd take to discipline a wayward child or brush aside a naughty kitten.

"I'm afraid I'll have to refuse your request," he said.

Baffled, she tore her gaze from his large, capable hand to meet his eyes, gleaming with amusement. She'd completely lost her train of thought. "What . . . what request?''

"For me to compose another ballad. 'Twould be impossible. Lady Beatrix just doesn't bring out the ardent lover in me. Fergus will have to offer music of his own composing tonight. What is the theme of your pageant, by the way? Maybe I can make up for my interference by assisting with that.''

"The Greek underworld," Joanna replied brightly, ready to knock some of that excessive overconfidence he wore like a crown into the dust.

He cocked an eyebrow at her. " 'Tis a strange choice for guests invited to celebrate a wedding.''

"I thought 'twas rather appropriate," Joanna stated.

"Persephone being carried off to the land of the dead and ravished by Hades." She cuddled the kitten under her chin and sent MacLean an ingratiating smile. "You can be Hades."

"The god of the underworld," he said with a quick laugh. "Is that how you see me? And are you to be Persephone?"

At the soft rumble of masculine laughter, Joanna felt a tingling sensation that tightened her scalp and set her insides vibrating. She fought the sudden urge to jump to her feet and race to the ladder and safety. Shaking her head, she started to edge away—slowly, so he wouldn't notice and reach out to stop her.

"Idoine will take the part of the goddess," she replied. "I'm to be Pan."

Rory fought the compelling urge to touch her, to bury his fingers in her thick coppery curls and kiss her until she gasped for breath and begged for his caresses. Instead he lay back against the pile of loose hay and tucked one hand behind his head. "Now why doesn't that surprise me?" he asked.

With supreme effort, he kept his gaze from drifting over his wife's slender waist and softly rounded curves, well aware that she was a hair's breadth from bolting. "In any case," he continued, "I prefer to be a spectator rather than a player in your little pageant. You can give the role of Persephone's ravisher to Andrew. 'Twill do the youth good to exhibit a bit of wholesome lust."

"Andrew's too young and inexperienced for the part," she replied. "If you won't do it, I'll ask Tam."

"Tam has other duties to attend to this afternoon." Rory smiled, softening his refusal. "Why not ask Fearchar? If any man can throw Idoine over his shoulder and carry her off, 'tis my giant cousin."

Joanna considered the suggestion for a moment and then nodded. She released the spotted kitten to play with the others, while she studied Rory from under her lashes.

"How did you know I was up here in the loft?" she asked. "Were you following me?"

"I saw you enter the stables from the battlements and decided to join you," he told her, his tone amiable, his posture one of complete relaxation.

When he'd seen her slip into the building, he'd suspected that Joanna planned to take Bebind for a solitary ride. He had no intention of allowing her to leave the castle without a MacLean escort.

From beneath lowered lids, he studied the fine-boned face, its faint sprinkling of nutmeg illuminated by the shaft of sunlight streaming through the stable's high western window. Her thick lashes fluttered as she cautiously peeked at him. Doubt and wariness clouded her violet-blue eyes.

Rory tucked his other hand behind his head as well, telling her without words that she was free to leave, if she chose.

Joanna shifted restlessly. Finally, she turned toward him, her low voice filled with hesitation. "You're not angry with me?"

"About what?"

His question caught her by surprise. He could all but see the windmills whirring. She didn't want to remind him of last night's confrontation or the part that her idiot cousin had played in loading the crossbow for her. Nor was it the moment for him to apologize for calling her parents vile names. The wounds were too fresh and too painful.

"About my sleeping in a separate chamber," she replied with a lift of her chin.

"We'll discuss that later this evening," he said blandly. "Tell me more about your pageant. What will you wear as Pan?"

"A short toga," she said, breaking into a shy smile. Her freckled nose wrinkled with a pixie's irreverent humor. "And a wreath of ivy in my hair, which will be pinned up like a boy's."

Rory gave a mock shudder. "Not under that hideous stocking cap, I hope."

She laughed, and the deep, husky sound of her contralto made his breath catch in his throat. " 'Twasn't as ugly as all that," she protested with a giggle.

He grimaced as though in excruciating pain, encouraging her lighthearted laughter. "Hell, I should have burned the damn thing days ago."

Her indigo eyes sparkling, she leaned over him with a teasing smile. "I would never have allowed you to destroy my favorite headdress, MacLean. Why, I'm thinking of having it trimmed with pearls to wear as a nightcap."

The thought of seeing Joanna in bed garments, pearl-trimmed or otherwise, brought a vision of the evening to come, when he would lift the flowing nightdress from her bare shoulders and cover her pale, slender body with his own. Rory's heart thundered and shook as a sharp, knife-edged longing sliced through him, bringing a hunger no man could deny.

"Kiss me, Joanna," he said softly.

Her eyes widened at his unexpected request. "I think not," she declared, as though he'd asked her to partake of poisoned wine.

"Ah, then, 'tis afraid of me you are."

"I am not!"

"I'll keep both hands clasped behind my head," he promised, his tone mild and soothing. "They'll stay right where they are now. You've nothing to fear."

" 'Tisn't that I'm afraid," she scoffed. Her cheeks grew rosy with indignation. " 'Tis simply that I've so much to do this afternoon, what with guests scattered from one end of the castle to the other, and all of them looking for relief from their boredom. I don't have time to kiss you or anyone else."

"Just one kiss, lass," he goaded, "to prove you're not afraid of me. Then you can go."

Joanna searched MacLean's mocking gaze, reading the certainty that she'd scurry away like a frightened wee mouse if he made so much as a move toward her.

Holy hosanna, she wasn't *afraid* of him.

She just didn't trust him.

"Macdonalds aren't cowards," she muttered.

He shrugged complacently. "If you say so, lass."

Joanna bent closer, glaring straight into his taunting green eyes. "I do."

He said nothing more, but the smile curving the corners of his sensual mouth dared her to prove it.

Bracing one hand on his solid chest, she dipped her head and brushed her lips across his in a brisk, feather-soft movement. "There," she stated with a jerk of her head as she straightened back up. "That proves I'm not afraid of you."

"It does?" he asked incredulously. "Is that what you Macdonalds call a kiss? That insignificant little peck?"

She leaned forward, propping her forearm on his chest. "Not everyone kisses like you do," she informed him righteously.

He raised his brows in bafflement. "Like I do?"

"You know what I mean . . . with your tongue."

"Everyone does, but Macdonalds," he replied with a jeering laugh. "Hell, I shouldn't be surprised that you don't know how to kiss properly. Your clansmen are known for their ineptitude, especially in the bedroom. 'Tis the gabble of the Scottish court."

She gasped at his effrontery. "I've never heard such a rumor!"

"You've spent a good part of your life in Cumberland, lass," he reminded her smugly. "Being part-English, you were shielded from what the rest of the world knows to be a fact. Sassenachs and Macdonalds have ice running through their veins." Rory made a slight move, as though to rise. "We might as well go, Joanna, if that insipid wee buss is the best you can do."

"Wait," she insisted, pressing her hands against his chest. " 'Tisn't true! Macdonalds can kiss as well as anyone. Better, I'm certain."

He grinned, the insufferable, conciliating look on his

sharp features more eloquent than words. "If you say so, lass."

"I don't have to say so!" she exclaimed. "I'll prove it."

MacLean shrugged indifferently in halfhearted permission for her to try.

Joanna clasped his bronzed, sea-weathered face in her hands and pressed her lips to his in a kiss so passionate, so fervid, so intensely provocative his toes would curl up in his fancy buckled brogues.

He failed to respond.

She pressed harder, tracing the tip of her tongue across the tight seam of his closed lips. When MacLean remained maddeningly impassive, she tapped his chin with her fingertips, urging him to open for her.

He reluctantly obliged.

Joanna touched his tongue with hers, timidly at first, but the shiver of expectation that went through her at the feel of his moist warmth erased all hesitation. Her entire body responded to the smell and touch of him in a sudden, wild tremor of longing. Angling her face across MacLean's, she smashed her open mouth against his and stroked his tongue with hers in mounting excitement.

The kiss went on and on, till her heart was hammering against her ribs and her pulse grew frantic. Finally Joanna started to pull away, then changed her mind. MacLean didn't seem nearly as stimulated as she felt. She didn't want to stop too soon. She had to make certain he never repeated such an idiotic rumor about the Macdonalds again. After this scorching kiss, Rory MacLean would never again accuse her of having ice in her veins.

"You could help by putting your arms around me," she whispered against his lips.

"Like this?" he asked softly.

"Like that."

Joanna resumed the kiss, delving into his mouth, as her fingers slid across the emerald earring and into his golden hair. Wondering frantically if he could feel her heart stammering and her body trembling in nervous agitation, she resolved to elicit some response from her dispassionate husband before breaking the kiss.

She slipped her arms around his neck and rubbed her breasts against his chest, for no other reason than it simply seemed like the best way to get his full and undivided co-operation. To her surprise, her breasts seemed to have grown fuller and heavier beneath her clothing. They shimmered with sensations as their peaks tightened and contracted.

The feel of Joanna's sweet, luscious curves moving against his hard body proved Rory's undoing. With a warning growl of male sexual intent, he pulled her slim form atop the full length of him, his hard-won control evaporating in the space of a moment. Cupping her buttocks, he rocked her slowly, lingeringly against his engorged sex, as he continued the searing kiss.

Panting, Joanna braced her hands on his shoulders and drew back, her innocent eyes enormous. "I-I should go," she insisted breathlessly. But in spite of her words, she lowered her head and kissed him once again.

Desire tightened every fiber in Rory's body. He rolled Joanna beneath him, careful to brace his weight on his forearms. He traced his open mouth along the curve of her jaw and down her neck, his heart leaping at the soft sound of her sigh. He kissed her silken breasts above the low, square neckline, then loosened the ties of her bodice and camisole and slid them downward. Heated blood raged through his veins as his gaze moved over her creamy perfection.

"My God, you're exquisite," he murmured. "I'm going to explore every delectable inch of you."

Her fingers trembling, Joanna removed the bodkin that pinned the corner of Rory's plaid to his shirt. She fumbled with the cords at his neck, then pulled the shirttails out from beneath his belt and slid her hands under the saffron material and across his bare chest. His muscles tightened and clenched at the feel of her graceful fingers skimming over his ravenous body.

"Take off your shirt," she implored, her voice husky with sexual arousal.

Rory yanked the garment over his head and tossed it aside. He smothered a groan as she buried her fingertips in the thick wiry hair on his chest, grazing his taut nipples, then leaned forward to place gentle kisses on his fevered flesh.

"Ah, lass," he murmured. Graphic images of what he intended to do with his innocent bride sent a spear of white-hot desire through his groin. The holy medal around his neck dangled between them as he bent his head and suckled her. She whimpered in pleasure, and he moved to lave the other rosy peak, breathing in deep, intoxicating drafts of her elusive scent.

His heart about to explode from the mind-numbing tension enforced on his body by his iron will, Rory drew the hem of her gown up to her gartered knees, then pressed one leg between her satiny thighs. She moved against him spontaneously, a low sob catching in her throat.

"Rory," she gasped. The husky, breathless sound of his name and the near-surrender it implied sent a thrill coursing through him. Beneath the thick wool of his plaid, his swollen manhood pulsed with need for her. Only her.

"Yield to me, Joanna," he whispered in her ear, tracing the delicate folds with his tongue. "I'll make it so good for you, lass."

Joanna squirmed and writhed beneath MacLean's weight, searching for something she didn't understand. An irresistible longing to press ever nearer made her open her legs wider and thrust up against him. She wanted him to caress her as he had before. She wanted to experience that convulsion of unbelievable pleasure. Clutching his massive shoulders, she looked up into his eyes, and the naked, undeniable hunger in his gaze lit a conflagration within her.

"Oh, Rory, I want . . . I need . . ."

A smile of unutterable tenderness curved his lips as he reached down to touch her—and stopped abruptly.

Joanna's heart skidded to a painful halt. She made a muffled sound of disappointment deep in her throat, then was silent as he pressed one fingertip to her lips in warning.

Male voices drifted up from below. A party of hunters, who'd left early that morning, had returned and were stabling their mounts. The hunt must have been a success, for the men called to one another in high spirits. She recognized Fearchar's deep, booming bass shouting a jest.

Before Joanna had time to react, MacLean deftly replaced her bodice and rearranged her gown. Pushing away from her, he reached for his shirt.

"You stay here," he whispered as he pulled the garment over his head and refastened the plaid across his shoulder. "I'll get the men out of the building and into the drill yard as quickly as possible. Once they're gone, you can leave with no one the wiser." His green eyes brilliant with an unmitigated joy, he removed a wisp of hay from her tangled curls. Then he smiled and gave her a slow, thorough kiss. "Come evening, we'll take up where we left off, Lady MacLean. In the meantime, I'm looking forward to seeing a wee, red-haired Pan dance around the great hall in her toga."

Stunned and speechless, Joanna watched MacLean disappear down the ladder. The men below seemed to pay no heed to his sudden appearance, and in a matter of minutes the stable grew quiet once again.

Her befuddled gaze drifted over the loft. In another pile of hay, Tabby calmly lay nursing her brood, unmoved by her mistress's near-total capitulation to her fierce warrior husband.

Joanna clapped her hand over her mouth to stifle an agonized moan. God above, she'd almost coupled with him of her own free will.

The Sea Dragon.

Her clan's mortal enemy.

The King's Avenger, who'd been responsible for the death of her grandfather. Who'd labeled her father a devil and her mother a witch.

Dear Lord, what had she been thinking!

She dropped back into the hay and covered her eyes with her forearm. God's truth, she hadn't been thinking at all. Even now, her traitorous body ached for his touch.

It no longer mattered if she moved her things to a separate chamber or if she slept in the same bed with him. What just happened here in the loft proved that MacLean could take her wherever and whenever he chose, and she would be his willing partner.

Ewen had been right. She was no match for the diabolical and cunning Highland warlord. She had to leave Kinlochleven tonight, or there'd never be a chance for an annulment.

Joanna scampered down the ladder and out of the stable in search of Clan Macdonald's commander. The scheme Ewen had proposed for her escape would have to put into effect tonight. She and Andrew could use the secret staircase and no one would be the wiser—until MacLean retired to his bedchamber that evening and, finding it empty, started a search for her.

The pageant of classical antiquity was received with thunderous approval by the Scottish court. King James and his courtiers joined in, playing the roles of Greek citizens in procession to the temple of Athena. Every bedsheet and tablecloth in the castle had been called into service to provide their costumes. Lachlan graciously agreed to be Zeus and Keir enacted the sky god's brother, Poseidon, while Lady Emma portrayed a stunning Aphrodite and Lady Beatrix was Hera.

To everyone's delight, Idoine made a convincing, if petulant, Persephone. And though Seumas, as Hades, couldn't carry the plump goddess off without help—Fearchar having refused unequivocally even to try—Kinlochleven's steward certainly looked the part in the pasteboard crown and scepter painted black.

The center of attention, however, was the wily Pan, who played a pipe and led the cavalcade through the keep, out to the upper bailey, and back to the great hall. Violet-blue eyes twinkling, the mischievous imp insisted on draping her husband with garlands of spring flowers for the role of Narcissus.

" 'Tis your own fault," she whispered, tucking a sprig of bluebells behind one of his ears, "for refusing to wear the toga I sent you."

Rory watched the frolicsome mummery with growing anticipation, which he was unable to conceal from his two sharp-eyed brothers. Since no one except the bride and groom knew the truth about their wedding night, however, there was no more than the usual number of ribald jests among the men that evening. A new husband's second night with his wife, after all, did call for some comment.

When at last the entertainment was over and he could make his excuses and go upstairs, Joanna was nowhere in sight. He wondered if she'd discovered that her things had been returned to their chamber.

Since their unplanned tryst in the stables that afternoon, Rory hadn't been able to snatch a moment alone with her. She'd blushed delightfully every time she'd turned her head to find his gaze on her during supper, but she hadn't added more than a few words to the conversation at the head table. Her shy reticence was unexpected, after she'd all but surrendered in his arms.

Rory smiled as he mounted the stairs, confident Joanna would be eagerly awaiting him in their large canopied bed. When he entered the room, the low chest sat in its usual place, and Joanna's trifles were scattered across the press cupboard and bed table—but his chamber stood deserted. His jaw clenched at her intransigent Macdonald stubbornness.

He left the bedchamber and strode along the third-floor passageway, opening and slamming doors as he went. His temper soared with each empty room he found.

At the end of the hallway, he entered the chamber in which Tam and Murdoch had discovered Joanna's possessions. The coverlet lay smooth and undisturbed on the bed—and there wasn't a trace of his missing bride.

Rory strode to the window and jerked opened the casement to search the grounds below. The sound of activity caught his attention. Five Observantine friars, their hoods pulled up to ward off the chill, guided their horses across the lower bailey to the barbican. A single Poor Clare rode in their midst, her head bowed and her veil concealing her face from the torchlight. The guards at the open gate spoke congenially to the group and then waved the party through.

The monks hadn't far to go; the Priory of St. Findoca lay close by. The chapel's square bell tower could be seen rising above the moonlit loch from the window where Rory stood. Still, it seemed strange that they hadn't waited until daylight.

As iron-shod hooves drummed on the planks of the drawbridge and faded into the night, a chilling comprehension explained the presence of the solitary nun. Dashing from the room, Rory hurried down the passageway to the top of the stairwell.

"Fearchar," he bellowed, then returned to his own bedchamber.

After the pounding he'd given Andrew the previous night, Rory hadn't even considered the possibility that the lad might be reckless enough to interfere a second time.

Given what he knew of the two young Macdonalds, he'd bet a chest of guineas that Joanna was the one who had engineered the entire scheme. She must have talked the downy-cheeked adolescent into helping her once again.

Hell and damnation. If Rory had immediately demanded his marital rights, instead of gallantly trying to coax Joanna into his bed, none of this would have happened. He sure as hell wasn't going to let it happen again.

Fearchar came racing through the door. "What's wrong?"

"Find Lachlan and Keir," Rory gritted. "Tell them to meet me in the stables at once."

Fearchar gave a quick nod. "Anything else?"

"I'm leaving you in charge of Kinlochleven," Rory told him, as he buckled on his sword belt and jammed his broadsword into its sheath. "See that every MacLean is armed and at his post immediately. Be prepared for a possible attempt by Ewen Macdonald to take over the castle."

"With the king in residence, that'd be high treason," Fearchar said with a scowl.

Rory snorted in disgust. "I wouldn't put any treachery past the Macdonalds." He checked his eighteen-inch dirk and adjusted the small knife concealed below his armpit. "Once I and my brothers have left, alert His Majesty and let him know what's happened."

Fearchar's gaze roved over the empty bedchamber. "Er . . . exactly what did happen?"

Rory grabbed his gloves and started for the door. "Unless I miss my guess," he said with cold fury, "my wife has just eloped with her idiot cousin."

Chapter 18

They found the friars near Rannoch Mill. Their bodies lay scattered across the grassy riverbank, where they'd stopped to water their horses. Fear gripping his entrails, Rory dismounted. He scanned the sprawled, dark lumps in the moonlight, counting frantically.

Four.

None of them, thank God, the Poor Clare.

He drew in a bracing draft of the night air and realized he'd stopped breathing. Christ Almighty, how many corpses had he alone been responsible for in ten years of warfare on land and sea? The sight of dead men had never twisted his guts into a knot before. He looked down at his shaking hands, encased in the fine leather gauntlets, and cursed softly.

Joanna had to be alive and well. He'd find her, and she'd be as impudent and saucy and exasperating as ever.

That's all that mattered.

"Over here!" Keir called from a patch of bracken fern. "This one's still alive." He crouched on the ground and lifted the friar's head in the crook of his arm.

Rory hurried over and dropped to one knee. Just as he'd expected, the injured man was no tonsured monk, but a Macdonald. "Where's Lady MacLean?" he demanded, his voice hoarse in his urgency.

The clansman stared at Rory through the glazed, sunken eyes of the mortally wounded. He'd been stabbed several times. Blood soaked the front of the priestly habit he wore and trickled from the corner of his mouth. He'd die eventually. But death wouldn't be quick, and it wouldn't be easy. His lids drifted shut as he started to slip into unconsciousness.

Rory grasped a handful of the thick wool at his throat and jerked him up roughly. "Goddammit, you bastard, where's my wife?"

The dying man's eyelids flickered, and for a brief second he seemed to recognize Rory. "They took Lady Joanna and Andrew," he said on a shallow breath, then coughed up more blood.

Rory shook him, refusing to allow the wretch to black out before he'd answered his questions. "Who? Who took them?"

"Brigands," the Macdonald answered on a gurgle of blood. "Caught us unawares. A dozen, maybe more."

After rolling the other three bodies over with the toe of his brogue and reaching down to feel for a pulse, Lachlan joined Rory and Keir. He shook his head, indicating the soldier before them was the only one left alive.

Rory released his hold on the robe and rose to his feet. "Put him out of his misery," he said.

Keir quickly and efficiently slit the fellow's throat, wiped his dirk on the coarse black wool, and returned it to its sheath.

"She's alive," Lachlan assured his older brother, compassion softening his perceptive gaze. "Those bodies are still warm. They can't be far away."

Taut with rage, Rory swung up into the saddle. He gathered the reins, calming Fraoch with a steadying pat, as he waited impatiently for Keir and Lachlan to mount.

"We'll follow the loch," he said. "Hopefully they've camped in the woods, not knowing we're close on their heels. In the moonlight, we might be able to spot their smoke above the trees."

The three brothers cantered their steeds across the new May grass, moving westward along the north bank of Loch

Leven, with the thick stands of birch and oak on the hillsides to their right.

Still dressed in the brown habit of a Poor Clare, Joanna sat with her back braced against an ancient oak, bound, gagged, and tied to the tree with a fat rope. Similarly trussed, Andrew watched her from across the campfire, his eyes stark with terror above the strip of linen that covered his mouth. He wore the black robe of an Observantine monk. Its hood had fallen back to reveal his shock of thick brown hair, disheveled and falling over his wide forehead.

Thirteen men lay about the campsite sleeping; two more stood guard along its periphery. They were broken men, with no clan of their own. Desperate brigands, who gave their allegiance to none but their fellow outcasts.

When they'd taken Joanna and Andrew prisoner, their leader, a thickset man with the posture and build of a soldier, had assured her they'd not be harmed. The religious disguises hadn't fooled him. He knew their identity, for he'd called them each by name. She assumed they were to be held until Ewen paid for their release with bags of gold from Kinlochleven's coffers.

In answer to Joanna's heartfelt prayers to every saint she could remember, not one of the men tried to molest her. Aside from binding her tightly to prevent her escape, they'd treated her with polite deference.

She leaned her head against the trunk's rough bark and closed her eyes. Her wrists and ankles ached from the snug cords; her body felt stiff and sore from being anchored to the tree. To make matters worse, the itchy wool robe had raised welts on her shoulders and arms, and the linen wimple chafed her neck and chin.

Tears trickled from beneath her lowered lids. The past two nights should have been the most wonderful nights in her life. The kind of nights every young maiden dreamed of and longed for with such hopeful anticipation. The tales of Tristram and Isolde, of Fraoch and Mai, of Launcelot and Guinevere had entranced her as a child. She'd envisioned a romantic bower, a breathless meeting of two souls destined to love each other for eternity, and nights of courtly, tender passion.

The thought of what had actually happened made her half-sick.

After she'd threatened him with the crossbow, MacLean had stormed from their bedchamber, leaving her to cry herself to sleep in heartbroken misery. Who'd ever heard of a bridegroom leaving his bride alone in their bed on their wedding night?

In all the tales of knights and ladies she'd ever read, all the stories of Celtic heroes and heroines she'd ever been told, Joanna had never heard of such a spiteful, ill-mannered, contemptible thing. God's truth, she'd never forgive him.

And that very afternoon, he'd nearly succeeded in seducing her in the hayloft like a foolish, pea-brained dairymaid. Even now, her cheeks burned with humiliation.

Tied to the oak for the last three hours, she'd had more than enough time to review the events of the past two days. Her only excuse for accepting the kisses and fondling of that depraved fiend was that she'd suffered from a transient bout of lunacy. How else could she explain her willingness, eagerness even, to have him touch her so intimately? God-sakes, she hated him!

She had to hate him.

He was a MacLean, and she was a Macdonald.

She had no choice but to hate him.

And to seek an annulment.

When the permission came from Rome, she'd follow her clan's wishes and marry Andrew.

That consoling thought should have fortified Joanna's resolve. It should have made her eager to escape from the brigands' clutches. Yet some strange, pathetic voice inside her beleaguered brain reasoned that, during the time she was being held for ransom, neither the annulment of her vows nor the marriage to her handsome cousin could take place. And for some strange, pathetic reason, that fact held more consolation than her inevitable rescue.

A rustle of movement stirred in the trees near Joanna, disrupting her unhappy musings. She opened her eyes, expecting to see some small forest creature skulking about the edge of the encampment.

What she saw brought her thundering heart to a standstill.

Not ten paces away, one of the sentries crumpled slowly and noiselessly to the ground. She caught the flash of a blade in the moonlight as the shadowy figure that lowered the inert body to the grass withdrew his dirk from just below the dead man's rib cage. She knew the man was dead. Nothing but a corpse would lie that still.

Not a second later, the sentinel on the far side of the camp gave a strangled grunt and fell at Andrew's feet, his throat slashed by another intruder. Blood spattered across the lad's dusty brogues and checkered short hose. In the firelight, Andrew's eyes widened in shock, then turned to seek Joanna's steadying gaze. There was nothing either of them could do but watch the carnage that followed.

With broadsword in his right hand and dirk in his left, Rory nudged the man sleeping closest to Joanna. The heavy-set brigand scrambled to his feet with a shout of alarm, and Rory buried his sword in the man's thick chest.

Lachlan scattered the brigands' horses, sending them galloping through the surrounding woods. Then he joined his two brothers in the fray, slashing at his adversaries with blades in both hands.

Rory caught the next bandit, rushing at him from behind, sword upraised, with a downward thrust of his dirk. Pivoting to meet his third attacker, he sliced across the burly fellow's solid torso in a vicious upward blow.

Rory glanced around the clearing. Lachlan and Keir had dispatched two brigands each. In less than four minutes, the brothers had killed nine men, including the sentries. Not one of his wife's abductors would remain alive.

So terrified she could scarcely breathe, Joanna watched

her rescuers slay the remaining outlaws—who'd been trapped in the center of the camp—in a merciless display of close-quarter fighting that made her blood run cold.

With an almost casual elegance, Rory, Lachlan, and Keir each brought down two men at a time, one foe with the broadsword, the other with the dirk. In seconds there was no one left to kill. Keir and Lachlan paused, bloodied weapons in their lowered hands, and looked at one another with expressions of exhilaration.

Godsakes, they'd enjoyed it!

"Maybe we should have let one of the bastards live long enough to answer some questions," Lachlan said jovially, his breathing smooth and regular. His black bonnet, with the two chief's feathers, hadn't even been dislodged from his reddish-brown hair.

"What for?" MacLean asked. He wiped both blades on the clothing of one of his victims and then sheathed his sword. Stepping lithely over the littered corpses, he moved in Joanna's direction.

"We already knew they were guilty," Keir said with a grin as he methodically cleaned his weapons. "Why waste our time or theirs?"

Her mouth dry with fear, Joanna watched her husband advance, dirk in hand. Unlike his two brothers, MacLean wasn't smiling. The sharp swing of his plaid as he strode across the bloodstained grass gave clear warning that he wasn't very pleased with his bride at the moment.

The unmitigated fury blazing in his eyes now made his past anger seem like mere disgruntlement, and the ferocity emanating from his large frame reminded her of all the reasons he'd become known throughout Scotland as the King's Avenger.

He'd just killed seven men in as many minutes, and from the squared set of his jaw, he looked ready to murder her. He would become an exceedingly wealthy widower if he did, with only his two bloodthirsty siblings as witnesses to the truth. How capable was he of resisting such temptation?

She pressed back against the solid trunk, trying to widen

the distance, if only infinitesimally, between her and her furious husband.

"Mmph," she warned him through her gag.

He didn't bother to answer. He severed the thick rope that bound her to the tree with his dirk and then cut the bonds at her ankles. Grabbing the cord that tied her wrists, he looped the doubled length of the rope through it and yanked her to her feet.

The Poor Clare habit had belonged to a much taller woman, and Joanna tripped over its sagging hem.

"Tamph omph thh gah," she pleaded, stumbling awkwardly against him. She clutched the brown wool garment in her tied hands and lifted it scant inches off the ground.

MacLean ignored her. Holding the rope in one hand, he led her like a haltered cow on its way to market toward the three horses that Lachlan had brought into the small clearing. In the meantime, Keir had released Andrew and removed his bonds.

The lad immediately tore the cloth from his mouth. "Th-they came up fr-from be-behind us," he stuttered, looking wildly from one brother to the other. "W-we didn't have a ch-chance."

The trio of grim-faced warriors towered over him. They were liberally splattered with blood—none of which was their own. Next to the tall lairds—all three in their twenties, and all three with magnificent physiques—the spoiled adolescent's immaturity became painfully apparent, even to himself.

Keir's scornful gaze skewered the frightened lad, and he shook his head in disgust. "You wouldn't have had a chance, you jelly-footed gowk, if the Angel Gabriel had blown his trumpet to announce their arrival."

Joanna tried to bring her hands up to her mouth to pull away the gag, but MacLean refused to allow it. By the simple expedient of holding on to the rope, he kept her arms securely anchored below her waist.

"Lemph mph goph!" she said, trying to jerk free.

He didn't bother to look around.

"What shall we do with the laddie?" Lachlan asked his older brother in a bored tone. His green-eyed gaze paused for a moment on Joanna, and she could have sworn he was choking back laughter.

"I say we geld him here and now," Keir suggested with a corsair's grin. " 'Twill be the last time he tries to steal another man's wife."

Andrew's face turned as white as curds. Clearly nauseated by the conversation, he clamped one hand over his mouth. He looked at his cousin beseechingly. "J-Joanna," he gasped through his cupped fingers. "T-tell th-them it-it wasn't m-my idea!"

"Doph hmph hiph!" she pleaded.

Her husband's icy gaze flicked over her, his tacit warning more effective than the gag. She didn't say another word.

"Take the boy to Mingarry Castle," MacLean told Lachlan. "Keir can ride back to Kinlochleven and tell his father what's happened. We'll leave it to Ewen to talk his son's way back into the king's good graces. Maybe he can save the damnfool idiot from hanging for treason."

Keir held the point of his dirk to Andrew's smooth cheek. "Why don't I carve up these fine, fair features a wee bit?" he offered gleefully. "Just enough to keep the lassies from drooling all over him."

MacLean paused, apparently considering his youngest brother's suggestion. Andrew bent over, retching in the grass at their feet. Joanna stepped toward him in sympathy, pulling the rope taut in her husband's strong fingers.

"Take the lad home, Lachlan," the chief of Clan MacLean said in a cold, clipped voice. "My wife and I are going to spend a little time alone together."

Lachlan mounted and pulled the miserable sixteen-year-old up behind him. "Come on, laddie," he said with an encouraging smile. "We'd best be going before my brother changes his mind, and you end up leaving some of your favorite body parts here on the grass."

Keir swung up on his chestnut. In the firelight, his emerald gaze twinkled as he touched his blue bonnet in a polite salute. "Lady MacLean."

Joanna realized belatedly that he'd likely been jesting.

Godsakes, 'twas a jolly macabre sense of humor he had!

Without another word, the two brothers rode into the trees, taking her grateful and very relieved cousin with them.

"Wamph!" she called to their backs. "Domph goh!"

Joanna stopped short, suddenly and painfully aware of her circumstances. Alone in the woods with her irate husband, hands tied, mouth gagged, and surrounded by the hacked, mangled corpses of fifteen men, nearly half of whom he'd killed unaided, she felt her body grow clammy beneath the coarse wool habit. The pleated linen wimple felt like a noose around her neck.

Hauling on her bonds, MacLean brought Joanna to him, inch by terrifying inch. His sharp-featured visage, cold and implacable, never seemed so menacing. His contemptuous sea-dragon's gaze moved over the nun's garb with insulting deliberation.

Joanna dug in her heels and tried to resist the inevitable.

With a grimace of irritation, he brought her nearer, till she could feel his warm breath floating across her upturned face. Their hostile gazes locked in wordless communion.

She wanted to look away, but couldn't. Determined not to cringe, even if he raised his hand to her, she braced her shoulders and stiffened her spine.

"I can see you like to play games," he said, his low baritone vibrant with an unholy humor. "First you impersonate a stable boy, then you're an archer; this evening you pretended to be Pan, and now you're masquerading as a nun. What kind of game shall we play next, wife? Captor and captive? We might both find that one entertaining. I know I would."

"Stomph imph," she pleaded.

He bent closer still until they were nose to nose. "I have to warn you, though," he added, almost gently, "I like my sport rough."

He caught her by the waist, lifted her up, and tossed her over Fraoch's withers. She landed on her stomach with a muffled scream.

Then MacLean climbed into the saddle, kicked the black stallion's flanks, and the spirited horse took off at a gallop.

Chapter 19

The monstrous, diabolical, green-eyed avenger left Joanna dangling over his horse like a sack of barley while she screamed and howled bloody murder through the strip of linen covering her mouth. Finally, exhausted, she gave up and concentrated solely on breathing, as the jolting ride drove the breath from her lungs and the blood rushed to her head.

After what seemed like eternity but was probably only a few minutes, he stopped beside a frothing burn, where he could splash the blood from his face and hands. First, though, he cut the cord binding her wrists. Joanna jerked at the tight gag over her mouth and then fumbled in frustration with the knot behind her neck. With a harsh exhalation of air, MacLean pushed her hands away and sliced the fabric with his dirk.

She had tried vainly to speak to him and been ruthlessly ignored. Now that Joanna could harangue her odious husband, as he so well deserved, she refused to say a word. Not a syllable. Not so much as a peep.

MacLean took her icy silence in stride. He pulled a silver flask from his saddlebag. "Here," he said mildly, "this will help."

Joanna turned her back on him in uncompromising disdain. Suddenly dizzy and sick to her stomach, she leaned her arm against Fraoch's saddle and rested her forehead on her scratchy wool sleeve. She ached in every muscle. Her throat felt parched, and a blinding headache pounded in her temples. "I just need some water," she whispered hoarsely.

"Take a sip of this first, Joanna," he said. "Then we'll drink from the stream." The quiet authority in his voice left no doubt that she'd either drink it willingly or have the liquid poured down her throat.

Without looking around, Joanna reached back, took the flask, tipped and swallowed. The fiery potation burned all the way to her stomach. "Achh!" she croaked. She whirled to face him, grimacing in distaste. "What *is* that putrid concoction?"

MacLean smiled unpleasantly. "Aqua vitae. The water of life." He motioned toward the flask. "Now take a wee bit more. 'Twill fortify you for the ride ahead."

Unwilling to have him force the scalding spirits down her, Joanna gingerly lifted the small metal vessel to her numb lips. Thankfully, her mouth and throat were numb as well. A warm, soothing glow spread through her belly, and she sighed gratefully.

MacLean took the flask and swallowed, once, twice, three times, draining it. Then they both crouched at the edge of the burn, drinking the cold snow melt in their cupped hands, after which he filled the flask with fresh water and returned it to his saddlebag. He withdrew a piece of mutton pie wrapped in a square of white linen, and they shared it in hostile silence.

Mounting, he reached down and, without so much as a "by-your-leave, milady," lifted her up in front of him. Seated sideways, she clutched his arm to keep her balance as Fraoch bounded forward. But she didn't complain. 'Twas better than being planked across the stallion's withers on her stomach.

Joanna sat straight and stiff, making every effort not to touch her large husband. An impossible feat, of course, for he'd wrapped his sinewy arms loosely around her, holding the reins in one hand, the other resting lightly on her hip. Heavy silence bristled between them.

A chilly drizzle started about daybreak, a fitting end to

the disastrous night. Rory pulled an extra plaid from the roll behind his saddle and threw it around his broad shoulders. Joanna refused to shelter beneath the black and green tartan, since that would require snuggling against him. Her brown wool habit soon became soaked, right through to her freezing skin, but she rode upright as a pikeman, her pride intact.

"Joanna," Rory called softly. She'd been sleeping for the past few hours, cuddled like a newborn kitten against his chest. "Joanna, wake up—we're here."

She wiggled closer to him, her head buried beneath the plaid that hung around his shoulders. The feel of her lithe form, nestled delightfully between his thighs, brought a reluctant smile.

In spite of the cold rain and long hours in the saddle with little food, he'd learned 'twas damn hard to stay angry with your wife when every movement she made reminded you that her soft curves were fashioned especially for your hard, angular male body. Even the drenched nun's habit couldn't hide her tantalizing femininity.

"Joanna," he repeated insistently.

She stirred, rubbing her eyes, then hurriedly sat up. "I . . . I must have dozed off for a few minutes," she admitted with a dismayed glance at him.

Try a few hours, lass. "Look ahead," he told her.

Through the steady rainfall, Archnacarry Manor rose up from the heathered hills. The keep was nestled in a glen, with the rocky peak of Sgoran Fhuarain looming in the background. As a youth, Rory had been brought to the tower house to be fostered by Gideon Cameron and his first wife.

"Where are we?" Joanna asked in a panicked tone. She clutched his forearm, her fingers twisting the damp material of his jacket sleeve. "Where are you taking me?"

"We need to find shelter from the rain," he told her. "You can't stay out in this wet another night."

Joanna stared with misgiving at the gray stone building

with its four flanking towers. The ground floor was a primitive square keep, but the upper part blossomed into a castellated skyline of gables, turrets, and dormers. " 'Tisn't a Macdonald keep,'' she said suspiciously as they rode into the yard. "I don't know these people.''

His arm about her waist, he pulled her tighter and bent his head. "You're right,'' he replied, his mouth close to the ear hidden beneath the wimple and veil. " 'Tis in our neighbors' territory we are, lass. A man with a Macdonald wife needs all the allies he can get, so behave yourself, Joanna, or you'll be regretting it.''

The steward led them into the hall, where the owners, having been told of their unexpected and uninvited guests' arrival, waited in front of a roaring fire to greet them.

A personable laird in his early thirties met Joanna's worried eyes and smiled in welcome. Of average height, he possessed a lean, well-muscled frame and an air of polite introspection. His light brown hair curled over his collar, and his hazel eyes watched their approach with a scholar's detached curiosity.

Beside him, a gorgeous creature with rose-gold hair and skin as pale as cream tilted her head inquiringly. Her eyes widened at the sight of the soggy brown habit, the dripping black veil, and the soaked, wrinkled wimple, then turned their gaze on the pitiful nun's escort with mild censure. But not before Joanna had read the compassion for her shivering female visitor in the woman's sky-blue eyes.

MacLean took Joanna's elbow and led her up to the couple.

"Oh, dear lady, for God's sake, please save me!'' Joanna cried shrilly. She flung herself down on her knees before the startled woman and lifted her folded hands beseechingly. "I'm a traveling Poor Clare on a pilgrimage to St. Findoca's shrine. I've been abducted by the wicked, salacious, perverted Sea Dragon, whose intentions can only be of the most vile.''

"Shame on you,'' the beautiful woman scolded the Sea Dragon. She lifted Joanna up and gathered her in her arms, ignoring the fact that her caller was a sodden mess and had just created a string of puddles on her newly swept floor.

The lady smelled of lilacs and gingerbread. "How long have you been traveling in this weather, my dear?" she asked kindly.

"All night and all day," Joanna complained, "and I've had scarcely a morsel to eat since last evening's supper. That horrible brute forced me to drink raw spirits. He was hoping to get me drunk so he could have his way with a pure and penniless pilgrim."

The woman patted Joanna's cheek, a gentle smile on her lips. "Well, no one will force you to drink raw spirits while you're under my roof. That much I can assure you."

MacLean smiled down at Joanna, then addressed the surprised pair. "My companion likes to play dress-up," he told them, his wicked, salacious, perverted eyes glittering with mirth. "Today she's a postulant; tomorrow, who knows? Perhaps a gypsy, who'll tell your fortune for a penny, or maybe a minstrel, who'll sing and play the lute to your endless delight."

"Oh, I'm not a postulant, dear lady," Joanna told her with utmost sincerity. "I've already taken my vows. I took them two days ago." She peeked at her husband from the safe haven she'd found, daring him to call her a liar, for that much had been the Gospel truth.

Rory folded his hands behind his back. "She's said her vows, right enough," he cheerfully agreed. "Only they weren't the vows of poverty and chastity. Obedience, however, was certainly one of them, and I intend to hold her to it." He grinned at them and continued. "Alex and Nina, I'd like you to meet my wife. Lady Joanna, may I present Laird Alexander and his good-sister, Lady Nina."

Instead of throwing MacLean out on his dragon-tailed behind, as Joanna had hoped, Laird Alexander welcomed them with a smile of delight.

"You've arrived just in time for the evening meal," the amiable laird said. "Nina can help Lady MacLean change into something dry, while I find Rory a shirt and plaid.

We'll join you ladies in the upper hall in, say, half an hour?''

Lady Nina guided Joanna toward the door, one arm solicitously around her waist.

"Oh, dearest lady," Joanna said with a piteous sob, "you mustn't believe a word that man says. We're not really married. You mustn't let that depraved fiend touch me again."

The rich timbre of Rory's laughter boomed in the cavernous chamber. "Christ," he said to Laird Alex, "I should let her feel the stinging touch of my palm on her bum. Then maybe she wouldn't always be spouting such bilge."

Straightening indignantly, Joanna drew a sharp breath at his mocking words, but refused to look back at him. He was simply too churlish and vulgar.

Lady Nina gave her an affectionate squeeze. "Everything will seem better in the morning when you're rested, Lady MacLean," she said sweetly.

The steward showed Rory's wife to their bedchamber immediately following supper. Not that Joanna realized it was *their* bedchamber, or they'd have heard her screaming like a crofter's wife who'd been cheated by a tinker peddling shoddy wares.

Knowing how tired his bride was, Rory stayed up late into the night, talking with his two trusted friends. Only three years older, the present Cameron laird had befriended Rory the day he'd arrived to be fostered by Alex's older brother. Gideon, a wise and good man, had taught Rory more than just skill with weapons.

Gideon's first wife had died fourteen years ago, and the former laird married the lovely Nina MacVicker. Though much younger than her husband, Gideon's second wife loved him even more than his first. His tragic and untimely death had lain like the stark gloom of Lent over Archnacarry Manor for the last two years.

'Twas good to hear the Camerons laugh. Alex and Nina listened to the account of Rory's courtship and wedding and dissolved into gales of mirth. The tale of how he'd caught Joanna, dressed as a serving lad, peeking at Tam and the dairymaid in the stables had tears running down Nina's cheeks. Even the story of the loaded crossbow aimed at the stunned, unsuspecting bridegroom appealed to their sense of humor.

Retelling it, Rory admitted to his host and hostess that had the incredible wedding night happened to Lachlan or Keir, rather than himself, he'd be roaring with laughter, too.

But on parting in the corridor, before the three friends made their way to their separate rooms, Nina held up her taper to illuminate their faces.

"You know," she said quite soberly, "if I hear so much as a single female scream coming from your chamber, I'll come in there—wedding vows or no."

He grinned. "And if you hear a male voice calling for help?"

" 'Tis a big, strapping laddie you are, milord," she replied, her eyes warm with amusement. "You can consider yourself entirely on your own tonight."

"The first thing I intend to do," he said with a chuckle, "is check beneath the bed for a weapon. You do keep your loaded hackbuts under lock and key, I hope."

"We do," Nina said as she moved away. "Oh, and Rory," she added softly, "congratulations."

The next morning, Rory leaned against the bed's high walnut headboard and waited patiently for Joanna to awaken. She'd been so exhausted last evening, she'd probably fallen asleep the minute she laid her head on the pillow.

She hadn't wakened when he'd slipped under the covers sometime after midnight. It obviously hadn't occurred to the peacefully sleeping lassie that her husband would be joining her, for she lay sprawled on her back in the middle of the mattress, arms and legs outflung. He'd scooted her over to one side, and she promptly rolled back next to him.

The feel of her small form nestled against his naked body

had brought a swift, intense surge of lust. She stirred in her sleep, and the soft fold of her nightwear brushed across his rigid sex. The hard, insistent pulse of carnal desire spread like hot pitch through his abdomen and thighs. Rory had clenched his teeth and sworn silently in frustration. He turned his wife on her side, slipped one arm beneath her, and brought her softly rounded buttocks tight against his determined manhood. The full force of his need swept through him, and his big body shuddered like a ship foundering in a gale.

Only her obvious exhaustion at supper, when Joanna had nearly fallen asleep in her trencher, had kept Rory from removing the nightshift Nina had loaned her and waking his wife to the fervid caresses of his hands and mouth.

The unprecedented tenderness he felt for Joanna, in spite of everything she'd done to thwart and deceive him, had astonished and confounded him. He'd lain awake for hours, holding her in his arms and wondering how this impudent slip of a lass had succeeded in becoming such an important part of his life. He couldn't imagine living without her.

The rain continued in a steady downpour. With the pale morning light coming faintly through the drawn curtains, Rory listened to the raindrops beat against the window and gazed at his wife. Joanna lay on her stomach. Her delicate profile, with its dusting of ginger, was outlined against the white pillowcase. The profusion of curls, bright as newly struck pennies, spilled over her shoulders in lustrous disarray. He reached out and lazily wound the long strands around his finger, savoring their silken texture.

The thick, curving lashes fluttered, and she slowly opened her eyes. "What are you doing in my bed?" she whispered.

She remained perfectly still, as though too horrified to move, and stared at his bare skin. The bedclothes lay across Rory's belly, leaving everything above his waist in plain view. Her startled gaze eventually came to rest on the fire-breathing dragon wrapped around his right arm.

He grinned at her artless naïveté. " 'Tis my bed, too, Lady MacLean."

"Godsakes, you didn't sleep here all night!" she gasped.

"Usually a man sleeps in his bed," he replied, pausing meaningfully before adding, "among other things. But 'twasn't easy getting any sleep, what with being jabbed first by your elbow and then by your knee. I did get a few hours of rest. Most of the night, however, I just lay awake and listened to you snore."

"I don't snore."

"How would you know?"

Still on her stomach, Joanna cautiously raised herself up on her elbows and scowled at him. "Maude's never complained."

Rory leaned over and braced his hand on the other side of his wife, effectively trapping her in the crook of his arm. He bent to kiss her cheek, and she turned her head away. He buried his face in her disheveled hair and inhaled deeply.

"Who's complaining?" he murmured.

"I am," she said, her words muffled by the pillow. "You came to bed without your nightclothes again."

He laughed softly as he nuzzled the curve of her shoulder. Her shift smelled of lavender and woman. Sweet, adorable woman.

God, he enjoyed being so close to her. And he hadn't even undressed her yet.

"I didn't bring a nightshirt along," he said. "I left in such a hurry, I forgot to pack it."

"Then you're a barbarian," she muttered crossly. "Only barbarians leave home without their nightshirts."

"Ah, and I suppose 'tis your own nightshift, that you're wearing, Lady MacLean."

"Will you stop calling me that!"

" 'Tis your name, lass."

"Not for long," she snapped. "You tricked me into saying those vows."

Rory brushed her hair aside and pressed his mouth to the

pink shell of her ear. "You were caught in your own deception, Joanna," he said with a tender smile. "We're well and truly married."

He knew how confused she felt. Snared in a maze of conflicting emotions—emotions he couldn't understand himself, let alone express to his unwilling bride—he struggled to make some sense of the past two weeks.

He didn't believe in the romantic gibberish that lovers spouted to explain their silly infatuations and their clandestine affairs. The only thing he knew for certain was that he wanted Joanna in his bed, a willing and eager partner. Yet despite his overwhelming sexual desire for his wife, Rory couldn't ignore her tender feelings. He wanted their life together to begin with mutual trust and sincere regard.

"Joanna," he said quietly, "I'm sorry I called your mother and father those terrible names."

She rolled over to face him, her eyes huge and filled with gratitude. "Thank you for that," she said softly.

He dropped a chaste kiss on her brow, then pulled back to meet her eyes. A hint of tears brightened their violet-blue depths. "Say you'll forgive me."

Her bottom lip trembled. "I forgive you."

He gently brushed his lips across her flickering eyelids, her darling nose, her satiny cheeks. "Thank you for that," he whispered.

As he'd chased after Joanna and Andrew the previous night, Rory had had plenty of time to realize his second grievous error. Had he failed to catch up with Joanna before she reached Mingarry, her kinsmen could have declared the vows null and void on the grounds their marriage had never been consummated. He'd have immediately stormed their castle, but at a terrible loss of life on both sides. Not a harbinger of wedded bliss.

Rory knew, without being told, that Joanna didn't fancy herself in love with Andrew. When he'd caught up with them, there'd been no indication the two cousins were a pair of infatuated young lovers fleeing from the harsh dictates of the king. Dressed as a stable boy, she'd had over a week to attempt an escape from Kinlochleven. She hadn't bolted until someone told her of Rory's caustic denigration of her parents.

He'd bet his best Ferrara blade that the loudmouthed someone was Ewen. The Macdonald war commander had played on Joanna's loyalty to her clan and her love for her dead parents. Rory understood her feelings—but he wasn't going to make the same mistake twice.

He had no intention of allowing Joanna to leave their bed until he'd bound her to him in a knot that could never be unraveled. Not by her kinsmen. Not by an archbishop. Not even by the pope.

Chapter 20

~~~⌒⌒⌒~~~

Joanna knew she should jump out of bed that very instant, race to the door, and tear down the stairs in her borrowed shift and bare feet, calling for help all the way to the ground floor. But the knowledge that MacLean hadn't a stitch of clothing on his large, long-legged body sent a tingling sensation from the top of her head right down to her curling toes.

Oh, she fully intended to run from the room.

But not quite yet.

Later this morning, she'd inform her gentle hostess that until she left for Kinlochleven, she intended to sleep in her own *private* bedchamber or sit up all night, wide-awake, in their hall.

So since she'd never again lie beside MacLean, bare-arsed and splendid beneath the covers, this was Joanna's last chance to discover if what she'd been told as a bairn was indeed fact, or could be relegated to the realm of childhood fantasy. She had no intention of leaving the bed until she found out.

She met his heavy-lidded gaze and placed her hand on his arm in a gesture of friendship. "I didn't really intend to shoot you with that crossbow," she said sincerely. "I only wanted to learn the truth."

"I know."

Leaning on one elbow, he bent over her, and the ferocious, three-headed dragon on his upper arm seemed to stir

menacingly as his bicep flexed. But a fetching smile curved
Rory's mouth. His indolent gaze drifted over her hair and
face as he pulled on the narrow blue ribbon at her throat,
releasing the top bow of her nightshift.

Joanna studied his strong features, sharp as the blade of
a Lochaber ax. He'd removed the thong from his hair and
the smooth golden waves brushed against his shoulders.
She reached up and traced her fingers over his straight eyebrows, touched the precious jewel that glittered on his earlobe, then buried her fingertips in his thick hair.

"I hope you can find it in your heart to forgive me,"
she whispered.

"You're already forgiven."

She smiled tentatively, abashed that she'd dared to point
a loaded weapon at her formidable bridegroom. "Did I
frighten you terribly?"

His dazzling smile widened. He tugged on the ribbon of
the second bow, and Joanna frowned as her gaze dropped
to his long, capable fingers. She'd have to make her discovery soon or retreat without the answer she sought. And
God knew, she didn't want to do that!

"You certainly caught me by surprise, lass," he said in
a low, husky voice. "I had my thoughts on other things at
the time. I didn't hear you get out of bed, much less pick
up a weapon."

"What other things?"

"Things like this," he murmured, releasing the third
bow.

He leaned closer and covered her mouth with his. He
followed the line of her closed lips with the tip of his
tongue, coaxing her to open for him. When Joanna com-
plied his tongue plunged into her mouth, teasing and in-
structing, and she greeted his cajoling thrusts with
eagerness.

Setting aside her secret quest for the moment, Joanna slid
her arms around his neck and returned his kiss. His lips
were firm and purposeful, his tongue tantalizingly bold. Shy
and hesitant, she entered his mouth and found him avidly

awaiting her caresses. Slowly she explored his welcoming warmth, learning to give as well as to take.

Her husband broke the kiss to slide his parted lips along the curve of her neck, marking a path of flame with his tongue. She released a soft, quivery sigh as the heat spread beneath the lacy collar of her voluminous sleeping gown.

Taken unawares, Joanna opened her eyes, belatedly realizing that her nightshift gaped open from her throat all the way to her navel.

Godsakes, when had he untied the other three bows?

"Oh, my," she breathed. "I'm coming undone." She reached down to retie the ribbons, and he caught her hands in his.

Interlacing their fingers, Rory brought Joanna's hands up to the pillow and held them lightly on either side of her head. He scattered a shower of kisses down one edge of her gaping bodice and up the other.

Joanna's heart pattered to the beat of the rain on the window. "Rory," she said, unaccountably short of breath.

"Mm," he answered.

"I . . . I think we should wait and get better acquainted."

He chuckled softly as he nuzzled the embroidered material aside to reveal her pink crests. "We are getting better acquainted, lass."

Her breasts swayed gently beneath his kisses. Joanna released a long, drawn-out sigh at the marvelous feel of his warm, moist tongue sliding over first one nipple and then the other. As he licked the sensitive peaks into tight, wee buds, she fought to keep her mind on her goal.

She needed to learn the truth about the chief of Clan MacLean as quickly as possible, and then get her prying, inquisitive mind out of his bed, and her fascinated body along with it.

"You're becoming better acquainted with me," she pointed out in a shaky voice, "but I'm not becoming better acquainted with you."

"We'll take turns," he said huskily. "I'll go first."

He suckled her, and the exquisite pleasure caught Joanna

by surprise. Her indrawn breath hissing between her teeth, she arched her back, lifting her breasts higher in glorious response. A sensation of warmth spread through her belly, and with it came an urgency to draw closer to him. She felt an unaccountable frustration that the bedclothes still lay between their lower bodies, and she shifted her legs restlessly.

Rory released her hands to cup her breasts. "I intend to get intimately acquainted with every inch of your sweet little body, lass," he said, "and then I'll let you explore my big, hairy carcass to your heart's content." He flicked the callused pads of his thumbs over her taut peaks as he kissed her deeply.

Joanna knew she couldn't wait for her turn to explore—not if she wanted to leave the bed with her virginity intact.

Getting an annulment would depend on it.

And her clan was depending upon her.

Timidly, she ran her hands across his sun-bronzed arms and wide shoulders. The bulging muscles beneath her fingers had been cast in iron. There was nothing soft or yielding about him.

"Let's explore together," she whispered.

As he suckled her, Joanna slid her hands across his broad shoulder blades and down, down beneath the bedcovers, following the hard ridge of his spine to the curve of his lower back. Her heart pounding wildly, she smoothed her palms downward to the base of his tailbone, glided her fingers over his compact buttocks, and traced the cleft between with her exploring fingertips. She traced it once more, just to make certain.

Her feathering touch on his naked loins seemed to have a riveting effect on her husband, for he tensed and grew absolutely still beneath her curious inspection. Lifting his head from her breasts, he met her gaze in wonder.

"Joanna . . . darling . . . ," he said with a surprised little laugh. He brushed his mouth lightly across her lips. "You don't know what you're doing to me, lass."

Joanna giggled softly in relief and thanksgiving.

No dragon's tail—not the teeniest, tiniest trace of one!

"I'm learning about you," she told him happily as she clasped his lean flanks. Once again, she ran her palms across his bare bottom and smiled in satisfaction.

Too late, she realized that Rory had already flung off the coverlet. He caught the hem of her nightshift in his fingers and drew the loose, flowing gown over her head with practiced ease. Before she could attempt to cover herself, he captured her hands and leaned back on his haunches.

"My God, lass, you're bonny," he said, his voice a hoarse whisper as his gaze moved over her with leisurely, deliberate thoroughness.

"Holy heavens," she rasped.

At the sight of her husband's massive erection, Joanna knew she'd committed a major blunder. Her foolish, irrepressible curiosity had led her straight into the boiling caldron of unbridled male lust. She leaned on her elbows and tried to scoot away from him. She'd made some huge mistakes in the past, but this time Joanna Màiri Macdonald was really in trouble.

"If we don't get out of bed right this minute," she announced with a jaunty smile, "we're liable to miss breakfast." She jerked her fingers from his grasp and started to roll off the high mattress. "And 'tis starving I am."

"So am I," he said with a smothered laugh. He caught her by the waist and brought her up on her knees in front of him.

"Fine," she said, croaking like a frog. "Then we're both hungry." She braced her palms on his solid chest and leaned as far away from him as possible. "Let's go downstairs and get something to eat."

He imprisoned her hips in his strong hands. "There's nothing to be frightened of, Joanna," he said, his words low and silky smooth. "All we're going to do is get very well acquainted."

Unable to meet his gaze, Joanna lowered her lids and stared at the holy medal adorning his scarred, hairy chest. Her cheeks burned with embarrassment. She'd seen Tam and Mary in the stables, so she knew what her husband had in mind—he didn't mean a lengthy conversation about their favorite childhood games or the color of their first pony.

Her mouth suddenly dry, she swallowed with a noisy gulp. Tam wasn't as big as Rory, and the buxom dairymaid outweighed Joanna by a good three stone.

The words came out of her parched throat in a raspy whisper. "My cousin Ewen wants me to get an annulment."

"There'll be no annulment, Joanna," he said placidly.

Resting on his flanks, Rory leaned closer and laved her nipples. Shafts of pleasure shot through her, and she bit her bottom lip to smother a soft cry of delight. In spite of her determination to resist his erotic onslaught, her breasts grew firm and full beneath the persuasion of his adept, experienced mouth.

Joanna cleared her throat and tried again. "Ewen says I'm supposed to marry Andrew."

"Forget about Andrew," he told her with a growl. "I'm the only husband you'll ever have, lass."

He slid his hand between her bare thighs, and his fingers delved into her triangle of reddish-brown curls with seductive expertise. He played with her gently as he suckled her. A tremor ran through Joanna's tense limbs, awakening within her an unbelievable need to get closer, and closer still, to this powerful warrior who touched her with such heart-wrenching tenderness.

"Oh, my," she murmured.

He smiled and continued to taste and caress the most sensitive parts of her quivering body.

Joanna tried to recite the Macdonald clan motto in her head, but she could feel herself become moist and slick beneath his skillful manipulations. She moaned as the incredible pleasure pulsed through her secret places, trying desperately to concentrate on what she needed to tell MacLean before things went too far.

God's truth, she didn't want Rory to think her a wanton tease who'd give him license to fondle and then demand that he stop. The possibility that she might have gone too far already set her heart hammering.

"Ewen sent to Rome asking permission for me to marry my cousin," she said on a breathless sigh. "Maybe we should wait and see if it comes."

"We're not waiting," he told her. He slipped his finger inside her, and the feeling of fullness made her sob in pleasure.

"Rory . . ." she said in confusion. "I'm not sure . . ."

"Kiss me, Joanna." He covered her mouth with his in fierce possession. She slid her splayed fingers across his scarred chest, touching his tightened nipples as he had touched hers.

"God above, you're sweet," he murmured in her ear, continuing to stroke and fondle her.

Joanna lowered her head, burying her face in the curve of his throat. She breathed in the earthy male scent of him as she nuzzled his bare skin. Her fingers caught on the gold chain, and she clutched the holy medallion in a silent prayer to St. Columba.

Her whispered words were scarcely audible. "I think I'm too small."

She could feel his chuckle vibrate deep in his chest. "You let me worry about that," he said softly. "That's the bridegroom's responsibility."

"What's the bride's?"

"All you need do is enjoy it."

"Will I?"

"You will, Joanna. I promise."

Rory eased his wife down to the soft mattress and knelt between her slender legs. He crouched over her and kissed the swollen tips of her breasts. Her long russet lashes floated downward to rest on her silken cheeks. With consummate care, he opened her velvety petals, gently teasing the fragile tissues till Joanna writhed with pleasure.

The beauty of her, lying there before him, pale and slim, with the mass of coppery silk strands spread across the pillow and the nest of auburn curls at the juncture of her white thighs, struck a chord of tenderness within him that he'd never known existed. She belonged to him. To touch, and fondle, and caress. No man but Rory would ever know the loveliness of her naked body or the sensual passion glowing in her marvelous eyes.

"Touch me, Joanna," he urged.

Her lids fluttered open. When she shyly reached toward him, he took her hand and taught her how to stroke him. The sight of her dainty fingers on his turgid flesh rocked him with the full, primitive force of pagan lust. Rory clenched his teeth, the pleasure so great his need nearly overcame his will. His lungs constricted, and he grew embarrassingly short of breath—a hardened soldier of twenty-eight years brought to the point of surrender by his inexperienced wife's silken touch.

Rory bent over her, kissing Joanna with the unfettered joy of total possession. "I'm going to come into you now," he told her softly. "I'll be very gentle, darling." But despite his confident words, Rory's heart thundered in his chest. God, she was small.

Bit by bit, Rory edged his rigid sex into Joanna's honeyed warmth. He entered her as slowly and carefully as he could, but her tight sheath resisted his efforts to be gentle. Covered with a fine sheen of sweat, his great body shook with the effort to maintain control. He could sense her apprehension building.

He kissed her, his tongue stroking hers in silent encouragement. " 'Twill hurt a wee bit," he said thickly, "but only the first time, lass."

Holding her in place, he thrust deep inside her, tearing the virgin's membrane. Her surprised cry slashed across his heart. Her slender form grew tense and stiff beneath him.

He kissed her lowered lids, tasting the salty tears. "Ah, darling," he crooned, " 'tis sorry I am that I can't take the pain for you."

"Are we through?" she asked hopefully.

He smiled at her innocent candor. Considering his shortness of breath and his pounding heart, he felt as if he'd engaged in hand-to-hand combat wearing a full suit of armor. "Not yet, lass," he said. " 'Twas the difficult part, though, and 'tis over. Now the fine, fair, bonny part begins."

Rory pleasured his bride, worshipping her soft femininity with his hard male body. He built a slow, steady rhythm, watching the wondrous emotions play across her expressive features, as her curving lashes drifted downward to feather her cheeks. He lifted his engorged sex up inside her, increasing and sustaining her enjoyment. Knowing the uninhibited response she was capable of giving, he would settle for nothing less.

Tears started to trickle down Joanna's face, and Rory stopped in dread. His heart lurched and skidded against his breastbone. "Are you in pain, lass?" he asked, prepared to withdraw.

She opened her eyes and gazed up at him, a look of awe on her face. "There's no pain, Rory," she said in her husky contralto. "None at all. 'Tis only that it feels so . . . so . . ."

He renewed his rhythmic strokes. Smiling tenderly down at her, he urged thickly, "Tell me, darling. Tell me how it feels to have me deep inside you."

" 'Tis so very . . . very . . . wonderful . . ." She sighed as she smoothed her fingers across his chest, burying her nails in the thick mat of hair. " 'Tis so . . . very . . . marvelous . . . I couldn't keep the tears back."

He scooped her long hair aside and braced his forearms on either side of her head. "Wrap your legs around me, Joanna."

She followed his directions without hesitation. Her supple limbs clung to him as her vibrant muscles clenched around his male member, driving him wild with sexual excitement.

"We have as long as you need, lass," he assured her, keeping the cadence unhurried and constant. "Take all the time you want. Enjoy every movement, every tiny flicker of pleasure. There's more after that, and more again still."

Joanna brushed her open mouth over his shoulder and

upper arm, then nipped him with her sharp little teeth. Her breathing grew heavy and ragged. She tightened her arms and legs around him, trying to get closer and tighter, squeezing him in her uncontrollable passion.

"God in heaven, lass," he breathed, pure joy spearing through him. "You take my breath away."

"Oh, Rory . . . oh, Rory . . . oh, Rory . . ." she cried softly. Her slim body quivered and tightened in her fulfillment. He could feel the delicate tissues fluttering around his hard staff as she convulsed reflexively, once, twice, and then once again, before collapsing back on the pillow.

The thrill of her eager response ignited blazing sparks of sexual excitement within him. The seductive perfume of her female body assailed his battered senses, and Rory knew he could hold back no longer. He thrust into her tight passage, exploding in a climax so powerful that his large frame jerked and shuddered.

His heart thundering, his breath coming in great, raw gasps, Rory rolled onto his back, taking Joanna with him. She pushed up, her knees bent on either side of him, her forearms braced on his chest, and gazed at him with eyes filled with awe and wonder. Clearly dazed by what had just happened between them, she stared at him, speechless.

He bracketed her head in his hands, his fingers buried deep in her marvelous hair. "You are mine, Joanna," he said, his voice harsh with suppressed emotion. "Mine, and mine alone. I swear by God, I'll kill any man who tries to take you from me."

" 'Tis kind of you to join us in the kitchen, Lady MacLean," the black-haired lassie said politely. She stood beside the table, watching Joanna knead the floury dough. "Mama lets Cook make the cobblers and tarts, but only I get to help her with the gooseberry pies."

"Making gooseberry pie is one of my favorite pastimes," Joanna assured the thirteen-year-old. "And 'twas kind of you to loan me your gown." Joanna glanced down at the pale yellow wool to discover a green stain on the sleeve. "And look what I've done! I've ruined it!"

Lady Nina laughed as she moved the iron kettle from the smaller of the kitchen's two fireplaces, where the fruit mixture had been cooking, to the trestle table. "Don't fret about the gown," she said, her lovely face glowing rosily from the heat of the fire. " 'Tis one of Raine's oldest. She's growing so quickly, she won't be able to wear it much longer anyway. She'll soon be taller than I."

At the mention of her height, the girl's jet eyes grew serious. "Aunt Isabel said I'll be taller than Papa before I'm sixteen," she commented gravely.

Joanna glanced over at the lass, who stood across the table stirring the bubbling sauce with a large wooden spoon.

Raine was tall for her age, with a gangly frame that made her seem all thin arms and long legs. Unsure just where to put her hands and feet, she reminded Joanna of a newborn filly.

Lady Nina paused in her work momentarily to study her daughter from the corner of her eye. Then humming softly, she began to ladle the steaming fruit into the waiting pie shells as Joanna rolled out the pastry for the top crusts.

A huge white apron belonging to a kitchen maid had been wrapped twice around Joanna's small frame, and all their aprons were now liberally splattered with flour and gooseberry sauce.

Outside, the rain had turned to a light mist, and the warmth and cheeriness of the large kitchen lent a special camaraderie to their task.

Joanna had slept through the morning meal, coming downstairs only after everyone else had gone about his business. She'd learned that Laird Alex had asked Rory to look at a mare about to foal. The men had left for the stables immediately after breakfast.

Joanna's pulse quickened at the thought of her husband. After their impassioned joining when she'd first awakened at daybreak, Rory had held her in his arms, his nude body hard and unyielding beneath her softness. He'd taken her again and yet again, in a slow, lingering fashion, building up the wondrous excitement within her, till her response to his caresses had become wild and uncontrollable. She'd lost all sense of decorum and modesty, following his every whispered suggestion with a willingness that brought a flush to her cheeks. God's truth, she'd even scoured his back with her nails in the throes of her ecstasy.

What he thought about her uninhibited behavior, she didn't know. She'd fallen asleep atop him, spent and sated. When she'd awakened for the second time that morning, she'd been tucked snugly beneath the coverlet, her husband gone.

"So this is Somerled Macdonald's granddaughter," a cheerful soprano voice said from the doorway.

Pulled from her reverie, Joanna looked up from the flour-covered table to find a lady in a purple velvet gown and old-fashioned horned headdress regarding her merrily. Bits of oatmeal rested on her shoulders, sprinkled there to ward off the faeries, no doubt. A small pair of steel scissors, the greatest protection possible from the entire elfin race, dangled from a chain round her neck.

Joanna had been told at supper the previous evening that the laird's older sister was supping in her private parlor with her niece; and she assumed the newcomer was Lady Isabel.

In her late forties, fair-haired, average in height and squarely built, the woman favored Laird Alex to a striking degree, though an aura of otherworldliness seemed to hover about her. 'Twas possible the lady practiced white witch-craft.

"Come in, Isabel, and meet Laird MacLean's new bride," Nina said, continuing to spoon the bubbling mixture into the pie shells. "Joanna, this is my late husband's sister, Isabel."

Not waiting for Joanna to acknowledge the introduction, Isabel crossed the kitchen's stone floor to stand beside her niece at the table. "I can see the resemblance to Somer-led," she said pleasantly. "The extraordinary marigold hair and plum-colored eyes. 'Twould be hard to mistake you, even in a room full of redheaded Macdonalds.''

Joanna set the pastry roller down. ''You knew my grandfather, then,'' she said curiously.

Smiling benignly, Isabel paused to drop a kiss on her niece's temple, then met Joanna's intrigued gaze. Her hazel eyes glimmered with some unexplained mystery. ''So they haven't told you yet.''

Nina stopped her work and wiped her hands on the skirt of her apron. ''This isn't the time, Isabel, or the place—''

Isabel leaned forward and stated without a hint of rancor, ''Your grandfather was executed for murdering my brother.''

Chapter 21

A t her aunt's words, the wooden spoon Raine had been holding clattered to the floor. Her face drained of color, the girl raced out of the room.

"Raine!" Lady Nina called to her daughter, then met Joanna's horrified gaze. "I'm sorry, my dear," she said sadly. "I wanted Raine to get to know you first, before she learned you were the granddaughter of Somerled Macdonald."

Joanna stared at her in shock. "Your husband was . . ."

Lady Nina's eyes, the same brilliant cerulean blue as her gown, suddenly blurred with tears. Her pale brows pinched together as she nodded unhappily. "Gideon Cameron. The man your grandfather murdered."

"Grandpapa didn't murder your husband," Joanna said. "My grandfather would never have killed any man without just provocation."

"Gideon was struck from behind," Nina replied with quiet certainty. "No matter what the provocation, a true gentleman would never strike an unsuspecting man in the back."

Joanna's voice rose excitedly. "If Gideon was killed from behind by an unseen assailant, it proves Grandpapa didn't slay him. And because of your family's mistaken accusations, my grandfather was taken to Edinburgh and wrongly executed for a crime he didn't commit."

Rory and Alex came into the kitchen in time to hear her

last breathless statement. The two men, their hair and clothing damp from the rain, looked at her grimly. Standing near the doorway, they seemed to have brought the cold in with them, for the air grew frigid in spite of the crackling fire.

"You're wrong, Joanna," Rory said with clipped gravity. "We had unequivocal proof of the Red Wolf's guilt."

Furious that he would tell such a brazen lie about her grandpapa, she braced her floury hands on the trestle table and glared at him. "I don't believe it!"

Alex moved to stand beside Lady Nina. His placid eyes troubled, he put his arm around his good-sister's shoulders, offering her his support. "This is terribly painful for Nina," he said calmly, "but you should know the truth, Lady Joanna. Gideon's severed head was delivered to Archnacarry Manor wrapped in a tartan pinned with a Macdonald clan badge."

"That proves nothing!" she countered. "Many Macdonalds wear that badge. Someone could have stolen it."

Widening his stance, Rory folded his arms across the front of his saffron shirt and lifted a brow sardonically. "That particular badge was accompanied with the written compliments of Somerled Macdonald."

Joanna ripped off her apron and threw it on top of the pastry dough. "You're lying!"

Isabel smiled, her hands folded in front of her in unruffled detachment. " 'Tis no lie, Joanna MacLean. On that very table, your husband and his two brothers swore an oath on Gideon's head to bring the Red Wolf of Glencoe to justice."

Shaking with fury, Joanna clenched her hands at her sides. Tears burned her eyes, but she refused to give in to such a humiliating weakness in front of her grandfather's enemies. She met their gazes straight on, determined to show them she had the backbone of a true Macdonald.

Then she turned to her husband and addressed him with brittle disdain. "I wish to go home to Kinlochleven."

Rory's jaw squared; his eyes turned frosty. "We'll return home when I say, Joanna, and not before."

At his harsh words, Nina glanced at Rory, then looked back at her trembling guest, her lovely eyes filled with sympathy. With her silky apricot hair and creamy complexion, she looked like a compassionate angel.

But Joanna Macdonald didn't need the woman's pity. She didn't need anything from the Camerons. She believed in her grandfather's innocence with every ounce of her being. In their haste to seek revenge, they'd caused the death of a blameless man. They were the ones who deserved to be pitied.

"Had I known how you felt about my grandfather," she said through stiff lips, "I would have slept by the roadside rather than enter your home."

Before anyone could say another word, Joanna spun on her heel and left the kitchen.

Instead of returning to the bedroom where MacLean might follow her, Joanna entered a large chamber on the second floor, its door having been left wide open. She hoped to avoid a confrontation with her husband until after she'd regained control of her emotions.

She hadn't the least shred of doubt that her grandfather had been guiltless of Gideon Cameron's death. She'd been allowed a brief visit with her grandpapa the day before he was hanged. He'd clasped her to him, reassuring her of his love.

"Darling of my heart," he'd said, using the familiar endearment for the last time, "I swear to you on your father's grave that I am innocent of the cold-blooded murder of Gideon Cameron."

Joanna brushed the tears away and looked about her. The room was in semidarkness. The heavy damask curtains on the tall windows had been drawn, allowing the gray morning light to filter in. But no candles had been lit.

A harp and a virginal stood in front of the windows, telling her she'd discovered the music room. Bookshelves and portraits graced the walls, as well as a tapestry depicting Hercules slaying a lion. Armchairs and small tables were scattered about the room, and a high-backed settle faced the hearth.

Joanna walked to the cold grate with the intention of kindling a small blaze. When she reached the fireplace, she found Raine curled up on the cushioned bench, her head resting on a pillow. Startled, the girl immediately sat up, her long braids swinging.

"I'm sorry," Joanna said. Her heart ached for the unhappy youngster, who was the one truly innocent victim among them. "I didn't realize you were in here. I'll go."

Raine put out a hand as though to stop her. "Please stay."

Joanna hesitated, not wanting to upset the girl more than she'd been already. "If you'd rather be alone, I quite understand."

The lass shook her head, her dark eyes solemn. "I wouldn't. I'd like you to stay. Honestly."

Joanna sank down on the tufted gold cushion beside her, wondering what she could possibly say to the pensive girl who'd been told, wrongly, that Joanna's grandpapa had murdered her father. Then she noticed the piece of gray stone that Raine clutched in her hand.

"What do you have?" she asked kindly. "May I see it?"

Raine immediately handed it to Joanna with a bashful shrug. " 'Tis a faery arrow."

Joanna took the chipped piece of flint with genuine interest. Though she'd never seen one, she knew that tiny arrowheads such as this were used on mortals. Unable to throw the elf-bolts themselves, the Little People compelled a man in their power to hurl it at another human being. The person struck instantly lost the power of his limbs and was taken to the dwelling place of the faeries. She turned it over in her hand, studying it with curiosity.

"Did you find this?" she asked.

Smiling shyly, Raine nodded. "I found it two summers ago in the woods nearby. I kept it especially for you. 'Twill guard you from evil."

Touched by the warm-hearted gesture of friendship,

Joanna tugged on one of the child's long braids playfully. "Thank you, Raine. I shall treasure it always."

The youngster regarded her with quiet contemplation. "I knew I would meet you one day, Lady Joanna, though I didn't know your name. I saw you there in the birch woods the day I found the faery arrow."

"How could that be?" Joanna inquired with a dubious shake of her head. "I've never visited this glen before."

Unruffled, Raine met her guest's disbelieving gaze. Her sooty eyes shone with a tranquil confidence. "I have the sight," she said simply.

"You do?" Joanna took a deep breath as she leaned back on the settle. Although she'd never met anyone fey before, she knew that some Scottish people did, indeed, have the second sight. In fact the MacNeil clan was noted for it. "And you saw me in a vision?"

Raine nodded. "I want you to keep the elf-bolt," she insisted with an earnest smile. " 'Twill protect you from evil."

Deeply moved, Joanna took the lassie's slender hand and squeezed it compassionately. "Even though you believe my grandpapa murdered your father, you still want to give me this?"

Raine clutched Joanna's fingers, and her answer rang with conviction. "The Red Wolf did not kill my da."

"How do you know?" Joanna questioned eagerly. "Did you see that in a vision, too? Do you know the identity of the man who murdered Laird Gideon?"

Raine bent her head, her thick black braids hanging down in front of her poppy-red gown. Her shoulders slumped in discouragement. "I have no knowledge of the man who's responsible," she admitted. "But when I saw the note signed with Somerled Macdonald's name, I knew in my heart it was false. I tried to tell the grown-ups how I felt, but they paid me no heed."

"Oh, Raine!" Joanna cried, knowing how painful it must have been for her to lose her father in such a gruesome way. "I pray God, you didn't see—" She stopped, too horrified to continue. She threw her arms around the lass and hugged her close.

"I saw my father's severed head," Raine confided, dry-eyed. "I was in the garden when they tossed it into the yard." Though she didn't break into tears, she wrapped her thin arms around Joanna and clung to her tightly.

"I'm truly sorry about your father," Joanna told her softly as she bussed her temple. "Having met you and your family, I know Gideon Cameron must have been a very fine man."

Raine drew back and looked up at the portrait above the fireplace. "My mother misses him terribly," she said in a small, hurt voice. "I miss him too." A single tear slid down her cheek, and she brushed the crystal drop away with the edge of her hand.

Joanna followed the girl's heartbroken gaze. The gentleman in the painting resembled his younger brother. Built square and solid, Laird Gideon Cameron had the same reddish-blond hair and the scholar's detached expression. His eyes, like Alex's and Isabel's, were light hazel.

She looked at the dark-eyed girl and smiled comfortingly. Drawing her close, she brushed back the tight wisps of curly ebony hair that had worked free from her braids and kissed Raine's high forehead.

"I hope we can be friends," she said sincerely. "And that someday the identity of the evil person who killed your father will be revealed."

Rory stopped in the doorway of the music room, watching Joanna and Raine embrace. When his wife had rushed out of the kitchen, he'd stayed to apologize to Nina and Alex. Then he'd gone upstairs to his bedchamber, expecting to find Joanna spitting invectives. Finding the room empty, he'd hurried to the stables, suspecting she might have decided to ride back to Kinlochleven on her own. But the grooms assured him that Lady MacLean hadn't tried to saddle Fraoch or any other mount.

Growing angrier by the moment, he'd methodically

searched the great hall, the lesser hall, the solar, the gallery, the pantry, the buttery, the garderobe, and even the rain-soaked kitchen garden. Only chance had brought him past the music room's open door.

Joanna looked up at that moment and saw him. Without waiting for an invitation, Rory walked over to stand beside the two lassies seated on the bench.

"Raine gave me a faery arrow," Joanna told him quietly, "to shield me from misfortune." She offered the flint arrowhead to him, and he took it, absently turning it over to examine the chipped stone.

Relieved to find Joanna's fiery temper had cooled, he smiled at the dark-haired girl beside her. "You're spending too much time with your aunt," he chided fondly. "Soon you'll be making potions to ward off the evil eye and chanting rhymes to cure everything from the toothache to pleurisy."

Though he didn't approve of the middle-aged woman's eccentric ways, he suspected that Raine felt closer to Isabel Cameron than she did to her sweet, gentle mother. He also thought he knew why.

"Aunt Isabel knows nothing about the elf-bolt," Raine replied with utmost seriousness. "I want Lady Joanna to keep the arrowhead with her always. 'Twill protect her from danger."

"My wife needs no amulets or talismans," Rory told the girl affectionately. "I will keep Joanna safe."

The thirteen-year-old studied him, her intelligent eyes thoughtful. "When you are with her, Laird MacLean, no man will ever hurt her. But when she is separated from you, you will not be able to shield her from her enemies or yours."

With a confident grin, Rory took Raine's hand and placed the piece of chipped flint in her palm. "Then we have nothing to worry about, do we, lass? For Lady Joanna will never be separated from me. Now you'd best go downstairs and find your mother. She's been looking for you."

Raine dropped the elf-bolt into Joanna's lap, and with a

quick smile at her, hastened to the door, then paused. "I
have a gift for you, too, Laird MacLean," she called to
him, a sudden, impish smile lighting her youthful features.
"For the success of your marriage. I'll bring it to you
soon."

"Thank you, Raine," he said with a chuckle. "I appreciate your thoughtfulness."

When the child had closed the door behind her, Rory
gazed down at his bride. Even in the stained and faded
yellow gown fashioned for a much younger lass, Joanna
glowed from within, lit by some buoyant inner radiance.
At the moment, however, her usual spontaneous joy had
been carefully banked, and she watched him with troubled
eyes.

"Why did you bring me here?" she asked, the pain in
her voice not quite hidden by her obvious anger. Laying
the arrowhead on the cushioned seat, she rose and stood
rigidly before him. "Why here to Archnacarry, when surely
you must know how I feel about my grandfather's execution and the part you and the Camerons played in it?"

"I wanted you to meet Gideon's family, Joanna," he
replied. "I wanted you to realize what a fine, decent man
he was and what a tragic loss his family felt at his death.
I wanted you to understand why I had to track the Red
Wolf down and bring him to justice."

Her stormy blue eyes snapping, she faced him squarely.
"You and your brothers hunted down the wrong man,
MacLean, and the Macdonalds are not likely to forget it."

Exasperated at her stubbornness, Rory strode across the
rug to stand before a tall window, bracing one hand on its
heavy wooden shutter. Outdoors, a spring mist covered
Archnacarry Glen, bringing its soft moisture to the white
heather that bloomed on the hillsides.

He took a deep, calming breath, determined not to lose
his temper and shout at his wee bonny wife. The memory
of their passionate coupling had intruded on his thoughts
all morning. He'd never spent more than a moment or two
thinking about a night's dalliance with a woman before. To

be so enraptured by Joanna's naïve yet eager manner in bed was a new experience—one he thoroughly enjoyed. He was looking forward to this evening, when they'd be alone in the privacy of the bedchamber and ensconced in their warm, soft bed.

"The feuding between the clans must stop," he said in an even tone, "or it will destroy Scotland as a nation. With our marriage, lass, we have a chance to end the bitter fighting that has been tearing the Highlands apart."

"Don't place all the blame on the Macdonalds," she retorted. "There was no rebellion until James Stewart's father decided to usurp Donald Macdonald and make himself Lord of the Isles."

Rory turned from the window and returned to stand before her once more. "By bringing the Glencoe Macdonalds under the authority of the Crown, we—you and I, Joanna— can forestall the threat of another rebellion. We can save hundreds of lives and give our children something we've never had: a lifetime without war in the Highlands."

As the force of his words struck her, Joanna sank back down on the bench and absently picked up the elf-bolt. Head bent, she traced the uneven edge of the triangular stone with her thumbnail. "I don't wish to see the warfare continue," she said in a subdued voice, "and I harbor no ill-will for this family. Their deaths wouldn't bring Grandpapa back from the grave."

"I'm relieved to hear you say that," he replied. "More deaths would only compound the tragedy."

Her fine-boned features drawn and tight, she looked up at him warily. "I realize now why you and Gideon's family were so convinced he was guilty. You made a horrible mistake, Rory, but I do understand your reasoning. I could forgive you, I think, if only you'd admit you were wrong."

Rory felt as though he'd just been savagely kicked in the stomach. He dropped to his haunches in front of his bride and enclosed her slender hips between his hands. " 'Twas no mistake, lass. I would do it all over again, if I had to."

She slowly lifted her head to meet his gaze and teardrops

clung to the tips of her lashes. Her obstinate refusal to recognize her grandfather's guilt could be seen in the set of her jaw and the intractable cast of her delicate features.

"I must return to the kitchen," she said stiffly. "I left Lady Nina with the pies half made."

He longed to hold Joanna in his embrace, to rock her in his arms until the pain went away. Her pain and his. But he knew she needed time to accept the harsh truth. "Very well," he said quietly as he regained his feet.

Joanna rose from the settle and moved to the door, her spine rigid and unyielding. She left the room without looking back.

After his wife had gone, Rory stood gazing at the portrait of Gideon Cameron. The laird had earned the respect and admiration of all who knew him. Rory couldn't remember his own father; he'd been too young when the warrior had been killed in battle. Most of what he'd learned about the human race had come from his wise foster father.

Gideon had encouraged Rory to strive for high ideals, to fulfill his duties with honor and valor, and to place the good of his country over his own aggrandizement. Yet it had also been Gideon, the astute scholar of history and geography, who'd encouraged Rory to build a ship and seek his fortune on the seas.

Rory knew that his part in Somerled's death on the gallows stretched like a vast ocean between him and his wife. He couldn't change the past, nor would he want to. But until he convinced Joanna that the Macdonald chieftain had been guilty of murder, she'd always blame him for her grandfather's execution. Rather than being the chivalrous knight she'd envisioned marrying, Rory would forever play, in her mind, the role of wrongful avenger.

He leaned both hands on the granite mantelpiece and stared down at the cold hearth with unseeing eyes. Rory wanted Joanna to be as infatuated with him as his mother had been with his father. So infatuated that she'd willingly forgo her blind loyalty to her traitorous clan and cleave to her kinsmen's mortal enemy. 'Twas the reason he'd striven to make her wedding day perfect. He longed for his wife to see him through a smitten lassie's eyes, filled with idealistic wonder.

With a rueful shake of his head, Rory finally admitted his unconscious wish. While he and Joanna had been so intimately joined, he'd wanted Joanna to tell him she loved him.

"I brought your wedding gift, Laird MacLean," Raine said, and he turned in surprise to find her standing at his elbow. She'd moved across the rug with such noiseless grace, he hadn't heard her join him in front of her father's portrait.

The tall, thin lassie held out a padded square of linen embroidered with roses in pink and scarlet threads. "There's rosemary stitched inside," she told him.

"Ah, rosemary for remembrance," he said softly as he took it. "Thank you, lass. Lady MacLean will be pleased."

Raine fluttered her hand in warning. "Oh, you mustn't show this to your wife."

"Why not?"

Her raven eyes regarded him solemnly for a moment, then she smiled entrancingly. "'Tis a love charm," she confessed. "You must hide this beneath her pillow while she's sleeping. 'Twill make her love you."

He smiled at her fanciful imagination. "Now I know you've been spending too much time with Aunt Isabel. And do you intend to give Lady MacLean a secret love charm for me?" he teased.

Twisting one long braid through her fingers, Raine shook her head. "There is no need, milord. You are already deeply and irrevocably in love with your wife."

He scowled at the preposterous notion. "I don't believe in such foolishness," he said, more gruffly than he'd meant to.

Raine laughed, the sound tinkling like merry bells as she raced to the doorway. "Your mind doesn't believe in love,

Laird MacLean,'' she said from the open portal. ''But your heart and soul have already surrendered.''

Rory glared down at the damnfool token. God Almighty! What made the elusive and mysterious lassie think he was in love with Joanna?

About to toss the embroidered linen square on the bench, he paused. If Raine returned to the music room and found it lying there, her feelings would be hurt. With a soft snort of disgust, he dropped the cockamamie love charm in his sporran.

Chapter 22

Rory had learned in his years of warfare that timing wasn't merely important—it was absolutely crucial. The day chosen for the commencement of a siege, the signal to retreat from a lost battle, the knowledge of when to leave port to avoid the icy storms of winter, or the decision to begin boarding a pirate vessel, were all too chancy to be left to blind fate.

As he mounted the stairs that evening to find his bed, he reviewed the day's events with a newly married man's smile of anticipation.

Just as he'd hoped, Joanna hadn't been able to hang on to her anger for long. She didn't meet life's problems by remaining alone in her room to nurse her vexation and sense of ill treatment. No doubt she'd seen her cousin Idoine's limited repertoire of sulking and pouting and had taken a healthy dislike to such childish affectations.

His wife was too decent by nature to take her ire out on the sweet-tempered widow or the blameless young lassie; and Alex was shown the good manners reserved for one's host, be he enemy or friend. A truce had been established between Isabel and Joanna that proved easy to keep when the eccentric lady retired to her private apartments to fuss over her herbal concoctions and magical incantations. Joanna reserved for Rory alone the impersonal disdain one would give something green and slimy crawling on the underside of a leaf.

She'd joined the family for the midday meal, her demeanor chilly, though polite. The afternoon was spent in the music room, and little by little, her icy reserve toward the Camerons had thawed.

With Raine on the virginal and Nina playing the harp, Joanna picked up a lute, tuned the strings, and joined them. To Rory's amazement and the Camerons' delight, she played and sang by rote the ballad Fergus MacQuisten had warbled at their wedding banquet. She might not have rendered it perfectly—Rory wouldn't know—but when Nina exclaimed over the beauty of the piece, Joanna told them her husband had composed the music and lyrics in honor of his bride.

Rory had scowled, uncomfortable beneath Nina and Raine's effusive praise. He met Alex's canny eyes and knew the other laird, familiar with both Rory and Lachlan, had immediately guessed the truth. The reminder of how he'd made such a damn idiot of himself trying to please his imaginative young wife stung Rory's pride. To hell with her starry-eyed fantasies. He intended to be exactly who he was: a hardened, cynical chief of a formerly landless clan.

If Joanna thought her frosty treatment of her husband would dampen his ardor, however, she'd been mistaken. Seated beside her on the settle, Rory had enjoyed the sweet proximity of his wife to the fullest. While she plucked the strings of the lute, he'd toyed with her long burnished curls. His arm resting across the bench's high back, he caressed the base of her throat, running his fingertips lightly across the satiny skin above her collarbone. The Camerons, bless them, pretended not to notice anything amiss between the newly wedded pair.

After supper, Joanna had excused herself to retire early for the night. Engaged in backgammon with Alex, Rory looked up and politely wished her pleasant dreams. He'd finished the game shortly after that and leisurely followed her upstairs.

Rory paused for a moment outside the bedchamber, then swung the door open and went inside. He could hear the splash of water and his wife's soft hum of pleasure coming from behind the screen that had been placed in front of the fireplace by one of the servants. His calculations had been perfect. He'd caught Joanna just stepping into her bath.

Closing the door quietly, he walked around the movable partition to find his wife up to her waist in hot, soapy water, the creamy globes of her breasts with their velvety tips tilting impudently upward. In the midst of lathering a bathing cloth, she watched in frozen surprise as he unfastened his sword belt and dropped the weapon on the rug at his feet.

Someone had added acorns to the crackling blaze on the hearth and lit scented candles on the mantel. The room smelled of summer roses, winter holly, and pine trees drenched by the rain. Steam wafted around her, scented by the bubbles in the tub.

Joanna stared at him as he lifted the bowl of fragrant soaps and the white toweling from the three-legged stool, placed them on the Persian carpet, and sat down.

"What are you doing?" she gasped.

He smiled complacently while he feasted on the sight of her. The glorious abundance of auburn hair had been piled on top of her head and fastened with four ivory combs. Save for a wispy fringe of tendrils too stubborn to be tamed, her slender nape and the dusting of freckles across her shoulders lay exposed to her husband's gaze. Steam warmed her cheeks to a rosy glow, making her violet-blue eyes almost purple in her vivid face.

"What does it look like I'm doing?" he questioned with a sardonic lift of his brow. "I'm waiting for my turn to bathe."

"You . . . you can't stay here!" she sputtered. "This isn't your bedchamber." She jabbed her finger in the direction of the closed door. "Your room is down the passageway to your left. Didn't Lady Nina explain to you?"

"Oh, she explained all right," he replied, casually removing his stockings and brogues. "And then I explained to Nina that I sleep where my wife sleeps." He looked up from his task to shake his head in mock reprimand. "If you didn't like the chamber we were in, Joanna, you should have told me. Did the fireplace smoke or was there a draft I hadn't noticed, while we were getting better acquainted this morning?"

She brought the sopping cloth to the valley between her breasts and glared at him. "Godsakes, do you intend to wait here until I get out?"

He unfastened the bodkin that pinned his plaid to his shirt, tossed the corner of the black and green tartan wool over his shoulder, and pulled his long shirttails out from beneath his belt. "I'm not sure we'd both fit in that tub, lass, though I'm willing to try. On second thought, you're such a wee bit of a thing, it might work at that."

Her gaze swept over him in outrage as she shrank back against the side of the oak vat. "Ask the servants to fetch your *own* bath in your *own* bedchamber."

"This is my bedchamber." He dragged the shirt over his head and tossed it on the floor. "And why waste a perfectly fine tub of hot water? We'd only make more work for Nina's staff."

Tipping her chin upward in tight-lipped indignation, Joanna rubbed the lathered cloth over her shoulder and arm, then moved to her chest and stopped abruptly. "I can't wash myself while you're watching," she exclaimed. " 'Tisn't decent."

Rory unfastened his buckle. "I'll be happy to do it for you," he offered as he slid off his belt and dirk.

Joanna heaved an exasperated sigh. "Very well, Mac-Lean, you win. I'll get out." She reached over the edge of the wooden vat and snatched up the linen towel. Snapping it open, she held it modestly in front of her as she emerged from the water.

Rory regained his feet at the same moment, allowing his plaid to fall away from his naked form. He offered his arm in a gallant gesture, ready to help her step out of the bathtub. Her eyes promising fire and brimstone, Joanna reached down, scooped the soapy cloth out of the water, and flung it at him.

The sopping linen hit Rory smack in the face. Her startled gurgle of laughter as she stepped across the opposite side of the tub told him she hadn't sighted her target, but was definitely pleased with the results of her reckless aim.

"Why, Joanna," he said softly as he peeled the soggy material off his nose. "You should have told me you wanted to play."

Her eyes widened in alarm at his grin, and she clutched the toweling to her bosom, which rose and fell delightfully in her agitation. She stood in front of the blazing fire, the oaken vat of water steaming between them. A smile twitched at the corner of her mouth and her eyes twinkled with naughtiness. She took a tiny step back.

"Pray, pardon me, milord husband," she said, poised as gracefully as a hind about to take flight from the hunter. "I was merely trying to assist you with your bath."

He replied with all the silky assurance of a very large man. "First, I'll help you with yours."

He reached for her, and Joanna sprinted away. She dashed around the screen, leaving Rory holding the damp towel in his grasp.

At the success of her ploy, her laughter rang out. "That's a thoroughly indecent suggestion, MacLean. Your mother should have taught you better morals."

Rory didn't follow her around the lightweight partition as she'd expected. Instead he purposely knocked it over, and the stool along with it, as he moved between his wife and the door, cutting off her route of escape.

She whirled at the thud of the falling barrier and stopped in her tracks, caught near the bed, trying to reach her nightshift. Too late, she realized he'd trapped her.

"I don't want to get my hair wet," she admonished, merriment sparkling in her eyes. " 'Twill take too long to dry."

"You should have thought of that before."

Dripping all over the thick carpet, Joanna edged slowly

back toward the outside wall. She was splendidly naked, the water and soap bubbles glistening on her ivory skin. When she realized his gaze had locked on the single drop trickling off one rosy nipple, she sucked in her breath. "Stay back," she warned.

He moved leisurely toward her. "You're not afraid of a little wetting, are you, milady wife?"

She bumped her bare rear into a bed table and, glancing back, discovered a bowl of apples. He read her intention before she'd fully realized it herself.

"Don't do it, Joanna," he goaded.

As she reached for the first projectile, he jerked a round silver tray from the press cupboard behind him and warded off the fruit she lobbed at his head. High, low, in between, Rory met the flight of each missile with the flat of his makeshift shield.

"Come out from behind there, you coward," she taunted as he moved steadily forward beneath the barrage.

He'd nearly reached her when the apples ran out. With an ecstatic crow of discovery, she seized a basket filled with walnuts and hurled the entire contents at him. Showered with three dozen brown pellets, he held his defensive weapon above his head. The nuts peppered him like stone shot, bouncing against the engraved silver platter and rolling across the floor.

Bringing the targe down, he found she'd already picked up her shoes and, with a screech of exhilaration, scrambled across the wide bed, where she hurled them at him one by one. Four bolster pillows followed the shoes. Once again, he blocked them with his trusty shield.

Joanna waited with the ponderous canopied bedstead between them, panting and laughing at the same time. A comb had fallen from her hair, and several long locks dangled around her bare arm.

"I'm going to catch a chill," she complained. Her bottom lip jutted out adorably. "If I die of consumption, 'twill be all your fault." Indigo eyes shimmering in the candlelight, she jerked at the quilted comforter spread across the mattress.

He grabbed the other edge and whipped it out of her grasp. "I'll keep you warm," he promised. "Right after I scrub you down." He flung the green bedcover to the floor.

A second comb fell from her hair as she glanced over her shoulder. Until that moment, she hadn't noticed the compote of oranges on the massive court cupboard, which took up the entire wall behind her.

"Now, Joanna . . ." he cautioned, purposely egging her on.

Her eyes bright with mischief, she started hurling the precious fruit. Impervious to the cost of the imported luxuries, she tossed the bright orbs at him with abandon. She followed up with balls of brightly colored yarn from a wicker basket on the floor next to the bed.

Her aim was improving. She was, however, attacking a man trained in the arts of war. Dodging swords and dirks had given Rory ample practice in thrusting, feinting, and rushing his adversary. He could have captured her after the first apple launched, but her sparkling eyes and musical laughter made the game much too enjoyable to end it so soon.

He worked his way to the foot of the bed, boxing her into a corner. When all the oranges and balls of yarn had been lobbed, he tossed the silver tray down.

"You're going to have some explaining to do, come morning," he said mildly. "Nina will think you went berserk."

A third comb floated to the floor, and the lustrous hair tumbled about her shoulders and drifted to her waist. "She'll blame you," Joanna retorted on a ripple of laughter. "Everyone knows all MacLeans are slavering beasts."

He paused to admire her nude body, every delicate hill and valley glistening with moisture. His gaze roved lingeringly over the head of glorious coppery locks; cinnamon brows, lashes, and freckles; indigo eyes; rosy cheeks; cherry lips and pink nipples; and the auburn puff of curls at the juncture of her creamy thighs. Hell, she'd turn any man into a slavering beast.

"And what does that make you, Lady MacLean?" he inquired with a confident grin. He propped his hands on his hipbones, and her eyes followed the movement. Her mouth dropped open at the sight of his jutting male member.

"I told you not to call me that," Joanna admonished, color flooding her cheeks. "Now you'll be sorry." She waited for him to get three steps closer, then lifted the fat blue pitcher at her elbow and splashed the water into his face.

Like everything else she'd flung, he'd been expecting it. He anticipated her next move as well. As Joanna scrambled across the mattress once more, shrieking with feminine laughter, he met her on the other side, a vase of spring flowers from the cupboard in his hand.

Leaving the bed abruptly, she skidded on the walnuts concealed beneath the jade quilt. Rory caught her by the waist, held her upright, and calmly upended the urn over her head. Ox-eye daisies, yellow cowslips, lavender bluebells, and cold water cascaded over her gorgeous hair, taking with them the last ivory comb.

"You wretch!" she gasped, then shivered. Her brilliant eyes flashed with excitement. "Now look what you've done!"

Rory chuckled softly as his hands slid up to her breasts. "I'll help you mend the damage to your hair later."

"You've caused enough damage. You'll do no such thing."

She shoved against his chest, and he obligingly toppled over, taking her with him to land on the padded comforter at their feet. Bare legs tangling, he rolled beneath her to cushion the fall.

Startled, Joanna looked down at Rory, who was grinning like a naughty lad who'd successfully evaded a switching. He plucked a bluebell out of her tangled hair and tossed it aside. "There, 'tis bonnier than ever."

"And who's going to repair the damage to this room?" she inquired with a cool lift of her brows.

"If you're a good lass and apologize, I just might help you." He set her on the floor, rose to his feet, scooped her up in his brawny arms, and moved to the tub. "But first we're going to have that bath."

"Rory!" she cried softly. "That really is indecent."

"Would you believe, darling," he said, "some cultures do it all the time. Men and women bathing together sounds like a sterling idea to me, especially if you're the woman and I'm the man."

Scandalized, Joanna gazed up at her husband. His strong jaw was stubbled with a day's growth of beard. His eyes watched her with a predatory light glowing in their brilliant green depths.

The barbaric emerald twinkling in his ear and the primitive sea dragon etched on his arm should have alerted her, despite the holy medal hanging on his chest. He was a half-pagan warlord, experienced in the vices of the heathen world. Bronzed and sea-weathered, he exuded an aura of savage ferocity.

She'd have been blind not to notice that all the time she'd been pelting him with everything that came to hand, he'd been sexually aroused. The tension vibrating inside her own body had changed during their ridiculous, one-sided duel, though she'd scarcely been aware of it.

"Rory," she murmured huskily. She unfastened the leather thong at the back of his neck, slid her fingers in the wealth of sun-bleached hair, and pressed her mouth against his.

He kissed her, his tongue thrusting and withdrawing boldly in a clear imitation of what would soon happen between them.

When he broke the kiss, he stepped over the tub's edge, sank down into the warm water, and settled her in front of him. He lifted her slightly and wedged her rump between his corded thighs, so she lay back against his solid chest, her head resting on his shoulder, her soaked locks floating in the water around them. His rigid manhood pressed insistently against her bottom, and there was no mistaking his intent.

His arms around her, he cupped his hands and rinsed out her hair; then he lathered the cloth with perfumed soap.

"I should have ordered a bath," he said with a chuckle, "and scrubbed Joey Macdonald down the first day I spotted the cheeky lad standing beside Father Thomas, all covered with soot and grime. 'Twould have saved me a great deal of time and aggravation."

He ran the soapy washcloth over her breasts, rubbing gently back and forth across her nipples, and the strength of her own arousal came as a shock to Joanna. She'd felt so cross with Rory when he'd first come into the room that she hadn't realized until now he'd been playing with her in a sexual way, teasing her and then using her sense of humor to overcome her resistance.

The cloth in his hand began an unhurried descent down her belly as the water lapped about them. He bent his head and kissed her ear, his tongue following the curves and dipping into the hollows.

"Joanna," he said softly, "I didn't compose the ballad that Fergus MacQuisten sang at our wedding feast. Nor did I write the words."

"I know," she replied with a contented sigh.

"You do?"

She nodded, enjoying the hedonistic pleasure of sharing a bath with her husband. His soapy fingers glided over her wet skin, beguiling and seductive as he bathed her most intimate places. Shameful and indecent it might be, but 'twas marvelously agreeable, too.

"Who told you?" he asked gruffly.

"Hm?" she murmured. "Oh, no one. I just knew that you didn't write it."

He paused, and she could tell he wasn't flattered by her assumption—even though it had obviously been correct. His deep baritone rumbled in his chest as he continued his tantalizing endeavors. "How did you know, lass?"

She smiled at the annoyance in his voice. "I just knew the man who compared courting a lassie to feeding carrots and apples to his horse couldn't have written that romantic verse or the hauntingly beautiful music that went with it."

He halted as he considered her reply.

"Don't stop," she begged. A delicious languor curled through Joanna, and she released a long, appreciative sigh. "Who did compose the ballad?"

"I'll tell you after our third child is born," he said, kissing her temple. Joanna could tell he was smiling.

He touched her beneath the water, playing with her gently. The warm ripples swirled around his gifted fingers, creating tiny rills of pleasure.

"If you knew," he continued in a serious tone, "why didn't you say something that day? As MacQuisten sang the ballad, you looked at me as though you believed I'd composed it."

"Because I assumed you'd asked Fergus to create a tender love song especially for me. And the fact that you *wanted* me to believe you'd written it touched me deeply."

"I may not be able to write songs," he murmured in her ear, "but I can play your sweet, lovely body, Joanna, till you're sighing for me like a wee magic harp fashioned by the faeries to drive a mortal man insane."

The warm bathwater swirled around Rory's dexterous fingers, enhancing each touch, each light brush of his callused fingertips over her delicate folds.

When she was sighing like a faery harp beneath his caresses, Rory lifted her up in his strong arms. Leaving the tub, he laid her, dripping wet, on the bed, with her knees bent, her legs dangling over the edge of the mattress. To Joanna's surprise, he didn't join her on the bed, but knelt on the floor in front of her. His hands sliding over her sleek thighs, he lifted her legs over his broad shoulders.

"What are you doing?" she asked with an embarrassed little laugh. She couldn't imagine what he intended next. She tried to sit up, and with one quick tug, he tipped her flat on her back again.

"This comes under the bridegroom's responsibility," he said, his sea-dragon eyes sparkling with devilment.

"What's that?"

"Teaching you something new every night."

"And all I need to do is enjoy it?"

His wide grin was positively wicked. "I'll think of something for you to do later."

Rory smoothed his open mouth across the sensitive skin of her inner thighs and nipped her gently. She could feel his warm breath drift over her and the prickly graze of his whiskers. Her heart thumped wildly against her ribs as he parted the tight curls that covered her mound.

Holy heavens.

Dragon's tail or no, he was half-savage. Like some great primitive beast, he nuzzled her with his lips and tongue.

"Rory!" she gasped.

This had to be something he'd learned from the sea nymphs. Who else would do such a scandalous thing?

Joanna jerked in convulsive reaction as he touched her with the tip of his tongue, his hands reaching up to fondle the tightened buds of her breasts at the same moment. The feeling that knifed through her body bordered on ecstasy.

"Oh, my," she breathed. "Oh, my."

She now had no doubt about the truth. The chiefs of Clan MacLean cavorted with mermaids. That's why he'd wanted to bathe in the tub with her. 'Twas the blatantly sensual lure of the water lapping around his manly parts. And that's why he wanted her hair loose and dripping wet—so she'd remind him of a redheaded sea nymph.

He laved her delicate folds, moist and warm and scented from the bath, moister and warmer now from his skilled mouth and tongue. The world around Joanna shrank to just the two of them as he taught her the incredible pleasures he could give.

He held her hips imprisoned in his large hands, and she writhed beneath his erotic stimulation till she cried out his name in breathless female surrender. Floating in a languorous haze, Joanna realized that Rory rose and bent over her.

"I know you must be tender, darling," he whispered. "I'll be very gentle."

As the exquisite pleasure throbbed and pulsed through her slick, engorged tissues, Rory spread her legs and entered her carefully. The feeling of pressure and incredible fullness seemed so right, she sobbed in relief and longing, wanting to have more of him and still more. She wrapped her legs tightly around his lean flanks, refusing to let him be gentle.

"I need you, Rory," she said, her words hoarse with emotion. "I need you inside me like this, hard and strong. I feel like I'll never get enough of you." She arched upward, moving her hips against his straining loins.

"Then come with me, darling," he said, seeming to understand her frantic state. "Come ride with me through the stars."

He bent over her, plunging in swift, strong strokes, building a faster and faster tempo. Where that morning he'd been steady and rhythmic, tonight he pumped wildly into her body, taking Joanna on a breathless ride. They climaxed together, their bodies shuddering in their release.

Her husband slipped his hand beneath Joanna's rump and, rolling over, brought her up on top of him. Her body clenched him reflexively, and he groaned. "Ah, Joanna, 'tis an old man you'll make of me before my time, but I'll enjoy every minute of getting older."

She lay on top of him, panting. As her heartbeat slowed and her breathing returned to normal, she pushed up, bracing her hands on his shoulders. The strands of her long, wet hair dangled about them.

"What was it like?" she asked with a curious smile. "Doing it under water?"

He looked at her blankly. "Doing what under water, lass?"

"This."

"This?"

She frowned, surprised and a little annoyed. He was usually far more astute. "What we just did," she explained. "What was it like, doing it under water?"

Rory slid his hands up her back and lifted the damp locks away from her shoulders. "Joanna," he said with a bemused expression, "why would you think I've coupled with a woman under water?"

"Oh, not with a woman!" she exclaimed. "With a sea nymph."

A crooked smile creased his sharp features, his green eyes danced with suppressed merriment. "What makes you believe I've coupled with a mermaid?"

"All Macdonald children are told how the chiefs of Clan MacLean cavort with the water sprites. And that the MacLean chiefs have dragon tails, which are snipped short at birth so they can hide them beneath their plaids. That's why, this morning, I wanted to get better acquainted. I wanted to find out if it was true—if you really did have a dragon's tail." She giggled happily. "But you don't."

"You mean . . . when you were fondling my bare buttocks . . . you were trying . . . to discover . . ." A look of sudden comprehension lit his face. Then he roared with laughter. He bellowed so hard, she bounced up and down on his chest. "Oh, God, Joanna!" he cried between hoots and guffaws. "Oh, God, I don't believe it!"

"Shush!" she told him. "You'll wake everyone in the house."

He wouldn't stop laughing—or couldn't. She wasn't sure which. Finally she grabbed a pillow and smashed it over his face. That finally shut him up.

He lay there so still, Joanna grew afraid she'd smothered him. "Rory?" she whispered, lifting the pillow.

He immediately brought her face down to his, kissing her passionately. All of a sudden, he started laughing again. He laughed till tears ran from the corners of his eyes.

"I'm going to start getting angry if you don't stop laughing at me," she threatened.

He kissed her again. "Darling of my heart," he whispered against her temple, "how did I ever get so lucky?"

At the loving Gaelic endearment, Joanna became absolutely still. Grandpapa had been the only person who'd ever called her that. Anguish welled up inside her, flooding her already overwrought emotions to the brink. She pushed back and looked into her husband's mirthful gaze, her heart breaking.

Unable to help herself, Joanna burst into tears. She slumped down on his chest and buried her face in the curve of his neck. "Oh, Rory," she sobbed, "why did it have to be you?"

Stunned, Rory cradled his wife in his arms and listened to her heartbroken sobs. He stared at the green silk canopy above them, fighting back the galling disappointment. He'd hoped that tonight Joanna would tell him she loved him. Instead, she was crying her heart out because he, Laird Rory MacLean, was her husband.

Rory and Alex stood in the kitchen the next morning, eating oat porridge and hot buttered scones. The weather had cleared, and they intended to make a tour of the Archnacarry fields. As laird of Kinlochleven, Rory would need to become familiar with the yearly routine of plowing, planting and harvesting crops, as well as the raising of the sturdy, long-haired Highland cattle. Before setting out, he planned to return upstairs to get his weapons and to check on his wife, whom he'd left peacefully slumbering in the midst of the shambles they'd created the night before.

Suddenly the door leading from the great hall banged opened with a crash. The two lairds turned in surprise to find Godfrey Macdonald holding his sword on Archnacarry's steward, Malcolm. Immediately behind them came a hefty Macdonald man-at-arms with Raine held fast in his grasp and the blade of a dirk laid across her throat. Though pale with fright, the lassie remained calm.

"I-I'm sorry, milord," Malcolm said. "They told me they were Lady Joanna's family, come to pay their respects to the bride and groom. They'd hidden their weapons beneath their clothing."

Fists clenched, Alex glared at the beefy Macdonald soldier. Like Rory, he hadn't yet buckled on his broadsword and dirk. "Get your hands off my niece, you damn filthy slug," he ordered.

Godfrey snickered, his beady eyes glittering in his bloated face. "No one will be harmed," he said, "as long as you remain calm. Lady Cameron and the lassie will act as surety for your good behavior. But if either of you try to resist, the girl and her mother will be the first ones killed." He jerked the point of his dark, scraggly beard toward the door. "Now, gentlemen, shall we join the ladies?"

When they entered the manor hall, they found Nina encircled by five Macdonalds at the far end of the chamber. Rory paused to scan the large, high-ceilinged room with its gallery leading to the second-floor quarters.

Andrew, accompanied by a corpulent Observantine friar, waited in front of the great hearth. His brown eyes troubled, the comely lad seemed to have lost his zeal for marrying his cousin. The night spent with the brigands and the subsequent rescue had left its mark.

Along with Cameron's clansmen who'd been disarmed, the household servants had been gathered together and seated on the benches at the trestle tables under the surveillance of a dozen soldiers. One woman wept quietly, the only sound in the large room, except for their footsteps on the scented rushes. Isabel stood apart, guarded by two men. Joanna was nowhere in the hall.

"Get in there," Godfrey snarled as he shoved Rory from behind.

Rory reined in the urge to turn on the filthy cretin and wrest the sword from his grasp. Until he knew that Joanna was safe, he dared not take the offensive.

The remaining Macdonalds surrounded Rory, their weapons drawn, and quickly separated him from the Camerons. They led him to the center of the hall, and Rory allowed them to force him to his knees, five sword points held scant inches from his head.

A noise came from the gallery above, and all eyes turned upward. Gripping Joanna's arm, Ewen dragged the outraged lass remorselessly along behind him. She was still in her nightshift, her hair tumbling about her. Too far away to be heard from the lower level, the two were arguing bitterly.

On the second-floor arcade, Joanna tried to wrest free from her cousin's grasp. "Let me go," she insisted. "How dare you invade these people's home!"

Ewen's baneful gaze flickered over her rumpled shift and disheveled hair as he scrutinized her with open disdain. "We won't be here long, lass," he replied. "Only as long as it takes for you to sign the papers for your annulment."

"You're mad!" she told him scornfully. "There are no grounds for an annulment."

"There are always grounds, if a lassie is clever enough."

Her jaw dropped, and she gazed at him in bewilderment. "What justification could there possibly be?"

"Impotency."

"That's a lie," she hissed.

But he already knew that. He'd found her asleep in bed, surrounded by the evidence of Rory's presence and their impassioned mating. The room was littered with apples, oranges, walnuts, flowers, perfumed soaps, and articles of clothing. The tub of bathwater, cold now, still sat in front of the hearth, the toppled screen on the floor beside it. Her husband's sword and dirk rested next to the overturned stool. Nearby lay a coverlet of sable, where they'd moved during the night to be close to the crackling fire while he brushed her hair dry.

" 'Tis a lie!" she repeated. "And well you know it."

Ewen pivoted so only his back could be seen from the manor hall, neatly hiding Joanna from view. He pitched his words low, making certain the people watching from the ground floor couldn't hear.

"You're going to swear before God and man that MacLean is impotent, Joanna," he said with a sour smile. "I've brought the priest and the papers. Your Macdonald clansmen shall be the witnesses to your oath.''

She recoiled in disgust. "I'll never swear to such a lie. Never. 'Twould be blasphemy!"

Ewen drew her closer, his fingers biting into her arm. "Then you'll be relieved to know that you'll soon be a widow," he said. "Because either you swear that the marriage has never been consummated, or by God, we'll kill the baseborn miscreant here and now."

Joanna clutched the red and blue tartan wool pinned to Ewen's shirt. "Don't kill him," she begged. "I pray you, don't kill him."

His smile flashed cold and humorless in his silver-streaked beard. She could hear the faint rasp of desperation in his voice. "The decision is yours, lass. I'd rather not risk the King's retribution for killing his favorite Highland laird. But James Stewart and his bloody avenger be damned, MacLean lives or dies according to the next words out of your mouth."

He thrust her toward the gallery railing. Below, the Camerons and her kinsmen waited in mesmerized silence, their faces uplifted, their gazes locked on the two cousins arguing above them.

"Say it," Ewen snarled. "Tell them now."

Joanna flinched in horror as she looked down at the scene below. On the rush-covered stone floor, five able-bodied Macdonald soldiers held Rory at sword point. He was on his knees, Godfrey behind him. The sight of the magnificent golden warrior humbled by his enemies tore at her heart.

Her lips trembled. "I . . . I . . ." she began, then covered her mouth with shaky fingers.

"Say it, Joanna," Ewen commanded.

She gripped the carved walnut railing and stared down at the crowded hall. Within a cluster of burly men-at-arms, Lady Nina, white-faced and terrified, met Joanna's gaze, beseeching her wordlessly to save her family. Ebony eyes unwavering, Raine stood with the malevolent blade of a dirk resting against her throat, waiting with an air of contemptuous detachment. Laird Alex and Isabel had been separated from the others by a small knot of soldiers.

Rory watched Joanna with cool self-possession, his features composed. He seemed to be trying to give her some of his own strength of will, his concern for her welfare surpassing any fear for his own safety.

Joanna tore her gaze from his, unable to meet the piercing green eyes when she denied him. Instead, she looked at the priest in the hooded black habit of the Observantines, who stood beside Andrew at the fireplace. "I-I wish to . . . to apply for an annulment, Father," she said, her voice scratchy and thick in her bone-dry throat.

"Don't, Joanna," Rory called, an icy warning in his words.

"On what grounds, milady," the friar inquired smoothly. The portly man had been bribed and knew exactly what was occurring.

"On the grounds of . . . of . . ." Tears blurred her eyes, and she could no longer focus on the people below. She placed her fingers on her eyelids, pressing away the telltale drops.

"Don't do this, Joanna!" Rory shouted. The fury in his words struck her with the force of a riding crop across the face.

Her gaze fastened on the clergyman, she clung to the wooden rail, her knees nearly buckling beneath her. "The marriage between Laird MacLean and . . . and myself has never been . . . been consummated."

"Goddammit!" Rory cursed, turning his wrath on the friar. "She's being forced to say this, you cold-hearted son-ofabitch."

The priest ignored him. "Can you prove your statement, milady?" he inquired pleasantly.

"We . . . we have always slept a-apart," Joanna said, choking back a sob. "I tried to kill him on our wedding night and ran away the next evening, as my cousin Andrew can avouch. Since arriving at Archnacarry, Laird MacLean and I have . . . have slept in separate bedchambers."

The friar's tonsured head shone smooth as a sea-worn

pebble as he nodded gravely. "And this you solemnly swear to, Lady Joanna?"

Joanna wiped the tears from her cheeks, then twisted her hands together in front of her. "I swear by all the saints in heaven that, despite the holy sacrament of matrimony, I remain a virgin still."

"She lies!" her husband roared. His booming voice echoed through the hall in his wild frenzy. "We are well and truly married."

Rage tightening every muscle, Rory started to regain his feet, and the five men encircling him struggled to hold him down. With an oath, Godfrey grabbed a handful of Rory's hair, shoved a knee between his shoulder blades, and jerked his head back. He held his dirk across the stretched tendons of Rory's throat, the steel less than an inch away.

"Don't make another mistake like that," Godfrey warned, a sneer creasing his pocked, bleary-eyed face.

"You're a dead man," Rory told him calmly. The points of five broadswords moved closer at the soft-spoken words.

"Let me slit the whoreson's throat," Godfrey called to his brother. " 'Twill be faster than filing those damn papers in Rome." He moved to draw the razor edge of the blade across the exposed juggler.

"Wait!" Nina cried. Her rose-gold hair drifting about her shoulders, she held out one graceful hand in a pleading gesture. "Don't kill him. 'Tis true, what Lady Joanna says. I gave them separate rooms at their mutual request. Laird MacLean never slept with his wife." She paused, knowing every head was turned in her direction, every pair of eyes fastened on her. "I know it for a fact," she continued, her angelic face drained of color, her melodious soprano quavering pitifully. "I know because he slept with me, instead."

A hush swept through the chamber.

"And you'll be willing to sign an oath to that effect, Lady Cameron?" the black-robed friar inquired with an unctuous smile.

"I will swear to it on the holy crucifix," she replied, her

lovely azure eyes fastened on Rory. "Joanna Macdonald remains a virgin."

With a bellow of rage, Rory shoved a punishing elbow into Godfrey's soft paunch and sprang to his feet. The merciless crack of a sword hilt on the back of his head brought instant blackness.

Chapter 23

The wind sweeping across the loch carried the smell of the autumn harvest. From his dungeon window, Rory had only a tiny glimpse of the cloud-covered night sky and the faint sound of water slapping against the prison's thick stone wall. But he knew from the scratches he'd etched on the granite that the straw and hay would soon be stacked in the fields and the black-faced sheep brought down from their hillside pastures.

Five months.

Five months that seemed like eternity.

He lay on the pallet, his arm across his closed eyes, and recalled his last day of freedom.

The Macdonalds had set fire to Archnacarry's barns to aid their escape. When Rory regained consciousness, Alex and his men were battling the blaze and seeing to the safety of the animals. Rory had quickly found his weapons in the bedchamber where he'd left them. As he prepared to leave, he'd spoken briefly to Nina, chiding her for sacrificing her reputation for his sake.

"Did you think I'd let them stick you like a Martinmas hog merely to save my laughable reputation?" she'd asked, her eyes shining with bittersweet amusement. "I've been the subject of gossip for the last thirteen years, Rory. At least this time, 'twas of my own making."

He'd kissed her forehead compassionately. Since the birth of a black-haired, black-eyed daughter in a family of

311

pale-eyed blonds, Nina had been the target of vicious gossip about Raine's parentage.

"I know you for who you are, Nina. A decent and honorable lady." He squeezed her hands and offered a bracing smile. "And I'll happily kill any man who dares to say different."

Then he'd galloped off on Fraoch with the intention of riding to Kinlochleven, there to gather his men—and his brothers, if they were still at the castle—and lay siege to Mingarry. But in his blind urgency to regain possession of his wife, he'd ridden straight into a trap.

A large force of armed men had lain in wait for him along the road through Archnacarry Glen. He'd killed eight of them before they'd finally overwhelmed him. Bound, gagged, and blinded with a hood, he'd been brought to the prison fortress.

Thoughts of Joanna came with the dusk, as they always did. Rory dreamed of her nearly every night. He saw her now as she'd been on their last evening together. Her eyes flashing, her slim, pale figure scampering about the bedchamber and scrambling over the mattress. Her throaty laughter as she'd lobbed the apples at his head.

God, he ached for her.

After their frantic joining that night, he'd held his wife in his arms while she quietly sobbed. He'd taken her twice more, each time a slow, lingering mating that had left her breathless and moaning his name. But though she hadn't wept again, neither had he been able to coax from her the one admission he craved.

He'd wanted Joanna to tell him she loved him.

It no longer mattered that he didn't believe in romantic love. *She believed in it.* And he wanted Joanna to believe she was in love with him. He wanted it with a yearning that tightened like a steel band around his chest and sent a sharp, fierce need raking through his insides.

But she hadn't said the words he craved to hear.

Nor would she ever say them.

He'd known that night, without being told, that she was

waiting for his confession of guilt. Joanna wanted her husband to admit he'd been wrong to capture Somerled Macdonald, and that he now regretted it. But it was the one thing he'd never say to his darling wife—because it wasn't true.

Lifting his arm, Rory opened his eyes and looked around the dreary cell. Other than being chained and kept in solitary, he'd been well-treated. Apparently Ewen was simply waiting for the papers to come from the Vatican, which would pave the way for Andrew to wed Joanna. Once the cousins were married, there'd be nothing Rory could do, short of murder.

He didn't look forward to killing the poor laddie, but the Macdonalds were leaving him no choice. The deaths of Ewen and Godfrey, however, were a different matter. Hatred for the treacherous pair had festered like a chancre in his heart during his captivity. Imagining various and ingenious ways to kill them, all involving the greatest degree of pain for the longest amount of time possible, had occupied his idle hours.

The clink of metal in the passageway signaled the arrival of his evening meal. As the yellow glow of torchlight glimmered through the door's tiny, barred window, Rory slipped silently to his bare feet. Reaching for the iron shackles on the stones, he moved to stand beside the closed door. He'd been leashed to the wall by a length of chain, and it'd taken him five months to loosen the damn bolts with a tool he'd fashioned from a tin cup. But tonight Rory would either be a free man or a dead one.

When the turnkey stepped inside the darkened cell, Rory moved with agile speed, looping the chain around the big man's neck and jerking it tight. The tall fellow, not one of his usual jailers, fought back with astonishing ferocity. The sonofabitch grabbed the chain around his throat with both hands and wrenched downward, at the same time grazing Rory's shinbone with the edge of his heavy brogue and stomping viciously on the top of his attacker's bare foot.

Rory clenched his teeth against the intense pain and yanked the restraint tighter.

From behind came a polite tap on his shoulder. "Pardon me, Rory," Keir whispered with a chuckle, "but I don't think you should be garroting your own brother."

"Jesu," Rory hissed and, opening his clenched hands, released the chain. Keir deftly caught the iron links before they clattered on the stone floor.

Rory threw his arms around Lachlan, enclosing him in a fierce bear hug. "You damnfool idiot," he said hoarsely. He clapped his brother's face between his hands. "I could have killed you."

Lachlan returned the embrace, pounding Rory on the back. "When we get out of here," he said with a wry grin, "remind me to blacken one of your eyes. Right or left, it doesn't much matter." Impeccably attired as usual, he ran his sardonic gaze over his older brother's tattered rags. "And I can recommend a good tailor, if you need one."

"God Almighty," Rory groaned, returning the grin as he hobbled about, "you almost broke my foot."

"Talk later," Keir advised. The gold hoop in his ear glittered in the wavering torchlight as he handed Rory a sword and dirk. "Right now, let's get the hell out of here." Holding up the burning rush light, he signaled them to be quiet.

Rory followed his two broad-shouldered brothers up a narrow, winding passage. The sprawled bodies of three guards lay along their path, throats slashed. Keir led them up a spiral stone staircase to the battlements, where another corpse rested at a peculiar angle. Despite his breastplate and helm, the soldier's spine had been snapped like a piece of dry kindling. Rory knew exactly what had happened because he'd seen it before. Keir had picked the sentry up, brought him lengthwise across his bent knee, and neatly popped the backbone. For whatever reason, he'd slashed the unlucky bastard's throat for good measure.

"I wanted to make sure he didn't cry out," Keir said with a shrug as he stepped over the dead man.

"There's a permanent garrison lodged here," Lachlan explained to Rory in a low tone. "So we decided to slip in and out without raising a fuss."

The sound of footsteps climbing an outside stairway at an unhurried pace came from below.

"This one's mine," Rory told his brothers softly.

Barefoot, he moved stealthily along the castle wall and waited for the soldier to appear. In the blaze of the torches, the shadows danced on the stones as the guard, a replacement for the fallen sentry lying beside the parapet, drew nearer.

The moment he stepped onto the battlement, Rory clapped a hand over the sentinel's mouth and jerked him off balance. As his adversary staggered backward, flailing wildly, Rory clasped the back of the man's head in his other hand and in quick movement broke his neck.

The three brothers lowered themselves down the rope that Keir and Lachlan had used to scale the outer wall. At the bottom, Fearchar waited in a rowboat. He clasped Rory's hand and pulled him aboard.

"Wheesht," he said with his boyish grin, "when you disappear, man, you go underground like wee pawky mole."

Rory scowled at the pale-haired titan, suddenly worried that his possessions had been usurped by the Macdonalds, along with his wife. "Dammit, you're suppose to be guarding Kinlochleven."

"I put Murdoch to watching over your fine, fair castle, laddie," Fearchar replied, untroubled by his cousin's testiness. "And your Uncle Duncan left a detachment of his own men there when he rode off for Stalcaire with your lady mother. Kinlochleven will be waiting for you, sweet as a dimpled whore, when you're ready to return."

They rowed quietly away from the mighty citadel, which rose up from a small island in the middle of a loch.

Rory looked back in astonishment. "Where the hell was I?"

"Innischonaill," Lachlan told him grimly.

Rory met his brother's sober gaze, then turned back to study the brooding fortress, its black outline faintly visible against the cloudy sky. The castle had been the seat of the chiefs of Clan Campbell until they'd moved to Inverary on Loch Fyne when they became earls of Argyll. It was now used solely for a prison.

"Why?" Rory muttered under his breath.

His single eye glittering in the moonlight, Fearchar spat into the loch. " 'Tis a question we'd all like answered. Maybe we should pay a call on Archibald Campbell."

Rory shook his head. "First, I'm going to raze Mingarry to the ground. By God, I'm going to tear down Ewen's castle stone by bloody stone."

"No need," Keir said cheerfully. "Mingarry's yours."

Rory looked over his shoulder at his youngest brother in surprise. "How long did the siege take?"

"Five days," he replied. "We left Tam MacLean in command. The lad's young, but he's sharp and capable."

Rory tried to smother his increasing alarm. No one had yet mentioned his absent Macdonald wife. Recalling the heartbroken tears she'd shed their last night together, he had no notion whether Joanna had gone with Ewen and Godfrey willingly. He wanted to believe she'd sworn to her virginity from a desire to save his life, but she might have made use of the opportunity to rid herself of an unwanted husband. Whatever her reasons, he intended to get her back. He'd worry about her feelings later.

"And Joanna?" he asked tersely. "Did you rescue her safely?"

"She wasn't there," Lachlan answered with compassion. "Nor Ewen or Godfrey. That's why the castle fell so quickly. There was no leadership at all. Only a token garrison had been left to defend the stronghold. We didn't destroy a single tower or blow up a battlement; everything's intact."

"Where are the Macdonalds?"

"No one knows," Lachlan replied as he rowed. "They've disappeared, including Ewen's wife and two children and a large, well-trained force of Macdonald men-at-arms. 'Tis why we had such a hard time finding you. There was no one to question and no leads to follow.''

''Ewen and Godfrey have been accused of treason by the Lords Commissioners of Parliament,'' said Keir. ''We're not the only ones searching for the blackhearted maggots, but we'll be the first ones to discover them. 'Twould be a bloody shame for anyone else to kill them but us.''

Rory plunged his oar into the black water of Loch Awe, rowing rhythmically. The fresh night air and the physical activity acted like a potion, sending the blood coursing through every vein. His muscles responded joyfully to the pull and drag of the current.

He would get his wife back—he didn't doubt it for a moment.

''How did you find me?'' he asked.

''Well, if you dangle a large enough bait, you'll finally pull in a fish,'' Keir said in cadence to his strokes. ''There's a guard back there in Innischonaill sitting on several sacks of newly minted crowns like a hen setting a clutch.''

Fearchar laughed, the soft, humorless sound filled with derision. ''If he's canny enough and lucky enough to fool Archibald Campbell, the Judas may just live to spend his gold.''

As they brought the small boat to the shore and jumped out, Rory turned and looked back at the island fortress. Somewhere in those formidable dungeons, the young Donald Dubh Macdonald waited in chains to be rescued by his kinsmen. Imprisoned by his own maternal grandfather, the second earl of Argyll, the lad was the illegitimate son of the last Macdonald High Chief, Lord of the Isles. Should the youngster be released from his imprisonment, every Macdonald in the Highlands and Isles, and their allies with them, would rise up in rebellion against James Stewart. 'Twould be Rory's duty to crush them. He prayed God it would never happen. Not for his sake, but for Joanna's.

''We'd best ride to Stalcaire,'' Rory said as they mounted and prepared to leave. ''Duncan will know if the permission for the cousins to wed has arrived from Rome. And if the annulment has been awarded.''

A scowl on his bearded face, Fearchar shifted in his saddle and glared at his cousin with his one good eye. "Hell and thunder! Won't the litigation be dropped, now that you're free to tell the truth?"

Keir snorted disdainfully. "There's always a midwife or a physician who can be bribed to swear to a young woman's virginity. And for enough sillers, even archbishops have been known to look the other way."

"But whatever the outcome of Ewen's petitions to Rome, we need to call at Archnacarry first," Lachlan said, a smile lighting up his aristocratic features. "I've received a message from Isabel Cameron. She believes that her niece can tell us where they've taken Joanna."

Chapter 24

"Your Aunt Isabel wrote that you may know the whereabouts of my lady wife," Rory said to the lassie, who'd approached him with an odd mixture of diffidence and serene self-possession. "Did you overhear something the day she was abducted by her kinsmen?"

Raine studied him for a moment, unused to the full beard he'd grown while imprisoned and now kept as a constant reminder of how much he owed the Macdonalds. Then she shook her head, her long ebony braids swinging gently. "The men didn't say where they were taking her, laird. At least, not that I heard."

Rory sank back in the chair, frustration eating at his vitals. Fearchar, Alex, and Nina, along with his two brothers, had joined him in the upper parlor at Archnacarry while he questioned the girl.

"But dearest," Nina said, clearly disappointed herself, "why did you tell Aunt Isabel that you knew Lady MacLean's whereabouts?"

"I do," the child replied, her jet eyes bright with the unflagging surety of youth. "But not because I overheard Lady Joanna's clansmen talking."

Lachlan, his backside braced against a table piled with books, gave her a warm smile of encouragement. With his shock of auburn waves, his classic features, and his fastidious dress, he presented a picture of urbane refinement. "Then how do you know, child?" he asked patiently.

319

"I saw her in a vision."

"Christ!" Keir exclaimed, "I can't believe it!" He sprang up from the tufted stool he'd perched on and glowered at the girl. "You wasted our time on some blasted hocus-pocus?"

Raine straightened beneath his accusing glare. Tossing her head, she folded her arms over her flat chest and met his scornful green eyes. "I didn't waste your time, Laird MacNeil," she said with a mutinous lift of her chin. "I never even knew *you* were coming."

Rory raised his hand, cautioning his hotheaded brother. "That's enough," he said. "I'm sure the lassie meant well."

"Pray, let her speak," Isabel entreated. "My niece is fey."

She'd entered the room unnoticed, and they turned to stare at her in surprise. The lady stood just inside the door, arms folded and hands slipped inside the wide sleeves of her mulberry wool gown. Wisps of her gray-streaked fair hair peeked out from beneath the sloping headdress; her eyes flashed with a droll humor.

Nina moved to her daughter's side and put an arm around her narrow shoulders. "Why, Raine, you've never spoken of this to me."

The hurt in Nina's soft voice touched everyone watching. Her gentle nature enriched the lives of all she encountered. Yet there seemed to be a wall of misunderstanding between mother and daughter that all the lady's sweetness had never breached.

Rory had heard the servants' gossip. Hell, who hadn't? Superstitious people whispered that Raine had been sired by a black-haired elf prince. Some were ignorant enough to claim that the lassie was part faery and possessed magical powers. He didn't believe such blather. But like anyone who'd observed the sloe-eyed, dark-headed lass in the midst of a family of blonds, Rory felt certain whoever the child's father was, he hadn't been Gideon Cameron.

"Nevertheless, your daughter has the second sight,

Nina," Isabel said, her voice ringing with pride. "I suggest you listen to her, Laird MacLean."

They really had no choice—'twas the only straw to be grasped. Rory nodded to Raine and gestured for her to step closer. Taking the lassie's small hand, he leaned forward in the chair and spoke kindly. "You say you've seen my lady wife in a vision?"

Her dark eyes never wavered from his. "Lady Mac-Lean's being held against her will, milord," she told him eagerly. "She is with her kinsmen in a fortress far away. I've seen her standing at a tower window, watching the sea and praying for you to come rescue her."

A tiny spark of hope glimmered in Rory's breast. Was he truly grasping at straws, or could this inexplicable child lead him to Joanna? "Can you tell me what this fortress looks like, lass?"

"The castle is on an island," Raine said. " 'Tis built on the edge of low cliffs." She took a deep breath, bit her bottom lip in concentration, and then continued. "It lies on the tip of a promontory jutting out into the ocean. There are three sea walls, and the gatehouse is flanked by octagonal turrets."

Rory met Alex's eyes with a feeling of desperation. Any number of Scottish strongholds would meet that description, especially in the Isles.

Alex came and dropped to one knee beside his niece. He patted her on the back and spoke in a low, easy manner. "That's good, lass. That's good. Now try to picture the castle very clearly in your mind. Can you tell us anything about this particular one that makes it different from any other?"

"The keep has two square towers and two round ones, each with a bartizan," she offered.

"Anything else?"

Bending her head, Raine pressed one finger to her mouth while she thought. Then she looked up to meet Rory's eyes, her adolescent features animated. "Along the parapets are gargoyles in the shape of ferocious eagles, with their beaks opened as though screaming into the wind and a cluster of arrows grasped in their pointed talons.''

"Dhòmhuill," Lachlan said, his voice sharp with exhilaration.

"Good girl!" Alex exclaimed as he hugged his niece.

Rory rose and patted Raine on the shoulder. "Thank you, lassie," he said, his hopes soaring.

Castle Dhòmhuill on the Isle of Skye was the mighty stronghold of Angus Macdonald, chief of Clan Uisdean. Like Somerled before him, Ewen could have fled to another kinsman for protection.

"We'll need all three ships," Lachlan said, pushing away from the table.

"And what if the lassie's wrong?" Keir demanded. "'Twill take a full week to load the armaments and supplies, another to sail there, and another back. That's nearly a month that we could be using to scour the countryside."

"I'm not wrong, Laird MacLean," Raine insisted. "I'm not." Her lips compressed in a tight line, she clutched his sleeve and looked up at him beseechingly.

"Trust my niece," Isabel said. "She saw Lady MacLean before ever she came to Archnacarry. Raine described your wife's red hair and plum-colored eyes two summers ago, when first she saw her. Neither of us knew the identity of the maid in her vision, until you brought her here."

"Is that true, Raine?" Rory questioned in astonishment.

" 'Tis true, milord."

He crouched down before the child. "Is she well?" he asked quietly.

Raine smiled, her eyes flashing with happiness. "Lady Joanna is well," she said. "In fact, she is more than well."

"What do you mean, lass?"

"You will know when you find her, Laird MacLean."

Rory looked up at his youngest brother. "Keir? Are you with us?"

Keir's green eyes narrowed and his cheeks flexed tensely as he met Rory's inquiring gaze. "Hell," he replied in disgust, "I wouldn't let you leave without me, and you damn well know it."

"All three ships lie off Stalcaire," Lachlan reminded his oldest brother. "You can speak to Duncan about the status of the annulment before we sail."

Rory took Nina's hand and met her worried eyes. "Thank you, once again, dear friend. At least now we have something to act upon."

"My family will keep all of you in our prayers," she replied. "I pray God you'll bring your wife back safely home."

The Macdonald fortress sat like a stone monolith on the basalt cliffs above the Minch. From the high tower window, Joanna watched the three galleons approach. Her throat ached from holding back tears of joy. Their sails had been spotted the previous day. Now the ships were maneuvering into place in front of Dhòmhuill's formidable sea walls.

The *Sea Dragon* sliced through the waves, her sleek prow graced with a three-headed monster. From her mainmast flew a long black banner emblazoned with a ferocious Celtic sea serpent, its elongated green body slithering in the wind. On her decks, Rory MacLean, chief of Clan MacLean, scion of the Celtic-Norse sea kings of the Hebrides, and laird of Kinlochleven and all its lands and all its fiefs, studied the ramparts of Dhòmhuill with the practiced eye of a warlord trained in the fine art of the siege.

"So the man has finally come," Lady Beatrix said from behind Joanna's shoulder. She gazed out at the galleons and sniffed contemptuously. " 'Twill do him no good."

Standing in front of the solar's other window, Lady Idoine peered out. Dressed in a gown of fine ruby silk, she fidgeted with the gold bracelets encircling her wrist. As long as her parents remained hidden away in the isolated castle, there'd be no chance of their contracting a marriage alliance for her, and Idoine was growing more and more discouraged every day. She'd had little to do in the past months except fuss with her cosmetics and jewelry to while away her boredom.

"Will he kill us, Mother?" Idoine asked in her high-pitched whine. "Andrew said the King's Avenger would come with his brothers and murder us all."

Joanna leaned against the edge of the stone casement and grasped the iron grillwork, her fingers taut and whitened. Despite her outer semblance of calm, her insides quivered with each breath she took. She fought the feeling of faintness that plagued her, refusing to give in to the fear that Rory might not be successful in his attempt to rescue her.

But he was there. Rory was alive, and he had found her.

"Don't be foolish, child," Beatrix told her daughter with a brittle laugh. "Dhòmhuill is impregnable. In two hundred years, no enemy has ever taken this castle."

Joanna clutched the elf-bolt in her other hand, remembering Raine's promise that it would protect her from danger. She prayed that her husband would be safe and that he'd forgiven her for betraying him in front of his friends. The rage she'd glimpsed in his eyes before he'd been struck from behind haunted her still. Yet if she'd refused to go with Ewen, Godfrey would have murdered Rory while he lay unconscious on the floor.

At Joanna's shoulder, Beatrix spoke coldly. "Ewen's already told you that the papal dispensation has been granted. You're free to marry Andrew as we all wish. Why worry about the King's Avenger and his contemptible brothers? They can do no more than yap at us like curs prowling around a dunghill."

"The annulment is still being investigated," Joanna reminded the callous woman, her gaze fastened on the scene below. "And I am still the wife of The MacLean."

As the first ship took her position in front of a twelve-foot-thick curtain wall, the second galleon drew near. On the tip of her prow, a great hawk soared above the waves on outspread wings. The *Sea Hawk* rode gently on the crests, her tall sails dipping to the castle in a deadly greeting. Lachlan MacRath, chief of Clan MacRath, whose ancestors included the kings of Ireland and Norway, had come to pay a call.

"Well, at least there won't be any more foolish attempts to sneak out of the castle." Lady Idoine twined a wisp of frizzled hair around her finger and giggled spitefully. "Unless Joanna intends to walk straight into their cannon fire."

But Joanna refused to be baited. She'd take no chances. Not now, after five and a half months of carefully avoiding confrontation, lest one of her cousins, in their mounting anger, become physically abusive.

High on the mainmast of the third galleon, a raven, symbol of an ancient Norse deity, flew on a blood-red flag. Keir MacNeil, chief of the MacNeils of Barra and descendant of Celtic sea raiders, maneuvered his ship alongside the others. Then the *Black Raven* dipped her flag in salute to her sister ships as a skiff was launched to take her captain to confer with his two brothers.

"Your disloyalty to your clan is shameful, Joanna," Beatrix needled. "Ewen has only the best for you in mind, my dear."

"Ewen is driven by ambition and greed," Joanna replied, her frayed temper unraveling at last. "He's never been concerned with the good of our clan. My cousin is willing to do anything, including murder, to get control of my inheritance."

With a sweep of her flowing satin robe, Beatrix turned and walked to a cushioned bench beside the fireplace. Joanna could hear the smile in her voice as she sat down and picked up her embroidery. "There's no sense in standing at the windows, girls. There'll be lots of noise and smoke for a while, but in the end they will merely have to sail away."

Time stretched endlessly as Dhòmhuill's inhabitants waited in near silence. Men-at-arms were ranged along the high battlements. Arquebusiers and archers stood impatiently in battle position, while cannoneers took their places at the gun ports. 'Twas the breath-stealing quiet before the storm.

The men on the ships below were in no hurry. They were making careful calculations as they measured the range. Joanna's husband would take utmost care that no stray cannon shell exploded against the walls of the keep, knowing that his wife would be lodged in the highest, most secure tower of the castle.

Just when it seemed that the battle would never begin, the first salvo sounded, and a cannonball struck the northernmost curtain wall. Shouts rang out along the parapets. The clatter of swords on targes, beating in cadence, filled the air, and the Macdonald war cry lifted from the throats of Joanna's kinsmen: *The Heathery Isle!*

The siege of Castle Dhòmhuill had begun.

Chapter 25

❦

They bombarded the sea walls methodically, testing the strength of the ancient fortress. Rory's master gunners fired their cannons with the precision of surgeons dissecting a cadaver. As he'd suspected, the castle's outdated ordnance couldn't match his advanced naval artillery. Dhòmhuill's ponderous culverins boomed from their keyhole gun ports, but the iron balls fell far too short to do any damage.

As they searched for the weak spot in the castle's defense, the trio of galleons moved along the low-lying cliffs, well out of range of the stronghold's ineffective guns. They found what they were looking for on the eighth day. A crack appeared in the northeast wall.

After that, the three crews took turns pounding away, hammering through the old stone and dry mortar with relentless accuracy. The guns boomed day and night, respites given to the cannoneers only long enough to cool down and regrease the iron barrels and their pivoting mounts.

Thick yellow-gray smoke, pungent with sulfur, drifted heavily on the moist sea breeze, and the constant noise of the cannonade ate away at the defenders' spirits. The explosions shook the battlements on which the Macdonalds stood watching in cold dread as their enemy, true masters in the art of war, worked with dispassionate expertise.

By dusk of the tenth day, the weakened rampart had been breached. Rory stood at the *Sea Dragon*'s landward rail and studied the fortress that tomorrow would be his. The reflection of the ships' lanterns bobbed on the cold, black sea, creating a shimmering pathway to his heart's desire.

"She'll be fine," Fearchar said, standing quietly beside him.

Rory nodded, his eyes fixed on the highest tower of the keep, where a single taper shone in the window. He smiled crookedly. "My only worry is who my wife will be pretending to be this time. Will I find Joanna disguised as a hackbutter or a faery princess?"

Fearchar scratched his whiskered jowl and laughed deep in his chest. "The bonny wee lass knows how to lead a poor laddie on a merry chase, 'tis certain," he agreed. "Your sailing days are fair numbered. You'll be too busy at home to be looking for any trouble abroad."

Rory hefted the astrolabe up to shoulder height to sight the Pole Star. He'd soon be charting their course for the return voyage. "Lady MacLean has a penchant for playing dress-up that I'm only now beginning to appreciate," he admitted, the warm affection in his voice undeniable. "I think I'll gift her with harem pajamas for Hallowmas and teach her how to salaam."

Later, under the protective fire of his cannons and the smoke-filled midnight sky, Rory took a squad of men in a skiff, scaled the low slopes to the west, where the fortress walls reached nearly to the water, and blew open the castle's sea gate to create a diversion. As the Macdonalds rushed to protect the small, insignificant portal, the three ships' crews clambered up the cliffs to the east.

At daybreak Rory and Fearchar led the first wave of assault through the gaping castle wall and into the teeming outer bailey. Behind them rushed their clansmen, the MacLean war cry loud and fierce in their throats. Lachlan and his kinsmen, followed by Keir and the MacNeils, made up the second and third waves. Screaming and shouting, the Macdonalds met them with arquebuses, swords, dirks, pikes, and Lochaber axes.

Rory, armed with broadsword and dirk, slashed his way

through the initial line of defense. In the clamor and confusion someone bumped into Rory's back, and he whirled to find Fearchar, who grinned with a fearsome happiness.

" 'Tis a great day for a fight!" the colossus bellowed before wading back into the fray.

From the corner of his eye, Rory caught sight of Keir, pounding a Macdonald down to his knees with mighty blows from the pommel end of his heavy hilt. A second fellow attacked from behind, and Keir impaled the man neatly on the spike of his targe before turning to kill his first opponent.

Rory fought his way steadily toward the keep, continually scanning the melee for a glimpse of Ewen or Godfrey. Across the length of the inner bailey, three husky men in half-armor, one brandishing a long-handled ax, were charging Lachlan. Light-footed and resilient, he ducked just in time to avoid decapitation, then lunged low with his dirk, skewering the Macdonald axman.

As Rory raced to his brother's side, one of the remaining two foes turned in belated awareness of danger. Rory rammed the thickset fellow with his shoulder so hard his helm flew off, then struck his nose a vicious blow with his sword hilt. The soldier staggered beneath the shock. Rory adroitly kicked his legs out from under him and slit the bastard's throat with his dirk on the way down.

By that time, Lachlan had dispatched his third opponent. He scowled at his older brother. "Are you trying to spoil my fun?" he called over the tumult. "Find your own Macdonalds to kill."

"I'm trying to find Ewen and Godfrey," Rory shouted.

"Haven't seen them." With a salute of his sword, Lachlan hurried to meet two pikemen coming toward him. "Try the keep," he shouted back over his shoulder.

Once engaged in close combat, the Macdonalds proved unable to sustain the shock of the first charge, and the battle's outcome was quickly decided. The invaders' initial violent rush swept through the defenders, isolating them in pockets. MacLeans, MacRaths and MacNeils were now systematically annihilating any of the enemy who refused to surrender. By Rory's orders, prisoners were not to be killed and the wounded were to be tended. He didn't want any more Macdonald blood on his hands than absolutely necessary.

Knowing victory was inevitable, Rory raced to the door of the donjon, which had been left ajar, its guards dead on the flagstones. The vestibule stood empty. The tables and benches in the great hall had been shoved willy-nilly in a jumble of furniture and half-eaten food.

He crossed the floor, stirring up the scent of the herbed rushes, ironically sweet in contrast to the gore and mayhem just outside the thick walls. Halfway across the chamber a blur of movement caught his eye, and he turned toward an inside staircase.

Cool and collected, Ewen stepped down from the last stair. With a faint smile, he moved confidently to the wall by the huge fireplace, where a pair of claymores hung, their blades approaching four feet in length, and calmly dropped his broadsword on the floor at his feet. He took one of the great swords down, and with the large hilt grasped in both hands, whipped it about, testing its strength and flexibility. He appeared fresh and relaxed. Clearly, he hadn't bothered to participate in the defense of another laird's castle. He'd left the fighting to his unfortunate kinsmen, along with the valor.

"So it comes to this," Ewen said with a smirk of satisfaction as he moved across the floor. "We can decide now, just the two of us, once and for all, the ownership of Kinlochleven and the chieftainship of Clan Macdonald." He gestured for Rory to approach. "You want the other claymore? Come get it. Or is it your wife you've come such a long way to recover? Come and get them both, MacLean—for you'll not have one without the other."

Rory advanced cautiously, the broadsword in his right hand, his dirk in the left. Without forewarning, Ewen charged, swinging the huge, double-handed sword like the scythe of death.

Parrying the claymore with its wide, drooping cross-guard, Rory dodged and feinted, edging sideways across the floor, moving whenever possible in the direction of the hearth and the other weapon. Fighting for his life, he used his agility and fleetness to avoid the limb-severing blade.

Again and again, Rory retreated before his opponent's aggressive, slashing attack. Ewen narrowed the distance between them relentlessly. He struck the smaller, lighter broadsword with his heavy claymore repeatedly, the jarring impact vibrating up Rory's arm and numbing his fingers. Canny and skilled, Ewen stayed out of range of the two shorter blades as he hacked viciously, trying to drive Rory to his knees.

Emitting a sudden shout of rage, the Macdonald war commander struck downward with all his strength, and the violent impact forced the broadsword to the floor. As Rory sank to one knee beneath the punishing blow, his blade snapped at the hilt and the blue steel clanged, useless, on the stones.

Ewen stood over him, breathing quickly, with a look of triumph on his dark, bearded face. He raised the claymore high over his head for the deathblow.

Rory sprang out of his crouch and propelled himself forward, striking out at Ewen's exposed thigh with his dirk in search of tendon and bone.

Ewen jumped back, the razor-sharp blade missing him by a hair's breadth. Off-balance, he staggered, crashed heavily to the rush-covered stones, and rolled to his knees, weapon ready.

In those few precious moments, Rory dashed across the floor to the fireplace and reached the other claymore just in time to turn and meet Ewen's slicing blow. With the great sword in his hands at last, Rory moved directly into the attack.

The claymores exploded together as the two enemies fought fast and viciously. Lunging, traversing, wrenching, parrying, they moved around the floor. The blades gleamed, wicked and deadly, in the flickering candlelight thrown from the brackets on the wall.

Two swordsmen of great strength intent on beating down the other's blade, they eddied back and forth across the chamber. They stepped over benches and tables, kicking the discarded trenchers and flagons out of their way, both men gasping for breath. Sweat poured down their faces and soaked their shirts.

Ewen's strength slowly waned before the furious onslaught of his more powerful opponent. Chest heaving, eyes bulging, he was no match for a man who'd spent the last ten years training in close combat. Swordplay was embedded in Rory's bones. Getting his second wind, Ewen thrust, dodged, and thrust again. The blades rang and slid.

Then Rory saw the opening he'd been waiting for. He parried, feinted, and slashed. Ewen dropped his weapon and stared blankly, knowing the clang of his heavy blade on the stones sounded his death knell. With a final lunge, Rory administered the *coup de grâce*, sending his claymore straight through his adversary's heart.

Then drawing in great drafts of air, he turned and started up the stairs, claymore in hand. Andrew stood at the top of the landing, holding a broadsword and targe. The youngster stared down at his mortal enemy, his beautiful dark eyes wide and terrified.

"Your father's dead, lad," Rory said quietly as he hurried up the stairwell. "Don't make me kill you, too."

His face stark with fright, Andrew took a step back, opened his hands, and let the weapons fall to the stones. As his circular wooden shield rolled down the stairs past Rory, he leaned his back against the rough stone wall and slowly slid down it. Resting his arms on his knees, he hid his face from sight.

Rory paused on the step below. "Where's my wife?"

"Up there," the boy answered, pointing one raised finger to the landing above.

Rory climbed the stairs to the third floor and found a

door standing open. When he entered, Lady Beatrix flung herself at his feet.

"Don't kill us!" she implored, her hands lifted toward him in supplication. "Oh, my God, don't kill us! Idoine and I are innocent of any wrongdoing."

Idoine began to screech, her ear-splitting shrieks filling the room. She didn't emit a single comprehensible syllable, just screamed over and over and over in mindless terror.

His wife stood at the window, her slim, rigid back squarely to Rory. Utterly silent and immobile, she looked out on the carnage below, where her kinsmen had suffered an ignominious defeat at his hands. He had broken the power of the treasonous Glencoe Macdonalds.

Rory tightened his jaw. He'd let her rail and call him names with patient composure. She could scratch and bite and kick if it brought her heart's ease. Hell, he preferred her clever tongue to this composed, icy silence.

All the while, Idoine's strident wail, piercing and monotonous, never stopped.

To Rory's relief, Fearchar appeared at the doorway. "Damn," he muttered, sheathing his weapons and stepping inside.

"Get them out of here," Rory ordered, his gaze fixed on his wife.

"Oh, please don't hurt us, don't hurt us," Beatrix moaned as Fearchar caught her elbow and drew her up. With a soft snort of disgust, he pushed her gently toward the door. Then he clapped his big hand over Idoine's mouth, lifted her up, and hauled her bodily out of the chamber. The muffled sound of the girl's squawking could be heard going all the way down the stairs.

Still Joanna didn't turn. With one slender hand braced on the stone casing, she stared straight ahead. Rory had no idea what she was thinking or feeling, for she gave no sign. His spirit shriveled inside his chest at the possibility that she hated him.

With a mighty thrust, he buried the claymore's tip in the oak planking at his feet. Then he held out one hand and tried to speak in a cool, dispassionate tone, though his hoarse voice betrayed him. "I've come to take you home, Joanna. 'Tis time to go home to Kinlochleven."

Joanna bent her head and blinked back the tears. The words spoken in that marvelous deep baritone were achingly familiar. They were nearly the same words Grandpapa had said when he'd come for her at Allonby Castle. *'Tis time to be going home, darling of my heart. 'Tis time to go home to the Highlands.*

She didn't need a bonny knight in shining armor to come riding up on a white steed to rescue her. Her magnificent husband, in his green and black plaid and clan bonnet with the three chief's feathers, had saved her from her evil, perfidious cousin Ewen.

Night after night, she'd dreamed of Rory coming to get her and take her home. And now he was here.

Her heart soaring, Joanna turned . . . and gazed in paralyzed revulsion at the barbaric creature standing before her. Here was no romantic Highland chief. This stranger wore leather breeches and long black boots that came past his knees. His full, luxurious beard hid half his features, and his sleeveless jerkin hung in tatters about his grimy, blood-smeared chest. The upper part of his face and his clubbed hair were covered with splotches of soot, and he reeked of gunpowder.

Holy heavens!

She'd been captured by a pirate.

Shocked, Rory stared at his wife, who looked at him in soundless horror. He barely noticed the grimace of repugnance that marred her lovely face. Instead his stunned gaze fastened on her belly, and he grinned in perfect delight as an extraordinary joy filled his entire being.

Joanna was big with child.

His wee bonny bride was gloriously, marvelously, unequivocally pregnant.

"Joanna," he said, the single word a harsh rasp.

She lifted one shaky hand toward him, confusion in her violet-blue eyes. "Rory?" she whispered with a catch of hesitation, and then slowly crumpled in a faint.

He reached her instantly, sweeping her limp form up in his arms before she touched the floor. His heart in his throat, Rory looked down at his wife. Her long hair spilled over his arm in strands of copper satin. Her delicate features with their sprinkling of faery dust were shadowed with circles beneath the long lashes. The firm mound of her abdomen pushed tautly against her bright yellow gown. As he looked at the unmistakable evidence of his child growing within her small body, a feeling of awe came over him.

Rory turned and discovered Lachlan standing at the doorway, one hand braced on the jamb, the other loosely holding his broadsword. He had a superficial cut on his arm, but was otherwise unscathed. "Is she hurt?" he asked with a frown of concern.

Shaken to his boots, Rory gazed at his beloved wife. "She fainted, is all." His heart swelled with pride. He glanced over once again to meet his brother's worried gaze, and the unimaginable joy he felt made his deep, twenty-eight-year-old voice crack like an adolescent's. *"She's pregnant."*

"Well, there goes the annulment," Lachlan replied with a wry grin.

Holding her close to his chest, Rory carried Joanna Màiri Macdonald MacLean out of Castle Dhòmhuill's keep and into his surrendered heart.

Joanna sat on the edge of the narrow bed, listening to the muted sounds of activity as the *Sea Dragon* got under way. She could hear her husband's shouted orders to the helmsman and the muffled rattle of the rigging above decks as the sails were unfurled. Wrapped snugly in a warm plaid, she looked about her. Rory had been plotting the course home; the materials were spread across a worktable bolted to the wall.

Curious to see his things, she wandered about the cabin, touching the sandglass, the lodestone enclosed in a filigree case, and the unfamiliar maritime instruments.

Fascinated, Joanna studied the mechanical compass and rulers, the tables of high and low tides, the magnetic navigational compass, the mariners' maps and charts of the heavens. Like so many Scotsmen, Rory appeared to have a natural gift for mathematics and science. She'd ask him to show her how he used his nautical tools, though she doubted she'd understand the half of it. Her studies at Allonby Castle had centered on languages, deportment, and religion.

The baby kicked at that moment, a strong, sudden blow, and she pressed her hand to the spot. "Do you want to be a seafarer like your da?" she asked happily. "Who are you, I wonder, my wee love. Are you a comely laddie who'll sail to exotic places and bring back marvelous treasures, or a bonny lassie who'll stay home with your mama when she's old and gray-haired?"

Restless and impatient to see the babe's father, Joanna peeked out the stern windows to the castle, where a cloud of billowing black smoke drifted across the leaden sky. She finally sank down on the edge of the mattress and drummed her fingers on her knees.

Rory came inside less than twenty minutes later. He entered the cabin stark naked, and she jerked at the sight of his imposing figure, bare-arsed and splendrous. The three-headed sea dragon on his upper arm glistened in the lantern light.

"I washed up on deck with the other men," he explained with a sideways grin at her startled reaction. "Our clothes and hair stink of gunpowder after a battle, and we're covered with charcoal dust. So we strip and suds down, then empty casks of fresh water over our filthy hides before coming below."

There must have been lots of Macdonald blood to wash away as well, though he was too polite to mention that.

He came closer, and she could see a row of blisters on one arm, where he'd probably brushed against the barrel of a cannon. In addition, he had several cuts and scrapes on his hairy chest and long legs, though nothing appeared serious.

"You've been hurt," she said, pointing to the raw weals.

He shook his head briskly, and drops of water sprinkled about his wide shoulders. "Only minor scratches."

"And you've grown a beard. 'Tis why I fainted," she explained. "I didn't recognize you with the whiskers and the pirate clothes. Godsakes, I've never seen you in breeches before. You looked like an English sea rover."

Her husband smiled, not saying a word.

"I don't usually faint, I can promise you that," she announced, unnerved by his enigmatic silence. "Idoine's the one who passes out at the least provocation."

Rory came over to the bed and sank down on one knee in front of her. He took Joanna's hands and gazed at her, the light in his brilliant eyes dancing. God's truth, having just successfully stormed an impregnable fortress and vanquished his foes, he certainly had the right to be happy.

He traced the callused tip of his forefinger in a half-circle beneath her lower lashes. "Have you been ill?" he asked tenderly, though the smile never left his eyes. "You look a bit pale."

So he hadn't noticed. Well, wasn't that just like a man who'd spent all his time being the scourge of the seas? What would a dragon know about women and babies, anyway?

Joanna had regained consciousness just as Rory laid her on the bed in his cabin. The moment she looked into those mesmerizing green eyes, she'd realized her foolishness. She'd forgotten back there in the tower room that her husband *was* a pirate. A predatory, half-civilized sea raider, who'd gone to great pains to ensure that his bride had the most romantic wedding day possible—until she'd ruined it by threatening him with a crossbow.

But they hadn't had time to talk then. He'd only stayed a few brief moments before returning to the castle to oversee the final stages of the siege, collecting the prisoners, treating the wounded, tallying the movable ordnance, and loading the sacks of shot and casks of gunpowder onto the skiffs to be taken to the waiting galleons.

"I haven't been sick, exactly," Joanna said as she adjusted the ample yards of wool tartan about her swollen body. She'd wait until the right moment to tell him he was going to be a father. "What happened to Beatrix and Idoine?"

"They and the other women, along with Andrew, are on board the *Hawk*. Lachlan will return them safely to Glencoe, where they can find shelter with kinsmen. After Dhòmhuill's arsenal is dismantled and the remaining armaments loaded into the holds, Laird Angus will be on his way to Edinburgh with Keir on the *Raven*."

" 'Tis a shame Ewen's greed and ambition brought another man down with him," she said. "I told the chief of Clan Uisdean the day I arrived that I was being held against my will. He refused to help me leave."

"Joanna," Rory said in a thoughtful tone, "we searched the entire castle and never found Godfrey."

"He was never there." Inhaling the clean scent of her husband's freshly scrubbed skin, she caught the medal of St. Columba on the tips of her fingers and rubbed the pad of her thumb absently across the engraved gold.

"When did you see him last?"

"He left us on the road out of Archnacarry Glen, after they'd fired the byres and outbuildings. Beatrix and Idoine were waiting on a fishing boat in the loch, which took us to the ship in Loch Linnhe. Apparently Godfrey was supposed to meet us at Ballachulish, but he never came, so we sailed without him. I don't think even Ewen knew his whereabouts."

"Godfrey's been declared a fugitive from the law. He'll eventually be brought to ground." As Rory talked, his fingers slid along the edges of the plaid covering her, and Joanna clutched it tighter.

"I'm cold," she said, feigning a shiver. Actually, the cabin had grown cozy from a glowing brazier in the corner.

Her husband glanced around the small space with a

scowl, and his voice grew sharp with displeasure. "Hasn't Arthur seen to your comfort?"

"He's been very helpful," she said in the young man's defense. "He brought me food and drink and lit a fire in the stove."

Satisfied, her husband began to peel away the sheltering green and black tartan once again.

"Rory, there's something I have to tell you," Joanna blurted out, clasping the plaid to her. She could feel her color rising as she wondered frantically how best to approach the delicate subject of fatherhood.

He lifted her tangled hair off her shoulders and smoothed the stray wisps away from her face and lashes. Then, as he cupped her cheeks in his rough palms, the smile in his eyes faded.

"Joanna," he said quite seriously, "I know how you must feel about this. Believe me, darling, I'm not happy about it myself. Often we have no control over the events in our lives. We must learn to accept the tragedies fate brings us and carry on."

For a moment, she thought he meant the unborn babe, and her shoulders drooped at the possibility that he felt such repugnance. Then she realized he was talking about the siege and the spilling of Macdonald blood.

"That's so true," she said softly. "And sometimes wonderful things happen without forewarning—at least, I hope you think it's wonderful, because I certainly do."

For the third time, Rory began to lift the wool from her shoulders, and Joanna gripped his fingers and held them in place. Though he outmatched her strength tenfold, he waited patiently for her to go on.

" 'Tis been over five months since we were wed," she stated in her most prosaic manner. "But we never really had a chance to get to know each other. That is, to know how the other one felt about . . . well, even small, inconsequential things."

He nodded encouragingly. "Such as?"

She took a quick breath and the words came out in a

rush. "Such as how you feel about children."

In sudden and jubilant relief, Rory comprehended the cause of Joanna's creased brow and the troubled look in her eyes. His wife didn't blame him for Ewen's death or the deaths of her other kinsmen. She recognized that her clan had left him no choice. But for some inexplicable reason known only to Joanna, she believed he was unaware of her pregnancy.

He spoke to her with perfect solemnity, though the effort not to laugh nearly strangled him, as he quoted an old Gaelic proverb. " 'A house without a dog, a cat, or a little child is one without affection or merriment.' " He pressed his lips to her forehead, then added, "I think 'twould be a sad thing for a man not to have several offspring, at the very least."

"You do?"

"I do."

The violet-blue eyes flashed with happiness as she released his fingers. "Then I have something to tell you." She shucked off the plaid that wrapped her small figure, flung her arms wide, and smiled delightedly. "I'm carrying your child."

"I noticed."

Her throaty contralto squeaked in surprise. "You did?"

"I did," he said softly, busy removing her shoes. Sliding his fingers up her shapely leg, he brought down one garter and hose.

She braced her hands on Rory's shoulders, scarcely aware of his movements or of his body's fiercely intense reaction to her nearness. "Are you happy about the bairn?"

"I'm very happy." He disposed of the other stocking, and cupping her high arches in his hands, he massaged her dainty feet until she sighed with pleasure. Then he lifted the hem of her gown and brought it up to her hips. "And now I'm going to show you just how very happy I am, Joanna."

Easing her legs apart gently, Rory kissed her bare thighs. Slowly, tenderly, he pushed the yellow gown higher and drew it over her head, then removed her petticoat and chemise. His heart thudding with elation, he sank back on his haunches and gazed at his pregnant wife.

She blushed as he studied her in wonderment. Her small breasts had grown fuller, their pink nipples slightly enlarged. Her previously flat belly protruded in a firm, compact ball.

Lifting her in his arms, Rory laid Joanna on the bed, where he searched for any bruises that might indicate she'd been mistreated. When he found no sign of injury, he breathed easier.

"No one hurt you?" he asked gruffly as he bent over her. His manhood brushed intimately against her thigh, hard and pulsing with need.

"I wasn't harmed," she assured him, then gave him a trembling smile. "Though my cousins were certainly unhappy when they noticed my condition." She touched his bearded cheek, her eyes bright with unshed tears. "I attempted twice to escape. After the second time, I was never left alone. I think Ewen planned on trying to do away with the baby once it was born. That's why I prayed for you to come day and night, Rory. I was so frightened you wouldn't find me in time."

"I was imprisoned in Innischonaill." He kissed her fluttering lids and the tip of her nose. "Otherwise, I'd have been here much sooner."

"Why were you put in that horrible place?" she asked in alarm. "Who took you there?"

"I don't know, lass. 'Tis something I'll have to find out later. Right now, I'm just grateful you're safe and here in my arms where you belong."

He kissed her deeply, tasting her sweetness, and their tongues met with frantic eagerness. Joanna threaded her fingers through his wet hair as Rory moved across her body, raining kisses on the creamy skin. He caressed her soft breasts, laving their crests; then he progressed lower and kissed her distended belly. The babe stirred in her womb, and tears sprang to his eyes as he saw the living proof of the seed he'd sown. The seed her body had so lovingly nurtured.

His vision blurring, Rory pressed his mouth again to Joanna's rounded abdomen. His heart ached with happiness as his hands roved over the smooth, taut mound. Teardrops crept down his bearded cheeks. Had anyone who knew him been told that the chief of Clan MacLean broke down and wept, he'd never have believed it.

"Rory," she whispered, touching her fingertips to his face, "you're crying."

"They're tears of joy, lass," he said. He caught her fingers and pressed them to his lips. "Joy that I've been so undeservedly blessed."

He lay beside her and spoke quietly. "I'm going to take you now, darling, but I promise to be very, very careful."

"Oh, Rory, I've wanted you so," she murmured against his lips, then kissed him passionately.

He turned Joanna on her side, her back against his chest, her rump pressed enticingly against his thickened sex. His aroused, eager body reacted with a sexual energy that pulsated through every muscle and vein. The vibrant ache of lust threatened to steal his control, and Rory clamped down hard on his rampaging instincts. He clenched his teeth and set his jaw, promising himself he'd be slow and gentle if it killed him.

His arms around his precious wife, he caressed her breasts, playing tenderly with the tightened buds. With his other hand, he delved into the nest of auburn fluff at the juncture of her thighs and lightly teased her silken folds until she grew sleek with moisture. She arched her back and released a long sigh of gratification.

"Does this please you?" he whispered in her ear as he stroked her delicate nub with the pad of his thumb.

"Mm," she hummed, moving against his hand. " 'Tis unbelievably pleasurable, milord dragon. I can't think why I wasted so much time dressed like a laddie. 'Tis *so* much more enjoyable being your wife than your gillie-in-training."

He nibbled on her earlobe and inhaled the perfume of her hair. "I was afraid I'd have to guess what guise you'd adopted this time. I wondered if I should look in the armory for an armorer's wee apprentice or search the donjon for a redheaded barber's assistant."

She laughed softly. "I'll wager you didn't expect to find me costumed as a pregnant lady."

"Not in my wildest dreams, sweetheart," he said with a low chuckle.

Carefully, Rory lifted her slender thigh to allow him better access and eased into her. Their physical joining nearly robbed him of his breath, the tight warmth of her narrow passage squeezing his turgid erection with dazzling currents of pleasure. He was far too big to sheath himself to the hilt in her diminutive body. When he bumped cautiously against her womb, he paused and waited. He closed his eyes, marveling at the wondrous feeling, as he enfolded his wife in his arms while buried deep inside her. He just held her, wanting the moment to go on forever.

"Oh, God, Joanna," he whispered. "How many nights I have dreamed of this."

She laughed softly and brought his hand up to her bulging tummy. "Not quite like this, I don't think."

He grinned and nipped her shoulder. "Only because I'm too much of a jackass to even think of such a splendid thing. I spent months worrying about an annulment that could never have been granted."

Slowly, leisurely, Rory moved inside Joanna as he stroked and caressed her with his hands. He kept the pace steady, using more restraint than he'd ever thought himself capable of.

Joanna made a short, breathless sound in the back of her throat, part sigh and part sob.

"Tell me if I'm hurting you," he said thickly, though 'twould be the death of him to stop now.

Her breath coming heavy and fast, she ran her hand down his arm and lightly touched his fingers, urging him on. "It feels wonderful. Don't stop, Rory. Oh, please, don't stop."

He played with her gently as he thrust steadily in and out, bringing her to fulfillment and then prolonging her pleasure, till she grew limp and relaxed in his arms. Drawing her closer to his straining body, he climaxed with great, shuddering jerks. The physical ecstasy heightened the overpowering feelings of tenderness and caring that Joanna and the baby had awakened inside him. The joy he experienced at that moment surpassed everything he'd ever longed for, ever dreamed of.

"Ah, Joanna," he said on a hoarse rush of air, "darling of my heart, I love you."

Rory stopped, dead still, as he realized what he'd just said. The words had come unbidden and unrehearsed, torn from deep inside him.

Her head came back sharply against his shoulder, but she didn't say a thing. He could tell she was as startled by the admission as he'd been. For breathless moments, he waited, hoping against hope that Joanna would tell him she loved him in return.

But 'twas not to be.

Rory bent his head and kissed her cheek. The taste of her salty tears seared the open wound that once was his unconquerable heart.

He told himself that it would be all right. In the years to come, he'd teach her to love him. But his pragmatic brain warned his battered soul that Joanna might never love him—not unless he confessed to a guilt and repentance he didn't feel for the capture and execution of Somerled Macdonald.

Rory eased his wife around in his arms and cuddled her close, and while she quietly cried herself to sleep, he silently and bitterly cursed the Red Wolf of Glencoe.

Chapter 26

February 1499
Inverary Castle
Loch Fyne

"The incompetence of your guards at Innischonaill cost me my freedom," Godfrey complained bitterly. "I don't dare show my face outside these walls. I might as well be clapped in a dungeon myself."

Archibald Campbell peered at Godfrey from the corner of his eye with cold indifference. They were in the laird's suite of private rooms at Inverary Castle, seat of the earls of Argyll. The present earl was having his portrait painted.

"MacLean and his brothers took the lives of some of my finest men-at-arms," Argyll replied in an unruffled tone. "You don't hear me ranting like a madman."

One hand on his hip, the other on the hilt of his broadsword, Argyll stood in the feeble light of the window, flanked by four freestanding candelabras. Draped across the back of a settle beside him was a banner with his coat of arms; on the cushions lay a magnificent claymore. A brass-studded targe, throwing back the candlelight, had been propped against the bench leg.

"Finest men! Pah!" Godfrey replied with a snort. "Andrew said over a dozen of your soldiers fell beneath the three brothers' blades in a matter of minutes. Only their gross incompetence kept MacLean from guessing the brig-

345

ands were actually Campbell clansmen in disguise. My God, if your men couldn't abduct a bit of a lassie and an awkward lad, they were worthless to begin with."

Godfrey glanced over at the artist with a scowl of annoyance. Upon his arrival in the sitting room, Argyll had assured him that Jan van Artevelde spoke no Gaelic; they communicated with each other in French.

The earl, in his attempt to preserve himself for posterity, had engaged the Flemish painter while meeting with the king at Castle Stalcaire. The short, stocky man from Ghent had painted both Duncan Stewart, earl of Appin, and James IV of Scotland. 'Twas the height of vanity, not to mention vulgar ostentation. Wisely Godfrey held his tongue and didn't mention either subject.

"MacLean killed eight more of my clansmen singlehandedly on the road from Archnacarry Manor," Argyll said pleasantly as he flicked a piece of lint off his sleeve. Attired in a predominantly black tartan, he sported a forest green jacket, a sleek badger sporran, and a black bonnet adorned with three plumes. He looked over at Godfrey, and his umber eyes reflected the gleam of the candlelight in cold, calculating appraisal. "You shouldn't have gotten the big fellow so damn mad, my friend. It took twenty husky men-at-arms to drag him down from his horse, disarm and bind him."

"I should have slit the sonofabitch's throat when I had the chance," Godfrey snarled. The artist looked up from his palette, mild astonishment in his eyes at the openly hostile tone.

Ignoring the baldheaded foreigner, Godfrey clenched his fists, longing to have MacLean on his knees before him once again. This time he wouldn't hesitate. Since the day he'd learned that the bloody bugger had escaped the island fortress on Loch Awe, he'd been shaking in his brogues.

Argyll smiled at the display of impotent anger. "I had hopes that the annulment would eventually be granted. In faith, I planned to free MacLean from Innischonaill after

Joanna and Iain were safely wed. There's no argument more convincing than a fait accompli.''

"My brother had other plans for Joanna," Godfrey reminded him bitterly. "What makes you think Ewen would have relinquished the heiress once he obtained an annulment?" In mounting irritation, he watched van Artevelde putter with his brushes and oils. Damnation. Argyll hadn't even shown the good manners to meet with him in private.

"You forget," the earl said placidly, "I have far more influence with the king than Ewen Macdonald ever had. Without James Stewart's permission for his ward to wed, no marriage contract would have stood up in the civil courts. And in the Western Highlands I *am* the civil courts."

What he said was true. Argyll obtained Crown charters of forfeited lands and bought up other chiefs' debts and mortgages. Using his overwhelming power in the Argyllshire courts, he obtained legal decrees giving him possession of their lands. And the earl wasn't afraid to use force, if necessary. He and his Campbell clansmen backed up their unscrupulous strategies with sword and dirk.

The earl looked down at the hand he'd braced flamboyantly on his hip and studied his large ruby ring. A nauseating complacency curved his thin lips, and Godfrey hoped to hell the portrait painter would capture it.

"With MacLean missing, presumably dead," Argyll continued, "the youngest son of the chief of Clan Campbell would have been a fine political choice for Lady Joanna's husband. But I underestimated MacLean's determination. This time I agree with you, Godfrey. He needs to be killed. And I'm going to give you a second chance to rid the world of the King's Avenger."

"What good would it do to kill him now, for Christ's sake?" Godfrey demanded. "There'll be no annulment. Not only does the rutting bastard have his wife back home at Kinlochleven, she's presented him with a son."

Argyll stirred restlessly and readjusted a fold of his plaid. The Fleming stepped from behind the easel, a frown on his intent features, and twitched the fold back in place. When the Scottish laird turned a thunderous scowl on him, the chubby fellow shrank behind the bulwark of his canvas.

"I'm well aware that a healthy male child has been born to Laird and Lady MacLean," Archibald Campbell replied in a sullen tone. "I had a very uncomfortable interview with the large gentleman in the presence of the king two weeks ago. It took all my wiles to convince James Stewart that I had nothing to do with MacLean's interment at Innischonaill."

His jaw clenched, Godfrey's words came sharp and stilted. "I suppose you placed the blame squarely on me."

Argyll shrugged and lifted his brows. "Whom else could I blame, my dear fellow? I told His Majesty that you and your clansmen had taken The MacLean to the fortress on Loch Awe and, through guile and deceit, convinced the captain of the garrison that you were acting under my orders."

Godfrey sank down on a low chest and covered his bearded face with his hands. It was worse than he'd expected. He was a dead man.

"Don't despair," Argyll told him smoothly. "There's still a way out of this mess."

Godfrey looked up, and his voice held the hoarse ache of utter defeat. "How, dammit?"

With a wave of his hand, Argyll signaled van Artevelde that the sitting was over and came to stand in front of his fellow Scotsman. "If you kill MacLean," he said without a trace of emotion, "the lovely widow will have to remarry for the sake of her clan and to safeguard her fortune. Given the chance, I know I can convince James Stewart that my son Iain would be the right choice. With my unqualified support, the alliance between the Glencoe Macdonalds and the Campbells would strengthen the king's hold on the entire western coast of Scotland."

"But MacLean's brat will inherit Joanna's estates and the chieftainship of the Glencoe Macdonalds," Godfrey retorted. "Not her second husband or the issue of that marriage."

"The lives of small children hang by a very fine thread," Argyll replied. He went to stand in front of the easel, studying his unfinished portrait intently. "A fever, an unfortunate accident, can snuff out their young lives in a matter of hours, minutes even."

Godfrey rose to his feet and straightened his shoulders belligerently. "Why should I take the chance?"

"*Très bien*," Argyll said, nodding his approval to the artist, then turned to Godfrey. "Because you are the one who knows Kinlochleven like the back of your hand, my dear fellow. And no one, least of all MacLean, would expect you to show your face within fifty miles of his castle."

A tiny flicker of hope sprang up in the midst of Godfrey's despair. "Getting into Kinlochleven wouldn't be easy," he said, half to himself.

"There's to be a christening in two weeks," the earl told him. "Relatives and friends have been invited to a grand banquet to celebrate. At Lady MacLean's request, even Beatrix and Idoine, accompanied by a small retinue of Macdonalds from Mingarry, are planning to attend. It seems the besotted husband is willing to grant his wife's kinsmen a pardon, provided they swear their loyalty to him on the dirk."

"I'm sure that pardon doesn't extend to me," Godfrey said with a humorless laugh.

"I'm afraid not," Argyll agreed. He picked up a decanter from a table nearby and poured sherry into three glasses as he continued. "But the celebration will provide an opportunity for you to slip inside the castle unnoticed. If you lie in stealth and take MacLean completely by surprise on what will certainly be one of the most joyous days of his life, you'll have a chance to rid us both of the King's Avenger once and for all."

Godfrey took the glass he offered. "And if I succeed?"

"If you succeed, I will see that you are safely transported

to France with enough money to last through your life-time—provided you're frugal.''

By God, it wasn't much. A refugee's life in some dreary, backwater village. But if Godfrey stayed in Scotland, he'd eventually be apprehended and hanged. MacLean wasn't called the Avenger for nothing.

He met the shrewd earl's unblinking gaze and read the unspoken ultimatum. If Godfrey knew what was best for him, he'd do exactly as he was told.

''You'll kill him?'' Argyll questioned amiably as he handed Jan van Artevelde a glass.

''What choice do I have?''

''Then I propose a toast,'' Archibald Campbell said with a smile of immense satisfaction. ''To the death of Rory MacLean.''

He lifted his glass, and the Flemish portrait painter, beaming happily, joined them.

The three men downed the wine in one hasty gulp. When Argyll dashed his glass against the hearthstone to seal the bargain, Godfrey did the same. The little Fleming looked from one man to the other in frank curiosity, then, with a grin, followed suit.

The day had been gray and stormy, but Kinlochleven sparkled with candlelight and swaths of green and black tartan. In spite of the chilly March weather, guests had come from as far as Castle Stalcaire to attend the christen-ing of James Alasdair MacLean. Everyone had assembled in the great hall for the lavish banquet following the High Mass and baptism ceremony. There'd been jugglers in bright silks and jesters with painted faces, muscular acro-bats in doublets and hose, minstrels playing harps, flutes, drums, and bells; and mysterious dancing gypsies with black flashing eyes.

After the feasting and entertainment, the titled visitors mingled, shoulder to shoulder, with the castle staff and gar-rison in the high-ceilinged chamber—laird and lady, stew-ard, scullery maid, and soldier—in celebration of the marvelous day. Even Ethel and her shy daughter, Peg, their dimpled cheeks aglow, came from the kitchen, blushing and smiling and hiding behind their lifted apron skirts, to join in the toast to the bonny wee bairn.

When Joanna and Rory had returned to Kinlochleven after the storming of Dhòmhuill, the Macdonald men-at-arms had been angered at learning that he'd killed their war leader. But Joanna told them how Ewen had abducted her, after forcing her to lie under oath to save her husband's life. She related her suspicions that Ewen had planned to do away with her baby once it was born. Each clansman had then willingly sworn an oath of loyalty to his chieftain's husband.

Joanna's household servants had been frightened of their new laird as well—after all, they'd helped her deceive him. But Rory had been willing to overlook past mistakes. He demanded only their loyalty from that day forward. His courage and intrinsic honor had shown in his actions these past five months. He'd been decisive and fair when it came to matters involving the castle, estates, and tenants and had proven himself a capable and just chief.

Now Seumas and Davie, Jacob Smithy and his burly son Lothar, Jock Kean, Abby, and Sarah stood beneath the gallery, where the musicians had started playing a lively round. Mary and several other pretty dairymaids whispered to one another in a corner, casting covert glances at a group of tall, rugged MacLeans and wondering if they were going to join in the dancing that was about to begin.

Lady Beatrix, Idoine, and Andrew had also attended the baptismal Mass, escorted by Tam MacLean and a small contingent of Macdonald men-at-arms. They'd stood a little apart from the throng of well-wishers in the great hall until Joanna approached, offering her hand in welcome to each. She knew her cousins had been dominated by Ewen's forceful personality. They were her kinsmen, and for the sake of her clan, she'd forgiven them. With Rory's acquiescence, she'd allowed the dispossessed trio to reside once again at Mingarry Castle.

Rory had begun, at Joanna's request, the subtle negotiations necessary to find Idoine a suitable husband. When Joanna had told her cousin they'd settled on a likely prospect, a joyous smile lit her round face, revealing the comeliness hidden behind the past sour disposition. Idoine had fussed over Jamie, her longing for motherhood tangibly expressed in the way she held the bairn close and kissed the wisps of golden hair. Away from their father's self-centered influence, both Idoine and Andrew would mature into the responsible adults they were meant to be.

Joanna moved from group to group in her role as chatelaine, making certain that everyone was enjoying the festivities. She waved to Lady Emma and her brother, Laird Duncan, from across the chamber, then threw a kiss to the Camerons. Lady Nina had graciously consented to be the baby's godmother, and Lachlan became the proud godfather.

The next chief of Clan MacLean was upstairs with Maude, sleeping peacefully in the cradle beside his parents' great canopied bed. Joanna had noticed Fearchar following her dear friend up the stairs and smiled to herself at the possibility that the two would soon ask their laird's permission to marry.

Murdoch and Tam chatted with Father Thomas by the blazing hearth, while Isabel and Raine Cameron, seated at a bench beside one of the trestle tables, visited animatedly with Arthur Hay. At another table, Keir and Lachlan were engrossed in a game of chess. Rory watched over their shoulders, offering acerbic advice to both.

After pausing to compliment Ethel and Peg on the delicious food they'd worked so hard to prepare, Joanna joined Lady Nina and Laird Cameron.

The rich blue satin of Nina's gown brought out the rose tones in her gold hair and complemented her peaches-and-cream complexion, reminding Joanna, once again, of a celestial being.

"Tell us about this tapestry in your bedroom that has Lady Emma so intrigued," Nina implored with her warm-hearted smile. "I understand it's quite unusual. Rory's mother believes the figures may be based on little known Greek mythology."

"Oh, 'tis not exactly *Greek* mythology," Joanna replied. "Originally, I had a scene of a knight in full armor bringing gifts to his lady fair hanging on my bedroom wall. I'd brought it with me from Cumberland, but my husband wasn't overly fond of it. So I had it removed to please him."

"What's so intriguing about this particular knight and his lady?" Alex asked, his hazel eyes inquisitive. At the mention of mythology, his scholarly interest had clearly been aroused.

"Nothing," Joanna admitted. " 'Twas the tapestry Rory hung in its place that's . . . well, different." At their looks of fascination, Joanna continued reluctantly. " 'Tis the depiction of a Highland laird who has a dragon's tail. He's . . . ah . . . frolicking with a sea nymph."

"Sounds rather scandalous," Alex said with a good-natured smile.

Rory joined them at that moment, and the two men exchanged distinctly masculine glances that spoke volumes about the differences between men and women and what they considered humorous.

Her eyelids lowered, Joanna smoothed her hand down the jeweled edge of her girdle. "For some strange reason," she said in a perplexed tone, "my husband thinks the laird in the tapestry is supposed to be the chief of Clan MacLean."

Nina's musical laughter rang out in startled surprise. "Why ever would he think that?"

Joanna met her husband's sparkling eyes. "Who knows?" she replied brightly. "I can't imagine where he would get such a nonsensical idea."

Nina and Alex turned their gazes on Rory, impatiently awaiting an explanation.

"That's something I intend to keep to myself," he said. He touched Joanna's long curls and grinned complacently.

"But I will tell you that my wife insisted the sea nymph be given bright red hair before she'd allow the tapestry to be hung in our bedroom."

As their friends laughed, Joanna wisely held her tongue. Sometimes in the evenings, Rory would look at the colorful wall hanging and burst into laughter all over again. She'd scolded him the last time, demanding to know if he was ever going to let her forget her mistake, but he'd been guffawing too hard to answer.

They'd spent the long winter evenings before Jamie was born sitting in their big bed, with a roaring blaze in the hearth nearby, learning about each other. Joanna had told Rory of her girlhood years at Allonby and Kinlochleven. He'd entertained her with stories of his marvelous adventures at sea. And she'd learned, though not to any great surprise, that the perfidious, diabolical, salacious Sea Dragon had a very sharp and very wicked sense of humor.

Rory put his arm about his wife's waist and drew her apart from the chattering guests. "I don't want you getting overtired," he told her quietly as he searched her face for any sign of fatigue.

Joanna had insisted on nursing Jamie herself, rather than allowing a wet nurse to nourish the babe. Resting against the pillows, she'd sit in their bed at night, cuddling him in her arms and cooing while he sucked greedily at her milk-swollen breasts. The loving tableau never failed to stir Rory's deepest emotions. He'd watch in awed silence until Jamie, milk pooled at the corners of his tiny pink mouth, fell asleep and was tucked in his cradle nearby. Then Rory would gather his wife in his arms and hold her against his heart, till they were all sound asleep once again.

"I'm not a bit tired," Joanna assured Rory now. "God's truth, I'm so happy, I'm floating." Her eyes agleam, she reached up, pulled his head down and kissed him lightly on the mouth.

He took the kiss and improved upon it, as greedy as his little son. "What's that for?" he teased.

She patted the lace on his shirt collar and fiddled with the gold buttons on the jacket he'd worn on their wedding day. "For bringing the Welsh troubadour all the way from Allonby Castle to sing at the banquet," she replied. " 'Twas a wonderful surprise." A smile curved her lips, and her face glowed with happiness. "How did you know I loved his ballads as a child?"

He touched the tip of her freckled nose playfully. "Maude told me about him. She said you used to sigh like a moonstruck lass over the verses he'd trill about the gallant knights-errant."

"Well, I don't anymore," she said pertly. "I'm not a dreamy-eyed lassie any longer. I have a real flesh-and-blood hero, who sleeps beside me every night."

He pulled her closer. "Do you now, lass?"

"Umhm," Joanna replied, scarcely able to keep from laughing. "And his name is Jamie." She wrinkled her nose impishly. "Let's go take a peek at him."

"Let's," Rory agreed. He caught Keir's eye as he guided Joanna toward the doorway of the great hall, signaling his brother that he was going upstairs.

Upon his arrival two days prior, Duncan Stewart had brought his nephew a message from Jan van Artevelde. Rory had spoken to the talented artist at Stalcaire, when he'd met with the king and the earl of Argyll a month ago. Upon learning that the little man from Flanders had been offered a chance to paint Archibald Campbell's portrait, Rory encouraged him to go to Inverary Castle and learn what he could about the connection between Godfrey Macdonald and the earl. Van Artevelde had quickly agreed, adding that the chief of Clan Campbell was unaware of his knowledge of the Gaelic, which had continued to improve since his shipboard studies with Lachlan.

From the painter's letter, Rory knew that Godfrey intended to sneak into Kinlochleven and assassinate him, most likely on the day of the christening. After conferring with his brothers and Fearchar, Rory had decided to go unarmed—except for the armpit knife hidden under his shirt—in an attempt to lure Godfrey from hiding.

From the day Duncan arrived with Lady Emma, the sentries had been alerted at the gatehouse and all entrances to the keep had been well guarded. But Rory hadn't told Joanna of the threat; there was no point in worrying her needlessly. Either Fearchar, Lachlan, or Keir, fully armed and ready for a surprise attack, would be with her and the baby at all times.

Chapter 27

～～ＱＣ～

Rory caught Joanna's elbow as they climbed the stone stairwell and drew her to a halt. It was the first moment they'd been alone since awakening that morning.

" 'Tis in a terrible hurry you are, lass," he said with a chuckle. "And for no very good reason that I know of."

"Was there something you wanted to tell me, sir dragon?" Joanna asked, a naughty smile peeking out enchantingly. "Or did you merely wish to reassure me that you haven't sprouted a scaly green tail since last I checked?"

She stood on the step above him, nearly eye level. Bracing her hands on his shoulders, she leaned forward for his kiss.

Rory covered her lips with his open mouth, stroking her velvety tongue with his own as he rejoiced in her sweet femininity. They hadn't coupled since the birth of their son, and he was wild with ardor.

During the months before the babe's birth, he'd longed for Joanna to tell him she loved him. Each time they'd joined physically, he'd waited in eager anticipation for her to voice affection for her husband. The eagerness had turned to disheartenment, and he hadn't made the mistake of speaking of his own love again. Rory had too much pride to embarrass Joanna by trying to force a declaration she couldn't make.

He'd also learned to avoid calling his wife by a certain

Gaelic endearment, for it always brought tears. The tender phrase revived painful memories, and he didn't have to be a gray-haired philosopher to guess what they were.

But he hadn't given up hope entirely. Lately he'd taken to hiding the love charm that Raine had fashioned under Joanna's pillow while she slept and removing it in the morning. Not that he believed in such rubbish. Still, a man who'd fallen helplessly in love with his strong-willed wife—a wife who refused even to consider the fact that she might be mistaken—could use all the help he could get.

When he broke the kiss, Joanna brushed her lips across his clean-shaven cheek and spoke in his ear. "We're supposed to wait for a month. That's what Maude and Lady Emma both told me."

"It's been a month," he reminded her. His hands about her waist, he drew her nearer still.

"Ah, so it has," Joanna replied with a winsome smile. She lowered her eyelids, feigning a maidenly shyness he knew for a sham. "Then tonight is the night, I suppose." She fluttered her long russet lashes outrageously. "That is, if you're willing, milord husband."

"I'm willing," he said huskily. She started to turn around and continue up the stairs, but he caught her elbows and held her fast. "Joanna, have I told you how happy I am? Seeing you with Jamie in your arms, watching you suckle him at your breast, seeing the love for our son glowing in your eyes. 'Tis the most wonderful sight a man could behold."

A hint of tears brightened her luminous gaze. She started to speak, and he placed two fingers against her lips.

"The night our son was born," he continued in a low, hushed voice, "I was beside myself with fear. Fear because you had to suffer the pain of childbirth, and there was nothing I could do to prevent it. Fear that the bairn wouldn't be healthy and strong. But most of all, lass, fear that I might lose you. I learned that night, as I prayed on my knees in the chapel where we were wed, that though our marriage had been contracted as a political and economic alliance, my life would be meaningless without you. The castles and the estates and the fiefs be damned. If you'd come to me, with nothing but the clothes on your back, sweetheart, I'd still have stormed that island fortress for you.''

''Oh, Rory,'' she whispered unsteadily. ''I . . . I . . .'' She paused, and the anguish in her violet-blue eyes nearly brought his heart to a standstill. Her lower lip quivered as she clasped his face in her shaky hands. ''I'm . . . so very . . . touched by your words.'' She pressed her lips against his in almost frantic desperation.

Rory could only hope that one day the memories of Somerled would fade, while his own presence would remain vivid and constant. More than that, Jamie's birth had forged a bond that could never be broken. And their future children would bind Joanna to him as nothing else could.

At last, Rory understood why his mother had run away with a man who owned no lands, no castles. The power of love was greater than any power on earth or in the heavens.

He broke the kiss and ran his fingertips across her satiny cheeks, brushing the teardrops from the tips of her lowered lashes. ''Come, milady wife,'' he said tenderly. ''Let's go see our bonny son.''

His arm about her waist, her head resting on his shoulder, they continued up the stairs side-by-side.

Just as they stepped onto the stone landing, a brightly clothed jester, his face painted in a comic mask, moved out of the shadows in a blur, catching them unawares at the very brink of the stairwell. The flicker of a blade gleamed in the dimly lit passageway.

In automatic reaction Rory threw his arm up, knocking the man's blow aside, while at the same time pushing Joanna forward and out of danger. She fell on her knees on the hard floor with a sharp gasp of pain, and Rory glanced to see if she'd been hurt. That brief instant gave his adversary the time he needed.

Using the momentum of his surprise attack, the man struck out viciously with the palm of his left hand, hitting Rory squarely on the jaw and cracking the back of his head against the wall behind him with a sickening thud. Momentarily stunned, Rory fought the blackness that threatened and slid to the floor, his back braced against the rough stones.

Sprawled on all fours, Joanna stared up in horror, unable to comprehend what was happening. The castle was filled with friends and kinsmen, many of whom were armed. But that day Rory wore no sword or dirk.

Wild-eyed and grinning deliriously, the buffoon in gaily spangled blouse and tight hose stood over her husband, his long, glittering blade poised to strike a lethal blow.

"Don't!" she gasped breathlessly. "Stop!" She flung herself at the man's back. With one arm wrapped around his neck, the other reaching to scratch his painted face, she hung on to him with all her weight.

The jester gave a feral snarl and brought the point of his razor-sharp blade back over his shoulder, stabbing Joanna. Shocked by the blow, she released her hold and tottered backward. The agonizing pain brought her to her knees, and darkness overtook her.

On the landing at Godfrey's feet, Rory kicked out with one foot, catching his enemy in the back of his ankle and knocking his leg out from under him. The portly man crashed on his back and slid down the stairs head first, the dirk clutched tight in his grasp. Rory drew his short armpit knife from beneath his shirt and scrambled after him.

Winded and dazed, Godfrey staggered to his feet in the middle of the stairwell. He braced one hand on the wall to catch his balance. As Rory approached, he struck out wildly with the eighteen-inch blade.

Rory twisted aside to dodge the frenzied blow. Certain of his advantage, Godfrey moved upward on the stairs, closing in on his foe in the narrow space. He lashed out with a low, strangled grunt, missed, and jumped back from the shorter blade just in time.

Rory wrenched past his opponent, gaining the lower step, where he ducked and dropped to one knee, avoiding the dirk's blue steel once again. Springing up from his crouch, he slashed out with his armpit knife, ripping across the man's paunch.

A look of disbelief contorted Godfrey's painted face. His weapon fell from his slack hand to rattle and bang its way down the length of the stairs. Incredulous, the brilliantly costumed jester looked down at his stomach. With a whimper of despair, he leaned one shoulder against the wall and slowly sank down, blood oozing between his fingers.

"Get me the priest," Godfrey moaned.

"You can find a priest in hell, you bloody bastard." Rory turned and raced up the stairs.

At the top of the landing, Joanna's still form lay prone on the cold floor, blood pooling on the stones beneath her shoulder. Rory turned his unconscious wife over gently, lifted her in his arms, and carried her into their private chamber. Maude and Fearchar, who'd been standing together at the window, turned in surprise.

"Christ, what's happened?" Fearchar asked, moving swiftly across the spacious room.

"Godfrey stabbed her." Rory laid Joanna tenderly on the bed and lifted her long locks away from the bleeding wound. "She was trying to save my life," he added, his voice raw and hoarse.

"My poor lambkin!" Maude cried as Fearchar headed for the door, sword in hand.

Rory glanced at the cradle. The sight of his sleeping son's cherubic countenance reassured him. His eyes closed, the laddie sucked noisily on his thumb.

"Godfrey's dead," Rory called over his shoulder to Fearchar's wide back. "But you can get my mother. And tell Lachlan and Keir what's happened without disturbing the guests."

Together, Rory and Maude bent over his wife's inert figure. "Damn," he cursed softly, "why couldn't it have been me?"

He took the scissors she handed him and carefully cut away Joanna's blood-soaked gown, bodice, and shift. At the sight of the clean cut, he breathed a prayer of thanksgiving.

Joanna had been struck in the fleshy part of her shoulder above the clavicle. In the glancing blow, the dirk had missed bone and major artery. The blood had already started to congeal. Considering the size of the two-edged blade and the smallness of her body, it'd been nothing short of miraculous. Rory would take his miracles any way he could get them.

Maude sighed with relief. " 'Twill need a few stitches, but my wee chick will be fine. She'll have a slight scar to remember the day by, is all.''

Rory met the woman's sensible gray eyes, grateful for her cool-headed presence.

"I won't try to revive her just yet," he said quietly. " 'Tis better if she's unconscious while we sew her up.''

He pressed the folded linen cloth that Maude handed him against the wound while she prepared the needle and thread. Brushing the coppery strands away from Joanna's pale face, he gazed at her drawn features. The freckles across her nose and cheeks stood out like a sprinkling of nutmeg on snow.

In only minutes, Lady Emma entered in a flurry of lavender satin. Immediately behind her came Keir. Rory's mother hurried to stand beside him at the bed, assessing the damage with quick, expert moves.

"She'll be fine, Rory," she assured him.

"Rory," Keir called from the open doorway, "you need to come with me. There's something you should hear.''

"Not now," he answered curtly, making no attempt to hide his annoyance. His youngest brother had the single-minded determination of a wounded bear, but nothing could be more important than being with Joanna at that moment.

"It's all right, dear," his mother assured Rory with her usual serenity. "Go with Keir. Maude and I will stitch up the cut. There's nothing more you can do here at the moment, and you're needed below.''

"I'm not going anywhere," Rory said, but he moved out

of the way so Maude and his mother could work on Joanna's shoulder.

Lachlan appeared at the door, a worried frown on his chiseled features. "How is she?"

"Nothing serious," Lady Emma called. "Though she won't be carrying Jamie around for a while."

At her cheerful words, Lachlan strode across the rug and placed his hand on his older brother's shoulder. "This is important, man, or we wouldn't be calling you away."

"What the hell is it?" Rory growled in exasperation.

The anxiety in Lachlan's green eyes warned him that whatever the matter was, it needed his immediate attention. Muttering an oath under his breath, Rory turned and headed for the door.

At the bottom of the stairs, Godfrey lay supine on the stones, grotesquely costumed in the multicolored blouse and long hose of a court fool. On his knees beside him, Father Thomas bent over the dying man. Making the sign of the cross, the priest began the rite of Extreme Unction.

To Rory's astonishment, Fearchar cradled Godfrey's head and shoulders, helping him to make his last confession. "The MacLean's here now," the flaxen-haired giant told Godfrey the moment Rory sank to one knee beside them. "You can say your penance."

Godfrey had shaved off his dark beard to apply the black, white, and red pigment to his pocked, coarse features. 'Twas no wonder he hadn't been recognized. His glazed eyes moved to Rory, making certain he was truly there. Then he took a shuddering breath and began.

" 'Twas I who killed your foster father, MacLean, not Somerled," he gritted, clenching his teeth in agony. "I lost my temper when Gideon Cameron accosted me . . . alone on the road . . . and berated me as if I were one of his lackeys. I thought the gossip I'd repeated a week earlier was . . . no more than common knowledge. But God . . . I should have kept a civil tongue in my mouth that day."

Dumbfounded, Rory stared at the mortally wounded man

and felt the skin crawl on the back of his neck. He didn't want to hear this.

Dammit, not this!

Godfrey paused, his breath coming in shallow pants. Runnels of sweat covered his face, smearing the jester's mask in hideous streaks.

"Cameron threatened . . . to cut out my tongue . . . if I repeated . . . scurrilous gossip about his family again. Christ . . . I should have known better in the first place. Everyone knew . . . how fond the laird was . . . of his bonny wife."

Gasping and groaning, he stopped and waited for a moment before beginning again. The pain must have been excruciating. Only sheer willpower kept him from passing out.

Rory met Keir's eyes, too stunned to say a word, then looked at Lachlan, who stood across from him. Neither man's calm gaze betrayed his own inner torment.

"Hell," Godfrey wheezed, his stained mouth twisted with bitter irony, " 'twas obvious . . . the old fool had been cuckolded. One look at Raine Cameron . . . and any idiot would know . . . the black-eyed lassie's not the man's issue."

"So you sneaked up behind Gideon as he turned to leave and buried your dirk in his back," Rory stated angrily. "Then severed his head."

"That last part was none of my doing," Godfrey replied. He moaned, a low, whimpering, animal sound, and then went on determinedly. "Archibald Campbell discovered me that afternoon . . . before I'd had a chance to flee."

"What happened?"

"Argyll hacked off Cameron's head with a claymore . . . wrapped it in my tartan . . . pinned it with my clan badge . . . and had it delivered to Lady Cameron . . . with the compliments of the Red Wolf of Glencoe."

Rory glanced up at Alex, who'd come to join them beside the man in the last throes of death, and read the startled comprehension in his eyes. A long-running feud had existed between Gideon Cameron and Somerled Macdonald over a land title, and Argyll had seized the opportunity to place the blame for Cameron's murder on the laird's hated enemy. The enmity between Gideon and the Red Wolf was the reason they'd all been so quick to believe the evidence against him.

"You had ample time to speak up," Rory told Godfrey, his harsh voice grating with suppressed fury. "You didn't have to keep silent when Somerled was captured and taken to Edinburgh for the hanging."

Godfrey tried to reach up and grasp Rory's sleeve, but didn't have the strength, and his hand fell to the floor. "Oh, I paid the price," he said, his words coming now as a faint, breathy whisper. "My silence saved my neck . . . but condemned me to be Campbell's pawn . . . for the rest of my life." He turned his faltering gaze to the priest. "For this . . . and for all my sins, Father . . . I am heartily sorry."

As Godfrey Macdonald's life ebbed away, Father Thomas anointed his forehead, lids, and mouth with holy oil, praying softly in Latin.

Rory rose blindly to his feet, feeling as though he'd just been struck at point-blank range with a cannonade of stoneshot.

Jesus, God Almighty.

He had delivered an innocent man to his executioners.

He had sent his wife's innocent grandfather to the grave.

Barely aware of the three men who'd helped him capture the Red Wolf, Rory stared blankly at the wall. Lachlan, Keir, and Alex stood near the dying man, mute with shock. They'd been so sure. They'd all been so damn sure.

Unable to speak, weighed down with guilt and regret, Rory turned and went back upstairs, carrying a burden that would last a lifetime. He would get down on his knees and beg his wife's forgiveness for what he'd done. Pray God, she would find it in her heart to forgive him.

Maude stood on the landing with Jamie in her arms. She must have heard something of what had been said at the foot of the stairs, for she gazed at Rory with heartfelt compassion.

Lady Emma met her son just outside the bedchamber door, her lovely features creased with worry. "Joanna's conscious and calling for you, dear. I can't seem to quiet her. She refused to believe us when we assured her you were alive. She's afraid you've been killed, and she needs desperately to tell you something. 'Tis something she's never told you before. I can't get her to explain what's wrong."

From the passageway, Rory could hear Joanna's terrified sobbing. "Why isn't he here?" she cried plaintively. "My husband would be with me if he were alive!"

When he entered, he found his wife propped up on the pillows and thrashing about restlessly. Afraid she'd endanger the stitched wound, Rory hurried to the bedside and knelt down beside her. He took Joanna's pale, shaky hand and brought the cherished fingers to his lips.

"I'm here, sweetheart," he said with a smile, though inside he was drowning in remorse. "I'm right here beside you. What did you want to tell me, lass?"

Bursting into fresh sobs, she reached up with one hand and slid her fingertips across his cheek. Her indigo eyes overflowing with tears, she pulled his face down to hers and rained kisses on his brows, lids, and cheeks.

"Darling of my heart," Joanna whispered raggedly, adding with each tear-soaked kiss, "I love you . . . I love you . . . I love you."

From her place in the open doorway, Lady Emma wiped the moisture from her eyes. With a tremulous smile, she withdrew, closing the door quietly behind her.

Epilogue

~~~OQO~~~

April 1503
Kinlochleven Castle

Jan van Artevelde had fallen in love with Rory's wife.

Hell, Rory couldn't blame the fellow. Her vivid coloring and vibrant temperament had proven an artist's delight. The portrait of Joanna in her bridal gown hanging above the mantel in Rory's library was a masterpiece. The mass of coppery hair framing a gamin's heart-shaped face, with its startling violet-blue eyes and luxuriant russet lashes, would enthrall any man with a breath of life in him. But to the talented little Fleming, Lady MacLean offered an opportunity seldom realized by those few portrait painters whose innate sense of beauty was combined with a Flemish love of realism and a brilliant mastery of the techniques of oil painting.

The adoration lavished upon Joanna by the short, pudgy, balding foreigner was purely of an aesthetic nature, of course. Still, Rory would be thankful when the present portrait had been completed, and van Artevelde could pack up his palette and paint pots and return to Stalcaire, while the family resumed the normal routine of daily life.

"Jamie, hold still," Joanna cautioned their son. " 'Twill not be much longer, dearest, and then Mama will give you a sweetie." She peeked up at her husband from beneath her long eyelashes and flashed him a dazzling smile. "You, too, milord husband," she added with a throaty laugh. "Try to be patient for a wee bit longer."

"I've been patient for the past three weeks," Rory complained. "My stewards are waiting for the final decisions on everything from the acreage of oats and barley to the beginning of the new barns."

"Only a few more minutes, milord," Jan called in his heavily accented Gaelic from behind the tall easel. "Then we'll be done. I can put the finishing touches on it tomorrow without you."

Van Artevelde had arranged the family grouping in the upper hall near a corner well lit by two windows. Rory, in his Highland chief's finery complete with feathered bonnet, stood beside his seated wife. Attired in a lavender velvet gown, Joanna held their two-year-old daughter in her lap, while Jamie was supposed to be standing next to his mama with one arm perched on her knee. Coaxing the active four-year-old to stand still had been nearly as difficult as getting his busy father to find a spare moment for the sittings.

"I'll be good," Jamie promised for the sixth time that morning. "But I'm getting *very* tired just standing here."

"Dada, Dada," Christine chattered, "up, up, up."

"My thoughts exactly," Rory told his squirming daughter as he lifted her into his arms.

Jamie's green gaze and golden hair reflected his father's, while Chrissy had been blessed with her mother's brilliant coloring. She patted her father's cheeks with her dimpled hands and pressed a dewy kiss on the side of his nose. As always, Rory's heart did a quick somersault at the feel of his tiny daughter's soft, wet mouth and chubby fingers on his face.

Life couldn't get much better than this.

"Enough," Jan said, coming out from behind the wooden frame to beam at them. "We're done. Complete."

"Hurrah!" Jamie exclaimed and dashed for the door. "I can ride my new pony."

Lachlan nearly crashed into the child as he came through the open doorway. "Whoa! Not so fast, ye wee loon."

Scooping the laddie up, he tossed him toward the ceiling. "You can ride on your Uncle Lachlan's shoulders, while you say hello to your Grannie and Uncle Keir."

Jamie obligingly straddled his uncle's strong neck and grabbed a handful of the wavy auburn hair. "Gid'up, horsie, gid'up."

With a tolerant grin, Lachlan pried the small fingers loose from his tousled hair and held his nephew's hands for safety as he strode across the carpet.

Lady Emma and her youngest son followed Lachlan into the hall. Keir carried a stack of presents for Jamie and Chrissy, which he set on a press cupboard. They'd traveled from Stalcaire to celebrate the lassie's second birthday.

Joanna hurried to embrace them. "Oh, you've come at last," she said, standing on tiptoe and pressing kisses of welcome on their cheeks. "We were hoping you'd arrive in time for dinner. I thought we'd have our meal here in the upper hall today. 'Tis much cozier."

Rory relinquished Chrissy to her grandmother, dropped a kiss on both foreheads, and then turned to give his two brothers a handshake and a hearty whack on the back. After warm greetings were exchanged all round, everyone gathered in front of the portrait.

" 'Tis wonderful," Lady Emma said as she jiggled her chirping granddaughter on her hip. She looked at van Artevelde and smiled appreciatively. "You've captured them perfectly, sir. I've never seen a finer portrait."

The little Fleming grinned from ear to ear at the well-earned praise. "Thank you, milady. I believe 'tis my best yet."

Chrissy pointed to the painting excitedly. "Mama, Dada," she said with a happy crow of laughter. "Jamie. Me!"

"Too bad," Keir commented dryly, as he shook his head. His gaze traveled from Rory's face to the portrait and back to Rory once again. A smile twitched at the corner of his mouth. "The damn thing looks just like you, big brother."

Rory studied the canvas with enormous satisfaction. The time-consuming sittings had been worth it. Jan van Artevelde had captured more than just their exact images on the canvas. Wit and liveliness shone on Joanna's pixie face, the indigo eyes sparkling with inner radiance. The unblemished innocence on the two young countenances would have touched the hardest of hearts. And Rory's sharp, sea-weathered features, while revealing to the most casual observer his obstinate Scots pride and his readiness to fight for his convictions and his country, also subtly imparted his personal happiness and the deep, abiding love he felt for his family.

Engrossed in the portrait, Lachlan stood quietly beside him. "How did you ever get so damn lucky?"

"I ask myself that question every day," Rory replied, his gaze fixed on the image of his bonny wife.

For Joanna had forgiven him. Completely and without reservation. The summer following Jamie's birth, they'd brought Somerled's remains from Edinburgh to be interred in Kinlochleven's graveyard beside the old man's wife and son. A special chapel had been built in his honor at the Observantine Priory nearby, where Joanna could visit to light candles and offer prayers for the repose of his soul.

"You told me once," Joanna had said, as they stood at Somerled's freshly marked grave, "that we must accept the tragedies fate brings us and carry on. I know you acted with complete conviction, Rory, certain that Grandpapa was guilty of murdering your foster father. 'Tis a blessing we have a son who carries my grandfather's blood in his veins, and God willing, we'll have more sons and daughters in the years ahead. 'Tis their future we must think of now. Our devotion to each other will be the foundation for their happiness, as well as the security of both our clans."

The charges Rory had lodged against Archibald Campbell could never be proved. There'd been only Godfrey's word against the wily earl's, and Argyll furnished a dozen plausible reasons why the dying man had chosen to falsely accuse him. But James Stewart had made it clear that should anything happen to Rory, his widow's hand would never be given to Iain Campbell—or any other man of that clan. At Joanna's impassioned pleading, Rory had agreed to end the matter at that. A bitter and prolonged feud with Clan Campbell would serve no purpose, and Rory was committed to bringing peace to the Western Highlands.

Lachlan's firm hand on Rory's shoulder interrupted his solemn reverie. "I have some news to share," his brother announced to the room at large.

"What news?" Joanna asked eagerly. "Are you betrothed?"

A grin creased his classic features at the typically feminine question, and Lachlan shook his head. "Nothing quite so exciting. The king has appointed me as one of the Scottish escorts for his new English bride. I'm to go with his other ambassadors to London next month and accompany Margaret Tudor on her journey to Edinburgh in July. In honor of the occasion, His Majesty awarded me a new title. I am now the earl of Kinrath."

"That's wonderful!" Joanna cried. "Congratulations!"

No one else spoke.

James IV of Scotland had married the eldest daughter of Henry VII of England by proxy two years before, when the lass was only twelve. Now about to turn fourteen, she was old enough to come to her new country, where she would rule as their queen.

Because of Joanna's part-English heritage, the rest of the family was too polite to say out loud what Lachlan must surely be thinking at the moment: visiting the treacherous Sassenach court would be worse than stepping on a nest of vipers.

Joanna's questioning gaze moved from one silent member of the family to another. She waited, bright head tipped in expectation, for them to respond to the tidings.

"Congratulations on your new title," Rory said belatedly, and his surprised family echoed the sentiment.

At that moment, Fearchar and Maude entered the hall. Behind them came the servants carrying trays of dishes for the midday meal. The couple had been married for three years, and though there'd been no children from the union, the two were happy and content at Kinlochleven. Maude cared for Jamie and Chrissy in the same loving way she'd always cared for Joanna. And Fearchar served as the head steward of all their vast estates.

As everyone found his place at the table, Joanna hastened to Rory's side, and he immediately put his arm around her waist and drew her close. He could read the perplexity on her lovely features.

"Why did everyone stare at Lachlan in horrified silence at his good news?" she asked in a subdued voice.

Rory bussed her on the nose, then murmured in her ear. "We're afraid of what the Sassenach lassies might do to him."

Joanna half-smiled, uncertain whether he jested or spoke in earnest. "What might the English girls do to him?"

Rory slid his hand down to her firm little butt and gave his gullible wife a loving pinch. " 'Tis said the bold-faced wenches like to slip their hands beneath a Scotsman's plaid to discover if he really has a tail."

At her indignant expression, Rory burst into laughter. Ignoring the glances of his curious family, he lifted his spouse up for a long, thorough kiss. "I'll let you check again tonight," he whispered. "Just to make certain one hasn't sprouted in the last twenty-four hours."

"I intend to do just that," she told him pertly. "God's truth, a poor Sassenach lassie can never be too careful when it comes to wicked, diabolical Scottish sea dragons."

As he held her lithe figure securely against his large frame, Rory's happiness knew no bounds. "Darling of my heart," he said tenderly, "I love you so."

"I love you, too, milord husband," she replied, wrinkling her freckled nose and bestowing her impudent smile on him. "Even if you never do grow a decent dragon's tail."

We stand behind the rave reviews so much...

STARDUST
NEIL GAIMAN

...that we'll refund your money if you don't agree. When young Tristran Thorn loses his heart to beautiful Victoria Forester, he vows to retrieve a fallen star and deliver it to his beloved. If you love romance, we're sure you'll fall for this magical fairytale by bestselling author Neil Gaiman. If you're not beguiled, send in the coupon below along with your proof of purchase, and we'll refund your money. But be forewarned: You're about to discover a romance unlike any other...

Avon Romances—
the best in exceptional authors
and unforgettable novels!